## "KA'IN."

Kane recognized the voice at once. It belonged to Fand, the woman/being he'd met in Ireland. "Where are you?"

"Far from you,  close the distance."

Kane turned, senses to mo miss. "How?"

"By destroying the Black Altar. You've held it in your hands, almost unlocked the secrets."

"I can't remember," Kane said hoarsely.

"Let me be your memory for a time, Ka'in."

"She's a fused-out crazy bitch, Kane," a man's voice told him. "Better to put her down like a mad dog."

"Ka'in." Fand sounded weaker, more desperate. "You're in danger whether you stay or go. The Daemon Prince will not give up the hunt for you now."

As if in answer to her statement, brush crackled to Kane's left.

**Other titles in this series:**

# JAMES AXLER

# OUTLANDERS™

# NIGHT ETERNAL

THE LOST EARTH SAGA

BOOK 2

A GOLD EAGLE BOOK FROM

# WORLDWIDE®

TORONTO • NEW YORK • LONDON
AMSTERDAM • PARIS • SYDNEY • HAMBURG
STOCKHOLM • ATHENS • TOKYO • MILAN
MADRID • WARSAW • BUDAPEST • AUCKLAND

If you purchased this book without a cover you should be aware
that this book is stolen property. It was reported as "unsold and
destroyed" to the publisher, and neither the author nor the
publisher has received any payment for this "stripped book."

First edition June 1999
ISBN 0-373-63822-1

NIGHT ETERNAL

Thanks to Mel Odom for his contribution to this work.
Special thanks to Mark Ellis for his contribution to the
Outlanders concept, developed for Gold Eagle Books.

Copyright © 1999 by Worldwide Library.

All rights reserved. Except for use in any review, the
reproduction or utilization of this work in whole or in part
in any form by any electronic, mechanical or other means,
now known or hereafter invented, including xerography,
photocopying and recording, or in any information storage
or retrieval system, is forbidden without the written permission
of the publisher, Worldwide Library, 225 Duncan Mill Road,
Don Mills, Ontario, Canada M3B 3K9.

All characters in this book have no existence outside the
imagination of the author and have no relation whatsoever to
anyone bearing the same name or names. They are not even
distantly inspired by any individual known or unknown to the
author, and all incidents are pure invention.

® and TM are trademarks of the publisher. Trademarks indicated
with ® are registered in the United States Patent and Trademark
Office, the Canadian Trade Marks Office and in other countries.

**Printed in U.S.A.**

# NIGHT ETERNAL

# The Road to Outlands—
# From Secret Government Files to the Future

Almost two hundred years after the global holocaust, Kane, a former Magistrate of Cobaltville, often thought the world had been lucky to survive at all after a nuclear device detonated in the Russian embassy in Washington, D.C. The aftermath—forever known as skydark—reshaped continents and turned civilization into ashes.

Nearly depopulated, America became the Deathlands—poisoned by radiation, home to chaos and mutated life forms. Feudal rule reappeared in the form of baronies, while remote outposts clung to a brutish existence.

What eventually helped shape this wasteland were the redoubts, the secret preholocaust military installations with stores of weapons, and the home of gateways, the locational matter-transfer facilities. Some of the redoubts hid clues that had once fed wild theories of government cover-ups and alien visitations.

Rearmed from redoubt stockpiles, the barons consolidated their power and reclaimed technology for the villes. Their power, supported by some invisible authority, extended beyond their fortified walls to what was now called the Outlands. It was here that the rootstock of humanity survived, living with hellzones and chemical storms, hounded by Magistrates.

In the villes, rigid laws were enforced—to atone for the sins of the past and prepare the way for a better future. That was the barons' public credo and their right-to-rule.

Kane, along with friend and fellow Magistrate Grant, had upheld that claim until a fateful Outlands expedition. A displaced piece of technology…a question to a keeper of the archives…a vague clue about alien masters—and their world shifted radically. Suddenly, Brigid Baptiste, the archivist, faced summary execution, and

Grant a quick termination. For Kane there was forgiveness if he pledged his unquestioning allegiance to Baron Cobalt and his unknown masters and abandoned his friends.

But that allegiance would make him support a mysterious and alien power and deny loyalty and friends. Then what else was there?

Kane had been brought up solely to serve the ville. Brigid's only link with her family was her mother's red-gold hair, green eyes and supple form. Grant's clues to his lineage were his ebony skin and powerful physique. But Domi, she of the white hair, was an Outlander pressed into sexual servitude in Cobaltville. She at least knew her roots and was a reminder to the exiles that the outcasts belonged in the human family.

Parents, friends, community—the very rootedness of humanity was denied. With no continuity, there was no forward momentum to the future. And that was the crux—when Kane began to wonder if there *was* a future.

For Kane, it wouldn't do. So the only way was out—way, way out.

After their escape, they found shelter at the forgotten Cerberus redoubt headed by Lakesh, a scientist, Cobaltville's head archivist, and secret opponent of the barons.

With their past turned into a lie, their future threatened, only one thing was left to give meaning to the outcasts. The hunger for freedom, the will to resist the hostile influences. And perhaps, by opposing, end them.

# Chapter 1

Kane moved in the darkness like a wolf, padding soundlessly through the cavernous corridors of the Cerberus redoubt. He went shoeless because he liked feeling the chill metal against the soles of his feet. The cold was real, a tangible that he clung to at the moment.

Yesterday hadn't been real. And none of the days that had made up yesterday had been real. His mind told him that, and it almost got a little easier to believe after the few hours of sleep he'd had. His chron showed 4:13 a.m. local time, meaning there'd been damned few hours of rest.

When he took a deep breath, he could still smell the death around him from those lost yesterdays. It blended in perfectly with the odor of spent cordite and burned ozone. When he closed his eyes, he could see Brigid's and Grant's blood-encrusted heads rolling toward him, their last expressions filled with pure horror—and C. W. Thrush stood beyond them, the pistol in his hand spitting yellow lightning in the darkness.

Thunder had crashed against Kane's chest and he'd died. At least, as Lakesh had pointed out during the debrief afterward, one of Kane's selves had died.

It had been Lakesh's fault that Kane had perished, a victim of C. W. Thrush and the Third Reich, which had controlled the world—that particular world—for almost three centuries. But that Kane had deserved to die, since that self had served the forces of darkness. Kane had to keep reminding himself of that, as well, working to keep at bay the insanity that the lost earths—or alternate worlds—brought with them.

Yesterday hadn't been real, he reminded himself as he strode through the corridor. Not to him.

At least, not to this version of him.

He kept his eyes open, sweeping the corridor with his trained gaze. He relied on his pointman's senses to warn him of any danger. The chance of danger in the redoubt had dimmed when they'd freed Balam, then followed his quest, which had netted them the facets of the Chintamani Stone. Those facets, however, had only led to the greatest danger Kane had ever faced.

He forcibly pushed out his breath, relaxing his nerves and muscles, the way they'd trained him back in the Magistrate academy. He wanted to throw things, but the wound in his hip kept him even from the exercise floor in the redoubt where he and Grant sometimes went to work out their frustrations with Lakesh and his half-truths and full-blown machinations. Lakesh spoke out of both sides of his mouth, Kane knew, balancing lie and truth to achieve whatever effect he wanted.

Finally, his journey ended up where he knew it probably would—the ready room beside the mat-trans chamber that Lakesh had ordered altered to work with the trapezohedron that had birthed so many legends of his world. He felt a tightness across his shoulders and through his chest as he stared at the mat-trans unit.

Thick brown armaglass walls enclosed the hexagonal chamber, separating it from the control center lying just beyond. With the Project Cerberus technology that had created the mat-trans network, most of the world lay open to Kane and his group. Anywhere was just an eye blink away.

But with the Chintamani Stone linked to it, whole worlds were easily within reach. Kane had been to one of the alternate worlds. Two others remained yet to explore. He forced himself to breathe out, reminding himself that the conference table was of his world, not some other Kane's.

Except he didn't know that for sure. What if, when he'd thought he'd been returning to his own world, he'd ended up instead on still another Kane's world—one that was more closely akin to the one he'd ventured from but still wasn't home?

That thought had finally kept him awake, unable to return to sleep.

The air was still in the room, and the hum of the computers in the redoubt's control center was the only audible sound. The lighting was dim. Even with the door at his back, Kane knew when he wasn't alone anymore.

"Can't sleep?"

Kane turned smoothly toward the feminine voice, relaxing slightly. A rogue female, Beth-Li Rouch, was still within the complex, and he'd yet to figure out the possible extent of her duplicity. She'd given him the gunshot wound he carried at present. "Slept enough," he growled.

DeFore, the complex's medical expert, stood in the doorway swathed in the early-morning shadows. She was stocky and buxom, with bronze skin that made her ash-blond hair stand out even more starkly. As usual, she wore her hair in intricate braids and the formfitting bodysuit that was the usual attire by the redoubt inhabitants. Her face was chiseled and didn't reveal anything that might have been on her mind.

Kane was perfectly content to blow her off and ignore her. He had his own agenda despite being tied to Lakesh and Cerberus.

"Having second thoughts about going through that thing again?" DeFore asked.

"No." Kane made himself answer. It sounded better, more sure, when he said it.

She walked around in front of him, trying for eye contact again. "You're certain?"

Kane looked through her gaze, not meeting it at all. He'd learned how to do that, too, in the training he'd been given to become a Magistrate in Cobaltville. He concentrated on the brown armaglass walls of the mat-trans.

Despite his surly manner, DeFore sat down on the edge of the conference table. "There's a fresh pot of coffee in the cafeteria. I know because I made it. We could go there."

"If I wanted to go there," Kane stated brusquely, "I'd have gone there. And if I'd wanted company, I'd have found Grant."

"Grant's sleeping," DeFore said.

"I'd have woken him. It wouldn't have been the first time."

DeFore folded her arms across her big breasts and returned his angry glare full measure.

"It's not like you to be so social," Kane declared, particularly suspicious since he and DeFore had in the past shared vigorous differences of opinion.

"Must be the company." DeFore shifted in the chair and it squeaked. "I find myself positively inspired this morning."

"What are you doing up anyway?"

"I was talking with Lakesh."

"Till four in the morning?"

She nodded. "I'd have talked to him longer if he'd permitted."

Kane gave her a cruel smile. "Care to tell me how he kicked your ass out of his face?"

DeFore's eyes flicked over Kane, taking him in from head to toe the way she normally did when he came back from a mission that she knew had gone awry. Since he'd shown up at the redoubt and joined forces with Lakesh, she'd patched him up a number of times. "We were talking about you, Grant and Brigid pursuing an investigation through any of the other alternate earths."

Kane paused, considering. "Lakesh is all in favor of it."

"I'm not," DeFore said without preamble. "I think it's too dangerous."

A bitter laugh rose to Kane's throat. "I don't know why you would. Hell, we all got chilled on that last earth, and we're still here." He tried to make it sound light, as though it were nothing. But he felt it hanging in the air.

"Are you ready to step into another alternate earth in just a few hours?" DeFore lifted a doubtful eyebrow.

"Yeah," Kane agreed. "Ready." He paused, letting his guard down a little as he turned away from some of the anger and fear staring him in the face. "Just not too happy about it."

"What did it feel like?" the woman asked.

"What?"

"Getting killed." DeFore didn't pull any words.

Kane turned away from her intense gaze. Put him across a table with a slagger already pointing a blaster at him, Kane knew he'd still gamble that he'd be able to pop his Sin Eater and chill the slag before he was chilled himself. He'd done it before. But thinking about getting into the mat-trans unit again left him cold. "I didn't get killed," he said.

Still, the phantom shock and pain of the bullet smashing through his chest burned through his memory. As a Mag for Cobaltville, he'd been wounded a number of times. But this had been different. He hoped that the phantom pain was from one of those instances rather than the one he'd had yesterday.

"For all intents and purposes," DeFore said, "you did. If you want, I can show you the EKGs and EEGs from your time in the mat-trans unit. For an instant in there, you flat-lined. All of you did. Brigid and Grant flat-lined ahead of you."

Kane shook his head. "We didn't die."

DeFore paused. "Not this time. My argument to Lakesh, however, was about the next time. What about then?"

BRIGID BAPTISTE LUXURIATED in the warm bath and tried to convince herself not to feel guilty.

The bath was an extravagance, something her training and upbringing guided her not to do. The lilac-scented water and scented candles that burned in the darkness above her made it almost a sin.

Deep in the water, she tried to relax. Dreams had plagued her sleep, images from the lost earth she'd visited with Grant and Kane yesterday, and from even further back, when she'd first met Kane and had fled Cobaltville. Before her exile, she'd been an archivist, and her eidetic memory had been a boon in searching through all the files kept in Cobaltville's Administrative Monolith. If she saw it, she remembered it.

That photographic memory was a curse now. Images, complete with sensory impressions, flipped through her mind like a cheap nickelodeon. The most recent images included her "death" on the other earth. A chill touched Brigid even through the warm water surrounding her. Tightness filled her burning lungs as she remembered how she and Grant had been killed. They'd glossed over that during the debrief afterward with Lakesh. And Lakesh had returned the favor, she knew, by glossing over the medical feedback DeFore had gotten from the biolink monitors.

As a trained archivist, though, Brigid knew misinformation often began with reticent truths, then grew into speculative transitions as someone worked to record the event. No information was sometimes better than partial information.

Aside from her death, there were other recollections from her time in that casement, as Balam and Lakesh had insisted on calling the alternate earths. She remembered how she and Kane had been able to take over the lives of their counterparts on that casement.

Their counterparts had been drawn to each other, and they'd ended up making love. Or having sex. Brigid still wasn't sure what to call it exactly. She remembered plainly that it had been at once smoldering and erotic, somehow steely and tender. And it had been performed in a hot rush.

As she lay under the water, she remembered how Kane's hands had roved over her body, touching her jawline, her breasts, his thick fingers reaching into her deepest recesses and setting fire to every desire she thought she'd set aside when she'd been accepted as an archivist at Cobaltville. The head ruled the body; thinking came before emotions. There could be no other way in her chosen line of work.

She saw the dim light of the scented candles above her, but she felt her nipples swelling in erotic tension, felt her body blossoming at the memory. Her pulse throbbed inside her head, picking up speed as she recalled Kane's heat as he'd filled her. Her body tightened in its desire, blindly seeking release. Her hand slid along her thigh, knowing it would be so easy to trigger the memory into a sensation that would sweep her away now.

With the discipline that had pushed her up in the ranks of the Cobaltville archivists, drawing the attention of Lakesh, the head archivist, she resisted. She pushed the burning desire to the back of her mind, walling it away, telling herself that it was actually being eradicated. The emotion she felt was too confusing. Self-gratification wasn't taboo to her way of thinking, but involving Kane in it in any way was too far over the line.

She rose from the water, sucking in steamy breaths. She gazed at her candlelit image in the darkened mirror beside the big tub. Her reddish-gold hair strung down her back, picking up highlights from the candles. She stood up from the water, taking pride in the fact that her body was leaner and harder than it had been while she'd been at the Administrative Monolith. Tall and generously curved, she held a woman's shape on long, athletic legs. Even in the darkness, her eyes blazed emerald.

She toweled off, rubbing her body briskly to remove the last of the chill that seemed to have taken root in her body. Finished with the bath, she pulled the plug and watched the water drain for a time, focusing on it to marshal her thoughts.

The water went down into a natural limestone filtration system built under the redoubt. Once the water passed through and the chemicals, including the lilac scent, had been leached out, the water returned to the complex's water supply.

Built over two hundred years ago as part of the Totality Concept—the American government's clandestine research program—the Cerberus complex had been constructed to last close to forever. It had been designed to be the home of at least a hundred people. The actual population now was barely double digits. And shrinking, Brigid couldn't help thinking, remembering the losses they'd had.

Returning to her living room, she took a seat at the comp-equipped desk against one wall. There were few personal items on the walls, but she'd chosen reference books that she enjoyed leafing through on occasion. With the gift of her memory, she never had to look at a book more than once. But sometimes she liked to hold them while thinking. It felt good for her hands to have something to do.

She took a pair of glasses from beside the comp monitor and put them on while she switched the monitor on. The screen juiced with an electric pop, and she got to the menu the complex used. As senior archivist for Cobaltville, Lakesh had had access to a number of books, treatises and documents, including electronic ones. He'd made certain Cerberus had benefited from his bounty.

Despite her photographic memory, Brigid wasn't quite a walking, talking encyclopedia. While being extremely knowledgeable about a great number of things, there were some she wasn't complete expert on, including theories of quantum mechanics. Though she was conversant with everything Lakesh had brought up when talking about the casements, she wanted to know more.

She accessed the electronic media available to her and began browsing the selection. She found it unusually hard to focus on the subject matter.

Images spun in the depths of the monitor, memories from even further back than her first meeting with Kane. She saw him again, a young man of nineteen or twenty, sword in his hand as he charged to rescue her from the men who held her captive.

He'd died that time as well, she remembered.

The mouse lay inert in her hand, the cursor blinking back at her steadily. Kane had worn another name then, but she remembered the other name she'd had for him best: *anam-chara*. In the Gaelic tongue, it meant "soul friend." And the dreams they'd had during different mat-trans jumps and crisis points suggested that they'd lived past lives, each continually intertwined with the other in some manner, never knowing romance.

That, however, couldn't be said about the casement they'd visited yesterday. She ran her fingers through her hair and tried hard not to think about what that episode meant. But the images and the sensory impressions of Kane's hands on her wouldn't leave.

Maybe it's just too soon, she told herself. She

breathed easily. She was glad she and Kane hadn't discussed the issue any more. For all his fighting prowess—or maybe because of it, Brigid wasn't sure—Kane thought first with his emotions. That was alien to everything Brigid Baptiste held dear.

To survive, one needed a clear head. She worked hard to keep hers that way.

Still, she wondered if a case could still be made that she and Kane hadn't been physically intimate with each other. Or would be again.

That was what had kept her up most of the night, she knew. Jumping to another casement, another lost earth, she had to wonder if she'd be just as lost to herself as she had been the first time.

There'd only been flashes of memory in the other casement until she'd made love with Kane. Then she'd completely taken over her other self's body, only separating out again till her other self died.

If she did exhibit some control in the new self she was going to jump into today, she had to wonder if it would take making love with Kane again to re-awaken her in that other casement. And what if their other selves were bitter enemies? Would it take a conscious effort to have sex with each other to put them in control again?

Her mind continued whirling, stray thoughts licking out to pluck at her emotions. Forcibly, she returned her attention to the list of selections on the comp screen. What she needed was a book on sex and quantum physics. The search was frustrating. She earmarked five books she wanted to look at, then leaned back in the chair. It creaked in the quietness of the room, barely audible over the humming comp.

She thought of Grant, remembering how Kane had

talked to the big man and brought him to his senses. Sex hadn't been involved in Grant's awakening, but it had been linked to Kane, as well. She made a mental note to discuss the matter with Kane. Maybe the focus was on Kane because the Chintamani Stone had locked on to him. Sex might not have anything to do with the reawakening process; it might only involve Kane and them coming together again in whatever world lay at the other end of the next mat-trans jump.

She switched the comp off, then retreated to her bedroom long enough to get dressed in a bodysuit. Then she made her way to the library, intending to spend her time reading, hoping she might find another clue to what was going on in the other casements.

C. W. Thrush remained a constant on those other worlds, and as such he was a constant threat. He'd killed them all once, but spared their lives on another earth. She had no doubts he would never be so merciful again.

"THING THAT BOTHERS ME MOST, Thrush is going to be out there waiting for us," Grant began.

"You afraid?" Domi challenged.

"Be a fool not to have some reservations, now, wouldn't I?"

"Don't think that way. Think you going hunting instead."

Lying on his bed in his room, Grant rolled his head over and glanced at Domi, who was sitting on the trunk at the foot of his bed. He stood six feet four in his stocking feet, broad across the shoulders and thick through the chest. Gray showed in his short hair at his temples, but the down-sweeping mustache showed coal-black against his coffee-brown skin. Scars covered his body, most of them acquired back when he'd been a Magistrate in Cobaltville. Keeping a baron's peace was not an easy thing; living as an exile was fraught with even more danger. A cast encased his right leg from ankle to just below the knee. He wore a pair of blue silk shorts and a white tank top out of deference to his company.

Domi, however, didn't have any clothes on at all and was completely comfortable with the lack of apparel.

Grant couldn't help himself, grinning at her for the first time in what must have been hours. He'd slept little, and his thoughts during the waking time had been harsh and dark. "You would think of it that way," he told her.

"Survival's only riff you need," Domi asserted. "Start thinking you lucky be alive 'stead of deserve, you start depending on it."

"Mebbe we're all a little lucky. Now and then."

Domi shrugged. "As long as not looking over shoulder for it."

Grant ran his hands across his face, feeling his stubbled cheeks crackle against the friction. He wished he felt more like sleeping, or felt more like being awake. One or the other, because feeling like he did now was the absolute shits. "I've never looked for luck, and I've never depended on it. I made whatever I got in any situation, same as Kane. But getting your head bit off on a parallel earth—well, mebbe that gives a man cause to appreciate it a little more."

Domi shivered. She was albino, her skin beautifully white, unflawed except by scattered scarring from the hard life she'd lived. Grant knew from Lakesh that she was at least a teen, but she looked positively childlike, even with her small breasts and gently flaring hips. She wore her bone-white hair cut close to her head. Her eyes were crimson, the color of fresh-spilled blood.

Her designation, according to what he'd been taught in Cobaltville, was an outlander. He'd been trained to exterminate anyone who lived on the other side of the imposing Enclave walls.

"You remember getting head bit off?" Domi inquired.

"Yeah. Not something you're likely to forget. Even if you want to."

A gamine grin covered Domi's face. "Tell me about it."

Grant shot her a look. "Next time you get close to a mutie mountain lion, stick your head in its mouth. Get back to me, we'll compare notes."

"On another world, I'd try." She sounded serious.

Actually, Grant didn't doubt that she would. Domi's life in the Outlands had been savage, and survival had been the only key. She'd learned well, was able to kill as quickly and as surely as any animal in the wild. He'd seen her do it, and been appreciative of her skill. "Yeah, mebbe you would."

"Too bad I can't go with."

"Right."

"You meet another Domi there?" she asked.

Grant didn't want to remember that, either, but he'd found he couldn't forget it. Thrush's people had killed that other Domi through torture, stripped her life from her before his very eyes. "Yeah."

"What she like?"

Grant closed his eyes and covered his face with his

arm. "I don't know. They chilled her before I got the chance to meet her."

"Oh." There was silence for a moment, and he figured Domi was thinking about the whole situation, about the complexity involved in an infinite number of Domis, probably wondering how differently their lives had turned out, whom those other Domis had loved, maybe even the babies that—

"She prettier than me?" Domi asked earnestly.

It took a moment for Grant to realize she'd really asked what he thought he'd heard her ask. Then he laughed, hard and long, for the first time since they'd gotten back from that other casement.

Domi's face hardened, and no flush of embarrassment touched her cheeks. "Not polite to laugh, Grant. Men known wake up no balls in morning for less than that."

"I'm not laughing at you." Grant held his hands up in mock surrender. "I'm just taking another look at the whole situation. Here me and Kane been worrying about Thrush, thinking mebbe there's a way he's been using all these casements to mess up all the worlds with the Archon technology he's been using. And you wonder if the Domi on another world is better-looking than you."

"Still sound like you're laughing at me," Domi warned.

"No. You just reminded me there's more than one perception for everything. Instead of worrying about how I'm going to get chilled in my next sudden afterlife, I should be looking forward to my next opportunity to take Thrush out."

"Thrush is bastard dangerous."

"Yeah, but so am I." Grant's mind whirled with

the possibilities, and he felt like laughing some more. "Mebbe in this next casement, I will go hunting."

"Good." Domi relaxed her harsh look and unfolded, stretching toward Grant till she covered his body with hers.

Grant tried to remain still, not responding to the feel of skin against skin. It wasn't the first time Domi had tried to seduce him. Her flesh was warm against him, and she felt soft, soft enough that a man could hold her and caress her and get himself totally lost in the privilege and experience.

Only Grant was reluctant to do that. He knew that Domi was no stranger to sex. She'd sold herself into service as a sex slave to Guana Teague in exchange for being smuggled into Cobaltville, then freed herself by drawing a knife across the fat Pit boss's throat when he'd tried to change the terms of their agreement. She was no stranger at all. But to Grant she represented a kind of innocence that he didn't want to change. Then there was always the memory of Olivia, the only woman who'd ever truly claimed his heart.

Domi kissed Grant's face and neck, making the kisses long and passionate. She moved slowly, languorously, only enough to make sure every square inch of her heated flesh pressed against his.

Grant steeled himself, resisting the temptation she represented, but he enjoyed the attention to a degree. Domi's caresses warmed his heart, took away some of the fear he'd been feeling. He wouldn't even have confided that fear to Kane, his friend and partner for so many years. Admitting it to Kane would have meant admitting it to himself on a very deep level.

Curling a hand over the side of his face to pull his

gaze toward hers, Domi looked at him, then kissed him on the mouth. She sank her teeth into his lower lip, biting just hard enough for it to hurt a little. Her crimson eyes flashed with pleasure and daring.

"This isn't going to happen," Grant told her softly, having trouble speaking the words with her latched on to his lip.

She giggled, the sound coming from deep inside her throat. Her nipples burning holes against his chest. Her legs slipped apart, gliding effortlessly to lock around his waist, pulling him close. "No?" she asked, feeling his maleness press against her, separated only by the thin material of his shorts.

"No," he assured her, thinking it'd better stop damned quick, though.

She started a rhythm against him, pressing hard.

Grant reached for her and lifted her from him, his arms corded with heavy muscle. She struggled to hang on, but she stopped short of turning the battle of wills into a physical confrontation.

"Damn you, Grant!" Domi pouted. "What if this is last time I see you?"

"Now who's being negative?" Grant teased. He laid her gently beside him, leaving his arm draped over her narrow waist, holding her close. He liked the scent of her, all sex and musk, as natural as the smell of bread baking.

She quietly lay beside him, curling into his side, placing a hand against his chest. He knew she was feeling his heartbeat, and the way she'd got it going, he knew there was no way she'd miss it.

"Not negative," Domi said. "But good excuse."

"No excuses," Grant said. "What I'd like to do is just lay here together. Quiet. Okay?"

"Sure, Grant. But if feel like later, I be ready."

Grant smiled at her, but her presence at his side was comforting. Within a few deep breaths, he was asleep, with no thoughts at all of dying on other worlds.

KANE STOOD on one of the ledges outside the Cerberus complex, watching as pale rose rays of the morning sun burned away the shadows clinging to the rocky mountainscape around him. The precipice before him dropped a thousand feet. At the bottom was a pile of rusted vehicles.

It was cold enough that Kane's breath turned frosty gray when he exhaled, and it made him feel more awake than he had in hours even with the coffee he'd shared with the complex's medical chief. His conversation with DeFore had been unexpectedly conciliatory if not pleasant.

The remnants of a chain-link fence ran around the plateau Kane stood on, testifying to how careful the Totality Concept had been. He stared out at the broken land that stretched out beyond.

The multiton vanadium-alloy sec door opened like an accordion behind Kane almost soundlessly. His Mag training didn't allow him to stand still and ignore a potential threat. He turned smoothly, spotting Brigid Baptiste.

The sunlight set her hair on fire. She wore a white bodysuit, the mode of dress common in the complex. "DeFore told me I'd find you out here." She carried two cups.

Kane accepted one of the cups, smelling the coffee instantly. "Thanks."

"I wanted to talk to you," she said. "Before we made the jump."

"Not much time left," Kane said.

She came to a stop beside him, her attention focused on the countryside.

Kane knew she'd seen the landscape before, and with her memory she'd be able to draw it in detail without ever seeing it again. He waited, taking the opportunity to study her. She was a beautiful woman and he appreciated the chance to watch her. The bodysuit hugged her curves, giving him even more to appreciate.

As he watched her, he thought about all they'd shared so far, all the dangers and all the close calls. And if the jump dreams were to be believed, they'd shared much more besides.

*Anam-chara.* The term chilled him and warmed him all at the same time. Despite the fact that they were about to crawl back into the mat-trans unit for another mystery jump, a smile curled his thin lips.

She turned to him and caught him smiling. Her voice turned cold. "Something on your mind?"

"Just thinking."

"About what?"

"Happy thoughts," Kane assured her.

Anger tracked across Brigid's face, and Kane knew she thought he'd been somehow insulting. She folded her arms over her breasts, looking imposing but vulnerable at the same time. "I should have expected something juvenile from you, Kane. I guess I was surprised I didn't hear it yesterday."

The smile dropped from Kane's face, and the frustration Brigid Baptiste so often brought out in him returned. "That's not what I was thinking about, Baptiste."

"I find that hard to believe."

"Yeah, well, you might remember that not too long ago you didn't give me credit for thinking at all."

"So you've shown a slight improvement."

Kane swallowed a hot retort, not wanting an argument to ensue. "Mebbe you'd like to take in the morning alone." He turned and started to walk away.

"Kane."

Against his better judgment, Kane turned.

"I'm sorry," she said. "That was unfair. It's only natural that—that what happened would be on your mind."

Kane shook his head. "That wasn't what I was thinking about at all."

"What *were* you thinking about?"

Kane studied her, noticing the dark rings under her eyes and knowing she hadn't slept well, either. "Guess we're both running a little ragged here." He sipped the coffee again, wishing he'd brought a cigar out with him. "I was thinking that mebbe we got lucky yesterday, making it back out of that casement alive. Thrush knows more about this than we do."

"Balam knew more about the lost earths than we did," Brigid said.

"I've been thinking about that, too," Kane admitted. "He wasn't traveling through any of the other casements open to us through the Chintamani Stone. And he gave them to us."

"To you," she pointed out.

"I know. I wonder about that, too. And why give it up now? He could have told us about it a long time ago."

"I can't answer that," Brigid replied. "We don't know enough about Balam to make any real guesses as to his motivations. Maybe he didn't tell us because there was no need. Or maybe he didn't tell us because it was one of his race's deep secrets. One of many."

Kane silently agreed with that. Either suggested scenario was possible. "I've started wondering if this isn't some kind of trap. Or a false trail."

"Lakesh doesn't think so," Brigid said.

Kane snorted in derision. "Lakesh doesn't want to think so. That other world Thrush knew me, knew he'd seen me before."

"That suggests that all the versions of Thrush share a collective consciousness."

"Like a comp program," Kane agreed. "Able to run apart and able to work together."

"That line of thinking makes it imperative we discover all the secrets of the Stone."

"Mebbe." Kane drank more coffee, wishing he had better luck at untangling all his thoughts. As a Mag, he was accustomed to action, to relying on instinct, not to deep thinking. "But the one thing I am sure of while looking out over this morning, there's no reason we all have to be at risk going into that next casement."

"You can't mean that, Kane. We didn't even remember who we really were until we—until we met."

Kane grinned wolfishly. "Yeah, well, Grant and I didn't have to meet in order for him to come to himself. It happened. There's nothing to say it won't happen for me if I go alone."

"Lakesh won't—"

"Won't have a damn thing to say," Kane said roughly. "Unless he's willing to make the jump himself. For whatever reason, that Chintamani Stone and Colonel C. W. Thrush have focused on me. I want to know why, but I don't have to risk you and Grant to do it.''

"But you'll be alone, Kane, and in a world you don't even know."

He laughed bitterly. "I'm alone in this world, Baptiste, and I only fooled myself when I thought I knew this world. Everything I thought I knew has been turned inside out over the past few months. Hell, I'll probably feel right at home."

# Chapter 2

Kane stood up in the clearing, pushing himself unsteadily to his feet, his fist clenched around a sword that he'd never seen before but somehow found felt comfortable. It was a cloth-yard length of cold iron with a basket hilt. Blood filled the grooves cut into the sword blade, and dead men surrounded him in the forest. Most of them, he knew, he'd slain himself. The others had been his comrades in battle, men he'd led to their deaths. His great spear, Gae Bolg, stood upright just out of reach, buried in the body of one of the goblins that had ambushed them.

He was still breathing hard from the battle, his mouth dry from exertion. Muscle fatigue filled him, and he knew he'd been wounded. Rust-colored blood stained the front of the intricately woven chain-mail shirt he wore over a padded vest. The armor extended from throat to midthigh. Leather breeches covered his legs, tied up into handmade boots.

He felt dizzy and disoriented, and in the back of his mind he was asking himself if something had gone wrong with the jump. Mat-trans nausea often resulted in hallucinations like this, he remembered. Except that he found he couldn't remember exactly what a mat-trans unit was.

He stumbled through the battleground, feeling some of his strength come back to him. He kept his fist on his sword, at the ready. No one else lived, and what little he recalled of the battle had been that some of the goblins had lived. None of the true men.

They'd come there for a reason, seeking someone. Only the disorientation that filled his mind like molten lead wouldn't let him summon up the reason. Was the someone they'd pursued been friend or foe?

"Ka'in."

He recognized the voice at once. It belonged to Fand, the woman/being he'd met in Ireland. He took a deeper breath and forced his voice to work. "Where are you?"

"Far from you now, Ka'in, my love," she said in her heavy accent. "In this turn of the wheel, they've kept us far from each other. But you can close the distance."

Kane turned, sweeping the forest surrounding him with care, depending on his pointman's senses to monitor the things his vision might miss. He tried not to remember that all his vaunted skill hadn't kept the men who'd depended on him from dying. He stumbled over a tree root snaking across the uneven surface of the terrain, hidden by the lush grass that grew everywhere, and nearly fell. Still, the mixture of hope and despair in Fand's voice made him keep moving. There was a mission to be accomplished. "How?"

"By destroying the Black Altar."

Staring up through the leafy foliage of the interlocking tree branches over his head, Kane studied the sunlight that slipped through. The pale amber splintering against the branches, he recognized from experience, meant that it was afternoon. "What Black Altar?"

"The one the Daemon Prince plans to use to enslave all the worlds."

Kane struggled hard to remember, then gave up in angry frustration because he couldn't. "My lady, I don't know about this Black Altar or this Daemon Prince you speak of."

"You know the Black Altar, Ka'in. You've had it in your hands, almost unlocked the secrets. One of the dark gods who empowered the Daemon Prince even turned against him, giving you the means to destroy him."

"I can't remember," Kane said hoarsely.

"You're wounded. I can help you."

"I don't want help. I want to know." Without the exact memory at his mental fingertips, Kane knew he'd been lied to before. Nearly everyone he knew had lied to him at some time, about something they cared about. Everyone had an agenda. His was simply survival, but it depended on trusting those he came in contact with. But not too much.

"Let me be your memory for a time, Ka'in."

"No."

Fand's voice hardened. "You have no choice, my love. You are the spear carrier. Your destiny, nay, all of your destinies, were writ even before you were first birthed. You've been selected for this fight."

"She's a fused-out crazy bitch, Kane," a man's voice told him. "Better to fucking put her down like a mad dog than to let her close enough to bite."

Kane knew both statements were true. A vague wisp of a memory whirled around in his brain. He recalled Lakesh and his father, the bargains that had been struck. His DNA had promised his soul, and events had been triggered to shape him into what he was now. And he remembered another man, at another time, who'd talked with him about Fand. But he wasn't certain where his memory was clear and where the doubtfulness began.

"You can't escape your destiny, Ka'in," Fand told him more softly. "And the Daemon Prince can't escape you. With each of your deaths, you'll only be drawn in more closely to him. He can't know this because he is less than you. And more."

Kane gazed around the forest, desperately seeking some clue as to what he should do. The trees and underbrush were almost impenetrable, a wall of dark greens mixed with thorns.

"If you don't stop him here," Fand said, "his goblins will overrun the villages you've sworn to protect. They will come from caves in groups, heeding his maddening call, and they'll attack the aged, the women and children, all the defenseless who have no champion to serve them. The Daemon Prince's power, magnified through the Black Altar, will be the end of this island kingdom, and his dark reign will spread across this world. Will you leave them to the savagery that awaits?"

Kane knew he couldn't. Even though he couldn't remember everything that had transpired here, he knew Fand spoke the truth. The force scattered in death around him had been the last, best hope.

Now only he remained.

"Will you let their deaths be in vain, Ka'in?" she asked with an edge in her voice.

"No." He looked down at the goblin corpses mixed in with those of his men. Early afternoon should have prevented the goblins from being out, he recalled. Full sunlight destroyed them; even brief exposure often resulted in suppurating sores that wept infection constantly and seldom healed. The weakness had been handed to them by the bent and twisted dark gods that had made them.

Rad sickness.

The voice ghosted through Kane's mind, bringing with it memories that clashed with what he was seeing. He shook his head, banishing them. Concentration was required if a warrior was going to survive. He studied the dead goblins further, seeking to discover what was different about these that they should be able to march in indifference to the sun.

They were long armed and short legged as he'd come to expect. Greenish-gray skin sagged around their frames, loose and scaled, tough as leather armor and proof against an ill-aimed spear or sword blow. Their faces were broader from side to side than the heads were deep from front to back. Animal hides covered their genitals and had knife and sword sheaths woven into them. They carried primitive war hammers and stone axes, as well.

Memories stirred within Kane, naming the creatures as something other than goblins: muties, hybrids, Archon guinea pigs. The words didn't belong in the forest. Images overlaid the goblins, changing them to even grimmer creatures than those he saw spread before him.

The ones he remembered had been shambling mockeries of men, some more human in appearance than others. Their DNA had been tampered with, too, by the Archons as they experimented with the creation of hybrids that would do their bidding. The Archons had been on the planet for a long time, and

their genetic tampering had led to myths and super-
stitions, founded whole religions.

The muties from Kane's own world were often rad-
blasted, carrying weeping sores from their afflictions.
And they dressed no better than the creatures he saw
here.

"Ka'in." Fand sounded weaker, even farther away,
more desperate. "You're in danger whether you stay
or go. The Daemon Prince will not give up the hunt
for you now."

As if in answer to her statement, brush cracked to
Kane's left.

Instinctively, he stepped back, bringing the sword
up in a defensive position. Sunlight splintered on the
keen edge.

Three goblins raced from the brush, brandishing
war hammers and axes. They screamed in shrill
voices, fueled by a berserker fear and rage.

"SOMETHING'S WRONG."

Standing in the doorway between the central control complex and the anteroom that held the mat-trans
chamber, Brigid Baptiste glanced over at DeFore.
"What's wrong?"

Rather than answering, the woman looked toward
Bry, who manned the dedicated control console on
the other side of the big, vault-walled room. He had
short, curly copper hair and was a round-shouldered
man of small stature. His white bodysuit bagged on
him. Almost defensively, he said, "Everything reads
fine with the equipment. The calibrations are exactly
what we used yesterday."

DeFore shook her head, rechecking the med sensors she had tied into Kane's subcutaneous tran-

sponder. "I don't know what it is. His brain-wave patterns aren't like anything I've ever seen before during a jump. His baseline temperature has elevated two degrees, and his white-cell blood count has increased in every major organ in his body."

The subcutaneous transponder was a nonharmful radioactive chemical that had been injected into Kane's body and allowed monitoring of his heart rate, brain-wave patterns and blood count. Lakesh had ordered all of the Cerberus redoubt personnel to be injected with them. Based on organic nanotechnology created by the Totality Concept's Overproject Excalibur, the transponder fed information through the Comsat relay satellite when personnel were out in the field. Excalibur was the division of the Totality Concept that had dealt with bioengineering and was responsible for most of the genetic changes that had been wrought before and after the nukecaust that had cashiered the world on January 20, 2001.

"With the white-cell count up," Brigid said, "that indicates some kind of infection. What about the gunshot wound Rouch gave him?"

DeFore shook her head. "I checked Kane out this morning on a prejump exam, same as I did you and Grant. He came up clean. The wound wasn't all that bad to begin with, and it's healing fine."

Brigid wrapped her arms around herself, suddenly feeling cold. The phase-transition coils enclosed within the elevated jump platform produced the steady, high-pitched drone, an electronic synthesis between the device's hurricane howl and its downcycling hum.

Grant stepped up behind her, moving gingerly on his injured right leg. Domi hovered at his side wearing a short red gown that barely kept her modest. "What's going on?" the big man asked.

"Kane's having some kind of reaction to the jump," Brigid answered. She moved into the anteroom, walking to the gateway unit. Pressing her face against the translucent brown-tinted armaglass wall, she peered into the chamber. She saw nothing within it except vague, shifting billows of mist, shapes without form or apparent solidity. Somewhere within them lay Kane.

She knew the mist was plasma bleed-off, the ionized wave forms that resembled vapor. The mainframe computers had been reprogrammed with the logarithmic data recorded during Brigid's and Kane's transit from Tibet with the three pieces of the trapezohedron. The new program prolonged the quincunx effect, stretching it out in perfect balance between the phase and interphase inducers. To maintain the effect, the power drain on the energy resources of the redoubt was enormous. Several nonessential systems had to be taken off-line.

She remembered the jump they'd taken when they returned with the facets of the stone. When they'd arrived, there'd been three phantom Kanes accompanying the real one. Grant had even reached a hand through the real Kane.

Then Brigid realized how subjective she was being with that line of thought. They were all real Kanes. Just from different worlds.

"Then shut the thing down and get him out of there," Grant growled. "Don't have to be a goddamned Tech to figure that out." He shot a harsh glance at Bry, and the effort was pure Mag intimidation, Brigid knew.

The small man deliberately turned away from Grant and returned his attention to the readout screens. Sine and cosine waves stretched and pulsed across them. The instrument panel's design did not conform to the symmetry of the rest of the control consoles in the complex. Dark, long and bulky, like an old-fashioned dining table canted at a thirty-degree angle, it bristled with thousands of tiny electrodes and a complex pattern of naked circuitry. A switchboard at his elbow contained relays and the readout screens.

"Everything here is fine," Bry repeated.

"Can't shut down," Domi said softly, stepping in front of the big man. "Pull Kane out too soon, might fuck up brain worse than is." She laid a small hand on Grant's arm. "Be patient. Time cycle set. Only three more minutes to go."

Kane had chosen to take a ten-minute jump this time, figuring it would give him enough time to observe the other casement before the rest of them went through. Given the distorted time differential between the casements, Brigid knew, that ten minutes could translate into hours or days.

"Patient, my ass," Grant replied, moving toward DeFore. "Kane could be dying in there. I shouldn't have let him talk me into letting him get into that fucking thing by himself. We've been covering each other's back for too long to stop now."

"Friend Grant."

Brigid turned and watched Mohandas Lakesh Singh enter the room. He resembled an animated cadaver, small and hesitant in his steps. Thick glasses covered his rheumy blue eyes. A hearing aid was attached to the right earpiece. Sparse ash-colored hair looked disheveled, and Brigid knew he hadn't gotten much more sleep than any of them. Despite the appearance of advanced age, he moved better than he should have.

He'd been born in 1952, long before the nukecaust that had wiped out so much of the world. He'd been a scientist then, with degrees in cybernetics and quantum mechanics at age nineteen, and he'd worked for premier institutions afterward. Then he'd gone to work at the Project Cerberus site in Dulce, New Mexico.

At the time of the nukecaust, Lakesh had been put into cryogenic sleep for the next 150 years. When he'd been awakened, medics had replaced body parts that had worn-out with bionics and organ transplants. Then he'd been put to work to serve the Program of Unification. Only then had he seen what the scientists he'd worked with had truly wrought. That, Brigid knew, had dropped a burden of guilt on Lakesh that the man would never escape.

"I'm listening," Grant said, but his tone indicated he wasn't going to listen to much. Like Kane, he preferred action, and now the only action that existed was inside the mat-trans unit.

Lakesh walked over to join them despite Grant's threatening bulk. Though at the moment, Brigid thought, it looked like it would be a close contest with Grant's leg in a cast and knowing Lakesh'd had major reconstruction work done on his body.

"Friend Grant," the old man said, "darlingest Domi has plainly stated what fears exist for us to take into consideration if we're to protect friend Kane."

"Fuck that," Grant snarled. "That goddamned stone could be frying his brain in there as we speak. Get him out."

That had been a concern, Brigid knew. Since the Chintamani Stone divided into three parts, they'd each taken one last time. Lakesh had been the first to advance the idea that the trapezohedron wasn't meant to be fully assembled during a jump. When they'd jumped with the first two pieces, there'd been no real feedback. But when Kane had brought the third piece even just into proximity with the others, the strangeness had truly begun.

She remembered the three Kanes Grant had described to her and shivered. The kind of research they were doing now was like poking a stick into a snake hole to see if it was home. She preferred to have more information before she acted. Unfortunately, none existed.

"Like that when you in there," Domi told Grant. "Only not so bad. Had to wait."

Lakesh moved closer to Domi, which put him within reach of Grant. Brigid wasn't sure that was a wise move. Grant wasn't quite as emotionally driven as Kane, but both of them tended to explode before most of the personnel at the redoubt were prepared for it. And Mags weren't versed in aggression control. As Kane had pointed out, that would have made for one dead Mag.

Their propensity for violence, though, had also been responsible for some of their victories over Baron Cobalt and the others.

"The dear child speaks only the truth," Lakesh said to Grant. "The Chintamani Stone seems possessed of its own nature regarding these explorations into the other casements of the multiverse. We were fortunate in being able to ascribe a time cycle to the first jump. To try and preclude such a cycle could prove quite dangerous to friend Kane. If we arbitrarily shut it down, the trapezohedron could seal our Kane's consciousness over in that other casement with his doppelgänger.''

Grant looked back into the mat-trans unit, staring hard through the brown armaglass wall. His expression was harsh, but lights of compassion lit his eyes. ''So what's different than yesterday? Why didn't this happen to all of us yesterday?''

''Perhaps,'' Lakesh said, ''the very variable friend Kane chose to deviate on this excursion. The lack of the trinity. As you may recall, I attempted to discourage this particular foray but he remained quite vocal and obstinate about the whole matter.''

That, Brigid decided, was the perfect example of an understatement. Kane had delivered a riot act, full of the command that had made him one of the most feared Mags in Cobaltville.

''Then what are we gonna do?'' Grant demanded. ''I'm not one for sitting around with my thumb up my ass.''

''No, friend Grant, I would have to agree with you there. Since we preclude that as a possible response to this problem, let's turn our thoughts to other, more positive endeavors, shall we?''

Grant snorted.

''What about an antibiotic?'' Brigid asked.

DeFore shrugged. ''I don't know. I've got these readings from the transponder, but I have to wonder how true they are. They may be influenced by the activity going on in the mat-trans unit, and it could be that these signals are coming from some other Kane.''

''What?'' Grant asked.

"I said," DeFore told him, "that maybe these readings we're picking up are from Kane's doppelgänger."

"An interesting conjecture," Lakesh mused, "but I fear you may be reaching much too far for an answer. I surmise our solution will be found closer to home than that."

DeFore didn't look happy about Lakesh's comment. "Then what do you propose?"

"I propose," Lakesh said quietly, "that we make a comparison of yesterday's brain-wave activities and today's and discover if—and what—incongruencies might exist."

"We don't have all of today's readings," DeFore pointed out. "The cycle hasn't terminated."

"Perhaps," Lakesh said, "we have enough to make a working hypothesis. If Kane has truly picked up an infection and we can rule out an external source—and I'm basing that on the fact that none of the rest of us in this place has evidenced such a sickness—then we need to look inside the man."

"Inside the man," DeFore snapped, "was just fine this morning. Unless you want to dispute my findings."

"No, I shan't do that. But the brain is also organic. And since it seems to be that organ that is suffering most during this particular mat-trans effort and it is actually the mind that appears to transgress the boundaries between the casements, I prefer to do my initial searching there." Lakesh walked back into the control center, followed by Domi, obviously placing herself between the old man and Grant.

Brigid wondered which one the albino thought she was protecting more. Domi had a great friendship with Lakesh, but it was definitely no secret how she felt about Grant.

Brigid leaned her head against the armaglass, hating feeling helpless. In her old life as an archivist, her only problems had involved researching questions or documents. The time constraints were basically artificial. Lives hadn't depended on her answers. At least, she hadn't known it if they had.

"I hate feeling like there's not a goddamned thing I can do," Grant whispered hoarsely at her side.

"I know," Brigid said. "He's going to be fine." They focused on the chron, watching as it counted down the final two minutes of the jump.

Grant nodded. "What makes you so certain?"

"Because to think any other way is intolerable."

Grant leaned on his crutches and dropped a big arm across her shoulders, hugging her tightly. "You're a strong lady."

"I wasn't strong enough to stop him from going alone."

"Nobody," Grant said, "was strong enough for that."

Brigid watched Kane through the armaglass, finally seeing him take a breath. She realized then that she'd been holding her own breath.

Then the chron reached zero.

All of them moved closer.

The high-pitched whine did not break its steady rhythm. The jump didn't end, and Kane remained imprisoned in the other casement.

Grant whirled on Lakesh. "What the hell went wrong, old man?"

Lakesh blinked owlishly behind his thick lenses. "Friend Grant, I do not know," he answered hoarsely. "I haven't a clue."

# Chapter 3

His combat senses flaring, Kane pushed himself into
motion, racing to meet the goblins in the center of
the clearing. Retreating into the brush and trees
wouldn't have given him the room he needed to use
the sword.

The goblins were taller than him, and their flesh
was riddled with open sores that gave off a hideous
odor. He had to force himself to breathe.

Feinting with the sword, sending the goblin to his
left stumbling to the side to avoid the blow, Kane
spun instead, facing the middle goblin. The goblin
had its heavy war hammer lifted over its head, holding the four-foot-long shaft in both hands. Teeth
bared in a hungry grimace, the foul creature brought
the war hammer down.

Kane shifted, a grim smile on his face. At the moment of conflict, his headache and confusion disappeared. Fighting was the one true art he knew, and
he'd always been a man of action. He whipped the
sword forward.

Already committed to the move, dragged by the
weight of the forty-pound hammer, the goblin
squealed in panic as it saw Kane step lithely out of
the way, then swing the sword. The sword bit into
the goblin's midsection with a sound like a melon
splitting. Then its guts spilled forward, worming out

in all directions. It tripped on the intestines, its feet sliding out from under it.

Kane wheeled again, slashing backhanded with the sword. The keen edge sliced through the neck, popping the head free of its shoulders. Before he could move again, the third goblin was on him.

The creature swung its ax as hard as it could.

Desperately, Kane lifted the bloody sword, meeting the ax. Stone rang against iron, and sparks jumped from the impact, hot enough to burn Kane's skin. He moved again, instantly on the attack, knowing the first goblin was already getting to its feet to his left. His movements with the sword were quick and sure, parry and thrust, burying the point deep in the goblin's chest.

Incredibly, the creature managed to grab the sword blade impaling it in one hand, then pulled itself closer. The scream that issued from it was thin and piping, flecked with blood. It raised the ax in one hand.

Kane lifted his foot and kicked the creature in the face. The goblin's corpse stutter-stepped backward, blood spewing and mortally wounded as Kane freed his sword. He ducked under the remaining goblin's initial attack, taking the collision on his left shoulder. He wasn't able to stand against the goblin's charge, though, and wound up getting pushed back to the ground. The goblin fought hard, knotting a hand up in Kane's hair, holding on tight.

It hissed at him, its long, mottled gray tongue flicking out, covered in sores. Then its fangs searched for his throat, snapping closed when Kane levered it away. Still, it clawed at his eyes and face. Kane twisted his head, barely able to keep the goblin's fingers from his eyes. Then he dragged the sword up between them, placing the edge against its throat and shoved back.

Goblin flesh parted instantly at its throat, splashing across Kane's face. He sawed with the sword, letting the edge bite more deeply, rasping against the goblin's backbone. It shuddered and died, its limbs finally going limp.

The goblin blood burned in the scratches in Kane's face, and he knew more than likely that it had poisoned him. There were herbs and salves he could use to disinfect the wounds, but he didn't have any with him.

He stood with effort, legs trembling. The confusion remained in his mind, but he knew the battle was just. It was his alone to do.

"Where do I find the Black Altar?" he asked.

Fand spoke again, but this time her voice sounded much farther away. "You will be taken. Trust me."

Incredibly, Kane found he couldn't implicitly trust Fand. There'd been a separation between them, deceits and blood, but he was damned if he could figure out where or when.

"There's not much time," she implored.

But he knew that might not be true. He'd learned things about the time flow on the other earths.

"Time is elastic," an older man's familiar voice assured Kane. "When you jump through the windows to the other casements, time becomes very malleable. You could spend what seems like years trapped on a lost earth, yet only minutes will pass by here. We don't know if it's always true, and there's no way to be sure."

Kane silently agreed with the man, irritated that the

words were the truth. It made his present circumstances even more confusing.

"You must come," Fand told him.

Kane gazed around the forest. He couldn't find an opening in the tree line or underbrush, nor could he find a memory of how he'd entered the clearing. "I don't know how."

"A way will be made," the woman assured him. "There always is where you're concerned, Ka'in."

As soon as her words faded away, the sound of a horse's hooves drumming against hard-packed earth rang in his ears.

Kane shifted, moving away from the goblin corpses, getting room to maneuver. He breathed out, the way they'd taught him at the baron's keep—Magistrate school, the voice in the back of his mind corrected him—letting the oxygen come back into his system naturally. Perspiration covered him now and caused the leather garments to stick to his skin. He blinked salty tears of perspiration from his eyes.

"Rest easy, Ka'in," Fand said. "This is only an old friend."

Kane didn't relax. Salvo had been more than that, and Kane had taken the man's life to save his own in the end. And Kane slew his brother....

The horse charged through the tree line, bursting through the leafy green in a rush of power and color. With a challenging snort, the stallion galloped into the clearing and spun around to face Kane.

The animal's beauty took Kane's breath away, and sparked a joyous recognition within him. "Dibhirceach," he whispered before he knew it. Then, hearing the name in his own ears, he knew he was right.

The stallion's name was Dibhirceach, taken from the old Gaelic tongue and meaning *vigilant.*

At the mention of his name, the stallion turned his ears forward and nickered. He stood eighteen hands tall or more, broad through the chest and hips. Long muscles roped his mighty frame, giving light to the truth that he was bred for war and battle, able to carry a warrior with sure-footed grace. Cast in purest cinnamon color, with ginger coloring in his flowing mane and tail, he had hooves black as coal, matching the wide-set eyes. Scars crisscrossed his body, testifying to the battles the horse had already seen.

Kane held out a hand. "Dibhirceach."

The stallion whickered, then dropped his head and came forward. He wore no saddle or bridle. When he reached Kane, the horse dropped his muzzle against the man's hand.

The velvet touch of the horse's whiskered muzzle brought a smile to Kane. Despite the death and loss surrounding him, he felt his heart uplifted. He sheathed his bloody sword, not even bothering to clean it. From Fand's tone, he knew it would be wet with blood again before the blade had time to fully dry. He ran his hands along the horse's neck, reacquainting himself and the animal.

Dibhirceach lifted his head, bulling against Kane.

Kane got the message even before Fand's voice touched his mind.

"There is precious little time," she said.

"I know." Kane stepped away from the horse and crossed the clearing to the goblin with Gae Bolg buried in its chest. He looked down at the men, knowing their names now: Old Rassik, who'd been his shield mate through so many battles and had helped him unite the mountain tribes under one banner; Jax, whom he'd taught to hunt only this past winter when the snows had chased most of the game away; Torm, the blacksmith whose strong right arm had beaten most of their swords into shape to stand against the goblins; Hels, who was only a boy who hadn't shaved his first time but now was a blood-drained corpse.

They'd all been his friends, the only family he'd ever truly known.

Grant was missing, he noted from somewhere in the back of his head. His truest friend—there had never been any lies where Grant was concerned. The picture of the black man swelled into Kane's memory. He didn't know where Grant was now, but he felt certain that his friend wasn't part of this memory or this earth. And that felt wrong.

At least Grant was still alive. He hoped.

"Ka'in."

"I led these men and lost them," Kane said. "Now there's no time to mourn them. That's not right, Fand. They deserved more."

"You don't have to be with them when you mourn them."

"It's hard to leave."

"No harder than any of the others you've lost over these lives, Ka'in."

Kane didn't believe that was true; at least he hoped it wasn't. He didn't ever want to think of himself as someone so cold as to accept the loss of a friend's life easily.

"They will be taken care of," she told him.

Feathery sounds brushed against the sky overhead. Kane looked up, watching as hundreds of black-winged ravens settled onto the overhanging branches of the trees. They regarded him silently, their beady eyes bright and sharp.

Kane knew why they were there, and they waited to start their dark feast out of respect for him.

"The ravens will care for your friends, Ka'in," Fand said. "They will not lie here on unhallowed ground where their restless ghosts will be condemned to walk."

Wolves appeared out of the forest, as well, and sat on their haunches. They were lean, hungry beasts, black lips slightly parted to reveal the razor white fangs.

"Nor will their bones be allowed to remain here," Fand went on. "I can do that for you, but to remain here and not finish what you led them to do will only dishonor their memories."

Kane knew it was true. He had no words for good-bye, so he strode to the goblin that held Gae Bolg and yanked the spear free. Then he crossed to Narftil and picked up the standard the young man had carried into battle with them.

The standard was mounted on a staff eight feet long. A tricornered red banner with a wolf's head stitched on it in black thread hung listlessly. It had been his banner, he knew, the one he'd used to unite the rough mountain people. And it had never tasted true defeat.

"Come, Ka'in, leaving the dead warriors behind is never easy for you. But now is the time."

Reluctantly, Kane turned to Dibhirceach. The horse waited patiently, watching the man. Kane looped the heavy war spear over his back, working it in next to the iron sword. Then he grabbed a handful of the stallion's mane and swung aboard. He settled onto the horse's back, immediately feeling that he'd come home.

He took a final look at the dead men, at the ravens and wolves waiting his permission, then he screamed a savage war cry that came from his heart, unleashing the pent-up emotions. He'd lost his whole command in his war against the Daemon Prince, and his only lead was the mental touch of a woman who'd been sired by goblins herself, who'd insisted their fates were intertwined.

As he kicked his heels against the stallion's sides Dibhirceach broke into a gallop. Kane lifted his standard, shoving the butt against his boot toe to balance it. The banner flapped in the breeze created by the horse's fast pace.

Branches whipped at his face and upper body. He hunkered low over the horse, keeping hold of the standard as it whipped through the brush. He kept his body in sync with the stallion, becoming part of the big animal as Dibhirceach burst through trees and brush, following a path that was clearly marked in his head. Kane felt that path, as well—a chill that hung in the air, tinged with nausea.

The big stallion wheeled and galloped, driving deeper into the dark forest, hooves drumming the ground. Abruptly, the silver strand of a river glinted before them. Kane felt certain that the horse would avoid it. Corpses of men and animals floated, staining the whitecapped waters scarlet in some spots.

But Dibhirceach maintained a straight course. The horse's muscles bunched as he gathered himself and jumped toward the river from an overhang ten feet above.

Kane held on to the horse with his knees, grabbing

a last quick breath before they dropped into the water. They plunged under.

The cold water drove ice spikes of pain into Kane's body, clearing away the rage and frustration and guilt he felt. When they surfaced, only their heads above the roaring water, the falls thundering nearby as the current shoved them toward it, Kane's mind was clear, focused. He hung on to the horse as he floated free of it.

The stallion swam strongly, not giving in to the cold or the current's strength.

The corpse of a middle-aged man slammed into Kane, almost tearing him loose from his grip. He knew if he lost the stallion he was lost himself. He plunged under the water again, letting the corpse go by. By the time he resurfaced, they were at the other side.

He pulled himself to Dibhirceach's back again as the great warhorse climbed the bank. The stallion took off at a gallop again, not showing any signs of flagging strength.

As they galloped through the countryside on the other side of the river, Kane noticed the climate change. Here it was cold, almost freezing, and it wasn't just because of the dip in the river. Dibhirceach's breath fogged out in front of him in long plumes.

The tree leaves were a colder green, lacking luster, and the bark held a silvery sheen that looked like ice. Above the trees, the sky was slate gray, no longer bright blue the way it had been on the other side of the river.

''You've entered more deeply into the Daemon

Prince's territory," Fand said. "He knows you're coming."

"Saves me from knocking at the door," Kane said grimly.

"You're not looking for him," Fand replied. "You must find the Black Altar. With it, the Daemon Prince can enslave your world, and all the worlds of it that are shadows of each other."

The words flickered through Kane's mind, touching another memory that didn't belong here. "The lost earths?"

"They've been called that."

"Where will I find the Black Altar?"

"Ahead," Fand told him. "In the rowan tree."

Before he could ask where the rowan tree was, Kane saw it. The rowan tree stood tallest among all those around it. The girth of the trunk was huge, more than a man could hope to begin to encircle with his arms, probably more than any five or six men could encircle even joining hands.

Dibhirceach ran harder, powering toward the rowan tree.

Kane felt the tension, as well. The Daemon Prince didn't leave any of his secret places of power unprotected. That Kane was able to locate it at all was a miracle.

Less than fifty feet from the rowan tree, just as Kane started to notice the lack of leaves on the tree but the presence of blossoms somehow growing on top of the thick branches and the blobs hanging down from others, they were attacked.

Dibhirceach had just crested the final ridge that poured into a bowl-shaped depression when the goblins shoved up from pits in the ground, discarding the cut sections of grassy earth they'd used to disguise themselves. They carried axes and war hammers, swords and clubs, and attacked without fear, throwing themselves in front of the warhorse.

"DEAREST BRIGID."

She turned at the sound of her name, discovering Lakesh standing there. She hadn't heard him come up behind her. "You found something?" she asked.

An hour had gone by since the time cycle ended, and Kane's fever had increased as the phase-transition process continued.

"Perhaps," Lakesh answered. "There is a discrepancy in the EEGs registering through friend Kane's transponder."

Brigid nodded. "DeFore noticed that when Kane jumped back with the fragments of the Chintamani Stone. She said his brain-wave patterns had totally changed for a short time there."

"Yes. And they returned to their proper natures afterward. While we observed the three of you yesterday, we were able to accumulate an abundance of statistical information. Of course, we've not had requisite time to properly analyze and assimilate it, but it's been enough to make some guesses."

"Guesses?" Brigid asked in disgust. "We need answers, Lakesh. Kane is trapped in there, maybe dying. Guesses aren't enough." Her voice broke, and she found herself talking louder than she intended, almost shouting. "Get him out of there!"

Lakesh looked uncomfortable. He waited, thankfully giving her time to regain control. "I would if I could, dearest Brigid."

She turned away from him, not wanting him to see

her weakness. "Guesses aren't good enough at this point, Lakesh."

The old man touched her shoulder tenderly, offering his support. "Guesses, dearest Brigid, are all I'm afraid this old head has to offer. But I promise you, they will be my very best ones."

DeFore approached them wearing a concerned expression. "His temperature's still climbing. He's at 103.4 now."

"Another degree and a half," Grant said, on the med tech's heels, "and Kane's going to end up having his brain scrambled. Once a fever gets a man and goes too far, there's no helping him. I've seen it caused by rad sickness. And once the brain's been affected, what you have for all intents and purposes is a zombie. Living dead. For fun you can prop him up and watch him drool."

Brigid almost lost her temper. If it hadn't been for her archivist training and her temperament, she might have anyway. Grant's words were harsh and cold, but she knew the man loved Kane as much as—

As much as anyone did, she told herself.

"The fever is something we'll deal with once we can get to him," DeFore announced.

"Follow me," Lakesh said. "We'll talk and see if we can demystify some of the problem that faces us." He lifted an arm toward the control complex. "I've been studying the findings Dr. DeFore and friend Bry have accumulated relating to the other jumps."

Reluctantly, Brigid left the mat-trans unit. "Kane, hold on," she said to the armaglass before trailing after Lakesh into the control complex.

# Chapter 4

Wheeling, Dibhirceach avoided the first of the goblins. The stallion's hooves cut into the ground as he raced toward the outer edge of their attackers.

Kane reached over his back and pulled Gae Bolg free. He hung on to the horse as Dibhirceach reared and brought a big hoof crashing down on the nearest goblin's head. Bone splintered and crunched, and gray matter erupted from the broken space. The goblin corpse dropped.

Dibhirceach stutter-stepped again, a move Kane had instinctively prepared for, and butted into another goblin, catching it off balance and knocking it down the ridge. The trees on either side of the battle area were too close to allow them to go around the pits dug in the ground. If the horse stepped into one of them, chances were his leg would be broken. And the goblins would swarm over both of them.

With Gae Bolg in his hand, Kane ducked under a sweeping blow of a stone ax. He kept his fist near the middle of the war spear so he could move it, clinging to the horse with his knees. Bringing the standard up, he blocked the foul creature's next blow, then slashed out with the war spear's heavy blade. Gae Bolg took the goblin's head off with ease in a bloody arc.

Dibhirceach backed suddenly and reared again. The sharp-edged hoof raked across the front of the creature's skull. Shrilling in pain, the goblin clapped its hands to the bloody hole where its face had been and fell away.

Kane stabbed another goblin in the throat as it advanced on Dibhirceach, slashing the windpipe with the spear's edged tip. Gurgling and coughing, the creature swayed uncertainly till another goblin climbed its back and leaped toward Kane. Reversing the war spear with skill, Kane slammed the butt into the creature's ribs, breaking several and knocking it off balance.

The stallion gathered himself, and Kane sensed the animal's next move. Exploding suddenly, Dibhirceach hurled himself through the knot of goblins, slamming into them with his broad chest and scattering them like leaves as he drove forward.

Kane readied himself, holding tightly with his knees and fisting Gae Bolg and the standard. When Dibhirceach reached the edge of the pits dug into the soft black earth, Kane tightened his grip. Then the stallion was in the air, leaping over the pits.

The incline fell away on the other side of the pits, strewed with fallen branches and huge rocks. The leap was only feet out horizontally, but it was yards deep. Sharpened wooden spikes pointed up from the bottom of the incline.

Dibhirceach reached forward with his front hooves, skidding and sliding down the incline's steep face. The sharp hooves couldn't find purchase in the loose soil, leaving deep scars behind as it skidded toward the wooden spikes like a flesh-and-blood avalanche.

Kane leaned back, his knees locked behind the horse's shoulder blades, depending on the shared dampness from the river to help give him the friction he needed to stay seated. His back touched the stallion's rump, staying in line with the warhorse as much as he could. It leaped again, clearing the spikes by inches.

After thirty yards through tearing branches that left welts on Kane's body and flying earth clods that smacked wetly into him, Dibhirceach reached the center of the depression. The horse grunted with the effort of staying on his feet. Huge plumes of gray fog puffed from his nostrils. Then he got his feet under him, charging toward the rowan tree.

Kane sat up, melding back into the stallion's rhythm. He twisted, glancing back up, and saw the goblins stumbling in pursuit. They leaped and capered down the incline, throwing themselves in rolls to break their fall. Two of them ended up on the sharpened stakes, their gray-green bodies pierced in multiple places. They struggled to get free, screaming in animal pain.

The small clearing around the rowan tree was cluttered with dead crimson leaves that looked like bloody handprints overlaying each other. The ground was flat, desolate, and nothing grew there.

Kane scanned the rowan tree, expecting the Black Altar to be erected somewhere in front of it. Or perhaps an opening carved into the dead tree itself. He saw nothing except the aged bark covered in orange-and-yellow fungus that stood out in ragged blades between eight inches and a foot tall.

"The Black Altar," Fand told him, sounding stronger again.

"Where?" Kane demanded. His breath poured raggedly through his burning throat, gusting out in gray clouds. His face felt tight, and he realized when he raked a shoulder against it that the feeling was because the river water and perspiration had turned to a thin layer of ice in the changed climate he found himself in.

The goblins screamed their blood lust, rushing at him with upraised weapons. They closed the distance rapidly.

"In the tree," Fand told him.

Dibhirceach turned, placing his haunches near the tree and readying himself for the attack.

Kane glanced up into the rowan tree and saw the horror that awaited him. The Black Altar was a thick slab of ebony rock jutting out from the crown of the rowan tree nearly a hundred feet straight up. In addition to the fungus that clung to the tree, blossoms sprouted from the naked branches like festering tumors, proof that something evil flowed through the tree instead of sap. The blossoms were four feet broad, standing up from gray-green tendrils that gripped the branches like arthritic fingers, wrapping around the branches as well as themselves. The blossoms were the dirty white of old death, without any kind of a shine.

And then Kane saw what he'd mistaken for fruit hanging from the branches. A low, guttural growl escaped his lips before he could contain it.

Something had hung corpses from the tree branches, binding them there with spiderwebs. There were a dozen or more of them—old and young, men and women. They'd all died hard, bearing the marks of swords, blunt instruments and fangs.

The closest corpse was only twenty feet away. Kane saw her clearly. The dead woman hung by one foot, upside down, her arms and other leg flailing away from her body in the relaxed repose of death. She was naked, covered with a yellow, shiny, jellylike substance. Her red-gold hair was plastered together, hanging down in long strands.

Kane peered more closely, afraid of what he'd find. *Anam-chara.* The term leaped to his mind, as did Brigid Baptiste's name, but he kept them from his lips.

The jellylike substance coated her face, blurring her features. She looked lanky and lean, her skin hanging loosely from her bones. With a shudder, Kane realized the flesh was sloughing away from her bones, breaking apart in places.

"It's the rowan tree's need to be fed," Fand said. "The fungus produces an acid that dissolves flesh over a time. When the corpse rots, it in turn feeds the rowan tree, which feeds the fungus. One can't exist without the other."

It was a symbiotic relationship, Kane knew, though how he knew that term escaped him.

"You can't escape the goblins, Ka'in. You must climb. The Daemon Prince uses the rowan tree to guard his Black Altar."

Kane swung his gaze back to the approaching creatures, seeing the goblins were almost on him and Dibhirceach. He looped Gae Bolg across his back again, then lifted his standard butt-first toward the screaming goblinkin. He thrust with all his might, burying the sharpened end of the standard pole in the goblin's chest and shoving the creature back.

The dying goblin fell backward, clasping the standard pole in one hand as it threw the ax with the other. The ax missed Kane, but the goblin fell, dead before it hit the ground. The black wolf on the red field stood proudly upright, grounded in the body of Kane's enemy.

Springing lithely, Kane leaped from Dibhirceach's back into the lower limbs of the tree. The warhorse reared and brought his flashing hooves down on the nearest attackers. Kane knew the great beast would break free. Dibhirceach hadn't been sired to die at the claws of goblins.

The horse neighed out his challenge and broke through the goblins' ranks.

Kane noticed his hands burning; the acids the fungus produced weren't enough to disable him, but the pain was severe. His wished for a pair of gloves, but had none. And there was no time to try to fashion some sort of relief from the clothes that he wore.

Axes and hammers flew up at him, slamming against the rowan tree's bark and branches, sending thick chunks of the fungus flying. He kept climbing, feeling the burn of exertion along his back, legs and arms. His head throbbed, as if his brain had swelled three times its normal size inside his skull. He knew something was wrong.

*Get him out of there!*

The voice was feminine, but it didn't belong to Fand. *Anam-chara,* he thought. He kept climbing, feeling his limbs tremble. He estimated that he was halfway to the Black Altar, but his lungs were already screaming for more air. His vision blurred, doubling. He reached for a branch and missed.

For a moment, he hung out over open space, then he fell. His fingertips grazed the rough bark of another branch. He curled his hand around it, feeling the flesh on his palm shred and tear. He hung on in spite of the pain and pulled himself back up.

*Kane, hold on!*

Shuddering with effort, he pulled himself up, resting for just a moment as he tried to recover his breath. He peered down through the naked branches.

The goblins had surrounded the tree, chittering up at him in anger and fear. One of them reached out to the tree, getting ready to climb after him. As soon as it touched the bark, however, the misshapen creature exploded into flames.

Squalling in agony, the goblin released the tree and ran, as if trying to escape the fire spreading all over its body. The flames just burned hotter. Before it had taken half a dozen strides, the goblin collapsed, overcome by the heat and lack of oxygen. It died on the scattering of leaves that looked like bloody handprints.

"The Dark Prince comes, Ka'in," Fand warned. "You have no defense against him."

"IF YOU'LL REFER to the graphs and diagrams friend Bry established," Lakesh said, seated at the desk, "you'll note the similarities we documented."

Brigid took her glasses out and put them on. All the years of working in Cobaltville's archives had left her with astigmatism. She compared the beginning brain waves of Grant, Kane and herself. Although all three of them were different, there were some similarities regarding the deep-sleep and REM functions that were evidently associated with the brain activity demanded by the mat-trans jumps to the alternate earths.

"Looks like a bunch of damned gobbledygook to me," Grant commented. He pushed his copy of the reports away from him across the table.

Lakesh kept a calm demeanor. He took a soft towel from his pocket and cleaned his glasses. "The alpha states the mat-trans unit calibrates through the Chintamani Stone are evidently necessary to make the jump. The intervals DeFore had marked for your observation have twenty-seven common points, even taking into consideration the three different brain waves and two sexes. Even the jump friend Kane is now on had the same initial jump prerequisites. But fifteen minutes into it, those stats changed."

Brigid referenced the new readout on Kane's current jump again. The first fifteen minutes had been similar, but everything since looked alien: the graphs went from solid lines of peaks and valleys to a series of four intermittent straight lines of dots and dashes.

Grant's eyes narrowed. "Why did they change?"

Lakesh laced his fingers together, resting his elbows on the table. "DeFore and I believe it reflects a—a false casement."

"They're all false, old man," Grant said impatiently, "all shadows of our own time line."

"We've never verified that," Brigid interjected. "For all we know, we're one of the bent time lines springing from the central core."

"I refuse to believe that shit," Grant said.

"Why?" DeFore asked. "You've seen one of those other casements yourself."

Grant faced her and shook his head. "Because that line of thinking is stupe. Believing, even doubting, that we're not the true time line is one short step from madness."

"And there may be a dozen different Grants stating that very same belief at this moment," DeFore returned. "So which one is right if they all believe the same thing?"

"Me," Grant answered without hesitation.

"Have you considered the possibility that you're wrong?" DeFore asked. "It's possible that the 'real' time line's Grant is dead."

Grant smiled. "Exactly my point. If I'm going to pick a time line to save, I'm going to pick one that's got me in it."

"Grant's right," Domi said in a challenging tone. "Be real stupe to save time line and lose own ass."

"I keep forgetting," DeFore said sarcastically. "You're not exactly the sacrificing type, are you?"

Genuine laughter gleamed in Grant's dark eyes. "Hell, I don't mind sacrificing as long as I'm not the sacrificee."

"Mebbe we pick time line that has no DeFore," Domi threatened. "Save that one." Her crimson eyes pulsed like bleeding wounds. It was no secret that she felt jealous of DeFore. The albino believed that the med tech had some interest in Grant.

Brigid hadn't precluded that plausibility, either. Grant was an attractive man, and she'd seen DeFore looking. "Perhaps we could get back to our current problem before we move onto the others." She glanced through the ready room door and at the gateway unit.

"Of course, dear Brigid," Lakesh said. He flicked his rheumy gaze over to Grant. "We do face a certain amount of time pressure."

Grant waved the comment away. "Tell me about this false casement, then."

"It is pure conjecture," the old man said, "and we

won't be able to substantiate it until friend Kane rejoins us.''

"Don't you mean 'if'?"

Lakesh shifted in the chair, evidently choosing not to respond to the question. Opening a drawer, he removed a gray metal box, placed it on the desk and opened the lid. Within lay two black stones, nearly identical, roughly the size and shape of a man's fist. At first, and even second glance, they appeared to be chunks of obsidian, or some other dark mineral. Only by careful examination could the eye discern the marks of tools on them, or faint scratches that might be inscriptions.

"There were three facets of the Chintamani Stone, and there are the three of you. DeFore and I have talked, wondering what it was about you that you three had in common and would allow only you to access the casements with the stone's help. And we came up with only one answer."

"Kane," Brigid said softly.

Lakesh nodded. "Yes, dear Brigid. My belief is that Balam gave the Chintamani Stone to Kane and triggered it to align itself with his brain waves, making him unique among any others. When the two of you arrived from Tibet, only he was strangely affected by the jump, manifesting himself as three other selves."

"But that may have been because he had physical possession of the three facets of the stone at that time. If I'd had possession of it, maybe it would have aligned itself with me," Brigid argued.

"Perhaps, but I believe Balam knew exactly what would happen. Remember, he is essentially a planner.

Think about all the things he was involved in over the centuries.''

"So he selected Kane for the stone?'' Grant growled.

"I believe so, on whatever basis he made his choice. And I believe Balam knew a strong possibility existed for Kane—as well as the two of you—to foil the plots and actions of our adversary. I believe Kane's decision to make the next jump a solitary one was an enormous mistake.''

"Made sense for him to try to recce the next casement by making a short jump,'' Grant stated. "I'd have gone if he'd let me.''

"I think that the programming in the Chintamani Stone's crystalline infrastructure would have prevented that,'' Lakesh said. "I believe friend Kane has become the key by which egress into the other casements will be made. Whatever the three casements are that we have access to through the stone, I believe they are of extreme importance to Colonel Thrush.''

"There could be more than three alternate earths open to us,'' Brigid said. "If we find a way to alter the Chintamani Stone's internal vibrations.''

"As you say, dear Brigid,'' Lakesh acknowledged. "But I don't believe that undertaking could ever be as simple as modifying the frequencies inherent in a ham radio's crystal diode. At present, I want to restrict my active pursuit to these three casements presented to us. There is a reason why these are open to us, why Balam thought they would be vulnerable to our attempts to set things right.''

"The casement we were in yesterday,'' Brigid stated softly. "Kane said that Thrush admitted that casement had been altered.''

"And he appeared quite disconcerted about it," Lakesh agreed. "However, as friend Kane noted, the infamous colonel also seemed to possess some kind of memory of seeing Kane before."

"From the jump back over the interphaser," Brigid said. "We all saw versions of Thrush at different times in history."

During her trip to 1945, Domi had witnessed Thrush's execution of Adolph Hitler. In 1947, Brigid had watched Thrush remove and hide proof of the Archon presence in Roswell, New Mexico. Kane had arrived in Dallas, Texas, in 1963 to watch Thrush's involvement in the assassination of President John F. Kennedy. And in 2001, Thrush had spoken to Grant after activating the nuclear bomb in the Russian embassy, giving them his name and telling him there was nothing they could do to unravel the Gordian knot that had tied together all the scattered threads of time.

Even Lakesh had his memories of the man. Thrush had been a United States Air Force colonel connected with the Totality Concept.

"The bastard remembered all of us after a while," Grant growled, shifting irritably in his seat.

"Exactly," Lakesh said. "The question is, how?"

"It was in his past," Grant answered. "No goddamned mystery about that."

Lakesh nodded, smiling like a teacher who'd seen the light of intelligence finally flash in a dim pupil, "As you say, friend Grant. And now your visit to the casement yesterday is likewise in Thrush's memory. He will know that the three of you have traveled as 'silent invaders,' as he calls them. And he knows that you can now act in those casements he's nurtured so carefully. There's every chance that he will now be on his guard against you.''

Grant's eyes narrowed. "You think Kane walked into a trap? In the form of a false casement?''

"To put it succinctly, I think there's been every opportunity that Thrush constructed such a thing to intercept Kane's next foray into the alternate casements," Lakesh said.

"That could explain the wild EEGs we're getting from Kane now," DeFore said.

Lakesh warmed to the subject, his rheumy eyes fixing on a nether distance as he glanced at the ceiling. "We know that Thrush is somehow linked to the Chintamani Stone. Assuming the Archon Directorate had influence in Thrush's creation, perhaps they entered a codex into his makeup that makes the two interdependent on each other. The information one version of Thrush knows, mayhap all of them know.''

"There could be a lag," DeFore said, tapping a pencil against the tabletop. "We know there are time differentials between the casements.''

"One can only hope," Lakesh agreed. "It would be a weakness in the design that we could exploit.''

"I've got one more to toss at you," Grant said. He rubbed a hand against his lower face, his callused hand rasping against the stubble on his chin.

"What?'' Lakesh asked.

"Dividing the trapezohedron makes sense," Grant said. "Mebbe having three of them on a jump diffuses Thrush's ability to monitor the casements. He didn't know we were there until he caught us behaving out of character for the doppelgängers we'd taken over. Kane jumping into the casement alone—''

"Was the equivalent of leaping into a lion's

mouth,'' Lakesh finished. He nodded unhappily, looking more tired than Brigid thought she'd ever seen him. ''Thrush could simply kill him over there and leave Kane's true consciousness floating somewhere in in-between space, or trap him in a never ending loop of worthless experiences.''

The room got quiet as the dark possibilities occupied their minds.

Brigid looked through the doorway at the mat-trans unit's brown armaglass wall. ''The question remains,'' she said, calming herself, ''of how to bring Kane back out.''

# Chapter 5

Kane shoved himself into motion again, working with the double vision by verifying a branch was there with a hand or foot before simply assuming. The pain in his head grew more intense, thunderous. He was less than ten feet from the Black Altar when he heard the Daemon Prince.

"Kane!" The dry, whispering voice could only belong to the Daemon Prince.

Thrush, the voice in the back of Kane's mind argued.

Kane kept climbing, within three feet of the black stone table now. Then he lunged for the altar, gripping the stone in his fingers.

The headache disappeared immediately, and he felt refreshed. He breathed easily, grateful for the healing contact.

"Ka'in, no, my love. Don't give in to the Black Altar's seduction," Fand pleaded. "It is a truly monstrous and evil thing."

"Did you come here to die?" the dry voice asked, closer now. "Again?"

Kane slipped his dagger from his boot, turning to face his opponent.

The Daemon Prince floated up from the ground effortlessly, looking totally relaxed. He was as thin as a famine victim, but looked tall. His bald head was covered with black tattooing in archaic runes. His high cheekbones and thin-lipped mouth looked artificial, as though sculpted by a cold and passionless hand. A black bearskin cape, held together by a silver chain with large links, fluttered around him as he flew upward. He wore a black tunic and black breeches tucked into bearskin boots.

Colonel C. W. Thrush, Kane remembered.

"Destroy the altar!" Fand ordered. "It must be done now!"

Kane watched the figure rise toward him, remembering that they'd fought before. And the Daemon Prince had won. He'd seen his own death, then he'd lived through it.

"The human trait of stubbornness in the face of the true nature of things has always intrigued me," the Daemon Prince stated in a flat monotone. "You know your own limitations, your own weaknesses, yet so many of you fight to deny them."

"All you know are lies, hell-spawn," Kane said. He waited, the dagger blade held in his fingertips, wishing he had a bow or a Sin Eater blaster.

"On the contrary, Kane," the Daemon Prince said. "I know the truths. All of them. Things you and your little group can only guess at."

"Destroy the Black Altar, Ka'in," Fand pleaded.

*Hold on, Kane, damn you!* The voice belonged to still another woman, one Kane had talked to only that morning. He searched for her name, but the blade in his hand felt more certain and more true.

The Black Altar began to vibrate under him as if an electric current was passing through it.

The Daemon Prince halted on a level even with him. His cold gaze regarded Kane judiciously. "I've always found it curious that in every branching of the multiverse there exists a version of you. Not all of your friends are represented on the casements created by Operation Chronos.''

Kane listened, waiting for his opportunity. He felt his heart pounding inside his chest, too hard to be normal.

"Do you want to know how many times I've executed you on those other casements?'' the Daemon Prince asked.

"Doesn't matter. You'll have to keep killing me.''

"Seventeen times,'' the Daemon Prince said. "Seventeen times a version of yourself has put yourself in harm's way, and I've killed you or had you killed. I don't always have to do that. Sometimes you're serving me on those casements, and people fear you as much as I've taught them to fear me.''

Kane didn't want to believe that was true. But he knew it was possible. His other self on the first alternate earth he had jumped to with Brigid and Grant had been a willing part of the Third Reich, an officer even. "We changed things there, didn't we? All the carefully laid plans you were following collapsed on that lost earth, didn't they?''

"You were a failure there, Kane, just as you're going to be one here.''

"No,'' Kane roared defiantly. "Balam gave me the Chintamani Stone, and it's some kind of key to the multiverse. Three people, three worlds.''

The Daemon Prince regarded him coldly, and for a moment Kane thought he'd penetrated Thrush's calm demeanor. "You fool yourself, Kane. Balam gave you nothing.''

But Kane knew the man was lying. They'd first

encountered Thrush when they'd inadvertently tried to jump back to the Cerberus redoubt using an interphaser to open a gateway to the mat-trans unit. He, Domi, Brigid and Grant had seen Thrush scattered across four different time periods, taking part in important events that had shaped the world. Or the worlds. And later, in yet another time period, they'd found out he was a hybrid cyborg created to maintain the different branches of the multiverse.

The Black Altar continued thrumming.

Dark clouds swirled overhead, heavy with the threat of rain. Lightning flared through the clouds with wicked, narrow fingers. Storm winds suddenly blew up, lashing out at the trees.

Kane held on to the Black Altar as the wind tried to rip him from it.

"It's time to die, Kane," the Daemon Prince promised. Lightning flashed down from the clouds, gathering into a ball between his open palms.

Rain drenched Kane as the sky split open. He peered up at the Daemon Prince through slitted eyes, watching the lightning between Thrush's palms gain in intensity. The glare through harsh white light over him, hurting his eyes. He pushed himself to his feet, standing on the Black Altar. Reaching over his shoulder, he drew Gae Bolg as the Daemon Prince released the trapped lightning.

The lightning bolt sizzled toward Kane.

He had the war spear in front of him before the lightning struck him, planting the drenched butt against the Black Altar at his feet. The jagged lightning bolt seared a wash of heat over him, but it struck Gae Bolg's iron head in a blinding flash of energy.

Kane guessed that he might be electrocuted at once,

but there'd been no other moves to make, and blocking with the spear had felt natural.

The current raced through the spear's iron head and wet wooden haft, burning through Kane's hands. He was in agony, then everything went numb. The lightning slithered through the Black Altar, absorbing the energy.

"No," Thrush said hoarsely.

But the damage was already done. Despite the certainty that he was on the point of death, Kane grinned wolfishly. Static electricity made his wet hair stand out wildly, sparks jumping between the strands. He felt vague popping between his teeth. The hair on his arms stood out, as well. And Gae Bolg grounded more and more of the lightning bolts streaking down from the stormy skies into the Black Altar.

The vibration filling the altar continued to grow geometrically. Then it exploded, flinging chunks of black rock in all directions.

Kane fell, miraculously still alive, preserved perhaps because the Black Altar attracted most of the lightning's fury. He let himself go limp. Even if the goblins weren't still surrounding the rowan tree, hitting the ground from a hundred feet up wasn't promising. He hoped for landing on a branch, barely aware of Thrush still hovering overhead.

He kept his face protected as well as he could. Slamming against a branch drove the breath from his lungs, and he didn't manage a hold before he kept on falling. Then he landed sooner than he expected, striking a soggy mass that squished against him.

Stunned for a moment, Kane looked up, recognizing the petals of the grisly blossom parasites that bloomed on the rowan tree. His lungs ached for air, but he forced himself to move. His hands were still numb, and static electricity continued discharging from his body in small sparks.

Then the blossom petals wrapped down over him, hugging him close. They pulled him into the dead flesh already waiting to be absorbed, cloying his nostrils with the sweet musk of meat gone bad. The waiting dark swept over him, washing his senses away.

BRIGID STOOD OUTSIDE the armaglass and visualized Kane inside the mat-trans unit. A whirl of mixed emotions filled her as she focused on his image. Kane was at once the most attractive and most vexing man she'd ever known. If she'd allowed herself the luxury, and she didn't because she was too well trained for that, she told herself, she might have wondered what their lives might have been like if they'd been shaped by different circumstances, had lived in a different world.

"Kane," she said softly. "You've got to wake up, Kane. Come back to us here."

Silently, knowing the others had unanimously chosen her as the one Kane would most likely respond to, Brigid concentrated on the visions she'd had of him in the jump dreams. She pictured the younger version of Kane racing to her rescue with his sword lifted in her defense. Who had taken her then? She considered the question in the past briefly, but she had no real answers.

Thinking about the jump dreams brought up another possibility. Mildred Wyeth, who'd traveled the Deathlands with the warrior named Ryan Cawdor, had recorded the fact that their band of survivors had discovered the mat-trans unit. One of their group, a man named Dr. Theophilus Algernon Tanner, had given them the activation codes for the mat-trans units. He'd been an anomaly himself, a man pulled from the nineteenth century by Cerberus's time-trawling experiments, then shoved deeply into the twenty-first century after the nukecaust had happened.

She hadn't encountered Thrush in the jump dreams until they'd used the interphaser. She made a mental note to ask Lakesh about the possibility that Thrush had the interphaser frequencies monitored to watch for the Chintamani Stone. Or perhaps Kane.

The two men had recognized an eternal enmity between them on first meeting. The idea that she and Kane had existed at other times in other lives had seemed preposterous to her when it had first come up. Maybe it still would have if she hadn't experienced those jump dreams herself.

And if she weren't aware of the deep tie between herself and Kane.

They didn't know how long the creature that called itself Thrush had lived. They presumed he'd been created by the Archon Directorate. At least, the hybridized and cyborg parts of him had been. But what about the human part? How long had it been around?

It was too much to think about. Resolutely, Brigid pushed the conjectures away. What mattered here and now was Kane.

She pressed her palm flat against the chilled armaglass, feeling her own heartbeat echo through her arm. She concentrated on that vision of Kane: young and arrogant, indestructible. And she did what Grant had advised, believing he would be okay.

Because believing anything else would have been intolerable.

*"Anam-chara,"* she said, "don't go."

ANAM-CHARA, *DON'T GO.*

Kane stirred, drawn by the words. Even as he opened his eyes, the blackness that surrounded him didn't go away. He couldn't feel his body, couldn't feel the grotesque hell flower that had closed on him. He recognized the voice but couldn't put a name to it.

He tried to move in the darkness but couldn't tell if he was. He felt mired in the nothingness. There was no frame of reference, and as a Mag he'd never been totally lost.

*Kane.*

His lips parted and the name came out. "Brigid." Only he didn't normally call her that. He called her something else.

Without warning, the darkness changed. An even darker spot opened up in the space he considered to be facing him. He felt himself sucked toward it on gentle eddies. A cold ball formed in his stomach, not true fear, but a warning nonetheless. Instinct told him that if he entered that spot, only bad things would happen. However, he had no control over his own movement.

Then brightness entered the dark, chasing it away in peeled shadows. A woman's hand, followed by her arm, thrust into the darkness.

Looking at it, Kane for some reason thought a sword was missing.

*Kane, it's not time to leave yet. You're not finished.*

With titanic effort, Kane reached out for the hand, grasping it tightly. The warmth flooded his flesh, chased away the deep cold he hadn't even been aware that had filled him. He pulled, knowing he was leaving the cloying darkness behind. *"Anam-chara."*

AT FIRST, BRIGID THOUGHT she only imagined Kane's voice in her mind. She knew what he was saying and she said it with him. *"Anam-chara."* Tears stung her eyes.

DeFore surveyed her equipment. "The EEG has changed again."

Grant was there in a heartbeat despite the cast on his leg. He pulled the scrolling paper out and studied the markings. A broad grin split his dark stubbled face. He looked up at DeFore. "This mean what I think it means?"

DeFore nodded. "Yes. He's coming back."

Grant loosed a whoop of savage, unrestrained joy, then swept DeFore up off her feet with one big arm. "You did it! You kept him alive till he could do it for himself!"

Embarrassed by the display of emotion, DeFore tried pushing herself free of Grant's arm. "Careful, dammit. You're going to rebreak that leg, and I don't want to have to set it again."

Grant released her and stepped away.

And Domi looked daggers at the woman.

The expression brought back to mind Beth-Li Rouch's own jealousy to Brigid. At some point, she knew, Grant was going to have to pay attention to the dynamic between the two women.

"There is some reason for this joyous outbreak, dearest Brigid?" Lakesh approached from the control room, fatigue hanging over him like a second layer of skin.

"Kane," Brigid said, pointing.

Lakesh stared at the armaglass, and a slight smile curved his lips. "You can't kill him that easily," he whispered. "I planned too hard, built him too well for that."

And Brigid forgave him that bit of false pride. Whatever genetic manipulations Lakesh had performed on Kane's DNA, she felt certain the success belonged more to Kane's warrior spirit.

The keening drone produced by the phase-transition coils faltered, then faded. Brigid heaved up on the handle of the jump chamber and pulled it open on counter-balanced hinges. Wavering fingers of mist rose before her. Before she could enter, Kane sat up from the floor, voicing a savage scream mixed of anger and fear.

"Fuck! Lakesh! Goddammit, Lakesh!" He flung the facet of the Chintamani Stone blindly, and it bounced across the interlocking hexagonal floor plates. His facet was much larger than the other two pieces, and its surface was as smooth as if it had been polished and lacquered to acquire a semireflective sheen.

Lakesh put his foot on the stone to keep it from rolling out into the ready room. "I'm here, friend Kane."

"IT WAS A TRAP," Grant said. "The fucker was waiting on you."

Standing outside the redoubt and looking down over the countryside, Kane took a deep drag off his cigar. "This time," he agreed. Hours had passed since he'd stumbled out of the mat-trans chamber and into DeFore's lab. She'd given him a full round of antibiotics, a B-12 booster and analgesics for the fever and headache that accompanied it.

"Thrush knowing we're coming changes the

game," Grant commented. "We go over there totally stupe about who we really are, bastard's going to have an edge."

"Yeah," Kane agreed with a crooked grin, "but us not knowing who we really are is about the best disguise I could imagine." He hit the cigar again, then released a blue-gray haze into the air.

"Then, once Thrush figures out who we are, he tries to chill us."

"And we try to chill him," Kane agreed. "Because he can't figure us out for silent invaders until we figure it out for ourselves. Then it's him against us, and all bets are off."

"The bastard's got the home-ground advantage," Grant said. He struck a match with his thumbnail and relit the stump of his own cigar.

"I know."

Grant narrowed his eyes, studying Kane. "You weren't so happy about making another jump again this morning. At least, that's the way I remember it."

"You remember it right."

Grant pursed his lips and spit out a fleck of tobacco. "So what's changed?"

Kane stared across the western sky, noticing that the sun was starting to set. He tried to put his feelings into words, not for the first time learning how limited they truly were. He'd already briefed all of them on his experiences while in the casement. "You ever been really scared, Grant?"

Grant looked as if he was going to offer one of his usual wiseass remarks. Then he evidently reconsidered it. "Yeah. Been in that neighborhood a lot of times. Even when I was a Mag. With the way things are now, the shit we're slogging around in, I get that way a lot. Can't let it get to you, though.''

"I'm not," Kane assured him. "But when I was in that empty space, after the casement had played out...I don't think I've ever felt like that."

"Fear's a natural thing, Kane. Nature's way to get the adrenaline flowing. Pushes the physical up to peak performance, and takes away all the questions about right and wrong."

Kane rounded the ash on his cigar on the fence post, shaping it deliberately.

"That voice you heard," Grant went on, "you didn't say when you were giving us the brief, but it was Baptiste, wasn't it?"

"I don't know, Grant."

"Really?"

Kane nodded.

"And whose do you think it was?"

Kane eyed him levelly. "It was a hallucination. I don't want to think about it at all." But he couldn't get the memory out of his mind. Thrush's trap had almost worked; he'd nearly been stranded out there somewhere in an electron-charged nightmare between worlds. Only Baptiste's voice had saved him.

"Okay." Grant puffed on his cigar again. "So when are we going back in?"

"Now," Kane said.

"Finish my cigar first?"

"Sure. Hate to see a good cigar go to waste."

Grant blew a smoke ring that floated out over the edge of the precipice. "So tell me again that we're not going into the next casement because of some macho thing."

"Because I was scared?"

"Yeah."

"Fuck that," Kane said. "I was scared. I don't have a problem with admitting that to you." He stared hard into his friend's eyes. "We're not going in because I was scared, Grant. We're going in because Thrush was scared. I saw it in him. You know the way you feel it when the slagger who's trying to gut you is afraid, too?"

Grant nodded.

"That's the way it was. If we're going to take Thrush down, now may be the best opportunity we have to do it. That's why we're going."

# Chapter 5

Brigid stood in the mat-trans unit looking at the three tables that had been set up for her, Grant and Kane. She crossed her arms over her breasts and repressed a shiver. Bry was checking over the computers under Lakesh's direction, and DeFore was recalibrating the diagnostics equipment that would monitor them.

A rolling sensation filled her stomach. The memory of being killed was vivid, partly because of her photographic memory, but mostly because of the intensity of the experience. She knew she didn't want to go through it again.

But there was no choice because she knew Kane fully intended to make the jump again. And if she didn't go with him, the triumvirate would be broken and Thrush might be able to kill him this time.

"Having second thoughts, Baptiste?"

Getting control of herself, Brigid turned to face Kane. "I'm further along than that," she admitted.

"Can't back out of it." He spoke in a whisper, but his words sounded cold and hard to Brigid.

She replied in a voice chipped from stone as she turned and faced him. "I go when and where I please, Kane. You might want to keep that in mind."

Kane's nostrils flared, and white spots showed around his compressed lips. His blue-gray eyes glinted fire. "You weren't so daring when you were working in the archives. Mebbe this is a good thing.'' Without another word, he left.

Brigid watched him go, regretting her quick words. Maybe Kane hadn't started talking to her to ensure that she would be going with them in light of the trauma he had been through. But it hadn't come across that way.

She cursed quietly, damning the gestalt of their relationship; they were depending on each other one minute, then at each other's throat the next. Pushing out a breath, she went after him, intending to apologize. ''Kane.''

He turned, squaring off against her as he would any aggressor. She read it in his body language and lamented her being the cause of it.

''You didn't have that coming,'' Brigid said. ''I'm sorry.''

''Don't worry about it,'' Kane said.

''Dammit, Kane. I just tendered an apology. You should acknowledge it in some way.''

''Thanks,'' Kane stated.

Brigid bit back her anger. ''Perhaps I misunderstood your approach. We seem to have a problem with communication.''

He gave her a crooked grin. ''Not when it matters, Baptiste.'' He hesitated. ''I just came over to make sure you were okay.''

''Why wouldn't I be?'' she asked.

Kane nodded. ''Right. I've got to go check on some things.''

''Me, too,'' Brigid said.

Kane turned and walked away.

Brigid watched him for a moment, feeling hollow at the pit of her stomach. The memory of the kiss he'd given her when they'd taken the jump back in time to the eve of the nukecaust ghosted across her mind. It was no surprise that she should remember the kiss with her gift, but the intensity of that memory was extraordinarily clear.

That line of thinking, though, brought back the memories of the jump to the last casement, of her body pressing hungrily against his. Then she felt herself growing angry at Kane all over again.

She should have quit when she was ahead.

STANDING NEAR BRY at the control console, Grant watched the exchange between Kane and Brigid. He shook his head. In all the years he and Kane had been partners, he'd never known his friend to be as off balance as he was around Brigid Baptiste.

After a bit, Kane walked away.

Grant read the emotions in their body language. "Now," he said, "there is a picture of true misery."

Bry looked up at him. "What are you talking about?"

"Human nature," Grant said. "Something that can't be boiled down into alphanumeric code."

Bry gave him a knowing look. "You're talking about Kane and Baptiste, aren't you?"

Grant raised a surprised eyebrow.

"I sit here at these computers," Bry said. "That doesn't mean I don't take a look around now and again."

"I guess not."

"They have their own issues to deal with."

"I suppose," Grant said. "But with things the way they are between them, it'd be a damned sight easier if they'd just realize what they've got going between them.''

"What?" Bry asked. "Sexual chemistry?"

"Ah," Grant said, "I've got a feeling it's more than that."

Bry ran a hand through his copper locks tiredly. "Those two are too different. If they attempted anything as prosaic as a relationship, they'd self-destruct."

"I don't think so," Grant declared.

Glancing up at him, Bry shook his head. "You don't even see the problems you have."

Grant shot him a questioning glance.

"I'm talking about Domi and DeFore."

"That's stupe. There's no problem."

"Of course." Bry returned his attention to the computers.

"Fuck you," Grant said, and moved away on his crutches. He headed for the cafeteria. Lakesh's briefing wasn't scheduled for another hour. It gave him time for a cup of coffee and some downtime.

Only when he got to the cafeteria, DeFore and Domi were both already there, sitting at different tables, each studiously ignoring the other. Backing out of the room before they saw him, he traveled back down the hallway as quickly as he could.

"Decided discretion is the better part of valor?" Bry asked. The computer systems operator was coming up the hallway.

"You could have told me they were both in there," Grant complained as he limped past him.

Bry appeared to give that some thought. "Probably."

"Asshole."

Bry stopped in the hallway and smiled. "You know, I bet if I suddenly stopped here and yelled out 'Hi, Grant,' they could hear me in the cafeteria."

As suddenly as it had come, Grant's anger disappeared as he looked at the little man. Then he laughed. "You're a blister when you want to be, Bry."

"Yeah," the man said. "I am."

Grant passed back down the hallway and pushed thoughts of DeFore and Domi out of his mind. A tactical retreat back to his room was definitely his best move.

KANE SPENT A FEW MINUTES in his room, getting his head back together before the meeting Lakesh had scheduled. A fresh cup of coffee sat on the table, and he worked on the Sin Eater with practiced hands. The Sin Eater was a Mag's assigned weapon, almost a badge of office. He knew it more intimately than anything else in the world.

As he cleaned the weapon, he tried to keep his mind from Brigid Baptiste, but it didn't work. Sometimes the glimpses of past lives intruded on his dreams. And sometimes he wondered how things might have been different if they could have met under different circumstances. Still, she didn't like how volatile his nature was, and he disapproved of how cold and efficient she could be. There was no changing that.

He disassembled the Sin Eater and took out his cleaning kit. When the parts were laid neatly against the towel he'd put down to work on, he started cleaning them in earnest. The Sin Eater didn't make the jump with him to the other casements, but it occupied his attention now.

A big-bore automatic handblaster less than fourteen inches in length, the Sin Eater was carried strapped to a holster on his right arm. The magazine carried twenty 9 mm rounds, and the stock folded down when it was holstered along his arm. Actuators attached to the weapon popped the Sin Eater down into Kane's waiting hand when he flexed his wrist tendons, putting it there in an eye blink. There was no trigger guard, and when the firing stud came in contact with Kane's finger, the blaster would discharge immediately.

As he put the Sin Eater back together, he reminded himself that his anger at Brigid Baptiste must not interfere with the upcoming mission.

A slip like that could get them all chilled. There couldn't be any hidden agendas. Kane smiled wryly, thinking that was Lakesh's domain.

GRANT PUT THE BALL of his thumb against the white wall in his room. Covered with ink, his thumb left a print a little over an inch tall and over half that wide. He dragged a chair over and sat six feet from the mark on the wall. Working on his relaxation technique, he concentrated his neck and shoulders first, then worked all the way down to his toes.

When he was ready, he focused on his breathing, putting himself into a hypnotic state. He'd been trained to do it while a Cobaltville Magistrate, used it for handling pain when he'd been wounded or dealing with physical exhaustion.

He intended to use it for something else now.

After memorizing the thumbprint on the wall, he

closed his eyes, visualizing in his mind. He checked it twice, then when his mental image matched that of the actual print, he kept his eyes closed and went even deeper into the hypnotic state.

He made the thumbprint larger in his mind, till it covered the wall from top to bottom. Once it was big enough, he pushed his mind into it, standing inside the darkness. His heartbeat sounded distant.

He concentrated on Thrush, memorizing the hybrid cyborg's face, adding in every detail of the man he could recall from the times he'd met him. He added a mental command, something he hoped he could lock away in his subconscious even when they made the jump into the parallel casement. He hadn't been able to come to the forefront of the doppelgänger's mind in the alternate earth conquered by Nazi Germany until after he'd met Kane there. The silent-invader Kane instead of the one indigenous to that world.

With the hypnotic suggestion he was giving himself, he hoped to change that. If it was strong enough, he thought it might serve to move the doppelgänger Grant even if he hadn't taken over that Grant's body yet.

When he saw Thrush, he intended to chill the man. No questions asked, no quarter given.

"THE REPORTS ON KANE came back clean," DeFore announced. "The fever wasn't caused by anything biological in his system. The tests I ran came back with no evidence of anything being introduced into his system."

"What about the white-cell count?" Brigid asked.

"Even with the fever disappearing so quickly, there should have been some traces of the infection."

Kane sat quietly at the table in the ready room, listening but not really caring. The mission began with the jump, not with the preamble. And the hypothesizing the old man insisted on didn't advance any of the knowledge they had.

"There was none," DeFore said.

Brigid leaned back in her chair. "That's impossible."

"I know," DeFore replied. "But I also know what I found. There was nothing in his system."

"The fever and the infection had to come from somewhere," Brigid persisted.

"Yes."

Brigid turned to face Kane. "You don't remember being sick when you were in the other casement?"

"No."

"You're sure?"

"I was there, Baptiste," Kane said curtly. "I remember everything else. I don't think I'd forget that."

Lakesh cleared his throat. "Perhaps," he said, "we should move on to another topic that may be somewhat more productive."

Domi sat at his side, but she wasn't saying much. Her hot gaze focused occasionally on DeFore, and Kane noticed a certain lack of friendliness.

"Friend Kane," the old man said, "when we first discussed these parallel casements after you brought the fragments of the Chintamani Stone, you gave us a description of the three alternate earths you were given previews of, including the one the three of you visited yesterday. That could have been some effect of the programming inherent in the device. Should simple logic dictate truly, there will be only two casements left open to you when you make the jump this time. Without us attempting to recalibrate the trapezohedron, that is.''

"Right," Kane said. He'd already arrived at that conclusion, as well. "But how do you figure on picking which one will be next?"

Lakesh shook his head. "I don't presume to do so. However, my hope is that by talking about it now, we might perhaps lay a foundation that will help you once you get into the next casement."

"The one I was in earlier wasn't one of those two."

"Agreed," Lakesh said. "But I also believe that you were shown the three that you could most effect. If you could get them to fall—"

"Then mebbe the domino principle would kick in," Grant stated.

"Exactly. Furthermore, friend Kane, I think that those casements were revealed to you in a certain order for a reason."

"What?" Kane asked.

Lakesh lifted his bony shoulders and dropped them. "I'm quite sure I have no idea. Perhaps in order to enhance the domino principle we're endeavoring to jump-start, the casements are best approached in the order in which you perceived them."

"That's guesswork," Kane grumbled. He felt they'd be better served going into the next casement.

The old man fell silent for a moment. "It's all we have, friend Kane, and I'd like to make the most of it. You're going to make that jump in a matter of minutes."

"Lakesh is right," Brigid said.

Kane refused to look at her, afraid it would start another argument he wouldn't be able to control, because he didn't see it that way. Balam had given him the Chintamani Stone and charged him with finding a way to save his people, but he could have been wrong. Thrush had had over 250 years to put his plan into operation. At best, the people at Cerberus redoubt had days. He felt tired and worn from the experience earlier in the day, but he didn't want to wait until tomorrow. "Fine."

"Tell us what you remember of the second parallel casement."

Kane concentrated, trying to keep all his recent memories straight. He took a deep breath and reached for the memory he'd been given of the second lost earth. "We were at an embassy of some sort."

"Who is we?" Lakesh asked.

Irritation stung Kane. "Grant and me. Told you this the other day. If you can't remember it, why am I wasting my time telling you about it?"

"I'm hoping, friend Kane, that your memory of the event sharpens up as we pursue it this time." Lakesh flipped open a small hardbound notebook. "I assure you, I've got everything you told me documented within this volume."

"I don't have Baptiste's memory," Kane growled, "and I wasn't quite myself when all that shit was coming down."

"Perhaps you could be a bit more relaxed," Lakesh suggested.

Kane pulled a face. "I'm sitting here in this chair and nobody's got a blaster pointed at my face. That's about as much relaxation as I can imagine."

"If I may," Lakesh said, pushing his way up out of his own chair, "I'd like to attempt something."

"No," Kane replied.

Lakesh hesitated, a pained expression on his face.

"You haven't heard what it is yet," Brigid soothed.

"I don't need to," Kane replied.

"Maybe you should reconsider that your last adventure of going it alone didn't turn out all that well." Brigid's voice remained even. "Lakesh doesn't have the monopoly on misjudgment around here."

Kane started to say something, then realized that it would only be the opening gambit in a protracted argument. He stifled the rebellious streak that ran rampant inside him. He held Brigid's gaze for a time, feeling his neck muscles tighten to the point of pain. He released a slow breath through his nose and shifted his gaze to Lakesh. "What have you got in mind, old man?"

"Have you ever experimented with hypnosis?"

"You don't experiment with hypnosis," Kane replied. "You have it experimented on you."

"They used it some," Grant said. "Back in Mag school. Trained you to kick it in to minimize pain, control panic and learn reflex control in martial arts. Kane wasn't a big believer."

"And you, friend Grant?"

Grant showed him a crooked smile. "Like with anything else in this world, old man, I took from it what I thought I could use for my own benefit."

"Good. I'm glad you found it useful."

"Hypnosis isn't a bad thing," Brigid said. Her voice was softer. "During the unification program, it was used in the archives sometimes to draw testimony out of people for the records.''

"Those records," Kane said coldly, "weren't the truth and you know it. The only reason archivists would hypnotize those poor bastards would be to find out those who knew the truth and were trying to lie about it to preserve their own skins." Color appeared in Brigid's cheeks and he knew he'd offended her. He felt bad about that, wishing he could take it back. He'd spoken out of anger. But the truth was that much of Brigid's job had constituted creating revisionist history at the order of the barons. In general, when it came to important facets of their history, she'd covered up more of them than she'd uncovered.

She whipped her gaze from his and folded her arms across her chest. "You're an arrogant bastard today."

"Must be Lakesh's hypnosis," Kane snapped. "I'm telling the truth already." He turned to the old man. "Do your best. I was never a good subject back in Mag school."

"Very well, friend Kane. If the exercise ends in frustration, so be it." Lakesh reached into the pocket of his bodysuit and took out a silver pen. "Please follow the pen with your eyes and listen to the sound of my voice."

Kane did as he was asked, flicking his eyes slowly from left to right.

"Concentrate on the pen," Lakesh soothed.

The room's lights glinted off the pen, spitting silver.

"And listen to the sound of my voice. Don't think about anything else."

Despite the suggestion and the calm tone in which it was delivered, Kane couldn't help thinking about

Brigid and the tension that had built up between them over the past few days. There'd always been tension since the day they'd met, but the situation seemed to be eroding. And thoughts of the woman leaving him caused vague stirrings of fear inside him. A nerve twitched in his face.

"Relax, Kane. Relax and we'll find out what secrets your mind has been hiding from your memory. We will make clear what is hard to see. Breathe more slowly."

Almost unbidden, Kane's breathing deepened and he felt calmer. Brigid's tie to him couldn't be severed. He wouldn't allow it to be.

"Be at ease, Cuchulainn," an old man's whisper echoed in Kane's head. "Those life skeins with your lady, tangled and tossed as they may be, are the foundation of your existence. And hers. You will truly never be one without the other. There exists between you that which will not be destroyed. For one without the other is an abomination."

"Mebbe," Kane told the voice, "but neither are we together."

"That fault lies with the bane of your existence."

"Thrush?" Kane asked.

"You will know the bane with your warrior's heart, Cuchulainn."

"When?"

"It's not up to me to say. I cannot foretell you the future."

"Then how do you know," Kane demanded, "that we will not be parted?"

"Without her, you would not exist. Deep within yourself, you know this to be true."

"I've never needed anyone," Kane replied.

"You lie only to yourself, warrior. Your blade and your heart are true."

Kane reflected on his involvement with the Mags at Cobaltville. "Not so true in the past."

"In this past, perhaps. But you've never been long past redemption, Cuchulainn. The lady is your saving grace."

"Why?"

"I cannot say. But you know the truth when you hear it. You are about to be tried again, warrior. Trust the bond that belongs between you. The gift of the *anam-chara* is strong. She protects you from damnation—she is your credential."

Then the voice faded from Kane's thoughts, and even the silver pen ceased to exist.

# Chapter 6

"He's under." Lakesh stepped back from Kane and put the pen back in his pocket.

Brigid looked at Kane, filled with anger again at his cutting remarks, and knew she was at fault, as well. Kane wasn't a man to be bullied or pushed into anything. His whole mentality was to push back. But it was so damned hard to remember when she could clearly see the direction in which they should go and he wouldn't listen.

His voice was a whisper over the quiet hum that was an undercurrent in the ready room. *"Anamchara."*

"What's he saying?" Grant asked.

Brigid shifted uncomfortably. Neither of them had talked with the others about the possibility of having shared past lives. It wasn't a secret, but it had no bearing on what they were trying to do now against the barons.

"I don't know," Lakesh answered. "Perhaps it's residue from this morning's experiences. At any rate, we want to go back to the visions he had while under the Chintamani Stone's influence." He kept his voice lowered. "Travel back with me, Kane. Go back into the past."

KANE'S BREATH TORE raggedly through his throat. His eyes teared from the smoke already filling the building. Part of it was from the fires that had been started, and part of it was the riot gas that hadn't quite yet dissipated. His legs felt rubbery from the run through the hallways. He thumbed the magazine release on the Spectre, checking the load. The machine pistol's oversize clip still held thirteen rounds, and he had spare magazines in the combat harness he wore.

"What are you wearing?" the soft voice prompted.

Looking down at the black suit he wore, Kane found it was scuffed and dirty. One of the knees had a hole in it, and he was missing his tie. His ID somehow still dangled from his jacket's left breast pocket.

"Look at the ID, Kane. Tell me what you see."

It was standard ID, issued by the department. The director's signature was at the bottom. He pushed himself up, getting ready to go around the corner—

"Wait. Describe the ID."

The ID, Kane noticed was a rectangle with the usual red and black, with his picture and security ratings on it. He pushed himself up, getting ready to go around—

"What is your name? What does the ID say?"

He was Special Agent Kane, of the President's Department of Extraterrestrial Investigations. He pushed himself up, getting ready to go—

"What is your function here, Kane?"

The Department of Extraterrestrial Investigations, Kane remembered, had been set up over two hundred years ago, after the Cuban Missile Crisis in 1963 had escalated into a world-wide conflagration. It was his job to disprove all claims that an alien race had been at the root of the war that had destroyed so much of the world despite what the ROAMer underground

tried to create and give to the media. The Reporters
of Alien Manipulation had been a fist in the face of
the Western States Coalition—WSC—since the remnants of Congress had migrated to Sante Fe, New
Mexico, and set up the provisional government after
the nuclear bombing stopped. That had been after
they'd crawled back up from the fallout shelters in
White Sands. He pushed himself up, getting ready—

"What do you know of the Archon Directorate?"

Kane didn't know anything about the Archon Directorate. But the ROAMers maintained they'd had
contact with an alien race called the Archons, and
they'd maintained that the Archons had been the ones
who'd started the nuclear war. ROAMer propaganda
stipulated that the Archons had secretly allied themselves with the major governments of the world, that
they'd been at work for hundreds of years, influencing
the future of mankind. The mutants that had sprung
up in the Eastern Alliance of Former United States,
they said, were proof of the genetic tampering the
Archons had been involved in. He pushed himself up,
getting—

"Do you believe in the Archons?"

Kane started to say no, he didn't. But memory of
Brigid and how she'd died cut through his denials.
Everything had become so damned twisted. No, that
was wrong. It had always been twisted. He'd only
found out lately. The Archons did exist, and he was
here for revenge. He pushed himself up—

"Who are the Archons?"

They were the enemy, Kane remembered. They'd
promulgated the race wars immediately following the
nukecaust that had ripped the tattered remains of the
United States to pieces. Besides the Western States

Coalition and the Eastern Alliance of Former United States, a handful of other empires had sprung up around the country over the years, rising and falling as prosperity and a strong hand took them over. Some of them in the worst areas had even gone back to a kind of feudalism, swearing fealty to barons that ruled and survived by the gun and sword. He pushed himself—

"Where are the Archons?"

They were here, Kane knew, in this building. They'd been hiding in the diplomatic mansions that had been established for the ambassadors from other surviving nations in hopes of restoring more of the communications between the emerging powers. The WSC had the most weapons and tactical advantages, but the Russian People's Protectorate was gaining rapidly. The ROAMers postulated that the Archons were deliberately building up arms, getting ready for more nuclear strikes against the Eastern Alliance, as well as the European survivors. He pushed—

"What are you doing here now, Kane?"

"YOU'RE PUSHING HIM too hard," Grant protested.

Brigid silently agreed. Kane's face was streamered with perspiration. His blue-gray eyes were wide open but empty, staring past Lakesh as the old man asked him questions.

"I know I'm pushing him hard, friend Grant," Lakesh said. "But whatever information we can gather will only help the three of you arm yourselves better before you take this next jump. It will even help friend Kane."

"If you don't kill him first."

"I'm not going to injure him, I assure you."

"Mind-fucking leaves scars, too," Grant growled in disgust.

"Only a little further," Lakesh said.

Grant looked away, obviously displeased. Brigid silently agreed with the man's assessment. If Lakesh went much further, she'd stop it herself.

"This world," DeFore stated, "sounds much different than the last. At least the governments have survived to some degree."

"Yeah," Grant said, "but it sounds like the Archons have got control of them."

"Friend Kane," Lakesh began again. "I have only a few more questions for you."

"Yes," Kane replied.

WHAT ARE YOU DOING here now, Kane?"

Kane shoved the magazine back into the Spectre. He'd come there to kill Archons. And Thrush. He pushed—

"Where is Thrush?"

From the intel he'd been able to gather, Kane knew Thrush was somewhere inside the embassy, hiding with his alien controllers. Or maybe the man controlled them. Kane wasn't sure. And it didn't matter. They were all going to be chilled for what they'd done to Brigid Baptiste. He pushed himself up, getting ready to go around the corner of the wall ahead of him.

An embassy guard, wearing the sky-blue uniform they were assigned, came to a stop in the cross hallway. He wore the white boots and gloves, but both were stained with the blood of the people attacking the embassy. He brought his assault rifle to his shoulder, his face covered by the hard shell of the riot helmet, its surface a sky-blue mirror.

Kane lifted the Spectre first, going with the reflexes that had kept him alive for so many years in the Department of Extraterrestrial Investigations. He pulled the trigger, firing a 3-round burst, aiming for the reflective faceplate. Grant had supplied the ammunition, and they'd loaded up with armor-piercing rounds.

The bullets cored through the faceplate and slapped the helmet back. The dead man fell back and hit the floor.

Kane moved out, running hard, ignoring the burn of smoke and residual CS gas in the air. He struggled to remember the directions he'd been given, checking the markings tagged near the ceilings at the intersections.

He turned another corner and found he was right on track. The first-floor landing was ahead of him. Broad and white tiled, the landing held two giant Chinese dragon statues surrounding a flower-filled atrium in the center of the building.

Bodies were strewed across the floor, twisted in pools of blood and body parts. Most of them were embassy guards and a few of the rebels that had slipped across the Mississippi Wall for the raid tonight.

Kane glanced upward, spotting Thrush on the third level with two of the Archon hybrids, guiding them through the walkway. He thought about Brigid, about how she'd ended up. He raised the Spectre, set it on full auto and pointed it at—

"What about Brigid?"

Brigid was dead, Kane remembered, all blown to

hell. He'd been too late to save her. He raised the Spectre, set it on full auto—

"Who killed her?"

A bomb had killed Brigid. The stark image still stained Kane's mind. Thrush had ordered it. Kane pushed the memory away. He raised the Spectre—

"Why did Thrush have Brigid killed?"

"THRUSH HAD BRIGID KILLED because she'd found out," Kane said tonelessly.

A chill thrilled through Brigid when she heard about her own death. She glanced at Grant, wondering how the declaration would affect him.

"Don't mean it's going to happen," Grant told her. "This is only what Kane saw through the Chintamani Stone. We're there to change things, remember? Things can't happen like Kane's remembering them right now."

"Yes." Brigid kept her emotions in check. Maybe it would have been different if Kane hadn't sounded so emotionless.

"Friend Kane," Lakesh said, "how did Thrush find out Brigid was a threat to him?"

Kane shivered. Drops of perspiration dripped from his face. "Because of me. I led him to her, let him know that she was a threat." His voice turned hoarse. "I killed her!"

"Calm yourself." Lakesh spoke in a soft voice. "These things you're seeing, they're not true."

"Not true?"

"No. We're going to change them. You're going to change them. But we need to know more."

"Goddammit," Grant swore. "He's had enough."

Lakesh turned to the big man, his rheumy eyes

piercing behind the glasses. "Do we get the information or not? If you do not prepare for this journey you're about to take, it's already going to cause dear Brigid's death. At least on that particular casement. And if you do not achieve what you're over there to do, she at least will not be allowed another chance because her doppelgänger no longer exists. You and Kane can't reenter that casement without her." He paused. "Now, which will it be? Which course do you think friend Kane would choose?"

Grant pushed up from his chair and walked across the room. "Go for it. Doesn't mean I've got to like it, though."

"You presume wrongly when you think that I find any pleasure in this," Lakesh declared. He turned his attention back to Kane. "Can you get Thrush?"

KANE RAISED THE SPECTRE, set it on full auto and pointed it at Thrush and the two Archon hybrids. He squeezed the trigger, burning through the clip in a heartbeat.

The bullets chopped into Thrush and the Archons. The creatures fell, their overly thin bodies flailing helplessly as the rounds tore them apart. Thrush staggered, but he didn't fall. He held a hand up in front of his wounded face, light reflecting from the metal under the flesh and blood. "Kill Kane!" he ordered the guards below. "He's a traitor to the government!"

Immediately, a fusillade of bullets sizzled through the air where Kane had been before he pulled back to cover. One of them clipped the special protective helmet he wore, jerking his head forcefully enough to blur his vision and send a wave of nausea through him.

With shaking hands, he toggled the Spectre's magazine release, then rammed a fresh one home. He shot the bolt, stripping and chambering the first round. Then he took a stun grenade from his combat harness, pulling the pin and slipping the spoon. He whirled and threw it toward the knot of guards on the other side of the corpses.

The grenade detonated on the first-floor landing. The concussive wave crashed down the steps and lit up the marble-floored foyer with a bright orange flash. Kane felt the shock and the heat on the back of his head.

The rest of the interdiction team had taken up positions around the embassy reception hall, deploying like well-oiled parts of a machine, subguns leveled to cover every possible avenue of either escape or opposition.

Kane looked up the stairway, noting that four members of the embassy's security detail had been incapacitated by the stun grenade. His protective helmet's comm-tach buzzed, and Grant's voice filtered into his ear. "The west wing is secure—nobody here but a couple of hybrid grunts. The diplomatic staff must have been evacuated." The man sounded harried, out of breath.

"Resistance?" Kane asked, moving toward the first-floor landing.

"A little. Some of those bastards are armed with infrasound wands."

One of the stunned security guards on the stairs tried to bring up a weapon. Kane put a burst in the center of the man's chest, hammering him back down on the stairs. Then he shot the others to make sure, as well. He charged up the steps. "What about the ambassador?"

Grant's intel had indicated that Ambassador Cobalt of the Russian People's Protectorate was actually a hybrid the Archons had created. They'd put in place a number of replacements across the globe. Business between the civilized nations of the world was conducted by the Archons, and guided by them. If Kane and Grant could get their hands on Cobalt, they'd be able to prove that everything the ROAMers had printed was true.

Kane charged up the stairs. "What about the ambassador?" They both now knew Cobalt's security here in Sante Fe was coordinated through Thrush's infrastructure within the Department of Extraterrestrial Investigations. They had mapped his chosen evacuation routes from the embassy, which was actually a warren of tunnels. It stood to reason that Thrush would try to get Cobalt out through one of those routes.

"No sign of Thrush at all," Grant answered. "He may have been tipped off."

Kane grunted, not wanting to contemplate the possibility. That would have meant Thrush had some other source within Grant's people. Or he'd tracked Kane's own progress. "Stand by."

He ran up the stairs, keeping close to the curving, elaborate balustrade, taking three steps at a time, holding his Spectre autoblaster in a two-handed grip. The corridor was filled with astringent smoke. Through its shifting planes, he glimpsed four figures stirring feebly on the floor, their white faces streaked red from the blood oozing from hemorrhaging eardrums.

Kane stepped carefully around them, turning right beneath an arch into a long, carpeted hallway. Almost at once, a door opened at the far end of the hall, and a hybrid was framed there, with a fragile-looking infrasound wand in his hand. It flicked toward Kane, the three-foot silver length shivering and humming.

Kane threw himself against the wall, raising his side arm. Even with the special shielding inside his helmet, he wasn't sure he could take a direct hit, so he fired at once. The ultrasonic burst swept high, a barely detectable blur peeling long splinters from the wall over his head. The rounds from the Spectre caught the hybrid in the chest, hurling him backward amid a flailing of arms and a kicking of legs. The wand clattered to the floor.

Kane muttered beneath his breath, "So much for diplomatic immunity."

He carefully moved on down the hallway and paused by a window. He peered out past the broken glass. The grounds of the Archon embassy were filled with running, falling and shooting figures. Smoke boiled from a corner of the building, and flames licked out of a ground-floor window. An armored car trundled through the wreck of the wrought-iron gate, spouting 30 mm shells in a jackhammer rhythm.

He saw a Cerberus specialist surrounded by a pack of hybrids, their infrasound wands humming and popping viciously. The ultrasonic waves pulverized the man's joints and crushed the bones in his face. He opened his mouth to scream, and his teeth blew out of his mouth in a spray of splinters.

Kane put his blaster out of the window and depressed the trigger, firing a long, full-auto burst. Hybrids squealed as the high-velocity rounds struck them, knocking them down like puppets.

An explosion filled the hallway with rolling, thunderous echoes. A sheet of flame erupted, and the concussive roar broke the world behind him.

And the memory ended like a vid tape breaking.

KANE NOTED THE SERIOUS FACES surrounding him at the table. He guessed that they were disappointed that Lakesh's attempt at hypnotizing him had failed. "Told you it wouldn't work," he said.

"It worked," Grant corrected. "Mebbe a little too good."

Kane grew angry, realizing that he knew something that he now didn't know that he knew. It was further infuriating that they knew it, as well.

"Friend Kane," Lakesh began.

Kane looked at him, a barbed comment already at hand.

Then Lakesh said, "Remember," and everything he'd just experienced dropped into his mind, triggering an instant headache.

# Chapter 8

"You shouldn't go, Baptiste," Kane said. They stood near the mat-trans unit, their reflections deep in the armaglass. He was growing more frustrated with the argument he was having with Brigid. The meeting in the ready room had broken up. They'd discovered as much as they could about the next casement they were going to travel in. Provided Lakesh's theory was correct.

"You can't go without me."

"Lakesh could be wrong about that."

"And if he's not?" Brigid demanded. "You and Grant could make that jump and end up trapped between casements the way you were this morning."

"We don't know if that's what happened then, either." Kane tried to control his anger, but Brigid kept punching all the right buttons. "If you'd just listen—"

She whirled on him, emerald eyes flashing. "I have been listening, Kane. I've listened to Lakesh's theory that the Chintamani Stone may give us the opportunity to correct at least some of the damage that Thrush and the Archons have done to our world."

"That's probably bullshit."

"Then why did you make the jump yesterday?" Brigid demanded. "And why did you make the jump this morning if you didn't believe it could be true?"

"I'm exploring the possibilities that Lakesh is right," Kane answered.

"You said yourself that Balam gave that stone to you for a reason."

"Could have been revenge," Kane pointed out.

"You don't believe that, either, Kane."

His irritation grew past its bounds. "You don't fucking know what I believe, Baptiste. And it seems as if everything I believe in you find something wrong with."

She stood almost nose to nose with him, looking up at him fiercely. "We both believe that the Chintamani Stone offers a chance for us to do something about what the Archon Directorate has done. What I don't understand is why we're arguing over it."

Kane let out a deep breath. "We're not arguing about that. We're arguing about whether you should go."

"I should."

"Dammit, Baptiste, if that memory I had was correct, you're going to get fucking chilled over there."

"I got chilled in the last casement, remember? I'm still here."

"And what if Thrush has modified the Chintamani Stone now that he knows we're able to move through it?"

"Then it would be completely stupid for you and Grant to try to go alone. The Chintamani Stone was made of three fragments, Kane. Three. And it's three for a reason."

"Then let someone else go."

"Who, Kane?"

Kane grinned mirthlessly. "Lakesh comes to mind.

Do him good to see what it's like in one of those casements.''

"The Lakesh we met in the other casement was in worse physical condition than the one here. He wouldn't be much help.''

"Now there's a first lost-earths constant,'' Kane commented.

"That's not what I meant.''

"It fits.'' Kane leaned against the armaglass of the mat-trans unit, the rage in him dwindling somewhat. It was, he realized, as much due to fear as to anything Brigid said.

"And there's another possibility,'' she said. "What if the Lakesh of this parallel earth is already dead?''

"Wishful thinking,'' Kane grunted unsympathetically. He saw at once by the fire in her emerald eyes that the comment hadn't been well appreciated. But it was too late to take back, and he didn't think she'd allow him the saving grace of just pointing out the kind of day he'd been having. His head still throbbed incessantly.

"It's something to consider,'' Brigid said. "What happens to someone who makes a jump into a parallel casement and they don't have a doppelgänger?''

Kane shrugged. "The way I see it, that's another reason for you not to go. Your doppelgänger could already be dead.''

"So could yours from the sound of that explosion.''

"The last time I foresaw my own death, as well. But we jumped in well ahead of that. Grant's still alive at that time, but we could jump in after your doppelgänger's already been killed. You could end up trapped over there.''

"No."

Kane looked at her.

"I'm going, Kane," she said.

"Damn, but you're the most obstinate person I've met, Baptiste. You'd think you could listen to a little reason."

"Must be the company I'm keeping these days," she told him.

Knowing his frustration was pushing him over the edge of control, Kane held up a hand, then turned and walked away.

"Kane," she called.

He turned back, seeing that she was troubled, too.

"I don't want it to be like this between us before we go," she said.

He lifted his shoulders and dropped them. "Can't see it being any other way under the circumstances."

"Just because you don't have it your way?"

He looked at her and decided to give her the truth. "I don't want to think about losing you, Baptiste. And that's an ace on the line." He turned and walked away.

"Then don't," she said.

Surprised, Kane looked back at her, but she was already walking away.

BRIGID STRETCHED OUT on one of the three tables DeFore had placed in the mat-trans unit. Grant was to her left and Kane to her right. They were both already buckled in, the biolink contacts stuck to their heads and chests. Both men appeared totally relaxed.

She stuck the adhesive contact tabs to her temples, arms and between her breasts. They felt cold to the touch. Nestled in her hands was a piece of the Chintamani Stone. Grant held another and Kane the larger, primary facet. She turned her head to look at DeFore through the armaglass, going through the checklist connecting her to the med equipment.

DeFore gave her a thumbs-up, letting her know all the readings were coming through clearly.

Lakesh stepped up to the door. "Good luck, dearest Brigid. We shall await your return here."

"I'll see you shortly," Brigid said.

Lakesh closed the mat-trans door and entered the security code. The door locked with a hiss.

Brigid closed her eyes, feeling the vertigo starting deep inside her head. Even after the information Lakesh had extracted from Kane under hypnosis, she didn't know what to expect. Then the blackness opened up before her.

"See you on the other side, Baptiste," Kane said quietly.

She tried to answer him, but the darkness overwhelmed her, sweeping her away.

*Sante Fe Ville*
*Western States Coalition*

"WAKE UP, KANE," the feminine voice said. "Looks like we're in business."

Wearily, Kane opened his eyes and lifted his head, trying to figure out where the hell he was. A headache rattled around inside his skull, throbbing insistently. He felt disoriented, as if he'd had too much to drink and this was the morning after.

Kane shifted in the seat, discovering he was in one of the department's unmarked sedans. The heater labored, beating back the October chill that threatened to invade the car. Unpredictable weather was one of the legacies of the nuclear winter that had swept over the world on October 31, 1963, when the Cubans had chosen to attack instead of backing off when President John F. Kennedy had ordered them to.

"What is it?" he asked, finding his voice thick and scratchy.

"We've got activity. Looks like the intel on this op was an ace on the line after all."

Kane rubbed at his eyes, careful because of the graininess filling them. His palm scraped against beard stubble, letting him know it had been days since he'd been near a razor. He glanced over at his partner, remembering her name with difficulty—Rouch.

*Lying, selfish bitch.* The voice was an almost alien presence at the back of Kane's mind, but it receded as quickly as it had arrived. Beth-Li Rouch had been his partner for the past three years. She was in her early twenties, and kept her waist-length black hair pulled back in a braid. Her ancestry was Asian, the blood almost entirely undiluted, which wasn't surprising considering the careful monitoring of the gene pool by the Purity Control Foundation. Of course, that step only worked if people checked in with the gene techs before they started jumping each other. There were enough muties and freaks living as homeless on the streets in most major villes in even the Western States Coalition that Kane knew most people didn't bother with the gene registry. Sex was a coin of the realm in most areas for those who didn't have government jobs.

"What'd I miss?" Kane asked. He tried not to worry about the fact he couldn't seem to remember why they'd been staking out the area. He had too many things on his mind these days. He peered through the mud-smeared window at the line of buildings across the street.

The nukecaust that had destroyed so much of the world in 1963 hadn't left much of Sante Fe untouched. Two hundred years previous, the Cuban missiles, followed by the Russian ones, hadn't known about the government facilities that had been springing up under White Sands, New Mexico. By that time, Joe McCarthy and his Red hunters had ferreted out most of the Communist sympathizers and spies from Hollywood, as well as from Washington, D.C. That had been pretty much wasted effort because neither of those places existed anymore.

The buildings were squats, structures that had been damaged but not destroyed by the quakes that had rocked the western half of the United States. They'd have taken too much of an investment to repair once the survivors had started getting organized, and too much time to tear down. And they'd served as way stations for transients to stay while they were being absorbed into the ville. Or turned away. Life had been hard in those days, and only those who could contribute were allowed to stay there.

A few lights gleamed in the windows on all three floors, but they were so dim Kane knew they were candles or perhaps lanterns that the indigents had stolen from the ville's citizens. Some of those people in the buildings were going to freeze in the next few days when the first of the winter cold waves washed over the southern Western States Coalition.

"Sheehan made the show," Rouch said. Like Kane, she was dressed in a department-issue solid black suit, with black, formfitting gloves and calf-high boots.

Kane struggled with the name, wondering why he was having so much trouble remembering things. The headache continued unabated inside his head.

"Are you all right, partner?" Rouch asked. She glanced at him in concern. Her oval-shaped almond eyes were red streaked, and he seemed to recall that she was taking most of the shifts lately.

"Headache," Kane growled. "I'll be all right."

Sheehan finally clicked in his memory. He was a suspected sympathizer of the Recorders of Alien Manipulation. A ROAMer.

Their intel was three weeks old, but they'd found out Sheehan was supposed to be taking possession of an alien artifact that he was going to courier to the media for national exposure. Sheehan was one of the major players in the lobbying action that filled the President's mansion on any given day of a business week.

And business, the politicians had found out much to their chagrin, had become as important as the military units President Foggherty had control of. In the old days, the military had taken charge of doling out salvaged supplies to survivors and attracting people into the ville. That had been taken over by traders, who ran the supply routes and made a profit that was plowed back into getting more vehicles into the supply routes. Now the various traders had become a consortium: employing people, feeding people and giving the security to those people that used to be given by the government.

There were some, Kane knew, who compared the

trader consortiums to the barons in the wild regions. And they talked of them with just as much ill favor.

"You going to be able to cover my back?" Rouch asked.

Kane gave her a grin, wondering again why he hadn't ever fallen for Rouch. She would have clearly been a better choice for a marriage partner than what he'd ended up with. But he stopped that line of thinking before he got angry all over again.

"I've got your back, Rouch," he answered. "You can always count on me for that."

Rouch grinned mischievously. "Promises, promises, Kane. One of these days, I'm going to have to find out if you put on as good a show as you talk." She reached into the back seat and pulled on the standard-issue ankle-length black coat.

Kane smiled back, and tried to look forward to such an encounter. It didn't work, and he had to fight the echoes of the voice that had insisted Rouch was a selfish liar.

"Let's go." Rouch popped the car door and got out into the misty cold wind. She reached under her jacket and freed her side arm.

Kane took his own black coat from the back seat and shrugged into it. He stepped out into the October chill, feeling the mist splash against his face. His breath tore away from him in thin gray plumes. Lifting his jacket, he loosened the straps that secured his Spectre, freeing it in his holster.

The blaster was a scaled-down machine pistol with a special silencer built on, one of the new weapons that had rolled off Sante Fe Ville's limited manufacturing lines. Most weapons were World War II leftovers and gear that had been introduced in the 1950s and 1960s. When the nukes had fallen, productivity and invention had died with it. Solid black and with a wicked snout, the Spectre spit the special caseless 9 mm subsonic rounds at over 1200 rounds per minute. Normally, it carried a 30-round magazine, or an extended magazine with 60 rounds.

Rouch fitted hers with the Slayer configuration, a hex-shaped magazine that fitted on top of the Spectre, fully as long as the weapon. It more than doubled the weapon's weight and required that the user cup it against his or her forearm. But with a 200-round magazine, it was a pure bitch in a firefight. ROAMer proponents had given the Spectres a name—Whispering Death.

"Going in kind of heavy, aren't you?" he asked her. He didn't like killing unless it was necessary.

"I'm not going to fuck around," Rouch told him. Her long hair whipped in the misty wind. "I've been sitting in that car in one spot or another for the last five days and I'm in this at this point for a little get-back."

"Sheehan may not be the enemy," Kane stated. He trailed her across the street, staying slightly to the right so she wouldn't get in the way of his field of fire.

"You want to tell the director that, Kane?"

A worm of real fear touched Kane even through the fatigue and the depression that had settled over him for weeks. "No." The director of DEI didn't leave much leeway for questioning his orders.

Rouch gained the other side of the debris-strewed street as a trader consortium security vehicle whipped by, drenching them both with murky water gathered in one of the numerous potholes.

"Fucking bastard," Rouch complained as she gazed after the car. "Bet they don't have to worry about the heater in that thing."

The security wag was a 4WD jeep painted bright green, a holdover from the days when the trader caravans had used the color to identify themselves to outlying villes. And the consortium workers always had the best wags by rights of salvage. They'd operated by that precedent as the governments started coming into power again, and the first lobbying movement they'd muscled into the government docket had been to have it written into law. There'd been little fight.

The wag Kane and Rouch used was a big Ford sedan from the early sixties. The exterior would have fit anywhere in Sante Fe Ville. There were more wags on the streets these days, getting workers to and fro around the ville to do their assigned work. With huge rusting patches, dents and the missing front bumper, the DEI wag looked like any other on the streets. Underneath the hood, though, was where the DEI wag mechanics earned their keep.

A dozen or so homeless indigents sat huddled across the front of the building. Kane guessed that they were new and hadn't had a chance to set up squatting arrangements. Most of them were adults, people too old or too unskilled to be anything but a burden on the ville, but there were four children, too, all of them looking ten years of age and younger.

Kane felt bad for them, knowing they'd spend their young lives in sexual servitude either among the stronger of the homeless, or for sale to the working class in Epsilon District. Once they lost their appeal, they'd be killed or thrown out with the rest of the refuse.

A small girl of eight or nine watched Kane, her eyes big in her hollow-cheeked face. She had a ratty blanket wrapped around her and sat next to a man Kane hoped was her father. Otherwise, she'd already learned what the cost of the blanket was.

He turned away from her gaze, unable to bear it. He'd never really given much thought to kids. At least, not having any of his own. But lately in his marriage, he'd started thinking about it, wondering if maybe that might not be a way to share the love he felt for his wife.

That brought up a noise that was mixed between a laugh and a sob before he knew it.

Standing beside the main entrance to the squatter building, her Spectre held in both hands, Rouch gave him a hard look. "Kane?"

"Indigestion," Kane said. Dammit, he was used to being in control of his emotions. Too much pressure was coming down too quick, from too many directions.

"Let's get this done."

He nodded, unsheathing the Spectre. If Sheehan was holding for the trader consortium, he didn't think the man would be on his own.

Rouch pulled a small gold device from her coat and attached it to the side of her face. "Get your comm-tach on."

Kane lifted the comm-tach from inside his jacket and pushed it to the side of his face. Surgical steel pintels embedded in his jawbone slid through the flesh through callused grooves then sank into the comm-tach. A burst of white noise static filled his head, vibrating the headache that claimed him to the roots of his teeth. ''Damn,'' he swore.

''Let's do it,'' Rouch said.

Standing this close to the woman, with the audio pickup working on the comm-tach, her voice echoed inside his ears, picked up by his auditory canals and the sensors that transmitted the electronic signals directly to his brain. DEI built their agents well. Even if he went deaf, as long as he wore the comm-tach he'd still have hearing. He nodded.

Rouch pulled on a pair of wraparound sunglasses, then strode through the doorway.

Kane took out his own sunglasses and put them on, pushing them in till the nosepiece connected to the surgical steel gimbal mounted at the base of his forehead. The lenses juiced immediately, feeding off the natural electromagnetic field generated by his body. When they cleared a nanosecond later, he had photomultiplier vision, gathering all available light and making the most of it to give him night vision. A second setting included infrared.

He followed Rouch, sweeping the inside of the first room with the Spectre. Shelves had been yanked from the walls, the wood stripped and burned for warmth, as had the wallpaper and furniture.

From the structure's setup, Kane guessed that at one time it had been a shop. Now it was just another gutted squat filled with homeless.

The people on the floor cowered back from Rouch. His partner moved quickly, keeping her weapon pointing straight ahead of her, butt up against her shoulder and front muzzle resting in her left hand. Just the way they'd been taught in DEI's Magistrate Division, the strategic enforcement arm the agency maintained. Kane had been a Mag himself for a time. The work had been good; he hadn't had to think about things as much as he did now.

"Intersection," Rouch called out. "I've got left."

Kane automatically fell into place on the right side of the hallway intersection like the well-oiled machine they'd become. Then he noticed the three squatters crawling away on hands and knees, looking back into the hallway where Rouch and Kane were, and into the hallway to Kane's right.

"Right," Kane barked over the comm-tach.

"Got it," Rouch answered. "Those bastards fucking set us up."

Kane knew it was true. It wouldn't be the first time. The ROAMers had started sending a message over the past three years, trapping DEI field agents and chilling them, setting the tone for the battlezones. The first year the ROAMers had killed three. Nine the next year, and sixteen the year after that. This year they'd already gotten twenty-one, and there were two months left.

"On three," Rouch said.

"Ready." Kane held his position, watching the squatters scurry away even faster, already feeling bad for those that would probably get hurt in the coming firefight. Taking a deep breath, he readied himself to kill the men in the hallway. It wasn't something he'd have chosen to do if there was a choice, but for every one of them he chilled, it would be less risk for the squatters. He wrapped his hands around the Spectre.

"One, two, three!"

# Chapter 9

Kane exploded from his position, pushing away the fear as he raced across the hallway. Bullets peppered him, stopped by the Kevlar lining in the heavy black coat. Then he heard the whisper of Rouch's Spectre cycling through the caseless ammo. Her blistering full-auto hammered into the front line of attackers, lifting them from their feet and blowing them backward.

Hoarse screams of fear and pain filled the building, and blasterfire thundered in the enclosed space.

Turning, Kane slid into the hallway wall, slamming his back against it, ignoring the cries of anguish, knowing he'd hear them again in his nightmares. He raised the Spectre at once, pulling the trigger and unleashing 3-round bursts. He picked off two men with shots through their unprotected heads. They flailed and went down. But the bullets had cut a swath through the squatters, who were stretched out dead behind Kane.

"They're down!" Rouch called over the comm-tach. "They're down!"

Kane had already ceased firing. He scanned the hallway with the night vision, then switched over to IR. The thin walls offered no proof against the infra-red vision. He spotted the three men hunkered down in the utility closet at the corner of the doorway leading into the stairwell. He replaced the extended magazine with a Slayer ammo mag and strode rapidly toward the wall.

Outlined in thermal reds and yellows that gradually cooled to greens and blues, the three waiting gunmen shifted nervously. One of them had what looked like a string attached to a handheld rectangle.

Kane knew that he was able to see the string only because it was "hot," charged with some kind of energy. Experience told him it was an electrical cord, and it wasn't much of a guess at all to figure that it was attached to a bomb at the other end.

He moved through the hallway, kicking weapons out of the hands of the dead men, making sure they were down. His body was already aching from the impact of the bullets. The Kevlar weave might stop a round, but it didn't blunt the hydrostatic shock much.

"Rouch," he called.

"I'm here."

"We've still got company."

"I've got your back."

Screams of terror filled the building as the rest of the squatters came awake. The acrid smoke from the personal fires they'd generated to keep warm hung in the hallways. What looked like bundles of rags in the night vision view turned out to be thick bundles of cloth wrapped around human beings. The rag bundles suddenly sprouted legs and crawled rapidly away.

Kane stopped short of the corner where the three gunners hid in the closet.

No mercy, he told himself. He thought of the squatters. They might not have much of a life, but they deserved what they had.

He lifted the Spectre, then started firing and kept

the trigger down. The subsonic 9 mm rounds ripped through the wallboard and into the men beyond. They stood, trying to escape the hiding place that had suddenly become a death trap.

Kane exercised no mercy, spraying them until the Slayer clip cycled dry. The rounds had taken out a huge section of the wall, pounding it into a dry white chalky powder. The corpses beyond were bloody and twisted. "Down," he called out to Rouch in a shaky voice.

"I count eleven men so far," she said.

Kane switched back to night vision and changed magazines, outfitting the Spectre with another Slayer. It clicked solidly into place, then he shot the bolt and chambered the top round. He didn't look at the dead men any longer than he had to. "Only one way up, and Sheehan hasn't come back down. You're sure it was him?"

"As sure as I'm sure you're you." Rouch joined him, staying on the other side of the hallway from him so they wouldn't be as easy to pick off as if they'd stood together.

"Then he's got to still be up there." Kane took the point, moving up the stairs, following the Spectre's muzzle. Halfway up, he found a dead body dressed too well to be a squatter. A handmade knife stuck out of his groin, covered in blood, the handle still wrapped in the spring that had thrust it up from the step. The corpse's pockets had already been turned inside out, showing how quickly the squatters had moved on their prey. He stepped over the corpse and kept going. "Place is boobied, Rouch."

And that was getting to be a too common occurrence these days, as well. There was already talk about initiating a government program to burn the squats down. Once they were started on that, other congressional heads suggested doing the same for the black sectors of the villes. At least, the ones that weren't gainfully employed in the service areas.

A man wielding a machete rose up at the second-floor landing. He was wild-eyed, ratty hair hanging down well below his shoulders. "Get out of our house, you stupe bastards!" He swung the machete from shoulder level straight at Kane's head.

With no other option, Kane lined up the Spectre's muzzle and fired a dozen rounds. The stream of 9 mm bullets caught the man in the center of his stomach and rapidly tracked upward, punching him backward, then splitting his head open.

Walking over the dead man, Kane spotted another squatter cringing near the wall, pulling his much patched coat down over his head.

"Don't shoot me!" the man begged.

"Which way did he go?" Kane asked gruffly, knowing there was no way for the squatter to mistake whom he was talking about.

"Up," the man said, pointing at the stairwell. "They all went up."

"How many?" Kane demanded, glancing up to check the stairwell to make sure no snipers remained.

"Four men."

"Who did they meet?"

The man looked puzzled and fearful.

"Who?" Kane growled.

"Each other," he squealed. "Only each other."

"Rouch," Kane said, heading up the stairs.

"Copied over the comm-tach," she replied. "I'm at your heels."

Kane thought about the building. Three stories didn't leave Sheehan many places to go. An aerial pickup was possible, but even the trader consortium hadn't been able to put much together in the way of an air force. That left the street.

He charged up the stairs, driving his legs hard, knowing the director wouldn't be lenient if they let Sheehan slip through their hands. His breath came in gasps, burning the back of his throat. The smoke inside the building was gradually drifting to the top, climbing the stairwell and collecting.

When he reached the third-floor landing, Kane found the first of the bodies. She was a teenage girl, her skin already a catatonic blue even in the darkness. A dozen others sprawled out behind her, all equally still. From his own labored breathing, Kane knew they'd died from carbon-monoxide poisoning, losing all the oxygen out of the air in their attempt to stay warm.

He scanned the hallway that ran straight down the heart of the floor. The doors had been removed from the doorways to be used as fuel years ago. He kept the Spectre level as he ran, listening to Rouch's feet hit the landing behind him.

"I can't believe they went to all this trouble to chill a couple DEI agents," Rouch said.

"I don't think they did," Kane replied. "I think we were a damned bonus." He checked the rooms as he moved, briefly stepping inside and never losing the cover of the doorways. Rouch took the opposite side of the hallway.

Dead squatters were everywhere. The number was rapidly approaching three dozen.

"No one knew we were watching him."

"Somebody did," Kane growled.

"The director's not going to like this."

"He's going to like it even less if we lose Shee-han," Kane said. In the next-to-last room, he found an open window that looked down on the adjacent building, less than eight feet away. A foot-wide plank ran from the windowsill to the next building's roof-top.

Without hesitation, Kane stepped out onto the plank. "Rouch. In here."

He started across. Before he got halfway, muzzle-flashes flared from below and bullets ripped up through the plank, scattering splinters in their wake.

Kane shifted his weight, then pushed hard against the plank, intending to shove off and use the spring provided to leap across the gap. But the board, weakened by the bullets that had riddled it, broke in two.

Bullets slammed into Kane as he fell. Instinctively, he whipped an arm out, focusing on one of the small balconies projecting from the building next door. His right hand closed around the wrought iron, startling the squatters hunkered down inside the room.

"Kane!" Rouch yelled over the comm-tach.

Fingers wrapped tight around the wrought-iron rail-ing, Kane hung on expecting the full weight of his body and the drop to work together to pull his arm from its socket. Instead, he came to a stop.

Kane was amazed, not believing the sudden stop hadn't done damage to him. He felt he should know the answer why he hadn't been hurt, but the headache was still interfering with his memory. And things were progressing too damned fast.

No sooner had his fall stopped than one end of the wrought-iron balcony ripped free of its moorings with

long metallic screeches. He fell again, hanging on
stubbornly, flailing with his other hand for a more
secure hold. He lost the Spectre, watched it flip down
to land in the alley.

Bullets flamed into the side of the building, searching for him. Then, when the gunner got the range,
rounds thudded into Kane's back. Knowing he
couldn't stay where he was, he let go.

With the balcony dropping, though, he only fell ten
feet. He initially landed on his feet, then spotted the
gunner charging around the side of the building to
enter the narrow alley way. He fell backward, drawing himself into a ball and rolling.

The alley was choked with debris, filled with weeds
that grew up through the cracks. Broken glass glit-
tered across the damp black asphalt between the
buildings.

The gunner rushed on into the alley, screaming
loudly, his pistol firing. Another man followed behind
him, then his head came apart and his corpse slammed
against the nearby window, splintering the frames and
cardboard used to patch it up and keep the wind out.

Kane continued rolling backward one more time.
His right hand reached into his boot and took out his
combat knife. It was fourteen inches of hardened
steel, double edges honed to a razor sharpness. He
slid his hand down its length with accustomed ease,
finding the balance.

Coming up on his knees once more, Kane reached
back and threw the knife hard.

The blade flipped once, then caught the gunman in
the throat, sliding all the way to the hilt. Inches of
the bloody blade stuck out the other side of the man's
neck.

Shock filled the man's features, and he dropped the pistol he'd been firing. He made hoarse gagging noises.

"Kane!"

"I'm all right," Kane told Rouch. He pushed himself to his feet, breathing hard. "Get your ass down here, Beth-Li. Sheehan is still loose somewhere."

"On my way."

After retrieving the Spectre, Kane put his boot on the dead man's head and gripped the hilt of his blade, not looking at the man he'd killed so he wouldn't remember the face. Not this way—it was easier in a report. He pulled the knife free and wiped it clean on the corpse's shirt, then tucked it back into his boot.

A knife wasn't considered a civilized weapon in the villes like Sante Fe anymore. They hadn't been outlawed, but they were definitely frowned upon. The director had taken a stance against knives, not allowing them to be carried by his agents. Kane had lived too long with a blade always at hand to feel comfortable without one. Back then, he'd killed only when there was no other choice, just to live. He hadn't planned on becoming a killer, just in securing his citizenship in the WSC. But he'd ended up in the DEI, selected by the director himself.

Alerted by the thrum of the big motor, Kane ran out to the street. Glancing left, he spotted the 1958 Plymouth as it streaked at him. The wag hadn't completely gotten up to speed, but it was traveling too fast for him to avoid. The car knocked him from his feet, rolling him up across the hood and against the windshield, plastered facedown.

He recognized Sheehan in the passenger's seat of the wag, but the driver was someone he didn't know.

Sheehan was a tall blond man with sallow skin, his angular face pitted with smallpox scars when the disease reappeared after the nuclear winter that had engulfed the world.

The driver was small, with long hair and a full beard, and fisted a revolver. He yanked the weapon up and pointed it at Kane.

Scrambling quickly, Kane rolled himself up on top of the Plymouth just as two bullets crashed through the windshield. He flattened out on top of the car, hooking his fingers over the edge of the hood as the driver swerved the Plymouth all over the street. The tires shrilled as they climbed up on the curb, then the side of the car scraped along a building on the right. Golden yellow sparks flared out from the metal fender as the brick roughly kissed it.

A hole appeared in the wag top, followed immediately by the rolling thunder of shots being fired. A line of bullet holes chopped through the top, chasing Kane back until he lost his hold and fell.

He hit the street hard, intentionally landing on his shoulders so he could take advantage of the coat's Kevlar. The breath left his lungs in a rush. Fisting the Spectre, he rolled to his knees, hurting all over.

The Plymouth's red taillights flared in the night and the engine's roar echoed over the street.

Kane got to his feet and ran for the DEI wag. He opened the door and slid behind the wheel, keying the ignition at once. He put his foot on the accelerator and the rear tires spun as he brought the wag around in a tight U-turn. He spotted Rouch coming out of the squat building.

She raised an arm to flag him down.

Hitting the brake, Kane leaned across and opened

the passenger's door. Rouch got in and Kane accelerated at once, speeding after the fleeing wag.

The driver ran, fleeing back toward the center of the ville.

Rouch slapped a whirling light with a magnetic base on top of the wag, then flipped on the siren. "Should we call in a support team?"

"No," Kane said. "One way or the other, it'll be over before another team could get here." He shot past the poor neighborhood. The ville was structured around a hub. The interior of the city housed the Administrative Monolith, a massive, towering cylinder of white stone. Divided into levels, or districts, the monolith had been carefully constructed to maintain the integrity and security of its components.

The perimeter of Sante Fe Ville contained the squatter buildings. Adjacent to the squats was Lowtown, the black section of the ville; the President and the congressional offices continued to maintain the segregation edicts due to the possibility of genetic anomalies that were inherent in mixed blood.

Poverty-scale residences and shops filled the area. Most of the populace living in the black section worked in the service markets and in the cultivation, preservation and distribution of organic foods. None of that living was easy.

With the DEI wag's greater speed, Kane closed the distance between himself and the Plymouth. He flicked his eyes to Rouch. "Think you can take out the rear tires?"

"Yes."

"Get it done." Kane swerved the wheel, avoiding a sandwich pushcart being trundled across the street.

It was almost eleven o'clock and the mass transit was already shut down.

Gaudy sluts occupied a couple of the street corners near the bars, pulling the night shift for those interested in slumming. Despite government ordinance against fraternization, it still happened.

The gaudy sluts screamed in excitement, jumping up and down and cursing.

Rouch leaned out the window, her Spectre snugged in close to her shoulder. "Keep the damned wag still!"

Kane was finding that hard to do, since Lowtown's streets were filled with cracks and potholes.

The Plymouth pulled to the right again, going up on the sidewalk and breaking through a set of empty shelves in front of a small bakery. The shelves came apart in a spray of boards, some of them flying through the glass windows out front.

"Fucking do it!" Kane urged.

Rouch fired, the Spectre humming smoothly.

Bullets struck fire from the back of the fleeing Plymouth, chopped fist-sized chunks from the street, and knocked the back tires to pieces. Unfortunately, the bullets also penetrated the gas tanks. Dark liquid splashed out in a fine mist. Before Rouch could get her finger off the Spectre's trigger, a bullet chipped sparks loose from the gasoline tank and a cone of yellow flames jetted out.

"It's on fire!" Rouch yelled.

"Get in the car," Kane ordered. When Rouch complied, he sped up, pulling alongside the Plymouth.

"What are you doing?" Rouch watched the other wag in disbelief as Kane steered them closer.

"I'm not losing Sheehan." Kane pulled hard on

the steering wheel, ramming the wag into the Plymouth. Metal ground. Kane yanked harder on the wheel, muscling the Plymouth over.

The driver lifted his pistol.

Kane hit the brakes, then slammed the Plymouth's rear with the front of the DEI wag again. This time, the Plymouth driver lost control completely, and the Plymouth went nose-first through the wall of a shoe-repair shop. Braking quickly, Kane brought the wag to a halt. He and Rouch got out, Spectres in their fists.

The Plymouth driver got out, as well. His pistol blazed.

The pain hit Kane suddenly, burning into his right side, letting him know the Kevlar hadn't stopped the bullets. "Down!" he yelled to Rouch, lifting his machine pistol.

# Chapter 10

Rouch dived to ground at once, but lay prone on her stomach. The Spectre whispered death, ripping into the driver and jerking his body backward. Kane's weapon purred, as well. The pain in his side was bad, but he'd been hurt worse. He ran forward, not wanting Sheehan to escape in the narrow alleys and twisting streets of Lowtown. When sec teams flooded the area looking for criminals who'd committed crimes in the inner city, the streets became part of the arsenal used against pursuit.

Sheehan climbed unsteadily out of the Plymouth, bleeding profusely from a head wound. Crimson streaked his blond hair. His eyes were round, and he looked dazed. He carried a package in one hand.

"Sheehan!" Kane roared. Up and down the street, he noticed the number of black faces looking on in consternation, wondering if he was a pointman for another government-sponsored raid. Lowtown was definitely the wrong place for a white man to be at this time of night.

The trader consortium lobbyist's head snapped around toward Kane.

"Down on the ground," Kane commanded, "and I won't shoot." He walked toward the man slowly, the Spectre trained on the center of his chest.

Sheehan pulled the package in tight to his body.

Blood ran down his nose, splashing on his light green shirt. "You can't cover this up, Agent Kane." He shook his head. "Not you. Not your precious director. The ROAMers were right about you and those goddamned alien bastards, and the world's going to know about it. They're here to chill us, Kane. They've already been doing it."

The fire curled around the Plymouth's rear, growing larger.

"Get away from the car," Kane ordered. "It's going to blow."

Sheehan didn't appear to hear him. He looked around, panicked. Black smoke belched from the burning car behind him.

Kane cursed, then ran over to Sheehan, wanting to get the man out of harm's way. The lobbyist tried to get away, but there was nowhere to go and his legs weren't working well. Seizing the man by his jacket, Kane hustled Sheehan back out toward the street. Before he made it back to the security of the DEI wag, the Plymouth blew up, turning into a roiling orange-and-black fireball that Kane saw out of the corner of his eye.

Hot wind surrounded Kane, then a wave of concussive force slammed him to the ground. Fiery debris rained down around him in slow motion. Struggling, he managed to push himself to his knees, unable to draw a full breath.

Flames twisted and curled inside the shop, licked excitedly at the ceiling. The building was old and in an advanced state of disrepair, a firetrap watching for the match. It caught fire easily, burning in a whooshing rush.

Kane looked for Sheehan, discovering the man only

a few feet away. He shoved himself to his feet and limped over to the lobbyist. Holding the Spectre in one hand, he felt the man's neck for a pulse. He found one, strong and steady.

Then Kane noticed the steel shard sticking into the biceps of his own right arm. It was an elongated diamond shape. He couldn't remember it hitting him, didn't feel any pain now.

Not believing what he was seeing, Kane yanked his coat open. Blood stained his side, drenching his shirt and pants. But there was no blood on his arm. The phantom voice touched his mind briefly, increasing the pressure of the headache for a short time.

*What the fuck is going on with my goddamned arm?*

He pulled at the coat, twisting so that the light from the fire could fall on his injured arm. Now that he was aware of it, there was no way he could have not noticed the wound. On top of that, he saw that the armor-piercing ammunition the driver had used earlier had hit his arm, as well.

The armor-piercing rounds had smashed through his forearm in two places, leaving two holes big enough for him to stick his thumb into. At first he thought the material hanging down from the wounds was fabric from the Kevlar jacket or his shirt. And there should have been blood everywhere. He shouldn't even have been able to use his arm. Instead, his fist still fit comfortably around the Spectre's pistol grip.

Then he saw the wires that came from the inside of his arm. Four of them, in red, white, blue and green plastic sheaths, sparked briefly against each other, causing a clenching in his fingers. Kane didn't feel that, either.

*I'm a goddamned machine!*

"No," he whispered hoarsely, staring at the damage done to his arm.

"Kane," Rouch called.

"I'm all right," he told her, wondering if he was telling the truth. He pulled his jacket and shirt open farther, baring the wound where the shrapnel piece had pierced his arm. The skin looked lifelike, complete with tan and light covering of hair. But it wasn't real. The material felt spongy to his touch, warm even. He snaked a finger inside his arm, following the flat side of the shrapnel piece.

There was no blood, but an oily gel seemed to fill the hollow in the arm. Panic swamped him in a rush of nausea. He tore at the flap of artificial skin around the wound, tearing it larger. He peered inside, using the night vision provided by the wraparound sunglasses.

*How much of me is left? Goddammit, who did this to me? Where is my arm?*

He didn't understand the machinery that occupied the space inside his arm where muscle and bone should have been. He had known about the subcutaneous contact gimbal for the night-vision glasses and the comm-tach. Why the hell hadn't he remembered about the arm?

He wasn't sure if the rush of panic was coming from himself or from the voice in the back of his head. The headache throbbed harder. He forced his attention away from his arm, watching as men around him crowded in, knives and broken bottles reflecting the fire from the burning Plymouth. Kane knew it wasn't beyond the dissidents among the populace to take down a security patrol if the chance presented itself.

Kane struggled to get to his feet and lifted the Spectre toward the crowd. His mind reeled with the effort, and he almost threw up. The wound in his side wasn't too bad; it was the unsettled gnawing at the back of his mind that was making him light-headed.

"Stay the fuck back!" Kane warned. "This is official Department of Extraterrestrial Investigations business! Obstruction of a DEI agent in the pursuit of his agenda is first-class treason against the Western States Coalition. If you attempt to interfere in any way, you'll be shot!"

A thin black man with frizzed gray hair and a matching short-cropped beard stepped forward out of the crowd. He opened his hands, showing he had no weapons. He wore a homemade shirt and patched jeans.

"Stay there!" Rouch commanded, joining Kane.

"Got no trouble coming from me, white lady." A keen edge of anger threaded through the man's words. "Just got me a question. See, I own that shop. Feed my family out of it with the work I do with my own two hands. You people done come in here and destroyed everything I worked for. And for what?" He glanced at Sheehan. "White man's problems, and none of my own."

Tears dappled the man's seamed face, but Kane knew they didn't come from any sadness. They came from pure, unrestrained hate, and the inability to express it.

*Grant! Where the fuck is Grant?* the phantom voice demanded.

He also knew a black man in the WSC didn't have many rights to protest anything that happened to him. There were some villes that didn't even allow blacks in despite the national government's stance on allowable segregation.

*What happened to Martin Luther King and the civil-rights movement?*

Kane blinked again, the Spectre wavering at the end of his arm. Electrical sparks flared beneath his shirtsleeve, burning holes and throwing small shadows across the inside of the material. He felt the sweat beading on his head. Martin Luther King, he remembered from the history vids he'd seen as a child in federal school, had been executed by the prenukecaust government for fomenting rebellion among the nation's black population. King had been tied in closely to the ROAMers, publicly announcing that aliens were even then in control of the major governments around the globe.

"We've all got problems, citizen," Rouch declared. "Nothing can be done about the shop."

"My problems don't mean shit to you two, though, do they? You fucks live in some fancy apartment on Cappa Level, high enough up you don't see the people working to keep the streets clean around your precious Administrative Monolith." The man took another step forward, corded muscle standing out against his throat.

"Stay back," Rouch repeated.

"Got people in Lowtown making noises about fair representation," the man said. "Me, I think it'd be good if you bastards stayed the hell off our streets."

A youthful contingent of the group stepped in behind the shop owner. Their faces were filled with dark rage.

"We're going to have to shoot a few of them," Rouch whispered to Kane over the comm-tach, "to prove we mean business."

At Kane's feet, Sheehan stirred, blinking and looking up. He appeared groggy but whole. Kane lifted his booted foot and placed it in the center of the trader consortium lobbyist's chest. "No," he growled.

Sheehan groaned and slumped back. Then he laughed. "Looks like we're both going to die out here at the hands of these people, Agent Kane."

"Shut up." Kane blinked his eyes, struggling against the headache that pummeled his consciousness, straining to hold the Spectre level. His finger tightened on the machine pistol's trigger.

*Are you going to actually shoot these people, kill innocents?* the alien voice screamed.

Nobody's innocent, Kane told himself, arguing with the voice.

Despite the conflict filling him, Kane knew he'd pull the trigger if he had to. Survival came first, and that was reinforced by his commitment to the DEI.

Then the thrum of rotors filled the air, and high-intensity lights suddenly splashed the streets. The crowd moved back out of the lights at once, the advancing threat breaking like a wave over a rocky shoal.

"This is the Department of Extraterrestrial Investigations," an electronically enhanced voice announced from the speakers on the helicopter's underbelly. "You people are risking breach of the understood social contracts."

The lights played against the crowd, chasing them back into the buildings and alleys like shadows.

"The cavalry," Kane commented, trying to remember how many times DEI had actually dispatched one of its precious air-support craft on an exfiltration run. He gazed up at the vintage Huey, spotting the M-60 door gunners behind their armored shells.

"It was the director's call," Rouch said. "Surprised me, too."

The Huey flattened its approach, slowing to hover over the street. The rotor wash whipped up loose debris from the street and whipped it around in a miniature hurricane. The scream of approaching DEI wags echoed between the buildings.

Suspicion flared inside Kane. He ignored the buzzing feedback coming from his injured arm as he knelt down and fisted Sheehan's shirt and jacket, dragging the man up till they were nose to nose. "What did you get?"

"Fuck you, Kane. And fuck your goddamned director. DEI's not going to be able to keep covering this up." Spittle sprayed from Sheehan's mouth as he yelled to be heard over the approaching helicopter.

"We're not covering anything up," Kane replied.

Sheehan shook his head. "That's either a bad act or you're totally stupe, Kane. The aliens exist!"

"That's paranoia speaking," Kane insisted. "Goddamned terrorist propaganda. I don't know who got to you, Sheehan, but you're going to pay for your mistake."

"You think so, Kane?" Sheehan shook his head. "That helicopter is proof that I got my hands on the real thing." He blinked his eyes, turning away when the helicopter's strobe lights hit his face. "You think they sent that airwag after you?"

Kane didn't know what to think. Maybe the trader consortium lobbyist had overheard his conversation with Rouch.

*He's right. Take a look at the thing he was carrying,* said the voice, quietly insistent now.

He reached for the impact-protective bag Sheehan had been carrying. The chopper drifted toward the ground, coming around so the door gunners had clear fields of fire over the street.

"Don't believe me, do you, Kane?" Sheehan asked.

"No," Kane answered.

*Yes.*

"Go on," Sheehan challenged. "Take a look at the thing I'm giving my life for."

Kane didn't want to. Doubt was the ROAMer terrorists' greatest weapon. "Nobody's going to hurt you."

"The hell they won't."

"ROAMer sympathizers are incarcerated in the Tartarus Pits beneath the Enclaves." It was slave labor for the criminal and terrorist elements who took care of the city's sanitation needs, Kane knew, but it wasn't outright death.

"That chopper is here for something, Kane," Sheehan said. "It's not me, because you already had me. Right?"

Kane didn't answer, feeling the headache increase in his mind till it felt as if his head were being squeezed in a vise.

"So if it's not me and it's not you," Sheehan

stated, "it's got to be here for something else. Something important. Look."

Kane hesitated. He'd never broken DEI doctrine in his career.

*Look!*

He gave in finally to the command in the phantom voice in the back of his head. Lifting the bag, he tabbed the electromagnetic seal, opening it. Inside was what looked like a computer-circuitry card. Red, green and gold lights chased each other around the smooth surfaces, as if it was already operational. "What the fuck is this?"

"That's part of the heart and soul of what the aliens are calling the Genesis Project," Sheehan said.

"What's the Genesis Project?" Kane demanded.

Sheehan shook his head. "Don't know. The ROAMers are piecing it together. It has something to do with the Russians, the embassy. They know more than I do. They've got someone inside DEI. Someone who knows the truth and is willing to tell it."

"Bullshit," Kane grated.

Sheehan laughed. "There are those in DEI who know, Kane. An upper echelon. If you're going to cover something up, you've got to know what it is you're covering up. You can bet your ass the director knows."

The helicopter's skids touched the street, and Magistrates poured out, double-timing it to secure the area.

"Kane!"

He looked up at Rouch.

"What the fuck do you think you're doing?" she demanded. "You aren't supposed to look at anything you recover."

Kane felt guilty and afraid at the same time. Not looking was part of the DEI protocol. If an agent had knowledge of something, even if he knew it wasn't an alien artifact, it was harder to disavow knowledge of it. In the early days of DEI, agents had been taken by the ROAMers and tortured for information. Not knowing was actually a move designed to protect the agents, and the ROAMers knew about the protocol.

He opened his mouth, knowing he was going to lie to Rouch, wondering if it was going to be his first time and scared because he couldn't remember. He didn't know what the hell was wrong with his mind.

"Gun!" Rouch screamed, wheeling toward Kane and bringing the Spectre up.

"No!" Sheehan screamed, lifting his hands up in front of him.

For a moment, Kane thought Rouch was going to shoot him for looking at the contents of the bag. The Spectre's laser sights skated across his face in a ruby flare, then locked between the trader consortium lobbyist's wide-open eyes.

The Spectre flared, and the subsonic round kicked Sheehan's head back, squirting his brain through the hole in the back of his head.

Then it felt as if someone touched a Magistrate's Shockstick to Kane's temple. His senses exploded, finally drowning out the massive headache.

# Chapter 11

Kane opened his eyes and stared up at the soft fluorescent track lighting whisking by overhead. A swath of gauze covered the left side of his head, partially obscuring his view.

Med lab, he thought, and wondered where DeFore was. And Lakesh. Images swarmed in his head, pictures of the second alternate earth. He'd been an agent there, working for the Department of Extraterrestrial Investigations. He didn't know where Brigid and Grant were.

He had no clue why he'd be strapped onto a gurney. Something had to have gone badly wrong with the jump.

He struggled against the restraint straps. Finally managing to free his left arm, he lifted it and started pulling at the strap holding his head down.

"Please," a female voice said, "you have to remain still until we find out how badly you've been injured." A pair of hands reached for his arm, trapping the wrist and elbow and applying pressure to guide it back beside him.

"Get off me, DeFore," Kane croaked. Pain flooded his head, throbbing with a basso beat that felt as if it were going to blow the back of his skull out.

A young man in med-tech whites leaned into his perspective and shone a penlight into his eyes, moving the patch of gauze to access the other eye. Both of them were working. It meant he hadn't been blinded.

"Do you know your name?" the young man asked.

"Get me up off the table, goddammit!" Kane roared.

"You're injured," the man said. "I'm Med Tech Specialist Watson. Do you know your name?"

Kane realized that he was still in the other casement. He tried to, but he couldn't remember getting shot.

Had Rouch shot him?

"What's your name?" Watson asked.

"Kane," he replied. "My name is Kane."

Watson nodded, checking a handheld computer. "Very good. Do you know what happened to you?"

"I was shot."

"A couple times," Watson agreed, punching keys one-handed on the small computer. "You're going to be okay. Know where you're at?"

"Sante Fe," Kane said. His mind shifted as if it had been built on a mudslide. He felt another self pushing, fighting back, trying to get back in control. "In the Administrative Monolith."

"Right, Agent Kane." Watson dropped the computer into one of the big pockets of his white jacket. "We're going to get you into the ER, take a look around." He cut his gaze to one of the nurses accompanying the gurney down the hallway. "Get a bag started. He's lost a lot of blood, and I want him stabilized so we can find out how bad it is."

The nurse popped the protective plastic from an IV shunt, then started to pull up the sleeve on his right arm.

"Not that arm, dammit," Watson said. "That's a bionic replacement. Didn't you read his chart?"

"Sorry," the nurse apologized. She shifted to the other arm, and Kane felt the painful bite as it slid into his flesh.

The gurney hammered through the next set of double doors and entered an emergency room. Stainless-steel tables lining the walls and the bright lights above the bed in the center filled the room. The med techs slipped the restraints.

Kane tried to push himself up into a standing position. He had to get out of there. If Rouch had shot him, maybe she was on to him. And if she hadn't, someone else must have been.

"Whoa," Watson said. "Where do you think you're going?"

"Out," Kane replied. "I'm fine." His bare feet touched the cold tile floor, then a surge of wooziness overwhelmed him. His doppelgänger stirred around again in the back of his mind.

"You've been shot, Agent Kane," Watson said. "Twice at least. You're not going anywhere." He turned to the nurses. "Put him down and restrain him. Switch off his bionics. We're going to need a cybertech in here to get that repaired, as well. He has to be experiencing some feedback off it."

Kane tried to protest, but didn't have the strength. They put him on the operating table and tied him down.

Watson leaned into view, bringing a mask down over Kane's lower face. "Breathe deeply, Agent Kane. We'll have you back in one piece in no time."

Kane reached for the mask with his left hand, finding his other arm curiously limp. He caught the mask but found he didn't have the strength to hold the anesthesia mask back, as it clamped down over his lower face.

Then he saw the wedding band on his finger.

His doppelgänger was married?

"Easy, Agent Kane," Watson soothed. "You'll find we do very good work here. The director gave us very specific orders."

Kane felt the anesthesia flooding through his system, making his body feel heavier and heavier. His mind struggled with what he'd learned. Was Brigid already dead in this casement? And if she wasn't, where was she? Where was Grant?

The anesthesia washed his senses away before he could make a guess.

*St. Louis Outlands*
*Eastern Alliance of Former United States*

GRANT SWEPT THE SKIES with a pair of Bausch & Lomb night-vision binoculars. He'd taken them from a Mississippi Wall border guard he'd killed six years ago, a year before he'd become the chieftain of the largest band of Panthers in the Eastern Alliance of Former United States.

He lay in the rubble of the ville of St. Louis, staring down into the valley where the Mississippi River lay like a sluggish fat snake. The dark water flowed slowly on down to the Gulf of Mexico, winding through the rad-blasted lands of what had been Louisiana State before the nukecaust of 1963. Now, after the Cuban-based missile had slammed into the southern coastline, hammering the major villes down into nuclear-tainted dust, all that remained of Louisiana and most of the other Southern states were rad-blasted swamps filled with hellish creatures.

Across the river was the Mississippi Wall. Ten feet thick and forty feet high, it ran the length of what had been the United States and separated the Western States Coalition from the Eastern Alliance of the Former United States. Vulcan-Phalanx gun towers were mounted every thousand yards, offering overlapping fields of fire. Deathbirds also made scouting runs, but those were mainly during the day when they'd be more effective and less vulnerable. The Deathbird's IR systems could be fooled; Grant had placed his warriors in the delta mud so their body temperatures would be too cool to detect, then shot the Deathbirds down with rocket launchers, machine guns, rifles and even pistols if the occasion permitted.

The WSC had placed a price on his head, the biggest that had ever been offered for a Panther warrior. It was a distinction Grant took great pride in.

"They're late," Humboldt said beside him.

Grant gave the man a crooked grin but didn't take the binoculars from his face. "It's like every other WSC promise you hear about, brother."

"Yeah." Humboldt was long and lean, built for running and one of the fastest men with a blade Grant had ever seen. Like Grant, he wore Panther battle dress, T-shirt and heavy jacket, winter-ready black military pants. His beret was tucked into his back pants pocket. "One lie after another."

The bitterly cold prewinter season had settled into the land. The growing season was over, and even the scavengers were going to have a hard time making it through to the following spring if they didn't have enough supplies laid in and a place to take cover.

Grant scanned the gun towers, seeing the WSC sec men clearly behind the bulletproof glass. Nothing less than a rocket would penetrate the glass. Grant had found that out from harsh experience. The sec men's ability to quietly reside in their posts was supposed to serve as a demoralizer to Eastern Alliance and Panther forces alike.

After the nukes had stopped falling from the sky, the East Coast had been ruined. New York and Washington, D.C., had been obliterated. The Great Lakes, ripped apart by earthquakes triggered by the nuclear explosions, had become one large entity, spilling down into the Ohio River Valley and leaving those areas forever under flood once the nuclear winter had started melting off.

The WSC had come off with the better deal, which was why the Mississippi Wall had been built—to keep out those who had nothing, not to keep out pestilence and disease as the WSC government espoused.

Grant watched as the massive gates left near the twisted remnants of what had been the gateway to the West opened. Pack wags rolled through under the careful supervision of the WSC sec forces.

The sec wags preceded the pack wags, lumbering across the broken ground to the riverbank where the huge ferry lay. The ferry was long enough and wide enough for six wags to fit on at a time in a two-by-three configuration. The ferry made two trips.

When the sec wags returned to the Mississippi Wall garrison and the gates closed again, the pack wags got under way.

"They know they're still covered by the garrison guns," Humboldt said.

"Yeah, but they're moving into our territory,"

Grant said. "And they gotta do that to do the shit they're planning." He watched the pack wags moving along the battered highway that was more scar than actual thoroughfare now. But it was the only way into East St. Louis.

The pack wags moved slowly across the rough terrain.

"How long do you think we have?" Humboldt asked.

"A couple hours," Grant replied. "Mebbe more. Enough." He rubbed the back of his neck, trying to ease the tension spreading through his broad shoulders, thinking that was the source of the headache that had been rattling his skull for most of the evening.

"What's wrong?"

"Headache."

Humboldt smiled, his lips purple in the moonlight. "Go get laid. Always makes me forget about mine."

"I'll remember that. You stay here, keep watch. I'll have Kadeem stay below with the motorcycle. If they field another wag group, send him along to tell me."

Humboldt nodded. "They decide to put a couple Deathbirds in the air, could be a different story when you take that wag caravan."

"That's why I'm depending on you and Kadeem. Kid's a fucking kamikaze on that motorcycle."

"Motorcycle can't outrun a Deathbird, Grant."

Grant stood, shouldering the M-14 he'd brought with him. He was tall and thick, his body scarred by his lifelong war and by the time he'd spent in the Tartarus Pits in Sante Fe Ville with whip-happy taskmasters working off their prejudice. His hair flared out in dark curls, matched by his full beard with the patch of gray on his chin.

"They put a Deathbird in the air, I'll chill it myself."

"May lose some people doing it."

"Panthers don't back down," Grant told him. "We ever do, we might as well place our throats on the blades of those hunting us down."

"I know. Keep your head down."

Grant nodded and made his way down the game trail he'd followed up to the ridge line. Beneath the heavy overgrowth of brush and grass, the old ville of St. Louis still lay buried, its ghosts still sleeping.

He was bone tired from sleeping only a handful of hours spread out over the past three days, and the headache wasn't helping. Even when he'd been working in the Tartarus Pits, before he'd found a way to escape and make his way east, he couldn't remember ever having a headache like the one that haunted him now.

Two hundred yards farther on, down in the tangle of buildings that had been one of the marinas lining the St. Louis riverbank, his Panther regiment waited. Over two thousand men hunkered down in the darkness under tents and makeshift shelters, all of them sufficiently young and battle hardened to fight to the death. There could be no other way.

Grant was proud of them. They were the Panthers, bearing the prenukecaust name of the black warriors who'd fought for equality in the United States. The predark government then had linked them with the Russian Communists of the old world, then the ROAMers making them out to be bandit princes who practiced only sedition.

And talk had never earned the oppressed anything. Equality meant being willing to fight back against anyone who would deny them their freedom. They were still fighting. Only they'd gotten better at it over the years. They'd also added equipment to their arsenal: wags and firepower.

Grant walked through the men, being polite but staying focused. The mission tonight was important.

If things went right, he'd have new converts after tonight.

*Find Kane!* The voice overwhelmed even the headache, but only briefly.

He cursed when the pain of the headache slammed into him again. Nausea gripped him, making his stomach roll.

"Hey, Grant, you okay, brother?"

Grant looked up and found Kadeem standing there. The boy glanced at him with concern. "Yeah, kid," Grant said. "I'm fine."

Kadeem was a head shorter than Grant, but at sixteen still had a lot of growing years ahead of him. He kept his hair brushed out, giving him a wild and shaggy look. His skin was coal-black except for the pink-and-white scars at his wrists where slavers' bracelets had been three months ago. He carried an M-14 and wore a machete at his hip. Scalps hung from a leather tie, all dried and cracked, and still ripe in enclosed spaces. There were nine of them so far, and Kadeem had taken them all himself from slavers. No one told him to lose the scalps.

"We gonna get them WSC bastards bringing that trash in to our people?" Kadeem asked, tagging along.

"Yeah. You're gonna stay here with Humboldt. Be

a lookout. If this is a trap and WSC sends reinforcements over, you're gonna have to get to us before they do."

A dispirited look filled Kadeem's youthful face. "I belong on the front line, Grant. This war of ours, I'm a survivor and the only way I'm gonna continue to be a survivor is if I get out there and push it back down their throats."

Grant clapped the boy on the shoulder. "I'm counting on you to handle that motorcycle, little brother. In the night and across the terrain you're going to be rolling through, you're gonna be more at risk than I am. Can I count on you?"

"Every time, my brother." Kadeem made a fist out of one hand and dropped it on top of Grant's fist. Then he walked back toward the group he'd been hanging with.

They'd arrived late the night before and made a cold camp.

Grant made his way to the matte black Airstream trailer he'd claimed as his own. The Panthers claimed seventeen travel trailers among their motor pool, all of them set up to serve as a med facility as well as a command post. Constantly on the run and mobile, retreating from the war and advancing to the next battlefield, the Panthers had no home.

Hooker waited for him, sitting in the doorway under the copse of trees where the Airstream had been set up. The old man smoked a pipe, burning some of the marijuana they'd traded for at a small ville a few days back.

The old man was skinny as a stick, but moved like a snake, all sinuous grace. He didn't look like he was sitting as much as he appeared to be coiled and waiting to strike. His hair had retreated to a fringe the color of cotton, surrounding the gleaming bald spot that ran from the front of his head to the back.

Red-rimmed eyes stared at Grant beneath cottony ropes of eyebrows, and flecks of gray stained his stubbled face. He wore a Panther uniform, but the pants legs were folded up under him. He'd lost his legs at midthigh seven years ago after being run over by a war wag during an attack on a barony in the Shens. Hooker liked to claim that he'd been mean enough to survive it.

And he'd continued to lead the Panthers for another two years from a wheelchair before passing that leadership onto his handpicked successor. He was the closest thing Grant had ever had to a father.

"Is it shaping up?" Hooker asked as Grant pulled himself up into the trailer beside him.

"Twelve pack wags," Grant replied. He massaged his temples, aggravated that the headache persisted.

"Get a head count?"

"No. Didn't want to chance getting spotted."

Hooker took another hit off the pipe, held it for a moment, then released a lungful of sweet smoke into the night air. "Twelve pack wags, figure six men to a unit. And what's six times twelve, Grant?"

"Seventy-two. I'm taking two hundred men with me in jeeps and transport wags. We'll reach the rendezvous before they do. And if we find out they're carrying poison, we'll chill them there, see if Trieste's band wants to join up."

"Trieste isn't exactly going to be in favor of that."

Grant smiled. "Fuck Trieste. He's built his group up to four hundred people and ain't done shit about taking care of them. Half of them are warriors, but they're underequipped, underfed, no goddamned supplies put away for the winter. That's why they're going on the WSC dole. And that's what makes them a danger to us all.''

Over the years, WSC whitecoats had introduced plague viruses and diseases into the black communities roving the Eastern Alliance territory. Gene splicers from Overproject Excalibur had created the bugs in labs and moved them into the eastern lands. In the beginning, and sometimes still, Deathbirds had flown into the Eastern Alliance territory and dropped cultures onto migrant bands. At other times, they put plague cultures in food products and passed them out in the winter. One variant had been a virulent pseudopodia that had lived dormantly in blankets that had been passed out, then become active when coming into contact with chemical salts humans normally secreted from their skins.

The Eastern Alliance government had sometimes supplied antidotes for the diseases and plagues out of duress. Full-blown epidemics had also adversely affected the Eastern Alliance, which also suited the WSC fine. They'd only offered the technology they maintained out of self-preservation.

But at other times, whole villes of men, women and children, people who'd struggled to eke out an existence from the cold hard land they'd found themselves in, had been put to death to end a plague or virus strain.

Grant had ordered it done himself. He'd ordered them chilled, then ordered them burned, and stayed until the last ash had grown cold. He wasn't going to do it again if he could prevent it.

"You figure you got enough supplies to take on another four hundred people?" Hooker asked.

Grant nodded. "We're ready to grow again."

"Make a bigger target. Hard getting around with all them people wandering around after you."

"Not a bigger target," Grant disagreed softly. "A bigger hammer. We got people out there willing to listen, Hooker. Add in Morgan's band and Culberth's band, we got nearly four thousand people."

"Enough for a Panther enclave if you can find a place safe enough to put down roots." Hooker smiled proudly. "Wouldn't that be something?"

"Yeah. And we're about ready to do it. Fuck the WSC and fuck the EAFUS. We'll get our own territory, mebbe take some of theirs while we're at it, build on it from there."

"Goddamn but you're a dreamer. You got fucking big eyes."

Grant dropped a hand on the man's thin shoulder. "Had a hell of a teacher."

Hooker smiled and nodded. "You gonna ask ole Trieste if he wants to join up, too?"

"Fuck him, too," Grant said good-naturedly. "I'll bring you his skull back for a soup bone."

# Chapter 12

Kane blinked his eyes open, and felt the dull thud echoing in his head. His mouth was dry, the way it always was when he'd been put out on an operating table. Another dull pain echoed in his side. He turned his head slightly, taking in the white curtains all around him. He felt chilled to the bone, weak.

He breathed out, trying to relax. At least he was back where he belonged. When he'd first woken on the gurney, he hadn't felt like himself. He'd felt shoved way back into his own mind, trapped by some other self that had tried to take over his body. The problem was, he still didn't think he had all of his memory back. He lifted his left hand, staring at the wedding ring he wore. The other self had been so surprised that he'd been married. He'd sensed it in the other man's thoughts.

One of the curtains slid back with a metallic rasping of the rings dragging along the bar. A buxom nurse with short brown hair looked at him over her handheld comp. "How are you feeling?"

"Groggy," Kane admitted.

She took his flesh-and-blood arm in her hands and pressed the comp against his wrist. "Tell me your name."

"Special Agent Kane, Department of Extraterrestrial Investigations."

She reached up and peeled back an eyelid, shone a penlight into them. "Do you know where you are?"

"Recovery room," he answered. "I've been here before."

"Very good. How's your memory?"

Kane looked at her, suddenly paranoid. He wasn't sure how much he knew and didn't know. "About what?"

"Just in general," the nurse said. "Do you know how you ended up in the hospital?"

"I was shot," Kane said. He pointed at his side. "Here. I don't know what happened to my head."

"You were, in fact, shot four times."

"Tell me."

"Your side, twice through the bionic prosthesis you have, and the fourth bullet creased your head. Another inch over, and it would have emptied your brainpan. As it is, you'll probably have a few headaches over the next few days."

"That won't be out of the ordinary," Kane said. Once the nurse finished with her evaluation of his condition and told him he'd be assigned a room within the next hour, he lay back on the bed and closed his eyes.

He'd been shot in the head. But who had done it? Beth-Li Rouch?

Or someone else?

AN HOUR AND FORTY MINUTES after he'd been promised, Kane got a private room, which meant the director had influenced the decision. He didn't know exactly how to feel about that.

Being afraid, however, was a good place to start.

The director didn't put up with mistakes, and Kane wasn't sure what the night was going to be called.

The private room was spacious, and dim track lighting gave the room a twilight glow, and reflected in the window overlooking the ville.

Despite the wooziness he still felt from the lingering drugs in his system, he forced himself out of bed, sitting on the edge. The cold air swirled around him, pressed into the soles of his feet where they touched the tile floor.

A bandage covered the wound on his side. He stretched his right arm out to inspect the bionic replacement. Sensation had returned to the limb, and the buzzing feedback no longer troubled him. He tried to remember when he'd lost his arm, almost panicking when he didn't immediately know. How the hell could he forget something like that?

Before he knew it, his stomach heaved. He barely got his head over the small trash bin beside the bed before the contents of his stomach came up. There wasn't much—a thin yellow stream of bile the stomach pump hadn't suctioned out on the operating table. When he finished, he felt better.

And he remembered how he'd lost the arm.

The memory popped into his mind in a screaming rush. The alley had been dark and the ROAMers desperate. One of them had swung an ax before Kane had a chance to get completely out of the way. He'd have been dead if Rouch hadn't been at his heels, blasting both the ROAMers away before they could chill him. The ax had destroyed his arm and the shoulder, requiring amputation. Bionic replacements weren't ordered as a matter of course, even for special agents, but the director had arranged for the bionic prosthesis.

It had allowed Kane to return to work, and maybe it had saved his life. And yet he feared the director because he'd seen the things the man was capable of.

He crossed the room to the window and looked down at the ville. There were few lights, as keeping illumination in the ville twenty-four hours a day was a waste of energy resources. It also made the monolith a big target in the night.

The holes in his memory were the most dangerous to him, Kane decided. He twirled the wedding ring on his finger, but that only brought more hurtful thoughts even though he couldn't pin them down. The fact that he was alone in the hospital room and she wasn't with him made his wife's absence even sharper. He took a deep breath and put the thoughts out of his mind, grateful the headache wasn't as bad as it had been.

Turning, he spotted the file comp hanging from the end of the bed. He crossed the room and took the comp up. Flicking it on, he searched through the files, finding his own. Then he reviewed the information, anchoring each fact in his mind till it was his again.

The room door opened.

When Kane looked up, he saw Beth-Li Rouch outlined in the doorway. She was still dressed in street black, dirt and dust staining her clothing. She gave him a smile. "Still among the living, I see, partner."

"Yeah," Kane said after a brief hesitation. He put the comp away. He still couldn't remember who'd tried to shoot him in the head. But one thing he was certain of—if it had been Rouch, she'd been acting on the director's orders.

POISED ON A RIDGE above the remnants of the highway the pack wags traveled, Grant watched the first of the vehicles make the final turn into the pass. Half his forces were on either side of the pass. He wasn't expecting much in the way of resistance.

The wag engines groaned as they powered up the incline. The dim lights were weak yellow cones against the night.

"Stupe bastards would be better off running without lights," Reba said, standing beside Grant. She wore blackface to turn her invisible in the night. Though she was of true Panther blood, her complexion was fair enough for her to pass as white. Her shoulder-length dark hair was tied back by a black scarf. The military fatigues disguised the womanly figure Grant knew from memory that she had.

"Yeah," Grant agreed. But the lights didn't bother him as much as the headache that pounded against his temples.

*Find Kane!* the voice insisted.

Grant unlimbered his M-14 and moved through the brush along the ridge in a crouch. Reba stayed at his side, working as his comm officer. She carried one of the few handheld military comm units they had that were still operational. It was easier finding parts for the wags the Panthers used than to find comm components.

He sweated heavily under his jacket and the heavy pants, but wondered how much of that was due to the headache. He felt his thoughts growing fuzzy, surprised that he couldn't remember clearly what had happened as late as yesterday. Or even how they'd come to find out the WSC had agreed to send a mercy pack wag caravan in to Trieste and his band.

Fifty feet farther on, Grant found the trap they'd set.

Fresh-cut trees blocked an avalanche of rock on the hillside. They'd worked most of yesterday evening and all of today to prepare the ambush, filling it with tons of boulders. Two thousand members of the Panthers, and nearly all of them able to do manual labor. It was almost enough, Grant thought grimly, to change the face of at least the Eastern Alliance Outlands. Maybe in his lifetime.

He glanced across the valley and spotted the other pile of rock on the opposite side. Two more such piles occupied the other end of the valley, ready to seal off any retreat the pack wags might attempt once the ambush had been started.

"Reba," he called.

"I'm here, Grant."

"Ready the teams," he ordered, drawing the machete he wore at his hip. The wags' roaring engines echoed over the countryside.

The woman worked quickly, notifying the other teams.

"On my order," he said.

"Grant! Grant!"

Turning, Grant spotted Marcus rushing toward him. He'd stationed the man as the relay communications for the outer perimeter. "What?"

The man stayed low, remaining under cover of the brush. He was in his early thirties, short and squat, with powerful forearms that had choked the life from Panther enemies. "We've got movement along the outer perimeter."

"Sec teams?" Grant couldn't believe that the Mississippi Wall garrison had fielded ground teams that had outflanked him. His warriors were better skilled than to have allowed a hundred men to move through the countryside without notice.

"Not sec teams," Marcus said, gasping. "Trieste's people. They've closed in from the south, cutting off our way back to the cold camp."

"Warriors?" Grant asked.

Marcus shook his head. "Everybody."

Grant grew angry, knowing that something was wrong.

"This isn't the rendezvous point," Reba said. "Unless we got the information wrong somehow."

Grant shook his head. "We didn't get it wrong. Trieste set us up."

"What do you mean?"

"The fucking bastard's working for the WSC," Grant snarled. "While we're here trapping the pack wags, he's brought his band up behind us to trap us. Must have been the price he had to pay for the cargo."

Reba looked at Grant with liquid eyes. "If we fight our way through them, we're going to have to chill a lot of women and children. I don't want to do that."

"Me neither," Grant said, his mind flailing for a means of escaping the situation. The trap, he knew, was primarily designed to pull the teeth of the Panthers' assault forces. He'd brought the cream of his warriors into the valley, expecting to roll over the sec forces manning the pack wags. "If we try to run, we're going to leave our backs open to the pack wag sec men. And that goddamned poison they're carrying is still going to find its way into the Outlands."

The deep anger that he'd always carried with him, ever since he'd been a slave down in Sante Fe Ville's

Tartarus Pits, assailed him. His adrenaline level jumped, charging his system. He struggled for control, feeling as if he were going away from himself.

He'd fled across the WSC, following one of the underground trails that spirited his people east of the Mississippi Wall, till he'd gotten into the Outlands of the Eastern Alliance. He'd lived as an animal until Hooker had found him and taught him to love and dream. But he never forgot to hate, and it had been that driving force that had shaped him into the weapon against the villes.

As he struggled for control of his anger, trying to think through the situation that confronted him, the headache suddenly blossomed into an agonizing nukeburst that drove him to his knees. And he felt the other self slipping into his mind where he'd been.

*Move over, you son of a bitch, I'm coming through.*

# Chapter 13

Kane put the comp back on the bed, keeping his eyes on Rouch.

She stepped into the room and closed the door behind her. The Spectre hung at her side in the specially made elongated shoulder rig. Her black coat was open only enough to allow her to reach the machine pistol, not leave her too terribly vulnerable.

"Catching up on your reading?" she asked.

"Just checking to see how they were writing it up," he said. "What happened to Sheehan?"

"He's deader than virginity in a gaudy," Rouch said. "Should you be up?"

"I'm up," he growled back at her. "Goddamned anesthesia's making me feel like I've got a hangover. You shot Sheehan?"

Rouch smiled sweetly. "Right between the eyes. You know I don't miss. You still have a headache?"

"Not like it was," he answered truthfully.

"The director seemed more than a tad interested in your headaches."

A warning chill snaked down Kane's spine, but it wasn't based on anything he could recall. He wondered if it was something left over from the other. "That's not like him to be too interested in anyone's health."

Rouch raised her eyebrow. "He's always seemed

to make allowances in your case, Kane. That's how you got the prosthesis when a normal field agent would have been given his termination papers and the gold chron for meritorious service.''

''How did he find out about the headaches?''

''It was in my report. He's asked me to give him the specifics of any aberrant behavior on your part.''

Kane grew angry. ''He told you to spy on me, Rouch?''

''Hell, Kane,'' she retorted in a light, uncaring tone, ''you and I both know we spy on each other. This is DEI, after all. I told him that in light of all the shit in your personal life and the fact you'd gotten nearly no sleep at all, a headache was getting by pretty easy.''

Kane circled the room, aiming for the closet opposite the bed. ''He believed you?''

''What else was there to believe?'' Rouch asked. Her voice took on a suspicious note. ''Unless there's something you're not telling me.''

''No.'' Kane opened the closet. His personal gear was inside, still bloodied from his wound. But his Spectre hung in there, as well. With his back turned to Rouch, he took the machine pistol's butt into his hand. He slipped it free, flicking the safety off. He didn't feel like his normal self with all the anesthesia still circulating in his system, but if Rouch was there to chill him, he didn't have a choice. ''Hey, Rouch.''

''Yeah.''

''Back there with Sheehan, everything happened in a blur, so I don't know.''

''Don't know what?''

''Who shot me?''

Rouch answered without hesitation. "Sheehan did. He had a hideout gun you must not have seen."

Knowing she was lying, Kane whirled to face her, bringing the Spectre up in front of him, scanning for Rouch. Only the woman wasn't where he thought she'd be.

"GRANT!" Reba put strong arms around him and tried to help him to his feet.

"I'm okay," Grant answered. He pushed himself to his feet and looked around at the Panthers. All of the faces showed concern.

*Who the fuck are you?*

He listened to his doppelgänger's voice echoing weakly in the back of his mind. The last surge of rage when he found out he'd been set up by Trieste had been enough to complete the biochemical and electrical changes necessary to put Grant in charge of his doppelgänger's body. The headaches weren't quite as severe, either.

"What are we going to do?" Reba asked.

Grant accessed his doppelgänger's memories, finding he was able to get to most of them. He knew enough about who he was in this other casement to get by for the moment. When he looked at the anxious faces around him, their names were there for him.

"Marcus," he said, "how far out are Trieste's people from our twenty?"

"Five, ten minutes, mebbe," the man replied. "But they're fanned out. Chances of us moving two hundred warriors back through their line unnoticed—" He shook his head. "That's pretty much fucked."

Grant grinned. "Then we won't go back."

"What are we going to do?" Reba asked.

"Go forward," Grant answered. It was pure Mag mentality, and he was sure Kane would have appreciated the sheer audacity of the situation and what he planned. He affixed the bayonet to the M-14 to underscore his words.

"Into the valley?" Marcus asked.

"Hell, yes, into the valley," Grant told him. He raised his voice so they could all hear. "We're going down into that valley and do what we came here to do. We'll fuck those pack wags over, and if Trieste wants a part of that barbecue, then he's fucking welcome to it."

"They'll be expecting us," Reba pointed out.

"Fuck 'em." Grant grinned. "'Yea, though I walk through the valley of the shadow of death, I will fear no evil.' For I am the meanest motherfucker in the valley. Is everyone with me?"

A chorus of yeses spread through the men around him. The Panthers were survivors, warriors, men and women who'd fought for everything they had and knew they'd have to fight to keep it. Grant knew that from his borrowed memories, and their sense of purpose filled him with pride.

Grant lifted his machete and stepped up to the rope that held the web of ropes containing the avalanche of rock ready to be released into the valley. "Tell them now, Reba." He waited till she'd made the radio contact, then he swung the machete, cleaving it through the rope and into the tree bole beyond.

With a low grumbling that rapidly became a roaring rush of tons of falling rock, the man-made avalanche gathered steam and ferocity. Dust filled the air, torn from the sandy loam.

Grant ran for one of the jeeps, sweeping the valley

with his gaze. Three other dust clouds, one opposite the avalanche he'd unleashed, and two others at the back of the valley. The trap had been sprung.

Now it was a matter of seeing who lived and who died.

# Chapter 14

Lakesh stared through the brown armaglass, feeling his breath tight in his throat, struggling with worry and guilt over putting Kane, Grant and Brigid at risk once again. But he'd had long years of experience in dealing with those infrequent twinges of guilt over interpersonal relationships. The guilts he bore were of much larger design than that.

He'd helped build the bleak future that they all now faced. Working with the Totality Concept, he'd carefully laid that future, brick by brick and mortared with megalomania. Back then, he'd felt their science had made them near to gods.

Now, he knew how false that had been. Still, he manipulated, pulled and pushed, battered and protected, lied and stole, for the preservation of the dreams he'd once had for the world. That, he supposed, Kane would never understand.

Guilt was something he dealt with in his private moments, not something he allowed to influence the decisions he made, or the risks he took with the people he could command or coerce into doing what he wished.

At the moment, he felt exposed and helpless because the events he was overseeing were well out of his hands, beyond his machinations. He resented such a lack of control, but it was the price of exile at Cerberus.

Domi came quietly to his side, linking one of her slender arms within his. Her fingers caressed his skin.

"Ah, darlingest Domi, to have you at my side now is such a joy," he said.

"Too risky," Domi commented. "Should find other way."

"If I could, I would, darlingest one." He gazed over her alabaster shoulder, so deliciously unclad, and stared at the Mercator-relief map on the wall behind her. "But there is simply so much at stake. Kane understands that, as do Grant and dearest Brigid."

"Chintamani Stone evil."

"Ah, Domi, the trapezohedron is merely a contrivance. What makes such a thing evil is the people who use it. We seek merely to undo the wicked schemes that have already been constructed."

"I know, but what happens then, Lakesh, when everything back like was?"

"Why, everything will be better, of course."

"How?"

He stared into her crimson eyes and saw the uncertainty in their depths. "Because it will be the future we were to have achieved before the Archons' interference ended the world."

Domi appeared to give that some thought.

Lakesh glanced over at DeFore. The med tech was monitoring Kane's vital signs through his transponder. Bry did the same on the computer, trying to find out if Kane had been able to return to the casement.

"He's stable," DeFore stated. "They all are."

Bry continued to work at the computer console.

Domi gently cupped Lakesh's chin in her hand. She pulled his face toward hers. "What be different?" she asked, forcing him to meet her gaze.

"Darlingest Domi, I truly can't answer that."

"Where we be, Lakesh?"

If it had been anyone else, Lakesh knew he might have tried to lie. But he'd always been touched by the young albino woman's innocence. In his eyes, she was purity, with the heart of a savage.

"I don't know. Truly, I don't."

"Then why change? We here, we alive. Not need any more. Change things, mebbe none of us be here."

"We have to explore this option, dearest child," he told her.

"Why?"

"Because," he said, fumbling for words, truly wishing he could make her understand and take away her fears, "because things might be better."

"Take more than need," Domi said, "risk getting hand or arm cut off. Mebbe that's only outlander saying, and not make sense."

"It makes perfect sense, darlingest Domi, and never fear sharing your thoughts." Lakesh patted her hand reassuringly.

"Then share yours."

"For investigating what possible secrets are contained in the Chintamani Stone?"

"Yes."

Lakesh blinked, not able to squirm away from her eyes. "There is a power inherent in the trapezohedron. We must discover what it is, and what changes we can effect."

"Because it there?"

"Yes."

Domi disentangled her hand from his, withdrawing, something she'd not been in the habit of doing. Her behavior hurt him more than anything had in a very long time. "Because it there is like excuse stick head in mutie bear mouth to see if it bite. Mebbe will, mebbe not. Stupe reason all same." She turned and walked away.

Lakesh watched her, restraining himself from going after her or calling out to her. The only reason he didn't, he knew, was that he was certain she'd have rebuffed him. He forced his gaze back to the mattrans unit, feeling more alone than he had in decades. His eyes stung.

She had been right, though. He didn't know what would happen if they did find a way to change the events leading up to the nukecaust. If he had his way, he'd change it without hesitation. So would Kane, Grant and Brigid. But if they couldn't, if all they could do was end the threat of Colonel Thrush, he'd accept that. For now.

"Lakesh."

The old man turned to look at Bry.

The man said tensely, "We're getting power fluctuations, worse than the last time. We're going to have to take more systems off-line."

Without hesitation, Lakesh said, "Do it."

"Wegmann will squawk, you know." Bry referred to the redoubt's engineer and all-around mechanic. His domain was the lower level where the nuclear generators provided power to the installation.

"Let him. This is more important than keeping the coffeemakers working."

Bry's fingers played over a series of toggle

switches. After a moment, he announced, ''It's done.''

''Thank you, Mr. Bry.'' Lakesh turned his gaze back to the mat-trans unit. All he could do now was wait and hope.

BEFORE KANE COULD GET his finger around the Spectre's trigger, Rouch kicked the machine pistol out of his hands in a sweeping front kick that came within inches of his nose.

''What the fuck do you think you're doing?'' Rouch demanded, holding her fists up in front of her as she dropped into a martial-arts stance.

Kane raised his hands, taking up a stance of his own.

*You hesitated! The goddamned blaster in your hand and you couldn't put that bitch down!*

He listened to the angry voice in the back of his mind. The headache buzzed in his skull again. He felt the other pushing at him, trying to shove him away. Kane blinked and stood his ground.

The fact remained that he wasn't sure if Rouch was guilty of shooting him.

*Keep hesitating and you're going to get both of us fucking chilled.*

Kane ignored the voice, concentrating on Rouch's moves. They'd faced each other on exercise mats at the department and he knew from memory that he could take her. The other pushed at his mind again, lurking in the shadows of his thoughts, but Kane held on to himself. He was the center of the only world he'd ever known, and if he ever once lost himself, he would never truly be at peace again. That was something his wife had never seemed to understand about him.

"Somebody shot me," he told Rouch, circling to the right. The hospital room, though private, was still a small battlefield.

"Hell, yes, somebody shot you!" Rouch exploded. "And if I hadn't been there, fucking Sheehan would have busted a cap in your face and not just grazed you! I saved your goddamned life, Kane!" She kicked his Spectre clear, too far away for him to reach.

His head still swirled from the anesthesia and the presence of the other. "I didn't see a blaster, Beth-Li," he growled.

"So you didn't see it."

"You chilled him in cold blood. Then you shot me."

Rouch looked honestly surprised. "You think I shot you? Kane, that's stupe! If I'd wanted to chill you, I wouldn't have missed. And if I had, I'd have damned sure shot again."

"There was no gun."

"There was. It's the head trauma, Kane. You just don't remember because of the injury. That's not unusual."

Kane fought to remember.

*The bitch is lying!*

He pictured the scene in his head again, tried to remember how Sheehan's hands had been, if there was anything in them. They had been empty.

Hadn't they?

The headache increased, throbbing incessantly again. He focused on Rouch, mirroring the kata she

:ycled through, remembering her moves from past en-
counters.

"I wouldn't hurt you, Kane. And if I wanted to, I
know enough about you that you'd never see it coming." Without warning, she uncoiled into a spinning
back fist, aiming for the uninjured side of his face.

Before Kane could move, the fist exploded against
his jaw. Pain threaded through his consciousness. Instinctively, he turned with the blow, then dropped
down to the floor and swept her feet out from under
her with a leg block. His side suddenly felt as if it
were on fire, taking his breath away. He fell over on
his back, no longer even able to stay on his feet.

"Kane!" Rouch was at his side, looking into his
face.

The other almost slipped past his defenses, treading
on the heels of the white-hot pain racking him.

She loosened the tape holding the gauze bandage
in place. "You got lucky. The sutures are still holding."

Kane didn't say anything, looking up at her, trying
to figure out why he doubted her so much. Maybe the
blaster had been there.

"C'mon, let's get you back in bed."

He nodded, grabbing hold of her shoulder. She
helped him to his feet with difficulty, then over to the
bed. He lay on the bed gingerly, spreading out to
minimize the pressure on his wound. His head
throbbed, especially from the bullet wound on his
temple.

Rouch called for a med tech, and a young man in
whites entered the room long enough to give Kane a
shot. The other self tried to get Kane not to let them

administer the shot, but he was hurting too much. Sleep would erase the pain, and the doubts.

It still felt uncomfortable drifting off with Rouch standing there watching over him. Maybe even downright dangerous.

GRANT LED THE PANTHERS down into the valley. He sat in the passenger's seat of the jeep, one foot braced against the dashboard to give him more stability. The Panthers had liberated the vehicles from one of the National Guard posts Hooker had located with his treasure hunting.

The roiling mass of rock had poured into the valley, cascading across the highway. In seconds, forward progress was made impossible by the sheer tonnage of rock. The first two pack wags locked up their brakes and came to shuddering stops. One of the vehicles behind them slammed into the rear of the one ahead of it.

The avalanches in the rear cut off an escape route, and the rock and debris swept over the last vehicle, crushing it as it rolled over. As the dusty haze settled over it, Grant didn't think there were any survivors, which suited him fine.

Men poured out of the stalled pack wags, and the rear gunners opened up with the box-fed machine guns. Their full-throated death roars punctuated the night.

Panther snipers lined the ridges on both sides of the valley. Their training put them on their targets. The hollow booms of the 7.62 mm ammo cut through the ripping snarl of the machine guns, cutting down the sec men before they were engaged by the mobile forces.

"Here!" Grant ordered his driver.

The man nodded and hit the brakes, whipping the jeep sideways in a spray of rock. He stopped only inches from the lead wag's front bumper, a welded section of four-inch pipe filled with concrete.

Grant pushed himself out of the seat, followed by Reba and the three men who rode on the rear deck. He kept the M-14 up, firing twice at the man behind the pack wag's steering wheel. The bullets punched holes through the windshield, jerking the man in the seat, dropping a corpse in their wake.

Stepping high, Grant pushed a foot against the front bumper, propelling himself up on the wag's hood. It collapsed and bent under his weight, but he leaped onto the cab and took the high ground. He brought the M-14 to his shoulder and fired a round through a sec man's head. Before the dead man hit his knees, Grant acquired another target. The sec man turned, sweeping around with his shotgun, and got two bullets through his lungs before he could squeeze the trigger.

Reba stood at Grant's side, a Colt .45 booming in her fist. He knew from his doppelgänger's memories that Reba stayed at his side during battles, relaying his instructions over the comm link.

Half of the jeeps stopped and disgorged Panther warriors. The other half maintained a circle around the stalled pack wags, racing constantly to pick off sec men who tried to flee the battlezone.

Grant's standing orders were for no survivors. Except one.

Racing across the solid shell of the pack wag's rear cargo section, Grant met a sec man climbing up onto the vehicle. Grant kicked him in the face, sending the man sprawling. He shot him before he could get up from the ground.

Spotting two sec men dug in near the wheels of the next wag in line, Grant reached for Reba, grabbing a fistful of her blouse and yanking her down with him. She went willingly. Bullets split the air over their heads.

"Thanks, lover," she said, breathing raggedly.

Grant dropped the M-14's sights over one of the men and squeezed the trigger. The bullet slammed through the sec man's head, jerking him backward.

The next round of bullets from the surviving sec man crashed into the pack wag's side, tearing metal loose and driving sparks high into the air.

Shifting aim, Grant fired at the other sec man, missing by inches as the man pulled back into cover. Cursing, Grant moved, targeting the man's exposed shoulder. He squeezed the trigger.

The bullet hit the man in the shoulder and spun him out into the open. Grant missed with his next shot, then fired again, hitting the man below the neckline of his helmet, crushing the spine and ripping his throat out.

"I've always liked forceful men," Reba said, gazing up at Grant.

"Specially ones that save your ass," Grant said. "I remember that."

Reba pushed her face up at his, giving him a brief full kiss, her tongue snaking into his mouth. "Wait until you see how much I appreciate it later."

Grant grinned at her as he pushed himself up. Reba folded lithely to her feet without her hands. "Get Marcus on the comm," he ordered. "I want to know how far out Trieste's band is.'' He turned from her as she lifted the radio.

Below, the second pack wag suddenly erupted into motion. Its bumper crashed into the rear of the wag Grant was on, nearly throwing the big man from his feet. Then it powered by, heading up the incline.

Backing up, Grant ran toward the edge of the cargo space's hard shell. At the edge, he leaped, throwing himself toward the moving pack wag. Landing on his feet, Grant struggled to keep his balance as the pack wag bounced and rocked across the rough terrain. Bullets from a sec man who'd spotted him from one of the other wags scored the cargo's hull and ripped into Grant's jacket. He cursed and wished he had the Mag armor at that moment.

Grant ran to the front of the pack wag, then emptied the M-14's clip through the cab. The driver evidently lived for a time after being hit. The wag stayed on course, powering up the incline, then listed out of control, losing ground and slowly turning over on its side.

As the wag overturned, Grant threw himself over the side, away from the fall. He landed, going down into a roll, then came up on his knees. Sec men abandoned the pack wag's cargo area, spotting Grant.

Knowing the M-14 had cycled dry, Grant hit the magazine release, dropping the empty, and slammed a fresh clip home. He chambered the first round and lifted the heavy rifle to his shoulder.

Three sec men went to ground in the tall grass and brush. Grant ripped a couple rounds at them to keep them honest, figuring he didn't hit a damned thing. Then he went low himself, throwing his body to the left. Bullets tore through the brush where he'd been.

One of his stalkers got impatient, popping up like a rabbit. Grant lifted the M-14 and put a round into the center of the man's face, making certain of the kill. He stayed low and kept moving, sweat streaking down his face, back and thighs. He smelled the blood in the air.

Most of the opposition at the pack wags appeared to have been dealt with. The rushing circle of jeeps had slowed, their movements more deliberate as they sought out survivors.

Reba came running toward Grant, trying to get into position.

Grant raised his voice. "Get down, woman!"

Instantly, Reba threw herself down, and that was what saved her life. Bullets hammered the grass where she'd been, searching.

Unable to find the gunners in the morass of underbrush, Grant kept moving, depending on his Mag skills to keep him alive.

Two of the Panther jeeps vectored in on Grant's position, their headlights cutting through the darkness. He watched carefully, expecting one of the sec men to attempt to snipe them. When one of the sec men rose up, Grant shot at him, bullets tearing through the grass near him.

The gunner dived, disappearing from Grant's view. But the jeep driver had a lock on him, putting the accelerator to the metal and lunging after him, crashing through the underbrush. The sec man broke cover, running for all he was worth. Before he covered twenty yards, the jeep overtook him, rolling over him like a rampaging beast.

Caught up in the death race, Grant didn't notice the

third sec man till he broke cover. He aimed a pistol at Grant and fired, racing toward the big man.

Grant moved with all the speed that Mag training had demanded, and he squatted down to make himself a smaller target. The muzzle-flashes strobed out at him, burning yellow-white in the darkness, and the bullets went over his head. He brought the M-14 forward, not trusting a shot to stop the charging man before he was on top of him.

# Chapter 15

Stepping forward, Grant rammed the bayonet into the sec man's chest just as the man's gun arm came down. A bullet punched through Grant's jacket shoulder, and another clipped the lobe of his left ear. He set himself to take the sec man's weight as the guy impaled himself on the bayonet. Dropping to a knee and using his strength, weight and leverage, Grant lifted the man from the ground, brought him overhead and slammed him down, putting his weight on the M-14's buttstock to hold the sec man in place.

The man screamed, his face a mask of rage and agony. He pointed the pistol at Grant again.

Grant slipped his finger into the M-14's trigger guard and fired three shots with the muzzle pressed into the man's chest. The hydrostatic shock of the bullets driving home killed him.

"Son of a bitch!" Grant snarled, wiping the dead man's blood off of his face. He yanked the bayonet free and stood as the two jeeps closed on him.

Reba ran up to join him.

Mind already working, knowing Trieste's band was closing on them, Grant stepped up into the rear deck of the nearest jeep. He held on to the roll bar, surveying the battlefield ahead of him. "Take me in there," he told the driver.

The driver put the jeep in gear and roared across the valley.

Grant looked at Reba. "You okay?"

"Yeah. Might not have been if you hadn't yelled."

"How far out are Trieste and his band?"

"A couple minutes at most."

"Get the sniper teams," Grant ordered. "Have them close in."

She did, but then looked up at him, worry in her eyes. "Wouldn't it make more sense to get everybody here to spread out and retreat to the north? Trieste can have the pack wag cargo. There won't be any reason to try to confront us."

Grant shook his head. "They've got poison in those packages. We leave it for Trieste and his band and it's going to come back to haunt us. And I came down here to get converts. You feed and supply an army, that's an army you're going to keep."

"Sun-Tzu?"

"Mebbe," Grant said, getting the information from his borrowed memories. "Hooker said it for damned sure."

The jeep arrived back at the wrecked pack wags, where the Panther warriors were piling up the recovered bodies of the fallen sec men. Other warriors were already at work, field-dressing the corpses with practiced moves, not a motion wasted. The entire macabre tableau was lit up by a circle of jeeps playing their headlights over the scene and by homemade torches carried around by men inspecting the pack wags.

Grant watched the knives flash, slashing through the sec men's clothing and carving out great hunks of meat. All of them were white; the WSC didn't man the Mississippi Wall with anyone except white men who'd been taught to fear and hate black skin.

The harvested meat was thrown into burlap bags that had been brought for that purpose. Grant grinned when he watched it, appreciating what Hooker had set into motion all those years ago. There was no mercy for the enemy, and fear was the greatest weapon to wield.

He leaped from the jeep, raising his voice. "Who's got my fucking prisoner?"

"Here, Commander Grant."

There were three prisoners, each one with his hands tied behind him and roughly escorted by two young men in Panther black. They were brought before Grant and forced to kneel, a knife held tightly against their throats. All of them watched the butchering being done to their fallen comrades.

Glancing up the hillsides on either side of the valley, Grant watched the snipers coming down on the run. He swept his harsh glance back over the three surviving sec men. "Got too many prisoners."

"Which one do you want?"

Grant walked down the line, making the men sweat, seeing the terror in their eyes. He didn't feel sorry for them; they'd come on a mission to kill people in an even more horrendous way than with a gun or a knife. Even with the fear involved, he was giving them a clean death.

He pointed at the man on the right.

The other two men had time to scream and struggle briefly, then the knives split their throats. Their executioners held them by the hair of the head till they bled out.

"Throw them over there with the rest," Grant ordered. "And the rest of you make sure you get the bullets out of that meat. Don't want to be busting my teeth on no goddamned lead fragments."

"Fucking cannibal!" the surviving sec man screamed.

Knowing he was running out of time before Trieste's arrival, Grant turned his attention to the captive. He smiled, kneeling to get close enough to breathe in the man's face. "You're talking a lot of shit for a man lucky enough to still be alive."

"Fuck you, black man! Fuck you and your heathen ways!"

"You know," Grant said quietly, knowing the man's eyes kept straying from him to watch the butchering taking place, "I've found over a few years of doing this that a man can have a lot of pieces cut off him and live. Mebbe I should go ahead and take the meat off of your bones. Not enough to chill you, 'cause I want you to take a message back to the WSC bastards that sent you here."

The man pursed his mouth, trying to work up spittle.

Grant backhanded him, popping his head sideways and breaking his lips. Crimson glided down the man's chin, and he started crying. Grabbing the man's hair, Grant yanked his head back. "You know about my people, don't you? We used to be warriors in our homelands, before your ancestors brought us here and enslaved us, made us die in your cotton fields."

He knew some of the history from the time period because prejudice had hung on even in the Outlands. Only the prejudice there usually divided people into two groups: the haves and the have-nots. The have-nots hated the haves, and the haves chilled any have-nots who dared reach for something that wasn't theirs. And that kind of upped the ante for the have-nots, who sometimes chilled the haves for a little advance revenge.

"Back in our homelands," Grant said, "it was an honor to eat the heart of an enemy, a fellow warrior who'd died in battle after taking up arms against us. You people don't know any honor."

The sec man started to say something again.

Grant hit him before he could. Then he grabbed his hair again. "You came across the Mississippi River with the promise to feed the people here." He jerked a thumb in the direction of the flesh harvesting. "You're going to make good on that promise. Just mebbe not like you'd thought."

Tears ran down the man's blood-smeared face.

"I'm going to let you run, toy warrior," Grant said. "And when I do, you go back across that river and you tell your superiors that every unit they put over here is going to fill our pots. Tell them to keep sending people and not be stingy." He nodded his head at the warriors holding the sec man.

They released him and he backed away, thinking it was some kind of trick. But when he hit the edge of the area lighted by the jeeps, he turned and fled.

Grant stood and watched the ridgeline to the south. The first lights of Trieste's vehicles were starting to cleave the skyline.

"How many casualties did we have, Reba?" he asked as the woman moved into position beside him.

"Fourteen dead and twenty-three wounded."

Grant nodded. Those were acceptable casualties. The WSC forces had lost seventy-one men, and a pack wag train of poison. Better yet, if everything worked out tonight, he was going to replace those men nearly ten times over.

"There they are." Reba pointed at the southern skyline.

Grant walked along the line of stalled pack wags. The locks on the doors of the cargo bays had been broken open. He scanned the boxes and buckets of foodstuffs the WSC had sent across into the Outlands. "Marcus," he yelled when he saw the man.

"Yeah."

"Before that stupe bastard Trieste makes a mistake I can't fix, have somebody put up a treaty flag."

Marcus yelled orders out. Less than a minute later, one of the young men climbed to the top of a pack wag and waved a white flag.

There was no denying the flag, Grant's borrowed memories told him. The Outlands bands roving the territories respected the flag between each other. Sometimes a treaty flag protected necessary trades of goods or information that helped them all.

Trieste wouldn't be able to ignore it, no matter how much he wanted to.

Grant crossed to the back of one of the pack wags and climbed inside. He borrowed a torch and played it over the contents of the cargo bay. Boxes of canned goods, dry goods, dehydrated rations and powdered milk filled the space. He passed the torch back to Reba and selected a case of peanut butter.

Throwing it over his shoulder, Grant dropped to the ground and headed for the nearest jeep. A dozen other jeeps filled with Panthers started up. Grant stood up in the back, still holding the peanut-butter case. Reba sat in the passenger's seat.

Trieste had lifted a treaty flag, as well. The white

material flew from the rooftop of the stripped-down
cargo van that rolled down the hillside. A dozen other
wags followed the van, some of them sporting homemade armor.

"Let's go," Grant told his driver. He stared at the
approaching wags. He didn't know where Kane or
Brigid were, but the main thing at the moment was
to survive. He was sure that's what they'd be concentrating on.

BRIGID BAPTISTE WALKED through the streets of
Santa Fe Ville's Beta District and knew she was being
followed. What she didn't know was if the slim man
trailing her through the government office area was
there to merely observe or to chill her. She checked
her image in one of the passing office windows, and
felt as though she were looking at a stranger.

Her red-gold hair was cut short, barely touching her
cheekbones, parted neatly on the left. It was a new
look for her, and part of her didn't like it. She wore
a long green dress with wide sloping shoulders, a reflection of her status at Beta Level.

She also spotted her stalker: a man in a green Beta
Level suit with flaring white-blond hair and a deep
tan. He was of medium height, thinner than his build
suggested. His face held no expression.

She knew that because her eidetic memory allowed
her to memorize his appearance in the brief glimpse
she'd gotten of him. It only took a couple seconds for
her to search her memory for any link to the man
before. There was none. She didn't know him.

The cold fear that she'd been living with for weeks,
that she'd been so sure could never get any worse,
suddenly flared to new heights. She shook, afraid now

that her legs would no longer move, might not even hold her weight.

Her breath caught in her throat and her heart pounded harder, causing the headache she had to reach nauseating levels.

*Let me out. I can help you. You don't have to be alone.*

She turned from the window, no longer able to stand there. The voice in the back of her mind scared her, maybe even more than the danger lurking on the streets of Beta District. Over the past few hours, the voice had become more insistent, more demanding. She'd become afraid of losing herself.

The Beta District streets at this time of night had less activity than during the day, but the Historical Division worked a twenty-four-hour cycle. Much of the history of the predark world had been lost. It was the Historical Division's job to ferret it out, to rebuild the world that had been from the records that were recovered so that the world that was could be made stronger.

Brigid walked down the street, aware of the black-armored Mags stationed on catwalks over this part of Sante Fe Ville. They were assigned to the sec posts to prevent any loss of data. Violators were executed on the spot, their bodies put on display.

*He's still there, still following you. Why? Tell me.*

A sob escaped Brigid as she tried to push the voice from her head. She didn't dare think about why she was there. Rumors she'd picked up in the ville suggested that Overproject Excalibur had developed a mutant strain of humans with psi-capabilities. And if one of them read her mind...

She didn't know what to be scared of more.

Glancing behind, she didn't see the man trailing her. But she felt he was still there.

*Why don't you request protection?*

That, she knew, would have been the equivalent of signing her own termination warrant. Her only chance lay in escaping any notice.

She glanced ahead and saw the entrance she was looking for. Beta District's streets were pristine. Crystalline steel, so expensive and time-consuming to manufacture down in Epsilon District, sealed the streets thirty feet above her. More crys-steel sealed the streets off two blocks over, creating the Enclave know as Beta Hub, where she lived and worked. The security over the area was tighter than anything outside of Alpha District, where the congressmen lived and the embassies were located.

A man in a green suit, his ID marking him as a level host, stood at the podium in front of the office she needed to get into.

"Citizen," he greeted in a flat monotone.

"Citizen," she replied, listening to her voice crack. With all the stress she was under, all the carefully crafted lies she'd woven, all the things that she'd lost already, it was a wonder she hadn't gone insane. Her photographic memory was both blessing and curse. When it came to keeping her stories straight, she never forgot—and when it came to knowing the risks she took, she never forgot.

"You have business within the mapping unit?" the host asked.

"Yes," she replied.

"May I see your identichip?"

Brigid extended her arm.

The host played a handheld scanner over her wrist,

reading the transponder imprinted in her flesh. "Your identichip suggests that your normal place of work is in the written-records unit."

"Yes. I have been allowed special permission to visit the mapping unit at Division Master Frasier's request," Brigid replied.

"I'll need to contact Division Master Frasier to verify this."

"Of course." Brigid glanced over her shoulder, looking for the blond-haired man. She didn't see him, but she still felt him there.

The host opened up a comm-link to the inner workings of the mapping unit. In less than a minute, her clearance had been granted.

"Please step through the gateway, citizen. Do you have any recording devices or photographic equipment to declare?"

"No." Those devices weren't allowed in any part of Beta District.

*What are you hiding?*

She shut her mind down before she could dwell on the pain that thought stirred up.

"Please continue," the host said. "Grids are clearly marked on the floor after you enter the threshold. Division Master Frasier's color thread is red." He pinned a badge to the sleeve of her dress. "Please stay on that path. If you should happen to veer from that, you will be apprehended and charged with a felony for treason. Please state your compliance for the record."

She faced the recording device built into the wall. "I understand the provisions set forth for me in accordance with this limited visitation. I further understand and accept the penalties inherent in the acceptance of that visitation.''

The host shut the device off. ''You may proceed.''

Brigid nodded a quick thanks, then stepped through the gateway. The hallway was pristine white, illuminated in a murky half light. Anyone who spent all day staring at readers or physical records appreciated the dimness.

She found and followed the red line marked clearly on the floor. Three office doors later, Division Master Frasier was standing outside his door waiting for her.

# Chapter 16

Division Master Frasier was a portly man who strained the lines of his green suit. His black hair was carefully brushed back, and a thin mustache curved down on either side of his mouth. He was in his early thirties, an egotistical man who had a reputation as a womanizer.

"Ah, Archivist Baptiste," he said unctuously.

"Division Master." She inclined her head out of respect.

He gestured to his offices. "I appreciate you coming so quickly."

"We all work for the same goals, Division Master." Brigid entered his offices, glancing around at the wall-to-wall shelves filled with rolled maps and map books. A comp screen built into the center of a large square table displayed a multicolored map. "Each step one of us makes serves us all."

"Yes." He stepped into the room. "Could I get you something to drink?"

"No, thank you."

"Do you mind if I drink?"

"Of course not."

He crossed the room to a small refrigeration unit and took out a bottle. "Vodka," he said. "A cache of it was found recently in the excavation they're doing in Las Vegas Ville. Perhaps you've heard of it."

"The geographical location, yes," Brigid said. "I didn't know about any finds."

"Of course not." Frasier poured the vodka into a glass tumbler. "The excavations, now that the rad levels have dropped, have proven to be more beneficial than we'd believed." He glanced at her, his eyes sweeping her from head to toe. "What do you know of Las Vegas?"

Brigid searched her eidetic memory, finding the information quickly. Then she searched again, discovering how much of it she should actually know from her own studies. "It was a resort town, a vacation spot. Gambling appears to have been the only economy the area generated."

"True." Frasier sipped his drink. "A Mafia man named Bugsy Siegel built the entire ville, leveraging money from his associates. Do you know what the Mafia was?"

Brigid knew that was sensitive information. "No."

"It was a criminal organization at the time. And Bugsy Siegel was one of their favorite sons. However, with the building of Las Vegas, he fell out of favor with his superiors. They had him chilled, thinking his brainchild was never going to turn a profit." Frasier stepped closer to her, touched her bare arm with his fingertips.

Brigid steeled herself against the shudder that possessed her. She'd been warned of the consequences of her visit.

*Stay calm. Don't show him any fear. His kind thrives on fear.*

"Division Master," she said, reminding him of his position, of all he had to lose with the risk he was taking, "I fail to see what this has to do with me."

"What I'm about to tell you," he said, oozing self-importance, "is highly restricted. If you breathe one word of it to anyone else without the necessary clearance, you'll be brought up on charges and very probably put to death."

"I understand."

"In these treasures that have been taken out of Las Vegas Ville are certain documents relating to Bugsy Siegel's business. There were, ah, partners—for lack of a better term—that he had that his associates weren't aware of. In diaries and journals we recovered, we found several references to caches he made along the East Coast of what was then the United States."

Brigid's heart sped up. This was it. This was what she had been trying to learn for the past two years. She kept her excitement and fear from her face. "How may I help you?"

"I'm told you can read the Russian language." His fingers continued stroking her arm.

"Yes."

"Bugsy Siegel involved himself in some interesting candidates while searching for investors for his vision of Las Vegas Ville. He appears to have allied himself with a faction of Russians. Since the Russians had the Communist system of government—do you know what that is?"

Brigid searched her memory, finding it was declassified information. "A political system wherein only the state owns property and the people serve the state."

"Yes. So if Bugsy Siegel was getting Russian money, it had to be coming from the Russian government. Probably they were setting up a spying network within this fledgling resort ville, hoping Las Vegas attracted the American government heads of state, as well.''

Brigid waited, steeling herself against his continued touch.

"In those diaries and journals," Frasier said, "mention was made of these East Coast caches. We don't know what was there, or if it still exists. But I've been given instructions to find out. I had a Russian translator at one time, but he was struggling with these documents I am about to show you.''

"Perhaps I could compare notes," Brigid suggested, knowing it was an obvious conclusion, one she knew better than to disregard. "Two heads are sometimes better than one when difficult situations arise.''

"Yes. Well, if that were possible, I'd see that it was done. However, your predecessor in this matter was chilled in an industrial accident down in Epsilon District.''

Brigid looked at the man. "Epsilon District is not a normal territory for a Beta-class citizen to journey."

"No." Frasier shook his head. "It appears he had a certain predilection to sexual favors available in that district. You have no secrets, do you, Archivist Baptiste?''

"None that I'm aware of. I'm under a double-clearance evaluation." She looked at him, hoping to scare him off. "My husband works in the DEI.''

Frasier made a face and withdrew his hand. "So I've been told. However, I'd also been told that your marriage is on somewhat shaky ground.''

"Perhaps," Brigid said, "you'd like to tell my husband that.''

Frasier drained his drink, then made himself another. "We should take a look at those documents. Time is, under present circumstances, most pressing." He walked to the back of the room and gestured to worn volumes stacked on shelves.

"May I?" she asked.

"Of course."

Brigid took down the first volume. The first entry was dated in January of 1948. She scanned the page, trying to make sense of the words.

"Well?" he asked.

"It's in Russian," she confirmed. "That's obvious from the use of the Cyrillic alphabet, but it's a variation that I'm not familiar with." And that was true, as well.

Frasier suddenly sounded stressed. "Can you read it?"

Brigid flipped through the pages slowly. "Given time, I'm sure I can."

"Time is one thing we don't have."

She glanced at him, asserting herself. When it came to her education and her skills in that field, none of her normal lack of confidence assailed her. "And instant answers is another thing we lack, Division Master. I have my own duties, and taking on this assignment to help you would cut into the little personal time I have allotted to me."

"I can fix the time," Frasier said. "One comm-call and you'll find yourself reassigned here. Temporarily."

Turning more pages in the journal, Brigid said, "I'd welcome the opportunity as a challenge. But my working conditions are important to me, Division Master." She looked at him meaningfully. "I want no distractions. If there are going to be any, then please leave me at my present assignment. And if those working conditions aren't maintained, I'll seek redress myself. Do we have an understanding?''

Frasier didn't look happy about it. ''Of course. This assignment is very important. Do you have any idea when I can expect some results?''

''A few days.''

Frasier frowned. ''That's not soon enough.''

''That's the best I can do.'' Brigid knew she couldn't appear to be eager to see the information.

''All right.''

Brigid looked at the collection of books and documents. ''Would it be possible to start in the morning?''

''I'll arrange it.''

So close to her goal, it was hard for Brigid to walk away. At the same time, she needed to get away, to think. And she wanted to get something for the headache that was plaguing her.

As quickly as she could, she said her goodbyes and walked back out to the street. Once outside, she took a deep breath of the recycled air. It was the same as that in Frasier's offices, but somehow it didn't seem quite so cloistered.

Then she caught a glimpse of a shadow standing out just a little too prominently across the street.

*The man following you is still there.*

She didn't need the voice to tell her that. Her fear returned. She remembered when her husband had followed her, after he'd gotten suspicious of all her time spent away from their dorm. At home, she'd pretended she hadn't seen him there, and he pretended he hadn't been following her.

Out of habit, she touched the wedding ring she still wore for luck.

*I'm married?*

Maybe the man following her would go away. Only when she looked back, she saw that he'd given up all pretense of staying hidden. He strode after her, not even bothering to stay in the shadows left by the streetlights.

Brigid kept moving, her heart in her throat and the fierce headache pounding in her temples.

ROUCH WAS STILL THERE when Kane woke again. She slept in a chair beside the bed. He didn't know what to think about that, but his suspicions were aroused again by her presence. Maybe she wasn't there to chill him, but she was definitely keeping a close eye on him.

He still felt light-headed from the drugs in his system. He checked his chron, found it was over an hour later than it had been when he'd been given the injection. Thankfully, the headache seemed to have retreated.

He checked himself over, discovering that the wound in his side seemed to be doing much better. But maybe that was from the pain-killers cycling through his system.

"Do you want a drink of water?" Rouch asked.

Startled, Kane looked over at her.

"There's a pitcher of ice water by the bed," she told him.

"I can get it." He shifted in the bed.

Before he could reach the small table, Rouch took up the pitcher and poured him a glass.

Kane drank, sipping the water, taking time to think.

"Thanks." He handed her the glass back. "What are you still doing here?"

"I wanted to make sure things between us were okay." She gazed at him with those oval almond-colored eyes.

"Things are fine, Rouch."

*No blaster. Lying.*

The voice sounded very small and very quiet. For the most part, Kane had no problem ignoring it. All he needed was a good night's sleep.

She stood beside the bed, looking down at him. Not for the first time, Kane was intensely aware of what a beautiful woman Beth-Li Rouch was. But he was married, and in love. Even after all the hurt she'd put him through, all the lies she'd told him, he still loved his wife. And he wished he didn't.

"In all the time we've been partnered," she said, "you've never accused me of trying to kill you." She reached out, tracing the wounded side of his face with her finger.

"Blame it on the delusional effects of anesthesia," Kane advised. "I am." Despite the conflict of emotions, he found himself reacting to Rouch's touch.

Without warning, she leaned in close to him. Her soft cheek grazed his stubbled chin, and her breath warmed his neck.

"Rouch," he said, "mebbe we should call it a night."

*Take her. It'll make things right.*

As the voice in the back of his mind spoke, Kane's resolve seemed to dissipate with the rush of blood moving through his system. He lifted a hand and ran his fingers through her raven's-wing hair.

Her hand drifted down his bare chest, nails raking

his skin lightly, stopping just short of scratching and bringing blood. Then her hand was under the sheet, snaking down between his legs, seizing the part of him that was already at full attention.

"No," he said.

*Yes.*

Before he could say anything else, Rouch kissed him, driving her tongue past his teeth and into his mouth. Her heat filled his mouth, and the scent of her perfume filled his nostrils.

Then he was kissing back and Rouch was climbing into bed with him, covering his body with hers. And all his inhibitions weakened.

# Chapter 17

"Stop in front of Trieste," Grant instructed his driver. When the jeep came to a halt in front of Trieste's van, Grant waited for the other man to speak first.

Trieste pushed himself out of the back of the van. A line of wags formed a semicircle around him, backing his play, confronting the Panther wags ranged out behind Grant.

If any violence broke out under the treaty flag, Grant knew it would turn into a blood storm that would engulf both bands. Even though the Panthers were outnumbered, Trieste's band would be wiped out or nearly so, as would the Panthers. But the Panthers here on this battlefield represented the best the band had to offer.

"I told them," Trieste said in an accusing voice, "that you would be here to try to take the food I'd negotiated from the WSC, Grant. There were some who didn't believe me." He was in his late twenties, ten years younger than Grant, but at six feet eight, he stood taller and weighed more. Torchlight danced against his shaved head, reflected in the oil he wore over his exposed skin as protection against the cold and the mist. His goatee and mustache were neatly trimmed, and his face marked by tribal tattoos. The jeans, shirt and coat he had on all looked new. With his size, getting the proper fits would have been difficult. He held a Thompson submachine gun in one big fist, slick and oiled black.

"I came here," Grant stated, "to save the lives of our people, not take them."

"You're standing there, your men guarding the pack wag train that brought the supplies in, and you tell me you're going to give us those supplies?"

"Those supplies are loaded with poisons," Grant said.

"Lies," Trieste snarled. He moved the Thompson more in Grant's direction.

Immediately, the Panthers on either side of Grant shifted, bringing the arms up in warning. The move was mirrored by Trieste's warriors.

Grant waved the Panthers down, facing Trieste on his own. He knew from his borrowed memories that Trieste liked to work from cover, killing his prey and his enemies from hiding, without risk to himself. "I'm not lying, and you know it."

"Bullshit, Grant. Everyone knows how big you've made your band. A thousand or more mouths to feed and winter coming on, you're getting desperate."

Trieste's words carried weight with the men and women around him. Grant read it on their faces. They numbered four hundred and were in danger of not surviving the winter for lack of food and shelter. They couldn't imagine any band even larger than theirs surviving on its own.

"I'm not desperate," Grant rebuked. "You are, Trieste, and you're willing to sacrifice your own people to save your own sorry ass."

"Fuck you, Grant. This treaty flag is over. We're leaving."

"No," Grant said, "it's not over. And if you try going back up that hill, I'm going to chill you."

A murmur ran through the men on both sides of the sudden skirmish line. Grant felt Reba stiffen at his side, but she didn't say anything to him and she didn't look away from Trieste.

Trieste's eyes narrowed. "This is a treaty flag, Grant. You can't break the flag. It's a matter of honor between our people."

Grant's borrowed memories told him that was true. "I know what the treaty flag stands for." He swept his eyes along the line of men backing Trieste's play. They were the men he had to persuade. Trieste had his own agenda, and if he backed down he lost the small empire he'd carved for himself. Grant knew the man's ego wouldn't allow that. "And I know the blood that was shed before the bands agreed to recognize it."

"Yet you stand here," an old man said to Trieste's left, "prepared to break that treaty." He had hair that looked frayed, the color of dirty gray cotton and a matching beard. The wrinkles and scars on his face advertised the hard life he'd led. He carried a double-barreled shotgun at port arms.

"I have no choice, Laraque," Grant said, recognizing the man. In his time, Laraque had been a feared killer. He'd picked Trieste as Hooker had guided Grant. "If I let you take that food, another WSC-designed disease will sweep the Outlands and claim even more of our people. The Panthers are at risk, too. If not today, then another day. It'll be like leaving this valley with a goddamned gun to our heads. I'm not going to allow that."

"Trieste wouldn't betray us like that," Laraque argued.

"He betrayed you when he let your band get to the cold season without food and shelter, making you vulnerable to the WSC treachery," Grant retorted.

"Four hundred people are a lot to feed," Trieste snarled. He looked around him for support.

"There's game here in the Outlands," Grant stated. "And there are the baronies and the villes to take from. If a man's strong enough, clever enough and brave enough, a way can be made."

"You've been lucky," Trieste said. "How many other bands have you stolen from the way you're stealing from us?"

"I'm not stealing," Grant told him in a cold voice. "I'm preventing the sacrifice Trieste is willing to make to save himself."

Trieste almost raised the Thompson then, but Laraque shot out a hand, catching the weapon by the barrel. "Wait," the old man said.

Grant was certain that Hooker would never have undermined him in such a manner. A band lived or died by the authority the leader wielded. If he had any thoughts, Hooker would have questioned Grant in private, suggested some new avenues to undertake.

Grant directed his attention to Laraque, keeping Trieste tagged in his peripheral vision. He knew Trieste would take the change of attention as an insult. "I'm not here to disrespect the treaty flag," he stated.

"You got a fucking strange way of showing it," Laraque commented. "Get yourself chilled pushing like that."

"I could get myself chilled trying to keep you from

that pack wag cargo," Grant said. "Here, mebbe I chill you and Trieste before you chill me."

Trieste started to say something, but the old man quieted him with a look.

"Got no illusions about surviving yourself, Grant?" the old man asked.

"None," Grant replied. He felt his doppelgänger spinning around in the back of his mind, but stilled the voice, keeping it locked down tight. He couldn't afford the distraction.

"You willing to die here?" Laraque asked.

"Yeah. But so would you and Trieste. That's an ace on the line. That done, your band is fresh out of leaders. Be an even harder winter for your people."

"The Panthers would be short their leader, too," Laraque pointed out.

Grant shook his head, showing them his hole card. "There's always Hooker. Man's old and ain't got any legs, but he's got the heart and soul of a warrior. You know that."

Laraque sat up taller, on the verge of making a choice.

"I wouldn't disrespect the treaty flag," Grant went on, "unless I had to. Unless there wasn't any other fucking way. Lot of people fought and died to make that flag stand for what it does. After the nukecaust, when the villes kicked our people out or segregated us into starvation and dependence on their grudging generosity, our people preyed on each other because it was easier than going up against the villes' or barons' sec men. They kept on doing the job prejudice started all those years ago."

"You're talking ancient history," Trieste snarled.

"Ain't got nothing to do with what's going on here now."

"It's got everything to do with it," Grant argued. "Treaty flag came about so we wouldn't spend all our time chilling each other, taking from each other. The deal you made with the WSC breaks that."

"You don't know what you're talking about," Trieste said.

"Why did they give you the food?" Grant demanded.

"I said we'd help patrol this part of the Outlands," Trieste said. "With the hard season coming on, they figured the ferry would be at risk. A WSC sec force stationed here would only be attacked again and again, wasting weapons and manpower. They figured a band would be more accepted."

Grant knew it made a skewed kind of sense. "You were going to do this sitting out here in the cold and the rain? Waiting for the winter snow to come?"

"They were going to supply prefab buildings in follow-up shipments," Trieste said. "If we held to the bargain, they promised weapons."

"Why not now?"

"They had the food now. The prefab buildings were going to take time."

Grant shifted his gaze to Laraque. "And you believed that line of bullshit?"

The old man gave him a stony look, eyes narrowing. "The WSC has made pacts with the bands in the past."

"Damned right they have," Grant agreed. "But only if they wanted something in return. Bands have been traded weapons for help getting a WSC spy team into one of the Eastern Alliance villes at different times.'' Hooker had made a couple of those deals himself, trading for weapons, never for food, and he'd always checked to make sure the firing pins were in place.

"The St. Louis gateway into the WSC has always been one of the most endangered when attacks were made by the bands, the baronies and the eastern villes," Laraque said. "It was a reasonable request."

"You ever get around to asking yourself how I knew the pack wag caravan was going to be here?" Grant asked.

"It's no secret you have spies," Trieste spit. "And it's no secret you're gathering up bands, making treaties with others. You gotta supply those people. You found out about our deal with the WSC and you come running like a hound dog got his nose opened up."

"I found out," Grant said softly, "because you intended for me to find out. You knew I'd see this for the trap it is, and you knew I wouldn't allow it."

"Why?" Laraque asked.

"The damned diseases and plagues contained in the food products," Grant said. "I've got my people dug into this area, wintering."

"How?" Laraque asked.

"We're staying mobile," Grant answered. "During the summer, we put up meat, cured it, dried it, buried it under the ground so it'd keep. We cut deals with small villes that managed to have a surplus of grains, vegetables they canned themselves, pork and chicken they put up, too. Buried all of it in caches we been building for years. It's Hooker's legacy, and we've been building a future to pass on, building a chance to become something more than we've been."

"If the villes or the WSC find out your band has

grown so large,'' Laraque said, ''they'll take pains to hunt you down, break up the Panthers.''

The surgical strikes were an established procedure to reduce the threats of the roving bands.

''They did find out,'' Grant said fiercely, taking pride from his doppelgänger's accomplishments. His other self and Hooker had initiated plans that were coming to fruition. ''That's why they cut the deal with Trieste. To draw me out here.''

Laraque shook his head. ''He didn't know you would be here.''

''Yeah, he did,'' Grant said. ''He made a deal with the devil, Laraque, and we were all going to swing in the wind for it. The WSC wanted the Panthers, and Trieste couldn't face a winter he wasn't prepared for and knew you and the others would hold him responsible for. Some bands fall on hard times, they have a tendency to chill their leaders. Mebbe he even cut himself a better deal than just getting out from under.''

''Fucking liar!'' Trieste screamed. He started to lift the Thompson.

Laraque shoved the double-barreled shotgun's muzzle under the big man's chin, stilling him in a heartbeat.

Grant saw the hurt in the old man's eyes when the realization started to sink in that he might have been wrong in his selection of a successor to lead his people. Laraque had given his own life to his band, as strong in his own way as Hooker was. And now, with the challenge he'd offered to the man he'd picked to replace him, Grant knew that Trieste's authority could never be the same again. In that single move, Laraque had stripped it away and taken it back.

"The Panthers aren't just a thousand strong, Laraque," Grant spoke softly. "They're two thousand strong."

The old man looked at him, the air whipping his dirty gray hair and beard. His eyes were filled with pain. "No fucking way."

"Come see," Grant coaxed. "Not only have we put enough away to feed ourselves through the wintering, but we can feed your band, as well."

"You would do that?" Laraque asked.

"We're brothers of the skin," Grant said. "The Eastern Alliance and the WSC have tried to keep us apart. We don't have to be. Not anymore. We can become a nation and rise up out of the ashes here."

"You might be able to back the Eastern Alliance down," Laraque stated, "but you'll never stand against the WSC."

"Then we'll run and we'll hide," Grant said. "And every spare moment we find to ourselves, we're going to grow stronger, bigger."

"Has Hooker ever told you about the aliens?" Laraque asked.

"Yes," Grant said. He knew from the borrowed memories that his doppelgänger didn't believe in the aliens, thought they were an old wives' tale that had been handed down to Hooker.

"How can you hope to stand against them?" Laraque hissed.

Grant looked at him, willing the old man to believe. "We'll find a way."

Laraque locked eyes with him for a time, the shotgun muzzle never wavering from Trieste's neck. Then he asked, "Can you prove what you're saying about the food?"

Grant reached down into the jeep's rear deck and brought up the carton of peanut butter. "Mebbe." He flicked his gaze to Trieste. "Let's see Trieste eat some of this food he worked so hard to arrange. If he does, mebbe I'll be convinced." He popped the carton open, showing the peanut-butter tins inside.

Laraque looked at his student. "You gonna eat some of that peanut butter, Trieste?"

"Got your choice," Grant offered. "Smooth or crunchy."

Trieste didn't move.

"Eat," Laraque ordered. "Prove you're not a fucking coward willing to sell out his own people, his blood." He shoved the shotgun harder against the younger man's throat.

"No!" Trieste yelled back.

"Why?" Laraque asked.

"You're not gonna fucking make me, old man. Take this goddamned blaster out of my throat and I'll make him eat it. You can stake him down, watch him for a few days, see if *he* breaks out in sores."

Laraque's eyes twitched. "Spoken like the leader I trained. But are you just talking bullshit, or can you walk the walk?"

Trieste's eyes blazed as they focused on Grant. "I can walk."

Laraque gently pulled the Thompson submachine gun from Trieste's hands. "You'll get your chance, then." He raised his voice. "Grant."

"Yeah."

"You made an offer to take over responsibility for this band," Laraque stated. "You can only do that by rite of the challenge. Man against man. You willing to do that, Grant?"

Grant looked at the man, knowing Laraque was every bit as devious as Hooker was, and maybe as manipulative as Lakesh. If Grant won, Laraque's band would throw in with him, absorbed by the Panthers, and they would believe. If Trieste won, the band would believe in him and be ready to follow him; most of the damage done here would be undone.

And the Panthers who'd followed Grant to the raid would be chilled.

"I'm willing," Grant replied. Under the treaty flag, combat for band leadership was permitted. He leaped from the jeep to the ground. The wags pulled back, creating a circle of light thirty feet across, an impromptu battle arena. He looked at Trieste as the man-mountain stepped down from the van. "You pick the weapon you want to be chilled with."

Without hesitation, Trieste took the combat knife and camp hand ax he was offered. Grant accepted the same, feeling the heft of the weapons.

Trieste started circling, grinning malevolently. "Come and get you some, little man."

Grant moved into action, thinking about Kane, wondering what his friend would have thought. Kane was an expert at hand-to-hand combat and appreciated the intricacies of personal warfare.

# Chapter 18

Kane's hospital gown offered no defense against
Beth-Li Rouch's attack. Her mouth continued to explore his, and adrenaline flooded his system.

She ripped the gown, splitting it down the center
to bare his chest, then her lips moved from his mouth
to his left nipple. She bit hard enough to hurt even
with the anesthesia wrapping cotton around his brain,
but pleasure was by no means absent.

"No," Kane croaked. Guilt thudded at the edges
of his conscious mind. In all the years of his marriage,
he'd never been unfaithful. He wanted to push Rouch
away, but he couldn't find the strength to do it. With
all the lies she'd told him, all the sacrifices he'd made,
he deserved this. It wouldn't matter anyway.

*Let her.* But even hovering at the back of his doppelgänger's mind as he was, Kane felt the sharp stab
of guilt, too. *Anam-chara.*

Kane put the guilt away. The mission was important. This world's Rouch could be all he needed to
fuse him with his doppelgänger.

He reached for the woman, welcoming her touch,
telling himself he couldn't be faulted, telling himself
it was necessary.

Rouch moved lower, stripping the sheet back from
his groin. The muted light in the room added to the
eroticism, jangling Kane's senses. Her mouth closed

over him, hot and wet and slippery. Her touch was demanding and her moves full of confidence. She knew he wasn't going to turn her away.

She suckled him, bringing him to his peak, then stopping before he achieved his climax. She rocked back on her heels, throwing her coat off, dropping her shoulder holster beside the bed within easy reach. Peeling her shirt up, revealing she wore no bra, she bared her breasts, showing the thick, turgid nipples colored dark olive.

"Do you like what you see?" she taunted.

Kane looked at her breasts, feeling the guilt rise in him with the lust. He couldn't—couldn't stop.

He reached for her breasts, massaging them briefly, feeling the silk of hot skin beneath his fingers, then helping Rouch off with the shirt.

"Mebbe you like it a lot," she told him. She pulled his head close, leaning down to him to place her breasts on either side of his face.

Kane breathed in the sexual heat of her, smelling the musk that clung to her skin, the hints of soap and perfume that lingered after hours of being in the wag watching over the squatter building. She pushed against him, smothering him in flesh.

She reached down again, cupping him and stroking him, her long-nailed fingers grazing the skin, giving him a chill when he realized how badly she could hurt him if she wanted.

Then thoughts of his wife tumbled through Kane's mind. He felt the guilt that swarmed over him when he thought of her finding out.

He focused on the anger that came with those feelings. It didn't matter what he did; it wouldn't change anything.

Then he focused on the mission with a Mag's intensity. As a Mag, it didn't matter what he did; it would change everything.

Rouch broke away again, lying down on her back on the bed. She pulled his hands, tugging him after her. "Don't quit on me now, Kane. I'm only half-undressed."

Kane pulled her pants down, first stoping to pull off her boots. Growling with the lustful hunger that fired through him, feeling saddened that he'd never even felt this way with his wife, that all inhibitions had been removed, Kane hooked his fingers in the waistband of her dark gossamer panty hose and pulled.

"Be fucking careful," Rouch commanded, biting his ear. "Panty hose aren't manufactured in Epsilon yet, and the scavengers' fees are bastard robbery."

Then the panty hose were gone, and the lacy white bikini panties followed. The fleecy triangle at the juncture of her slim thighs beckoned.

Kane hesitated, on the edge of giving in to the insane lust that fired him.

He pushed at his doppelgänger's mind, beating down the defenses.

"Teasing, Kane?" Rouch smiled at him, not at all nervous about her nakedness. "You don't need to. I'm ready." She reached down between her legs, giving a sharp, soft cry at her own touch, biting her lip.

Kane moved his face forward, parting her delicate folds with his tongue. She moaned, and the sound of it tore down his final barriers. He feasted on her, driving her to orgasm twice. Then he pulled back, ready to plunge into her.

Before he could, she pushed him back and slid forward, taking advantage of his confusion to crawl on top of him. "I don't want you to hurt yourself, Kane. In case you feel ambitious again."

Kane felt like his brain was on fire, rushing toward a certain nuke-level meltdown.

Rouch straddled him, grinding her pubis against his. He felt her wetness against him and groaned. She reached between them and joined them, then started riding him with easy thrusts, posting up and down.

Kane knew he wasn't going to last long. He placed his hands on her hips, pulling her close, aiding in the motion.

"Yeah, that's it, Kane," Rouch cried excitedly. "This is what it's all about. If you're going to live your life on the edge, you don't hold back and cut yourself off from pleasure. You take what you want from this life—nobody's going to give it to you." She worked against him harder, and he knew she could feel his response within her.

Kane exploded, almost losing consciousness from the intensity of the moment. He hit his release, spending all the pent-up frustration and fear in a heated rush. Then he waited for the bio-chemical and electrical changes to take place and allow him to swap places with his doppelgänger.

Rouch gazed down at him, her hands pinning his shoulders to the bed. "Better?" she asked, leaning down to kiss him. The scent of sex and perspiration was an ambrosia.

Kane felt freer than he had in months.

But he was still trapped in the doppelgänger, a ghost in the back of the man's head.

CIRCLING TO THE LEFT, following Trieste's lead, Grant waited for an opening as the bigger man feinted. The combat knife was in Grant's left fist, held point down and blade out, and he carried the stainless-steel camp ax down and slightly behind him.

The Panthers and Laraque's band crowded around, drawn down from the hillside and in from the pack wag caravan. They surrounded the makeshift arena, already shouting support for their respective leaders. The lines of demarcation between the bands were already blurred.

"I trained in the pits in Banta," Trieste said. "Sport for the barons and our blood wasn't our own." His blade danced before him, weaving a glittering net of moon-kissed steel. The camp ax bobbed and danced like a cobra preparing to strike. His familiarity with both weapons was apparent. "I chilled fifty-nine champions from other villes, carved my name on their backs before I took their lives."

Grant watched his opponent as they circled through the area lit by the wags' headlights and the handheld torches. The shifting light, flaring out behind him and turning him into a shadow, made it hard to see Trieste at times. Grant marked the wags with the brightest lights in his mind so he could use them to his advantage. If his sight was thrown off by the different lights, he knew Trieste's would be, too. As a Mag, Grant had been trained to take every advantage that was offered.

"Did you spell it?" Grant asked. "Or did you just make a big *X*? A big *X*, hell, that's no fucking strain." He darted out, following the edged steel of the knife.

Trieste turned, caught off guard, not expecting Grant to go on the offensive so quickly. The knife razored along his stomach, slicing through his shirt and opening a long, shallow cut. Trieste gazed down at the weeping wound in disbelief.

"Hell," Grant said, "if an X was all it was, I'm halfway there."

Instead of losing his temper, Trieste kept moving at the same rhythm. He grinned coldly as a small patch of blood spread across his shirt from the wound. "A scratch, asshole. Cut me like that all day long and I'll still be standing when night comes."

Grant closed again, not bothering with the feint, trying for contact with the knife. Trieste blocked with his hand ax and steel rang on steel. He was strong enough to stop Grant's knife, then brought the hand ax down in a sideways slash.

Surprised by the big man's speed, Grant narrowly avoided the blow. The hand ax whistled through the air and sheared through Grant's coat before Grant was able to lock the arm out with his hand ax.

"Afraid, Grant?" Trieste taunted. "Come a little closer than you thought I would? Mebbe I'm a little better than you thought?"

Grant disengaged, dragging his weapons away from Trieste's. The big man came at him at once, exploding into motion. Giving ground before the charge, Grant kept the knife and hand ax flashing, meeting a half-dozen attacks in a row, sparks skidding in all directions as he met a dozen more.

He listened to Trieste's breathing, hoping all the months and years of being a band leader had softened him. But it hadn't. Trieste's steps stayed quick and powerful, always advancing.

Trieste's knife licked out, slashing Grant's upper arm through the coat. Before he could withdraw or change the angle of his attack, Grant head-butted him in the face.

Blood gushed from Trieste's nose like a burst blossom, eliciting a great roar of pained rage. He staggered back.

Grant pressed his advantage, launching a snap-kick that caught the big man in the chest. Trieste staggered backward, then set his feet and charged again, holding the camp ax high.

Staying loose, bouncing on the balls of his feet, his breath ragged in his own ears, Grant danced with death. Glittering steel edges slashed by his face, missing by scant inches, turned or parried by Grant's weapons or his forearms. Perspiration beaded under his jacket and shirt, drenching him.

Trieste brought the hand ax down in a vicious overhand blow, aiming at Grant's upturned face. Grant sidestepped, using all of his Mag skills and experience to avoid the big man's rush.

The hand ax hammered down, cutting its way through the engine hood of a wag. Trieste screamed in rage, pulling the ax free and swiping at Grant with the knife.

Closing his fist around the haft of the ax, Grant slipped his wrist in front of Trieste's wrist, blocking the blow with bone-jarring contact, hoping to knock the weapon free. But Trieste's grip held. Concentrating on his moves, keeping the weapon locked down, Grant brought a foot up and kicked Trieste in the side of the neck.

The kick knocked Trieste backward, but he managed to lift the hand ax. Grant dived in again, driving his opponent back with ax slashes and knife thrusts. Trieste managed to avoid them, but Grant kicked, as well, repeatedly scoring on the other man's torso and head.

The spectators' voices escalated, urging the battle on, firing up their champions.

Falling back, Trieste reassembled his defense. He was too good for Grant to move on immediately. For all his treachery and posturing, Trieste had been a pit fighter.

"You can give up," Trieste prompted with a bloody grin. "Mebbe I'll be merciful, chill you quick."

Grant lashed out again, turning the big man's blades away, but not able to beat through Trieste's defense. He landed three more kicks against the bigger man's side and stomach, but before he could disengage, Trieste's ax sliced a thin, shallow furrow under his chin. Grant felt the rush of blood running down his neck.

Trieste came for him, a juggernaut of flesh and blood and glittering steel. Grant's hands moved mechanically, blocking the attacks, feeling the man's incredible strength, listening to the quick scrapes of steel, taking in the twist of shadows as the lights surrounding them played over their bodies. He waited, maneuvering, using the terrain and the light. Then, when he had the wag lights behind him, he stepped back, knowing Trieste couldn't be sure of the movement in the combination of light and shadow.

The big man's attacks were thrown off, and Grant whirled into motion with renewed vigor. The knife and ax whipped out, digging into Trieste's body. Blood flew, spraying out over Grant. Mag training left him no mercy, no quarter.

Trieste lunged at him, but Grant sidestepped easily.

He rammed the knife blade through Trieste's ribs, hoping to drive it home into the man's heart. Trieste turned enough to make him miss his heart, and the blade was locked in the clutch of ribs. Trieste swung the camp ax in a backhand blow.

Dodging down, Grant caught himself on his left hand in a crouch, then shot his right foot out at his opponent's knee. He aimed the kick from the side, with Trieste totally exposed and vulnerable. Mag school trained him that it only took seventeen pounds of pressure to destroy a knee with a blow from the side. His foot struck Trieste's knee flush. Bone shattered.

Trieste screamed but didn't go down through sheer force of will. Flecks of blood expectorated during the scream, and Grant knew the knife might have missed the man's heart, but it was buried deep in a lung. Winning translated quickly into just surviving, letting the man drown in his own blood as his lungs filled.

But Grant didn't want that kind of win; he wanted a confirmed decision. Trieste was a veritable force, and watching him wear down, laboring for his breath, wasn't a clear-cut victory. Granted wanted it for himself because he was caught up in the battle, and for Laraque's band. A warrior led men into battle, not a cautious man.

Trieste flailed at Grant with all his strength. Grant timed the attack, feeling the cuts that streaked his body burning with the perspiration that covered him, feeling the aches and pains in his muscles and body from the battering he'd taken. He waited, then shot his left arm straight up as he stepped inside Trieste's ax blow. His arm blocked Trieste's arm, catching the man's forearm with his own. From the corner of his eye, Grant saw Trieste's other hand sweeping the knife in toward his opponent's face in a last-ditch effort at revenge. Grant brought his own ax down, crashing it through Trieste's forehead and burying it deeply in the brain. Twisting his right elbow and lifting it, still holding onto the ax handle and yanking Trieste's head toward him, Grant blocked the approaching knife. The point ripped a line of fire across Grant's back.

Trieste's eyes locked on Grant's for a moment, less than two inches away and blazing fury. But the big man couldn't bank the fire, and it died in his next shuddering breath. A blood-streaked mask of death filled Grant's vision, and for a moment, he stood in the dead man's embrace as he remained erect even on the shattered knee. With the shadows, Grant knew the onlookers couldn't tell for sure who had ended the fight, or if anyone survived.

Taking a deep breath, Grant shoved the corpse off him, watching Trieste collapse in a loose sprawl. Immediately, cheers rang out as the Panthers and Grant's supporters even within Trieste's own band showed their support.

Empty-handed now, Grant approached Laraque.

The old man lifted his hands, quieting his band.

"I chilled your leader, Laraque," Grant said.

"Yes."

"Then I need to know if you're going to follow me or walk away."

"My brothers and sisters need to be fed, Grant. Tell me that you can take care of them, and that you will." Laraque's gaze was defiant and daring.

"I can and I will," Grant said, responding to the tradition he knew from his doppelgänger's memories.

"Then I will follow you," Laraque answered. He gazed around at the people thronging the battle area. "If there are any of you who don't want to follow this man, leave now."

Grant gazed around, looking to the four hundred men, women and children he'd just accepted responsibility for. Even though this was his doppelgänger's world, taking on that load was still daunting.

The acceptance filled the valley.

Despite the fact that he hadn't found Kane or Brigid, and despite the fact that Colonel Thrush still lurked somewhere on this world, Grant felt the pride of victory course through him. He held his arms above him and screamed with them.

Then he heard the roar of a motorcycle engine approaching at full bore. Glancing back up the southern hillside, he watched Kadeem speed over the ridge, the motorcycle leaving the ground in a long jump.

Kadeem recovered the motorcycle when it struck, downshifting and powering toward Grant. The Panthers among the crowd moved the others back, letting the boy through.

Reba hurried over to Grant, handing the M-14 back to him.

Kadeem lifted his goggles as he looked at Grant. "Coalition gunships," the boy said.

"Clear the area!" Grant ordered, waving the rifle. He turned back to Kadeem. "How many gunships?"

"Three," the boy gasped. "Coming fast."

Grant thought furiously, considering his options. The WSC hadn't fully trusted Trieste to carry through on his part of the bargain, either because they didn't think the man could accomplish it, or because they intended to make the double cross even more successful over a shorter time.

Scattering in the dark wouldn't do the Panthers or Laraque's band any good. The gunships were equipped with infrared that would strip away the night.

But the gunships were expecting to come up on a firefight between the pack wag sec men and two bands.

Grant stared at the wags, remembering the machine guns mounted on the vehicles. He'd planned on taking those, as well. He looked down at Reba, names already in mind. And thinking like a Mag, he spoke calmly over the fear that seized the people around him.

# Chapter 19

Brigid Baptiste put her hand against the lock-out plate of her Enclave apartment building off the main street through Beta District. The print reader scanned her palm with a flash of bright light and the doors opened. As she stepped into the foyer, she glanced over her shoulder, looking for the blond-haired man.

He wasn't there.

*He hasn't gone away.*

Cold fear brushed against her again, robbing her of her short-lived illusion of security and chilling her to the bone even inside the foyer. The voice in the back of her head was still there, speaking all of her fears. Her temples throbbed, even worse than before, from the headache that slammed at her.

She wished it would go away, wished she dared go to the med labs and let them give her something to relieve the pain.

*Let me in. Once you let me in, everything will be fine. I can help. Trust me.*

The voice of the other sounded seductive. Brigid wished there was someone she could trust, someone within Beta District. She was tired of being alone.

But there wasn't anyone to trust here, and she couldn't go to the med techs because the DEI director's power extended even over those places. She'd made a powerful enemy.

Inside the foyer, she took a deep breath and headed for the elevator. She took it up to the seventh floor. The Beta District was ten stories tall, totally secured from the Cappa District below and the Alpha District above.

Arriving at her floor, she hesitantly glanced down the pristine walls devoid of color or images, anything that would detract from the focus of the orderly minds that inhabited Beta District. An older woman in a green suit approached her.

Brigid tried to remember her face but couldn't. With her memory, she knew that would have been an impossibility if she had seen her before. The terror returned; new neighbors were a rarity in Beta District. She swallowed hard and focused on her room.

She palmed the print reader and opened her door. The room on the other side was cool and dark, and soft chamber music provided an undercurrent. The music was the one luxury she allowed herself.

Her apartment was small and compact, neatly organized with a breakfast nook she used for all her meals. The primary furnishings were the desk and computer against the wall to the right. A small shelf above them held two ivy plants with purplish leaves under a grow light, and a stack of books she hadn't yet read. She never kept books after she'd read them; with her memory there was no need. But she enjoyed reading. A gifted author's words took her far from the world she lived in.

Aware that the dorm was probably bugged with more than the normal complement of transmitters, she tried to behave as though everything were normal. Even inside her own dorm, her life wasn't her own.

She went into the small kitchenette and heated water for hot tea. She poured the water into a cup and added a tea bag, enjoying the spicy scent. Then she noticed a program was running on her computer, the glowing symbols printing in columns, filling the display rapidly over and over.

When she walked back into the main room, an arm snaked around her neck from behind, shutting off her wind.

"Don't scream," a rough male voice advised.

Brigid dropped her cup and saucer, and they shattered across the tiled floor.

"We're going to talk," the man whispered hoarsely. As he lifted a knife, her reflection caught in the broad blade. But his was, too, and she recognized the thick shock of blond hair.

The headache suddenly increased in tempo and pressure, and she had the feeling of being shoved aside in her own body. Unbidden, she watched her hands come up to the arm around her throat.

GRANT LEAPED from the back of the jeep while it was still in motion, barely maintaining his balance when he hit the ground. Then he stretched his stride into a run, charging through the distance separating him from the pack wag ahead.

The bulk of the Panthers and Laraque's band ran up the southern slope of the valley, heading for the protection of the forest beyond. Even then, Grant knew, the IR systems aboard the WSC Deathbirds would allow the gunners to target them in the dark.

He leaped up into the wag's cargo bay, then pulled himself on top and ran to the front of the pack wag as the first of the Deathbirds appeared against the black sky.

The choppers had begun life as Huey-class helicopters before conversion in the WSC's munitions plants to their present configurations. Coalition sec forces now had more fighter jets in their ranks—a result of the small advances in technology—but the Deathbird was a standard of the Mississippi Wall defensive posture.

Grant swung behind the Browning machine gun around in a tight arc and put the front sight over the lead Deathbird. He checked the ammo belt, made sure the box was lined up so the feed wouldn't be interrupted and pulled the trigger.

Tracer rounds burned through the night, and Grant adjusted his aim, as the other machine guns manned by Panthers joined in. Then he had the Deathbird in his sights. He hammered it unmercifully, striking fire from the armor plating and drilling holes in the glass windscreens. The white-phosphorus tracers impacted and exploded in puffs of fiery smoke. Brass spun out in flashing arcs, spinning heat.

The Deathbird unleashed its arsenal of machine-gun fire and 20 mm rockets. Craters opened up in the ground, and other rockets rocked the pack wags. Cargo exploded in all directions, and Grant knew he was losing men, as well.

Grant was surprised that the Deathbirds targeted the pack wags. Grant's Mag senses flared in warning, but he couldn't nail down anything specific. He adjusted his aim again, targeting the Deathbird's pilot.

Reba pulled herself up beside Grant and worked the ammo belt feeds. "They're shooting the pack wags," she yelled above the thunder of the guns.

"Yeah," Grant replied grimly, "I noticed that." Laying the Browning's blade over the Deathbird's cockpit again, he squeezed the trigger as the helicopter tried to come around. The heavy bullets cut the pilot to doll rags.

Out of control, the Deathbird slid sideways in the air until the whirling rotors struck the hard-packed earth and shattered into gleaming shards. Grant dropped an arm over Reba and pulled her down an instant before the shrapnel peppered the side of the pack wag and sliced through the air overhead. The Deathbird exploded a moment later, sending a funnel of gray smoke streaking skyward. Muscling the Browning back on top of the wag, he took aim on one of the surviving Deathbirds.

Sudden greenish fog clouded up from two of the pack wags, caught in the downdraft created by the Deathbirds. In seconds, the heavy rolling fog filled the valley.

Grant breathed it in, feeling his lungs burn. "Dammit!" he yelled, suspicions forming immediately in his mind, none of them pleasant. He turned to Reba. "Tie something over your mouth and nose." He ripped at his own slashed shirt, tearing loose enough material to tie over his lower face.

The two Deathbirds took another pass over the area, emptying out their rocket ammo and blowing holes in the stalled pack wags. But the choppers stayed well above the garish green fog.

Grant finished off the ammo belts, succeeding in disabling the tail rotor on one of the craft as it climbed overhead. Tracers blazed through the night from other machine guns.

The Deathbird with the disabled tail rotor struggled to stay aloft, but finally turned toward the ground. It smashed against the northern hillside, breaking apart in large pieces on impact.

The third Deathbird hovered over the area, playing a searchlight over the ground. Two survivors from the helicopter crash stumbled out of the wreckage. They straightened and waved their arms.

Grant pushed himself into motion, racing for the nearest jeep. He kept the M-14 in one fist. His lungs burned as the fog invaded his lungs. The thought of what it might be made him afraid. Even though this world was only borrowed for the time it took Kane, Brigid and him to find Colonel Thrush, Grant found himself bound to it. He didn't want to lose, didn't want to see the people around him lose.

And he was afraid they already had.

Reba sprinted up beside him, dropping into the jeep's passenger's seat while Grant slid behind the wheel. The scarf she'd used to hold her hair back was tied around her lower face. "What's wrong?" she asked.

"The gas," Grant said, his voice muffled by the cloth. "The WSC set up a double cross all the way down the line." He jammed the M-14 between the seats and keyed the ignition. Other Panthers had climbed aboard jeeps and were also getting under way. He let out the clutch, all four wheels ripping into the landscape.

He sped around the wag caravan, watching as the Deathbird in the air dropped, angling toward the one below. The men ran toward the descending craft.

Then the wind changed, and the green fog rolled up over the wreckage of the Deathbird. The sec men on the ground tried to outrun the fog, fleeing in obvious panic higher up the ridge.

Grant steered for the ridge, shifting through the gears quickly.

The flying Deathbird rose into the area immediately, jockeying to get away from the rushing wave of fog. Once the pilot recovered, he headed back for the sec men, reaching them just as the fog overtook them in a billowing roll. Muzzle-flashes lit up the Deathbird's cargo bay. The sec men fleeing the fog fell, rolling back down the hillside and disappearing into the brush.

Cursing, Grant manhandled the jeep as he steered it up the ridge. The Deathbird faded in the distance, headed west, back to the Mississippi Wall. He killed the engine, then set the brake, throwing himself out of the vehicle. The fog continued burning his lungs, reminding him what tonight's victory had cost.

The first sec man he found was dead, nearly decapitated by the rounds that had hit him. Farther up the hill, the second man was crawling through the brush, trying to hide.

Grant covered him with the M-14. "Keep your hands where I can see them, you stupe bastard."

The man rolled over, keeping his hands in the open. Blood stained the WSC border-guard uniform at one shoulder and a thigh. He was young and clean-cut, and his blue eyes blazed hatred. "Go ahead and shoot me, black man." He laughed bitterly, tears running down the sides of his face. "It won't fucking matter."

Winded from the run and drained by the adrenaline starting to ebb in his system, Grant moved closer. He kept the M-14's barrel centered on the man's face.

"That mask won't help you, either," the man said. "It can get through cloth."

"What?" Grant demanded.

"Death," the man said. "You and all those apes you're running with are fucking dead. You just don't know it yet."

The woods on the hillside around the man filled with Panthers and Laraque's warriors. Grant amended his thinking; they were all Panthers now.

"What's he talking about?" one man asked.

"The fog," Grant said, knowing he couldn't keep it to himself. "It was some kind of poison, a chem or a biological. Some kind of WSC nasty."

"I feel okay," another man said. "If it was poison, I'd be coughing up my lungs or something. Mebbe shitting blood. Hell, I've seen the shit those WSC crazies use. Something would be happening right fucking now."

Grant was aware that was the most frightening thing facing all of them: they knew the horrors the WSC were capable of. Waiting for this one to manifest itself was agony.

"It's going to kill you," the WSC guard stated. "It'll kill you and everybody around you." He shifted his gaze to Grant. "And they knew all about you and these fucking Panthers, Grant. That is your name, isn't it?"

Grant didn't say a word, watching the man in silence.

"The DEI got information to us," the guard said. "They told us all about you. You can write off some of those underground railroads you fucks have been using to spirit away the help in the coalition. The DEI closed them down over the last couple days. Then they put out the termination warrant on you."

Every word hit Grant like a blow. He felt his doppelgänger's fear settle over him from the back of his mind. His borrowed memories rattled faces and names through his mind, people who were in the Panthers now, people that he was responsible for.

And people who were now at risk.

Looking over the sec man's head, through the trees, he saw the green fog finally starting to lie low to the ground, its damage done.

"They've been watching you, Grant," the guard went on. "They knew you were getting the bands together, that you thought you were building some kind of black empire over here. It made you vulnerable, too, though."

"What are you talking about?" Grant demanded.

"That shit they dropped on you, it's designed to chill you fucking blacks. It's going to spread through you animals like blood through a rad canker. None of you bastards are going to be left."

Grant slapped the man, turning his head and flattening him back against the ground. Then he grabbed a fistful of the man's shirt and slapped him again. Blood smeared the man's face from his split lips.

Grabbing the man again, Grant brought him up to his face. "You're going to tell me everything you know," he growled.

"Fuck you," the man said. "I only know three things. White makes right. Your name is Grant. And you fucks are all going to die. They didn't tell us anything about what was in those pack wags."

Grant slid his combat knife free of his boot and called for a rope. In seconds, the border guard was hanging upside down from one of the tree limbs. "We're going to find out what you know for sure, and we're going to do it the hard way."

"Fucking cannibal," the man yelled, wiggling at the end of the rope.

Grant whipped the knife out before the man could do more than flail helplessly. The keen edge sliced through his ear, shaving it off close enough to reveal the white skull and pink-meat musculature beneath. The bloody hunk dropped into the grass under his head, showered by crimson that ran black across Grant's boots.

The man screamed and cursed.

"You may really not know anything," Grant promised, "but you're sure as hell going to wish you did before I'm through."

# Chapter 20

Raising her boot, Brigid stamped down hard on her captor's instep, raking the edge of the heel down his shin. It was a move she'd learned from Grant and Kane in Cerberus redoubt.

The man yelped in pained surprise and loosened his grip.

Taking advantage of the shift in his weight, Brigid held his knife arm tightly and bent forward, putting all of her strength in the move. The man came over her back, and she controlled the knife hand, keeping it clear of her body. Still maintaining control of his fall, she dropped with him to the ground, bringing him down hard.

The breath left him in a whoosh.

Brigid stood, then kicked him in the temple as hard as she could. He groaned in pain and tried to claw his way up from the floor tiles.

The headache still thundered in Brigid's head, but not with the same intensity. Despite the transition she'd experienced into her doppelgänger's body, things didn't feel right. She was in control, but only just.

When the man rocked to his knees unsteadily, glaring hatred at her, she kicked him in the face, then again in the temple. He hadn't killed her outright when he'd had the chance. That put them on equal footing, because Brigid was reluctant to kill him. She didn't know what she'd do with the body for one, and for another, there were questions to be asked.

In the back of her mind, her doppelgänger screamed soundlessly. Her tension leaked out and threatened Brigid's calm. Someone on this alternate earth wanted her other self dead or injured or frightened, but she didn't have a clue what it was about.

The man slumped to the floor, too weak to move.

Brigid took the knife from the floor and backed away. Her senses swam as she tried to remain in control. It was harder this time. She couldn't help thinking that Lakesh had been right in assuming that Thrush had somehow put up safeguards against the silent invaders from other casements.

Brigid tried to sort through her tangled thoughts. Normally she had access to her doppelgänger's memories. At least, she had access to most of them. Now it felt as if she were trying to think her way through oatmeal, and she couldn't reach what she needed.

The one thing that Brigid could sense was that her doppelgänger's fear was real. She centered her attention on the blond man.

He had trouble focusing his eyes on her. They were black, blank, part of the mask of calm demeanor he exuded. "What are you going to do with me?"

"Chill you, maybe," Brigid said. She moved the knife slightly.

A small smile curved his face. "That wouldn't do." He touched his cheekbone where an irregular cut oozed a line of blood down to his chin. "They didn't tell me you knew self-defense. They led me to believe you were quite helpless." He took a handkerchief from his pocket and dabbed at his face. "I won't make that mistake again."

"There won't be another time."

"Oh, I think there will."

"Who sent you here?" Brigid asked.

"Playing coy, Baptiste?" He continued wiping at his face. "You know very well who sent me."

"The Director?" Brigid asked.

*No! You'll only make things worse!*

The blond man put his handkerchief away. "I'll be sure and give him your regards."

"What does he want with me?"

As he looked at her, a flicker of doubt registered in his eyes. "You know."

"No, I don't."

He was silent for a moment, moving his head slowly as if testing his neck muscles. "I almost believe you."

"What were you doing here?" Brigid demanded.

"Waiting for you."

"You followed me here. I saw you."

"You were supposed to."

"Why?"

His low, mirthless laugh sent a chill through Brigid. "To see where you went, of course," he answered. "And that's all the questions I'm going to answer here."

"I still have options," Brigid said. She showed him the knife. But she knew she couldn't do it. Killing wasn't something she did casually even when her life was on the line.

"You can't use that. If you could have, you already would." He pushed himself to his feet, staying well away from her, offering no threat at all. "By the way, the spoofer you have on your comp system linking you to the audiovisual pickups in this dorm is first-rate. And the encryption coding on your programs was quite elaborate.''

Brigid backed away, frustrated at her own lack of understanding about what she should do. If she possessed all of her doppelgänger's memories, maybe she'd know more. One thing she was sure of, though: a body would be a hard thing to get rid of unnoticed on the Beta District.

"Next time we meet," the man said, "I won't forget this encounter." He pressed his palm against the print reader, and the door whisked open. "Pleasant dreams." Then he was gone.

Shuddering with relief, Brigid let out a pent-up sigh. She kept hold of the knife, looking around the room. Kane or Grant could have handled action like that any time, she knew. She'd dealt with her share of danger, but it still left her shaken.

The headache pulsing at her temples didn't help. And she could feel her doppelgänger moving around at the back of her head. "I need more information," she told herself aloud.

Crossing the room, Brigid sat at the comp. She struck keys, following the logical progression she knew from the operating systems she was familiar with to try to pull down menus. Nothing worked and she stayed locked out.

Suddenly, Brigid realized the false lead the comp represented; her doppelgänger also had an eidetic memory and wouldn't store any incriminating evidence on the comp.

Brigid pushed up from the desk on shaking legs. The sudden movement sent a wave of nausea washing through her head. She almost lost control of her doppelgänger's body. Waiting for it to pass, she started searching the room. She concentrated, wondering how much like her other self she was. A fresh wave of nausea lapped at her conscious mind. Her knees buckled and she fell toward the floor. Her stomach heaved, trying to lose its contents. She clung to her control of the body stubbornly.

When the nausea passed, she forced herself back up again. Then she began a systematic search of the dorm, wondering about the unknown clock she was working against.

KANE WOKE, realizing he was alone. The scent of sex and perfume lingered in the room, but he knew Beth-Li Rouch was gone. He kept his eyes closed for a time, putting off seeing things as they were. He felt the morning sunlight burning through the room's only window.

When he couldn't stand the pressure in his bladder anymore, he opened his eyes and shifted in the bed till he was sitting on its edge. He felt sick to his stomach, his head still pounding with the headache.

Pain tugged at his side as he pushed himself to his feet and took his weight. When he saw his nakedness, thoughts of Rouch and what they'd done flooded his mind with carnal images. The guilt set in then, but so did his willingness to do it again.

He tried to remember where she lived but couldn't. He guessed that she lived somewhere in Cappa District in the Enclaves, the same as he did. Then he tried to remember where he lived. That proved impossible, too. Luckily, he'd gotten the address from the med tech file on the comp.

The headache remained a constant, dulled only by the anesthesia. He could sense the other still in the back of his mind, but the voice no longer seemed able to influence his movements.

Avoiding the bathroom for the moment, he crossed the room to the locker where his Spectre was stored. He took it out and quickly field-stripped it. Maybe his other memories had been tampered with by his other self, but the machine pistol was a constant.

The Spectre fell apart in his hands, and he spread the pieces over the windowsill. The morning sun creeping in through the crys-steel that secured this part of the ville soaked into the matte black finish of the weapon, warming the pieces.

Once he was certain everything was in order, he reassembled the weapon while watching a Deathbird circle in the blue sky above. When the Spectre was together again, he rammed the magazine home. Then he went to the bathroom, limping only slightly.

He relieved himself, then stepped into the shower cubicle. The gauze bandage was covered with a waterproof seal, proof against the shower's spray. He hung the Spectre from the shower caddy. The machine pistol had been designed by DEI to weather any conditions.

He scrubbed carefully, enjoying the heated water. When he finished, he shut off the taps and stood there, air-drying for a time. His mind worked constantly. If he couldn't think about the past, then he'd think about last night.

He pictured Sheehan in his mind again, trying to imagine the small hideout blaster the man must have been carrying. He still couldn't imagine it, but he couldn't imagine a reason Rouch would lie to him, either. He tried to remember why he and Rouch had first started trailing the trader consortium lobbyist. That was part of his missing memory.

He glanced at the wedding ring on his finger, feeling the other surge up in the back of his mind. The ring represented another mystery. He never had figured out what had motivated his wife to do the things she had.

He pushed away the bad memories, all the lies and hurt, and stepped out of the shower cubicle. He toweled down, then took up the Spectre and walked back into the hospital room.

"Agent Kane," a sibilant voice stated.

Kane looked at the man standing before him, recognition coming in a heated flash.

The man was tall and thin as famine, dressed in an elegant black suit with wide lapels. An equally black cummerbund covered his waist. Obsidian wraparound sunglasses hid his eyes. He stood relaxed, at military rest, in the center of the room.

"Director Thrush," Kane responded automatically. But his hand tightened on the Spectre's butt. Despite the man's calm demeanor, Kane knew Director C. W. Thrush was a living, breathing threat.

BRIGID BARELY MAINTAINED control over her doppelgänger, fighting the woman constantly. The headache had increased to the point of debilitation. The morning sun lit the crys-steel barrier guarding Beta District from attack.

She was tired and worn from hours of searching the dorm. If anything, this casement's version of her was even more obsessed about order and cleanliness than she was, and understood living with and keeping secrets. But her other self seemed more fragile than she was.

That was confusing, too, because if her other self was weaker willed than she was, she didn't think there was any reason her other self would be able to block her out. She wished she could talk to Lakesh. There had to be something else interfering with the transference.

Or maybe she and Kane had to be within a certain proximity of each other. In the last alternate world, Grant hadn't been able to break through until they'd confronted him with the truth. It had taken a face-to-face.

The realization gave her an idea. She went into the tiny bathroom, hardly big enough for the toilet and shower cubicle. But on one wall was a mirror.

Brigid leaned across the sink and stared into her image. The cropped hair still shocked her. It wasn't something she'd thought she'd ever do. And it wasn't a popular cut among the other people she'd seen in Beta District. Her perfect memory suddenly kicked in, bringing to her attention something she'd seen in the other room.

"You don't normally wear your hair short, do you?" she asked her image aloud.

A vague sense of anxiety and unease echoed in the back of her mind.

Returning to the bedroom, she took up the small holo protector she'd found during her search earlier. It played small disks that had pictures saved to them. The technology was only a little different from what she'd seen in the Cerberus redoubt.

She powered the device up, then flipped through the three-dimensional pictures that appeared six inches above the holo projector. All of them featured her doppelgänger with other people she guessed were her friends. All of them wore the Beta District green.

Brigid only glanced briefly at the other people in the pictures. She guessed that they were plants, left there for the people who regularly searched through her doppelgänger's dorm.

What caught Brigid's attention were the images of her doppelgänger. In every picture, her doppelgänger wore her hair long, not short as it was now.

"Why did you change?" Brigid asked out loud.

Not surprisingly, there was no answer.

Putting the holo projector away, Brigid returned to the bathroom. She stared into the image again. She focused on the emerald green eyes of her doppelgänger. Her greatest strength as an archivist had been her photographic memory, and she'd been able to devote her concentration to a singularity with a degree of discipline that had been for the most part unequaled.

And that talent for a photographic memory was something she shared with her doppelgänger.

Brigid breathed out, concentrating on her image, trying to get behind the familiar face to the unfamiliar thoughts behind it. Achieving a light hypnotic state, she picked up the bar of soap from the soap dish. Slowly, she willed herself to use the bar of soap to write on the mirror, reaching for one of the hidden secrets.

When she finished, she was shaking and in more pain from the headache than she'd been all night. Sweat covered her face, and her limbs felt like rubber.

But a word tracked across the mirror, streaked in white soap and crafted in childlike block letters.

GENESIS.

# Chapter 21

"How are your wounds?" Director Thrush asked. His featureless black gaze rested directly on Kane.

"I've been better," Kane said. He remained standing, naked, the Spectre in one hand.

Without warning, Thrush asked, "Where do you live, Agent Kane?"

"Cappa District, Suite 1483 Archer," Kane answered. But he didn't know it from his memory. He knew it from the file the med tech comp had on him. "You already knew that."

"Your birth date?"

Kane told him, then followed up with answers to other questions that Thrush asked in his cold, precise voice. Thankfully, all of the questions were from information from the comp file.

"Checking my memory, Director?" he asked when the questions finally stopped coming.

Thrush crossed to the window, moving as if his joints were ball bearings. Every movement was concise, immaculate. "I was told the bullet that creased your skull could have caused brain damage. I hoped that had not happened."

"No, sir."

"In light of the events over the last months regarding your wife, I know you've been overly stressed."

"I've been handling it." Kane crossed to the locker.

"Do you wish clothing?" Thrush asked.

"Yes."

"I brought some with me." Thrush waved toward a bag on the small table beside the bed. "I think you'll find everything in there you need."

Kane walked back to the bed and went through the bag. Inside was a black suit that looked almost exactly like Thrush's. The bag's contents included underwear and an overcoat that looked big enough to conceal the Spectre and its shoulder holster.

"Are we going somewhere?" Kane asked.

"We are indeed," Thrush answered. He looked relaxed, at rest, a statue carved grim and hard.

The thought triggered the voice in the back of Kane's head. He ignored it and got dressed.

"Do you feel well enough to travel?" Thrush asked when he was finished.

"Yeah." Kane fit the Spectre into its shoulder holster under his arm, then pulled the overcoat on.

"Then accompany me." With a single step, Thrush was in fluid motion, headed for the door.

Kane fell into step, moving gingerly from the wound in his side and head, and from the soreness in his muscles from his physical exertion with Rouch. "Where are we going?"

"To visit the trader consortium," Thrush replied. He crossed to the elevator bank on the other side of the hallway. Immediately, one of the sets of double doors opened, revealing an empty cage. The director strode into it, waving off a patient in a wheelchair and three hospital staff.

They gave ground immediately.

Inside the cage, Thrush punched the button for the basement level. Kane stood beside him. Without warning, the elevator cage dropped like a stone. The sudden rush also affected the headache. It felt as if his brain were getting fused. He massaged the back of his neck.

"Are you still getting those headaches?" Thrush asked.

"Yeah. How did—?"

"Agent Rouch told me about them this morning."

Kane couldn't help wondering how much Rouch had told the director.

Thrush reached into the pocket of his jacket and brought out a vial of pills. "I'd like you to take these."

Kane accepted the vial as the elevator cage came to a soft stop. He examined them through the amber-tinted plastic. They were large, maybe five hundred milligrams each, pearl-white. He rattled them in the container, then dropped them into his pocket.

"Please take two now," Thrush said, leaving the cage and stepping into a large underground parking area. There weren't many wags in the area.

Kane started to resist on general principle, but Thrush's somber face stopped the thought dead. He shook out two of the tablets and swallowed them. That was the control Thrush had over his agents.

"What are the pills?" Kane asked.

"Thorazine." Thrush made his way to a long black limousine. When he pressed a thumb against the modified print reader, the door lock inside popped up.

"That's a tranquilizer, isn't it?" Kane slid into the passenger's seat. He tried to remember if he'd ridden in the director's car before but he couldn't.

"A very powerful tranquilizer," Thrush agreed. He keyed the ignition, and the wag's engine caught smoothly, growling like some mutie beast. He dropped the wag in gear and screeched out of the underground garage, taking to the streets in a rush, narrowly avoiding a collision with a cargo wag.

The ville's streets had come to life. Shoppers circulated through the Epsilon District, purchasing the goods they needed.

"Why did you give me the pills?" Kane asked.

"Last week," Thrush said, "you might have gotten exposed to a new virus the ROAMers have developed. The determined ferocity they have for proving the existence of extraterrestrials on this planet continues to fascinate me."

"Yes, sir." Kane watched the streets blur around him. Thrush broke every speed limit in the ville.

"The tranquilizers are to help you control whatever side effects there might be from the virus."

Kane nodded, but somehow the explanation rang false.

"You and I perform an important job in this ville, Kane," Thrush said. "Sante Fe Ville is the leader of the WSC, a bastion of the future. If it should fall, the beacon of hope it offers falls with it."

"Yes, sir."

Thrush seldom touched the brake but kept the accelerator pinned. "That's why we can't allow anyone to tear down what we've worked for. We're entering increasingly difficult times." He swiveled his head, gazing at Kane with the black-lensed glasses. "Sacrifices must be made, but they must not be our sacrifices."

"Yes, sir."

"Some of the trader consortiums haven't been pleased with edicts recently handed down," Thrush went on. "According to information I've received, Sheehan's actions last night were condoned by his employers. I'm going to ask some questions about that this morning. I thought perhaps you'd like to be there for that."

Kane sat quietly in the street, knowing that Thrush's presence on the field during a questioning meant nothing short of a bloodbath. He felt the tranquilizers starting to kick in, filling his body with a warm lassitude. Everything was going to be okay.

AFTER WETTING A HAND TOWEL, Brigid scrubbed the soap-written letters from the mirror. Despite her continued efforts, she'd gotten no impressions more specific than her doppelgänger's fear at the sight of the word *Genesis* scrawled on the mirror.

Then she remembered the appointment she was supposed to have that morning with Division Master Frasier. Knowing how strict procedure was in Beta District from her doppelgänger's memories, she knew she couldn't risk missing the appointment.

She took a fresh green suit from the closet and headed for the bathroom. Turning the taps, she adjusted the water temperature. She undressed in front of the mirror, studying the figure that was revealed. In a way, it was oddly familiar and voyeuristic at the same time. This casement's version of her carried a little more weight in her hips than Brigid was accustomed to. There weren't any other clues as to what the woman was up to, or what she was hiding.

But as she was about to glance away from the mirror and step into the shower, she noticed that the heat from the water had steamed up the glass. Only one area a couple inches in diameter didn't look the same.

Going with her hunch, Brigid hooked her fingertips at the mirror's edges and lifted. The mirror came off the wall easily, revealing the recessed area beneath.

It held one of the disks for the holo projector.

Still naked, Brigid padded back into the bedroom and popped the holo disk into the projector. She keyed the projection, and the first picture flared to life. They were wedding pictures.

And the groom was Kane.

Without warning, the headache slammed into her with renewed fury, pushing her back over the edge of the precipice where she'd precariously balanced. Her doppelgänger rushed by her.

THE TRADER CONSORTIUM building was five minutes outside Sante Fe Ville, the hangars housing the wags sitting on top of a sun-blasted hill sprinkled with scattered scrub brush. Sand-pitted sheet metal that was rusted in places covered the buildings crowning the rise. The infrequent acid-rain showers drifting up from the Gulf of Mexico were merciless to exposed metal, and even harder on flesh and blood.

A number of pack wags stood outside the main buildings on the hard-packed earth, loading up from smaller wags and horse-drawn carts. People looking to trade brought their surplus to the consortiums, things they'd made or grown or salvaged. In exchange, they received a letter of credit from the trader consortium for use when the pack wags came back with other goods to trade.

Thrush roared into the middle of the pack wags in a roil of dust that followed him in from where he'd left the highway. He stopped the limousine, then reached between the seats and brought out a pump-action Remington shotgun.

Kane looked at him, then back at the two dozen or more wag drivers and teams. Dressed in camou and Kevlar, with tattoos and weapons in evidence, the wag drivers were some of the roughest in the business.

Without hesitation, Thrush threw open his door and got out with the shotgun in hand.

Kane got out the other side, leaving the Spectre tucked in shoulder leather. Every wag driver and guard at the post watched them.

"Nervous?" Thrush asked as they walked to the front office.

"Hell, yes," Kane answered quietly.

Thrush chuckled. "Don't despair, Kane. I'm not used to losing. In fact, I almost never do. I don't intend to do so today." He stepped up onto the wooden boardwalk in front of the building.

Few of the trader consortium buildings were permanent, Kane knew. They had to be able to travel with the trade, as nomadic as any group that made its living from mobility. New markets often opened up when scavengers made fresh strikes, digging through rubble down into the predark villes, and supplies had to be gotten into the other scavengers that joined them, as well as transport arranged for all the things they found. A permanent location would have been detrimental. Still, according to law, the floating trader consortiums had to formally register their locations when they moved.

A big man in overalls and sporting a wild beard stepped up and blocked the doorway into the building.

He carried a .30-30 lever action rifle, and his body was turned so he could bring it up at a moment's notice.

"What do you want?" he demanded.

Thrush slowly moved a hand forward, exposing the identichip in his hand. He pressed it against the print reader mounted at the doorway.

The display pulsed, putting Thrush's picture up on the screen, full frontal and left profile. "Director C. W. Thrush," a mechanical feminine voice said over the speaker, "Department of Extraterrestrial Investigations."

Thrush put the identichip away. "I want to see Broderick."

"Trader Broderick is busy," the big man said. "Mebbe you should make an appointment."

Three other men and a woman in the room shifted from the chairs where they sat at a small table playing cards. Jack chits occupied the middle of the playing area.

Kane scanned the room. It was barren of any creature comforts, possessing only a large metal desk and the half-dozen chairs scattered around the table and the windows. Nude centerfolds stripped from men's magazines occupied the walls between regional maps of the Western States Coalition. The interior was covered in plastic sheets, and the floor was poured concrete that had cracked in several places. The stench of human sweat and piss clung to the air.

Uncoiling almost too fast for the man to see, Thrush hit him in the mouth with the shotgun's butt, breaking teeth. The man flew backward, landing at the feet of the men and woman playing cards.

They went for their weapons.

Fast as they were, Kane was faster. The tranquilizers created a sluggish warmth inside him, but his reflexes were left intact. The Spectre came up, spitting subsonic rounds through the tabletop.

"Hands on the table," Kane said in a cold voice. "Pulling a weapon on DEI personnel is an executable offense in Sante Fe Ville."

The trader consortium people raised their hands. "You didn't have to bust Jamey up like that," the woman complained.

Director Thrush gave her a cold smile. "Interfering with DEI personnel in the performance of their duties is a punishable offense. Your friend is still breathing. Let's not forget our fortunes, shall we?"

Mute hatred stared back at them.

Although he didn't know what Thrush was doing at the trader outpost, Kane backed the director's play. He kept the Spectre leveled.

"Where is Broderick?" Thrush demanded.

"Here."

Kane moved to cover the man as he entered the doorway at the back of the room.

Trader Broderick was a big, beefy man with a rust-red beard and a checked shirt. Suspenders held his pants up over a large stomach. He sported two .357 Magnum pistols in a double shoulder holster. "What do you want with me?"

Thrush fixed him with his steady gaze. "I have some questions, Trader Broderick, concerning importation and exportation practices across the Mississippi Wall."

The man regarded him from behind hooded eyes. "Don't know what the fuck you're talking about."

Thrush held the shotgun at port arms, the barrel

leaning over the crook of his left arm. He approached the bigger man without fear. "I'm talking about your part in the underground railroad that takes the black men back and forth across the Mississippi Wall. Your group handles most of the supply routes to the wall."

"We do business there," Broderick said, "but any man says I been running them coloreds back and forth across the wall is a fucking liar."

"That man," Thrush said calmly, "is me."

Broderick straightened up, but his gaze broke away from the DEI director. "You're wrong."

"Am I?" Thrush shook his head. "The DEI has been looking at your trading network for some time, Broderick. My research accountants tell me they don't see any way you're making a profit during those excursions to the wall. My immigration bureau tells me that felons escaping from their assignments in the Tartarus Pits have been disappearing with astonishing regularity."

Kane watched the big man's face. Broderick wasn't keeping his composure very well under the onslaught of questions.

"The time lines for both problems do not seem unrelated," Thrush went on. "I'd like to take you to department headquarters and question you concerning those matters. I hoped you might feel amenable."

"You ain't making me take a fall for something I haven't done," the man said.

"Precisely." Thrush let the shotgun's muzzle point more in Broderick's direction. "Now would be a good time to accompany us."

The big man shook his head. "You don't have enough men to make me go with you."

The cold smile lit Thrush's face again. "I think that can be remedied, Trader Broderick."

Then the heavens filled with thunder, crashing and booming over the warehouse. The drivers and guards standing around the wags suddenly ducked for cover. Glancing through the windows, Kane spotted the dragonfly-shaped shadows of the Deathbirds racing unevenly across the ground.

"That," Thrush announced above the roar of the helicopters, "is the remedy." He rolled back his sleeve and consulted his chron. "You have ten seconds to decide whether you're going with me or whether you're going to witness those wags being blown to hell." He flicked his harsh glance back at Broderick.

"You'll have a hard time getting me out of here," Broderick said. "My friends aren't going to let me go just on your say-so."

"I happen to think they will," Thrush replied. "See, if you come with me, I'll leave the rest of them alone. This time. And they get to keep their wags."

The only sound in the room for a long time was the pulse of the Deathbirds waiting to strike. Then one of the men looked at Broderick. "You better get moving, Broderick. You ain't staying here and getting our wags shot to shit. Lot of other places to sign on at."

"You can't—"

Thrush lowered the shotgun to point at Broderick's stomach. "I believe they already have. Let's go."

"Sure," Broderick said. "I'm going to tell you everything I know."

"I know you will," Thrush stated.

The quiet calm in the director's voice sent a chill

down Kane's back. He knew the other self didn't approve of his superior's actions. The voice spoke in the back of his mind, but under the effects of the tranquilizer, he didn't hear the words.

Thrush directed Broderick through the door, keeping the shotgun pointed at him. Kane backed out of the room, covering the other people inside. The director walked at a sedate pace even outside, crossing to an open area below one of the Deathbirds.

The helicopter dropped to the ground, barely resting on its skids as the cargo door opened up and two men in black reached out for Broderick and hauled him inside. Seeing the uniforms, Kane felt an immediate affinity for the armored ebony.

Once Broderick was out of his hands, Thrush walked to his car. "Come on, Kane."

Kane took his seat in the limousine again but kept the Spectre out at the ready. He let out a tense breath, then realized pain in his side was creating a dull pressure.

"What did Sheehan tell you last night?" Thrush asked. "Rouch told me the two of you shared a few words."

"Very few," Kane said honestly. An image of the lobbyist popped into his head, showing him nothing but empty hands before Rouch shot him in the face. He pushed the image away, suspecting that it had been given to him by the voice lurking in the back of his mind.

"Did he try to bargain for his freedom?"

Knowing Thrush was fishing for something, Kane shook his head. "He spent his time trying to convince me of his innocence."

"By telling you what?"

"That there were aliens," Kane replied. "Standard ROAMer doctrine and a load of bullshit."

"Did he offer you any proof?"

Kane thought about the device he'd seen in the bag Sheehan had been carrying. "No. There wasn't time."

"Did he talk to Rouch?"

"No." Kane shifted in the seat, trying to find a comfortable position. The director was headed back toward Sante Fe Ville, but Kane didn't feel relaxed. The incident with Broderick had been for his benefit. Otherwise, Thrush wouldn't have had him along. And Thrush didn't usually dirty his hands to bring someone in himself.

"Then what happened?"

Kane looked at the man. And lied through his teeth. "Sheehan pulled a hideout blaster and Rouch chilled him." Then he waited to see what price he was going to pay for the lie because he was certain Thrush knew it was a lie, too. It just remained to be seen if Thrush knew he knew he was lying.

# Chapter 22

Brigid Baptiste stared at the wedding picture of herself and Kane. The sight of Kane in dress black broke her heart, especially when she thought of all the lies she'd been part of. Kane had been used as a pawn by Director Thrush, and she shared the guilt.

Tears spilled down her cheeks before she knew it. Despite the reasons she'd married him, she'd fallen in love. And in spite of the impossibility of their relationship, she'd felt that perhaps it was somehow meant to be. Being with Kane had been easy and comfortable.

Reluctantly, she put the holo away. Her chron told her only a short time remained before she was expected at Division Master Frasier's office in the mapping unit. Everything Lakesh had worked for was coming to fruition today.

She showered and dressed, trying not to remember the man who'd invaded her apartment. She felt more vulnerable there than she ever had. With Kane, even with the duplicity between them, she'd always felt safe. Until at the end of their relationship, when her lies turned their marriage into the masquerade that it was, he'd lost all faith in her. Violence lived in him, even though he tried not to deal with life that way.

In the end, she'd become afraid of him, and she'd been advised to maintain distance between them. For a moment, she wondered if Kane had sent the man to her dorm last night. She took a final look in the mirror, trying to see behind her emerald eyes. She no longer felt the other in her mind. The fact that Kane and she had been married seemed to surprise her.

Reluctantly, she left the dorm, reinitializing the sec monitors over the dorm after punching the spoofer built into her computer. Lakesh's people had designed it to circumvent any attempts to spy on her. The sec monitors only picked up months-old tape of her doing pedestrian things around the dorm. Lakesh had advised her early on to set up a routine, one that would be boring and one that didn't deviate, one that didn't include guests in her private quarters.

She walked through Beta District's streets, the sun blazing down through the crys-steel barrier high above. She'd never been lonelier in her life than after she'd met Lakesh. Then again, she'd never felt like her life meant more.

So much had been covered up, so much lied about.

She kept watch over her back trail, looking for the blond-haired man. The thing that frightened her most, though, was that it wasn't the blonde anymore—it was someone else.

The voice in her head bothered her a lot, as well. The aliens had powers like that. She knew because she'd seen them herself.

GRANT STAYED UNDER the shower spray, soaking up the heat. His head felt clearer this morning, the headaches in abeyance. His doppelgänger was still somewhere in the back of his mind, but he was beginning to think the presence had weakened after last night's defeat snatched from the jaws of victory. The other

Grant had become a dreamer, feeding on Hooker's belief that the bands come become a nation by uniting. All that had died with the raid last night.

Anger smoldered in Grant, though, and he wasn't ready to just give up and die. Thanks to his Mag training, that anger was transformed into implacable determination.

He placed his palms against the tiled wall of the shower beneath the spout and opened his mouth. He drank deeply, as if the hot water might wash out whatever chemical he'd breathed in last night.

So far, no one had gotten sick, and whatever disease or plague they'd been exposed to hadn't shown any signs yet. But it was there. Grant imagined he could feel it coiling in his heart and stomach, digging in with prehensile claws and waiting to strike.

He'd racked his mind all night, and he'd raided his doppelgänger's memories, as well, but no plan of action had suggested itself. Hooker and his doppelgänger had shown no mercy when eradicating small roving bands and villes that had been infected with the designer plagues.

The door opened and Reba stepped through. "How are you doing?" she asked.

"Feeling pretty damned good for a dead man," Grant snapped.

"Mebbe I should have left you alone a little longer."

Grant saw the hurt in her face and eyes, and regretted his response. She was scared, too, and since he wasn't actually the Grant she remembered, he'd surprised her by not wanting to be with her last night.

"No," he said, "it's okay." He felt like company. The cool gray of morning had been held over in the fog rising from the torn countryside outside, and he felt more vulnerable now than he had last night.

"You're sure?"

"Yeah. I'll get out and you can have the shower."

"No," she said. "Just scoot over." Without preamble, she took her clothes off, hanging them over a towel bar on the other side of the bathroom. She had a good body, filled with womanly curves instead of the leanness of youth, the kind of curves a man could trace for hours with his hands. Her breasts hung heavily.

Reba stepped into the shower with Grant. Water dappled her light-colored body from the spray. Without a word, she took up the bar of soap they'd scavenged from the ville and started lathering herself.

Grant watched the woman with interest. It wasn't sexual. The sight of a woman washing herself was somehow reassuring, making all the fear that raced around inside his head seem overstated. Only he knew it wasn't.

The border guard he'd captured hadn't known anything. He'd died under Grant's knife, screaming and crying, cursing and begging. When he'd breathed his last rasping breath, Grant still wasn't any closer to knowing what had happened.

Grant wasn't too afraid. If this casement operated like the last one, when this world's Grant died, he'd end up back in the Cerberus redoubt. But he didn't like waiting on the end to come for him, especially not when there were six hundred plague victims in waiting, hidden in the tunnels the Panthers had dug below St. Louis.

And if he ended up dead after all, trapped somehow for real in the other Grant's life, he knew he'd be sorely pissed that he didn't do something about achieving a little get-back on whoever had put the genocide plan together.

He continued watching Reba clean herself, drawn into the act. Memories of Olivia came to him then and filled him with a bittersweet longing. He still missed her, and now he found himself missing Domi.

Quietly, giving in to the memory and the sight of the flesh-and-blood woman in front of him, wanting to recapture the illusion of being about to captain his own destiny, he took the soap from her hand. She glanced up at him over her shoulder, searching his face warily.

Grant rubbed the bar of soap in his hands, creating a handful of white lather. Then he smeared the lather over her back, working it gently into the skin.

"There's nothing you could have done about last night, Grant," Reba said softly.

He kept massaging her flesh, taking care with what he was doing. "I got all those people chilled, Reba. Mebbe not now, but I got them chilled all the same."

"If you hadn't gone to destroy that pack-wag caravan, they'd have been killed anyway. Mebbe a lot more besides."

Grant kept his hands moving. "Instead, they sit here in this dead city waiting for death to come knocking."

"Doing this was the only way you could contain it," Reba said.

"It's a fucking early grave, Reba."

Reba touched his face, stroking his cheek with a callused palm that still remained tender. "You talk like we're already dead, Grant, and that concerns me."

"Haven't you thought about it?" Grant asked.

"I have to," Reba said, "but that doesn't mean I have to give up. I didn't think you would, either."

"Mebbe I haven't," Grant replied, "but we need to know more about the designer plague in that fog. And the WSC is too fucking big to go searching through."

"I know."

"And if we had the tech available, mebbe we'd have a shot at creating some kind of antidote."

"Hooker's going to talk with some of the sympathetic Eastern Alliance villes. Mebbe he'll find someone who can do something."

"Mebbe," Grant said, reluctant to take her hope away. But his own line of thinking was that the WSC wouldn't have sent over a plague they'd been exposed to before. Most of the previous plagues had eventually died out, and there was no way for the WSC to be certain which ones had been circumvented by Alliance med techs.

He'd contacted Hooker over the radio last night and explained the situation. Despite the old man's hard-edged outlook on the world, the conversation had become very emotional. Grant hadn't gone unaffected himself, and those were the first tears he'd shed in a long time. He'd guessed that most of the feelings that he'd experienced had come from his doppelgänger, surfacing even through his control, but he knew some of them had been his own.

Hooker had taken the rest of the Panthers and drifted farther south. With the plague in evidence, there was little chance of the WSC trying to establish a beachhead during the coming wintering.

"We've go to hope, Grant," Reba said. "What else is there to do?"

Grant had no answer. But a plan started to form in his mind. By all rights, Kane and Brigid were still out there somewhere. He hoped they had more answers than he did.

Reba turned and reached for him, wrapping her arms behind his head and pulling his mouth down to hers. Grant resisted her at first, then surrendered to his own needs, as well as to hers. He kissed her passionately, losing himself in the press of flesh against flesh.

His hands traveled over her body, running down the smooth lines of her back to the swell of her buttocks. He found himself erect in seconds, his breath tight in his throat. A calm part of his mind told him that the adrenaline surge he was feeling would probably spread the disease throughout his system even faster. But he didn't care.

Reba took his lower lip into her mouth, biting it just hard enough to hurt a little. Her hand drifted between them, grasping him and urging him even harder. She pulled him against her till he could feel the wiry brush of her pubic area glide teasingly across him. His hips bucked instinctively.

She smelled of soap and water, and felt clean and soft. Kneeling, she took him into her mouth, bringing him close to the edge. Grant's hips bucked again, but she pulled away before he could finish.

"Patience," she admonished. Then she faced the wall with the spout, leaning into her hands. The hot water spumed down her back, running over her buttocks. "Now come to me."

Grant moved toward her, and she reached between

her legs to join them. He penetrated her, felt the moist heat wrap around him. She moaned lightly and he thrust himself into her to the hilt. He reached under her, seizing her breasts, feeling her nipples press into his palms, and he gave himself over to the lovemaking.

# Chapter 23

Kane stood on the upper observation deck looking down into a room that was set up like an ER. Stainless-steel equipment and cabinets filled the small space. The big stainless-steel table was the centerpiece.

Trader Broderick lay strapped to it, only minutes dead. Hoses went into and out of his body, but none of them inhibited his ability to speak. The man had talked as Thrush had worked ceaselessly with his gleaming instruments for the past two hours, and he'd died hard in the end, pinned like a butterfly to the table.

Gutters in the stainless-steel table had carried away the blood Thrush's attentions had drawn, as well as the man's urine and feces when his body had excreted them. Thrush hadn't interrupted his ministrations for anything except to listen to the man's words.

The harsh lights illuminated the cuts that lined the trader's big body. Crafted with surgical precision, most of them had been superficial, not life-threatening, but extremely bloody. Toward the end, Thrush had begun a series of organ removals and amputations.

Now, Trader Broderick resembled a picked-over main course at a macabre feast.

Down in the torture theater, Thrush ripped off the

blood-covered white surgical gown and threw it onto the corpse. He turned the lights off, leaving the room in darkness.

Looking down on the director, Kane had to admit the man never seemed more at home.

*He's not human. Find Baptiste!*

The voice whispered through the back of his mind, and the headache increased in intensity again. He closed his eyes, concentrating to make it go away. Then he took the vial of tranquilizers from his pocket and shook a couple out into his palm. He felt numb around the edges already, but the pain from the headache was getting unbearable.

Thrush caught him swallowing the pills. He'd come up from the DEI torture chamber by way of the curving stairwell.

"The headaches?" the director asked.

"Yeah." Kane put the vial away. "The med techs checked for a concussion but didn't find one. They didn't have an explanation for the headaches, though. Just told me to keep them updated."

"I'll have a talk with them and get you back in for more tests if you like."

"No. Mebbe after I get some rest, they'll go away all on their own. In the meantime, the pills help."

"Good." Thrush nodded, but his black-lensed gaze gave nothing away. "I want to get you back into the field as soon as possible, Agent Kane. I have need of your talents."

"Yes, sir."

Thrush took the lead, walking through the featureless hallways of DEI's inner sanctum. The agency had a public facade, but Kane knew its darker heart was revealed inside these hallways. Trader Broderick's body would disappear the way so many others had, dissolved by organic bacteria and flushed away through the waste-disposal systems that served the ville.

"Trader Broderick is part of a much larger problem facing the WSC," Thrush declared.

"The underground railroad?" Kane asked. "I didn't know that losing felons from the Tartarus Pits was such a grave concern."

"No," Thrush said. "It's not the loss of the felons. We can always simply draft more felons from Lowtown to replace whatever cheap labor we may lose. But the underground railroad has been found working both ways."

"Bringing people into the WSC?"

"Precisely." Thrush stopped in front of one of the unmarked doors that lined the hallway. Only he had access to them. He palmed the print reader, and the door slid back, revealing a small conference room with stainless-steel walls and floor. A desk-sized table occupied the center of the room. Two plush chairs sat on either side of it. "Join me and I'll explain."

Kane walked into the room, his unease increasing. He knew that this wasn't Thrush's office. No one was allowed to see that.

"Sit." Thrush pointed at one of the chairs.

Kane sat, discovering that the chair was mounted in the floor, able to tilt and turn, but remained locked in place.

Thrush sat on the other side of the table and took a remote control from his pocket. At the touch of a button, a section of the back wall opened up to reveal a monitor. The display pulsed dirty gray snow.

"The administration has decided upon a new

tack," Thrush said, "in dealing with the Eastern Alliance and the other problems that spring from that area. New threats loom on the horizon within WSC territory, and it was decided that no threats will be allowed from the eastern sector."

"What threats?" Kane asked. "The ROAMers?"

"The ROAMers remain a hostile force within our region," Thrush said, "but they've not become a true threat that we can't handle. They still seek to prove the existence of aliens in order to turn more people against our present government. However, the practicality of the government, the security that this administration has been able to provide, have all spoken—nowhere on the rad-blasted remnants of this globe has life become better." He paused. "We are the future, Kane, and I'll brook no interference on that score."

"Yes, sir," Kane replied.

"You and I have both seen in the past that the ROAMers have organized strikes to reveal the existence of an alien presence. They stormed Roswell, looking for downed alien spacecraft that were supposed to be kept there by the United States Air Force as early as 1947. You were part of the defense teams that turned back the last strike two years ago."

Kane nodded, remembering. "They refused to back off even after one of them was allowed in to vid the empty hangars."

"Of course, and started their new tack of saying the alien spacecraft had been moved to underground crypts under the installation. They knew we could show them no such installation because it didn't exist. But if they were able to infect the rest of the coalition with their paranoia, the administration's diplomatic

relationships with other surviving powers, as well as
with the regions within the WSC, would fall apart.''

The headache slammed into Kane with a renewed
fury. He closed his eyes and pressed against the un-
wounded side of his head.

*The prick is lying! Every bastard move that's made
here has his damned fingerprints on it!*

''That'd be stupe for them to do,'' Kane said, wanting to put it into words for that voice lingering in the
back of his mind. ''Without the administration coor-
dinating events between the different governments,
they should realize how far back they'd go. We're not
that far from the barbarism of the baronies now.''

''They don't realize this,'' Thrush said. ''They
don't realize how far they've come and how far
they've yet to go.''

''If the ROAMers aren't the threat now,'' Kane
asked, ''what is? The Eastern Alliance isn't that
strong.''

''Not the alliance,'' Thrush replied. ''The bands of
disenfranchised blacks. By stomping out their sedi-
tious behavior here, we've only strengthened their
numbers in the Eastern Alliance. One of the bands,
the Panthers, has actually set up a network of caches
of food and supplies. And its leaders have begun ne-
gotiations with other bands, as well as the Eastern
Alliance powers, to unite even more of them to a
common purpose. By the logistics I've been referenc-
ing, if the bands are left unchecked, they could well
become a formidable military force that we'll no
longer be able to deal with without incurring large
losses ourselves.''

''The trader consortium has been working with
them?'' Kane asked.

"Not with them," Thrush corrected. "For them. And for the ROAMers."

"The eastern bands are working with the ROAMers?" Kane asked. It was the first time he'd imagined the arrangement. "But that doesn't sound possible. The eastern bands have reduced themselves to sheer savagery."

"True," Thrush replied. "But they've begun pulling the other way." He pointed the remote control at the wall display.

The picture juiced and revealed the features of an old black man. The photograph was blurred, shot from a distance, and the man had obviously been on the move.

"This is Hooker," Thrush said. "He first started organizing the eastern bands."

"I can see what the bands could use from the ROAMers," Kane said. "Weapons, tech, food supplies. But what would the ROAMers get from the eastern bands?"

"A military arm," Thrush replied.

"But how could they trust the eastern bands to do what they wanted?"

"I could conjecture a dozen things within ten seconds," Thrush replied. "The fact of the matter remains that the ROAMers are desperate, wanting to prove their insane dogma. What we need to focus on is the fact that those two groups together would create more problems than we need to deal with."

"This is what Sheehan was working on?" Kane asked.

"Sheehan was a major part of the union between the ROAMers and the eastern bands. The trader consortium has been underwriting many of their dealings in the past months.''

"Why?"

"Because," Thrush replied, "if the ROAMers are successful in undermining the authority of the present administration, what force would become the strongest west of the Mississippi Wall?"

Kane only had to think for a moment. "The trader consortium."

Thrush smiled coldly. "You see, then, how this wicked little web they've woven has become quite malign?"

"Yes," Kane answered.

"That's why Genesis Project has been put into operation," Thrush said.

Kane waited, remembering it from the mention Sheehan had made of it. But he'd talked about the Russians, as well. And the embassy region was found in Alpha District.

"The Genesis Project was designed to give the Eastern Alliance lands a rebirth," Thrush said. "A plague has been introduced to that area, and it will destroy eighty-three percent of all life there."

"YOU'VE ONLY GOT ONE CHANCE, Grant."

Staring through the binoculars at the Mississippi Wall on the other side of the broad river, Grant watched the garrison sec men at their posts. Their numbers seemed to have doubled overnight.

He listened to Hooker's voice over the walkie-talkie, interspersed occasionally with bursts of static. Reba lay at his side, a silent shadow crouched down in the ruin of the ville beside him. Fully a dozen Panther warriors had fanned out around him, also hidden.

"I know, Hooker."

"Even then, there's no telling if the techs among the ROAMers can come up with an antidote," Hooker said.

"It's the only chance we've got," Grant replied. "And to believe any other way is intolerable."

"I agree."

"I'm going through the caves this morning," Grant said. Despite the presence of the wall, what had been Missouri State was still honeycombed with caverns. The earthquakes that had ravaged the area had broken them up, collapsing some and extending others. Hooker had explored some of them, lured on by the rewards of finding whole buildings that had sunk beneath the surface, ferreting out supplies that had been preserved during that time. "I'll catch a ride with one of the trader consortium drivers and be in Sante Fe late tonight or early tomorrow morning."

"That sounds find, son." Another burst of static shattered the conversation for a few seconds. "Gonna be out of radio range in a few minutes."

"I know."

"Want to wish you luck," Hooker said, his voice thick with emotion.

"A man makes his own luck, Hooker. You taught me that yourself."

"Yeah." Hooker laughed gently. "I guess I did at that. You take care of yourself out there, and get back to me when you can. My heart's gonna be an empty place if you don't."

"Mine, too," Grant said. For a moment, feeling the love his doppelgänger had for the old man, he wished that he'd known someone like Hooker, someone other than the Mags who'd shaped him.

Then he remembered Kane, realizing that he had someone he could care about, and who cared about him. And somewhere out there, Kane had to be searching, too.

The radio communication died in a final burst of static. Grant handed it to Reba, who took it without a word. Grant thought longingly of the time they'd made love that morning. He hadn't felt like that in a long time, but it had been awkward, too, because he didn't really know her and she loved the Grant that was native to this casement.

He studied the wall again, watching the crisp efficiency of the sec men. After the attack on the wags yesterday, it stood to reason that the security would have been beefed up and that watch commanders would have been more alert. But the effort he saw now bordered on the fanatical.

Then two rabbits broke cover less than ten yards from the Mississippi Wall, foraging, just as a sec team arrived back on the western shore from the ferry. Sec men atop the wall yelled a warning, and the sec team on the ferry brought their rifles to bear. Bullets chopped into the ground, tearing fist-sized craters in the soft loam.

One of the rabbits exploded in a bloody puff of fur that flipped end over end. Confused and frightened, the second rabbit raced straight for the men aboard the ferry. They scattered, one of them accidentally shooting another in the legs as he tried frantically to shoot the rabbit. A burst from sec men on the wall killed the second rabbit just as it reached the brush.

The sec men from the ferry hurried back to the wall's gateway and scrambled inside.

"They're scared of rabbits?" Reba asked. "I don't understand."

"I do," Grant said, a cold knot forming in his stomach. "That fucking plague affects more than humans. This isn't a controlled attack on the bands. This is genocide."

"PLAGUES HAVE BEEN TRIED on the bands before." Kane remembered, but he'd never liked the idea. Killing an enemy when he had a weapon ready to use was one thing, but the wholesale slaughter of an unsuspecting population was hard to accept.

"Not like this one," Thrush stated. "This one has been engineered to affect animal life, as well as human life. Even should seventeen percent of the human life survive, there won't be enough animal life to hunt for food. And I intend to break the trader consortium's ties to the Eastern Alliance, as well."

Kane nodded, realizing how big the effort really was.

"With the way the eastern bands are growing and evolving," Thrush said, "it won't be long before the Mississippi Wall will no longer hold them back." He pointed the remote control at Kane. "There is, however, one more question I must ask you."

*Move!*

The command thundered through Kane's mind, bringing with it a fresh rush of nausea from the headache. He was torn between either obeying the order because of Thrush's threatening move, or staying put to discourage his superior suspicions.

Before he could move, steel bands shot out of the chair and wrapped themselves around his chest, stomach and thighs. They blocked his access to the Spectre, and his only means to defend himself. He made himself remain calm and looked at Thrush. "What's going on?"

"My question, Special Agent Kane. Those bands serve not only to restrain you, but to monitor your responses. I'll know if you're lying." He tapped the display panel that had lit up under the table's surface only inches in front of him. Kane had never seen any instrumentation like it.

"What do you want to know?" Kane asked, masking the anger and fear that filled him. He maintained eye contact out of stubbornness.

Thrush pointed the remote control at the wall display again. The picture changed, showing the face of another black man.

Kane looked at the man. He didn't know him, but he heard the voice in the back of his mind.

*Grant!*

"This man is the leader of the Panthers," Thrush said. "Do you know him?"

Looking at the face that seemed vaguely familiar, knowing that the other that existed in the back of his head, Kane wondered if he could lie. Because even telling the truth might show up as a lie.

"Do you know him?" Thrush repeated, slipping his hand under his jacket.

# Chapter 24

Brigid's hand trembled slightly as she closed the book she'd been studying. Her head hurt from all the frantic memorization, and the other had returned to her mind.

She closed her eyes, pulling up map after map, matching up what she'd read in the text about the areas. So many secrets had been hidden for so long.

*Find Kane. He'll help you.*

She didn't know why Kane had been on her mind. When she'd continued to consider the possibility that one of the aliens had somehow gotten into her mind, she'd ultimately had to reject the idea. It was something else. If one of the aliens Director Thrush and the DEI protected had managed to read her thoughts, she'd have been killed.

The bruises across her neck and chest had already started turning purple. She'd checked in the bathroom earlier when she'd taken a break. Division Master Frasier hadn't been too lenient in the matter, demanding constant updates on her progress. She'd tried gently to let him know that the interruptions served only to slow her down. As soon as she had information, she entered it into her comp and sent it over to his. But only the information she was willing to share with him.

And the lies she'd had to tell had grown constantly bigger. The story that they'd first found had only intimated at the wealth of information that the division master's books actually contained.

Her stomach rolled, the nausea never leaving her now. She stood up from behind the table where she'd been working and stretched the kinks out of her back and shoulders. She cleaned her glasses, then put them in her purse.

Division Master Frasier stopped her at the door. "Wherever are you going, my dear?"

"To lunch," Brigid replied.

"But you can have lunch brought in."

"I'd rather go out."

Frasier scowled. "Think of the work you'll be missing."

Brigid made herself stand straight and meet the man's gaze head on. "Division Master Frasier, might I remind you that immersing oneself in one's work is sometimes counterproductive? I need a break. If I did not need this time away, rest assured that I wouldn't be taking it."

"Senior officials are waiting on the information we can get from these books," Frasier reminded.

"I'll be back in a short time," Brigid said firmly, surprising herself.

Frustrated, the big man gave in.

Brigid walked out of the office and to the Beta District streets. It felt good to be out of the dim rooms and in the warm sunshine banked by the crys-steel barrier. She felt free, but she knew it was an illusion. Everything about Sante Fe Ville was an illusion: safety, security and the care shown to the citizens.

She stopped at one of the meal dispensaries in Beta District and ordered her usual meal. Most of the peo-

ple got their meals to go, not attracted at all to the
sterile, featureless environment of the dispensary.

Brigid didn't like it there, either, but she knew she
couldn't stomach going back to Division Master Frasier's offices. She sat at one of the tables. The soup
was bland and thin, filled with pasta and little in the
way of vegetables. The sandwich had a protein spread
between dry pieces of unleavened bread. Both were
designed to fill, not necessarily to satisfy.

As she was finishing her meal, trying not to think
what the headache signified, a man in a green suit sat
at a table beside her. She recognized him at once.

"Lakesh wants to meet with you," the man whispered.

Brigid didn't know whether to feel relieved or more
threatened. She ended up being both.

KANE MET DIRECTOR THRUSH'S gaze directly. The
black man's picture remained on the display screen
on the wall.

*Grant. Where the hell is he?*

"No," he answered. "I don't know this man."

Thrush's hand remained beneath his jacket. The
sunglasses moved only a little as he looked at the
readout panel in front of him. Then they flicked back
to him. "Have you ever seen him before?"

"Not until today." Kane answered.

Thrush checked the measured response. "Do you
have any sympathies with anyone connected with the
ROAMers?"

"No."

"Did you talk with Sheehan the night you tried to
apprehend him?"

"Yes." Kane answered without hesitation. From

experience, he'd learned Thrush never asked any questions unless he had the answers already.

"Did he talk with you?"

"Yes."

"Did he mention the presence of aliens on this planet?"

"Yes."

"And that he was going to try to prove their existence?"

"Yes."

"Did he say anything further?"

"Yes."

"Did it pertain to the same matter?"

"Yes." Even though Sheehan had told him about the Russian embassy and the Genesis Project, they'd been part of the same argument to get Kane to believe in the presence of aliens.

"Have you had any contact with your ex-wife since your divorce?"

"No."

"Do you still love your ex-wife?"

Kane felt the anger grow in him but couldn't restrain it. "Yes."

"Would you do anything for her that would put your work at DEI in jeopardy?"

"No." A thin worm of fear crawled into Kane's anger as he realized Thrush was still hunting for something. He had no idea what it was.

"Would you protect your ex-wife?"

"The question's too broad, Director," Kane said. "If you're asking if I would protect her from harm, the answer is yes. If you're asking if I would do anything for her that would bring me into conflict with DEI, the answer is no."

"Not even if it meant her life?"

"No."

"Do you believe aliens exist, Agent Kane?"

"No."

Thrush's hand came out from under his jacket, and he smiled. "Did Agent Rouch shoot Sheehan last night?"

"Yes."

"Do you know who shot you?"

"Yes."

"Was it Sheehan?"

Kane hesitated, then went for the truth. Whatever game Thrush was running, this particular truth wasn't going to hurt him. "No."

"Was it Agent Rouch?"

"Yes."

"Do you have any idea why she would shoot you?"

"No."

*Because Thrush told her to. Don't be stupe.*

Thrush pressed another button on the remote, and the steel bands withdrew. "Very good," he said in his monotone.

Kane remained seated. The tranquilizers had kicked in so hard he barely felt his arms and legs. The anger inside him roved like a live thing, and kept the headache constant.

"I'm counting on your help in this mission, Agent Kane," Thrush said. "If the current administration is left in place, able to function as it was designed, we'll be entering a brave new world. But we are at a delicate crossroads now."

"I understand," Kane said. "But I believe in what DEI stands for. I've never questioned that."

"I know, but I still had to ask those questions and hear the answers for myself." Thrush thumbprinted open a drawer in the table, then took out a file. He laid it on the table without opening it. "Your resolve in this matter is going to be tested quite thoroughly before the threat of all the opponents we face is resolved."

"How?"

Thrush flipped the file open and pushed a color pic across. "Do you know this man?"

Kane took the pic and studied it closely. The man in the pic looked older than anyone Kane had ever seen. But he had the feeling he was somehow familiar. "No."

"His name is Mohandas Lakesh Singh," Thrush said, "and he's become one of the most dangerous men living."

BRIGID ENCOUNTERED no resistance at all in descending to the Tartarus Pits. Sante Fe Ville went from a sterile environment to one that resembled an archaic medieval dungeon.

When the ville had recovered from the damage done by the nukecaust, it had gone underground for a time to escape the hellish cyclic winds that had ravaged the area. The survivors had dug in and scavenged during the calm times. Once the winds had diminished and conditions became more livable on the surface, the ville inhabitants had built upward again. And the aliens had appeared under the guise of other survivors, shaping and guiding the ville to the head of the WSC.

She walked down the service hallway that led to where all the waste and sewage were disposed of.

Felons were stamped with indelible ultraviolet tattoos that showed up in the black light bulbs set into the track lighting overhead.

Crafted of sandstone bricks, the Tartarus Pits stank of old earth, human sweat and excrement. It wasn't a place anyone who lived in the surface parts of the ville would want to visit. That was one of the reasons Lakesh and the ROAMers hadn't been discovered. The sec patrols the DEI occasionally dispatched into the area weren't bright enough to search for and find the hidden tunnels and passageways the ROAMers had constructed after the upper ville had been built.

That had been after Lakesh had discovered the evil that he'd truly sold his soul for 250 years ago.

None of the sec men noticed her. The sanitation uniform she wore hid her curves and blended her in with the colorless environment. She followed the mine train tracks used by hand-pumpers to supply the pit dwellers. A hundred yards from the entrance to the track, she counted fifteen stones up and pressed.

A section of the wall opened on well-oiled hinges, exposing a deep, dark-throated tunnel. Brigid followed it in.

Several minutes later, past a series of security doors disguised as walls, she found Lakesh laboring at the comp console that tied him in with much of what was going on in the upper ville.

His pallor was gray as death, and his hair wild and uncut for several years. He'd been eleven years old at the time of the nukecaust, recognized as a child prodigy. The aliens had already been securing children who'd excelled at mathematics and music, and offering free schooling at programs for gifted children. He'd been part of the Totality Concept for five years before the nukecaust, and his education had been completed by the Brain Trust in a bunker in Boston, overseen by the Archon Directorate.

The room was floor-to-ceiling circuitry and display screens. Only Lakesh's specially modified chair, a desk and a chair occupied the stone floor.

"Come in, dear Brigid," Lakesh said in his reed-thin whisper. He blew on an air-powered controller beside his chin. Smoothly, the wheelchair turned around to face her, jerking as it stopped.

Over the years of his long life, due to the impressive creativity of his intellect, the Archons had ordered replacement organs and prostheses for Lakesh, struggling to extend his value to them. Despite the pain and suffering that had gone with each successive operation, Lakesh had stubbornly hung on to his health. The cost of every one of those years showed in the seamed lines of his face and wattled neck. He wore a gray coverall that looked to have been stripped from a vagrant scarecrow.

"Lakesh," Brigid exclaimed, looking at the disarray he was in, "hasn't anyone been in to take care of you?"

"I can take care of myself," the old man whispered. His last vocal-cord transplants had worn-out three decades ago. So had much of his body, constraining him to the wheelchair.

Brigid's heart went out to the old man. Seventy years ago, Lakesh had broken faith with the emerging Archon Directorate. He'd faked his own death and disappeared into exile in the Tartarus Pits, and started waging his own struggle against the Archons. Over the years, he'd created the ROAMer movement and slowly built up connections with the Eastern Alliance, the eastern bands, and the trader consortium.

Now he was trying to pull the threads of the tangled skeins together. All that was needed was irrefutable proof that the Archons existed. He called the underground resistance movement Cerberus, a sly reference to the guardian of the underworld in Greek mythology.

"That remains to be seen," Brigid admonished as she sat in the chair across the table from him. "Why did you call for me? I'm supposed to be at Division Master Frasier's at this moment."

"You've gotten in to see his books?"

"Yes."

In their sunken hollows, Lakesh's eyes twinkled. "You found the information we were seeking?"

Despite her fear, Brigid couldn't keep the excitement from her voice. "Yes. It's there, Lakesh. It's really there. All of it."

KANE CONSIDERED THE PIC of the old man again, trying to see him as a danger to the administration. He couldn't. "Why don't you pull him in? He doesn't look like he can do much."

"We can't find him."

"Where do you think he is?" Kane was intrigued. No one ran from the DEI for long.

"Absurdly enough," Thrush replied, "we believe he's here."

"In the Administrative Monolith?"

"In Sante Fe Ville," Thrush amended. "But we've no idea where. The Enclaves and the main tower itself are honeycombed with service tunnels and false walls as the new buildings and wings arose. We also believe that Lakesh is the man responsible for the ROAMer organization.''

Kane handled the information slowly, turning it around in his head, trying to find all the angles. Thrush was still leading him somewhere. ''Why would he do this?''

Thrush's black-lensed sunglasses gave nothing away. ''Lakesh used to be involved in the research-and-development section in the main tower. As you can see, he's a very old man. The med techs diagnosed his condition as dementia. You know what that is?''

''Progressively developing hallucinations,'' Kane answered.

''Very good, Agent Kane. Apparently, Lakesh's condition deteriorated more rapidly and more completely than the med techs could keep track of. One day, he simply disappeared.''

Kane nodded. The pain from the headache twisted and coiled in his head.

*Lies. All of it. Ask him why Lakesh would start imagining aliens.*

Kane remained silent, not giving in to the other's pressure to ask something so damning at the moment. Thrush didn't allow free-thinking; it got in the way of the truths he handed out.

''We also have reason to believe your ex-wife is working with him,'' Thrush said.

Suspicion flared through Kane as he realized what Thrush had really brought him in to tell him. ''Why would she be doing that?''

''I don't know,'' Thrush answered. ''But I wanted you to be aware of the situation.''

Kane translated that as being information the director didn't want to divulge. But he was definitely aware of the situation Brigid was in if she was a suspect. His pulse ran thready.

*Believe him, you stupe bastard, and you're going to get Brigid chilled.*

He cleared his throat. "What did you want me to start working on, Director?"

Thrush watched him quietly, and Kane got the impression that it was the same look of fascination a spider might give to a fly trapped in its web. The director placed his long fingers against each other. "I'll keep you apprised, Agent Kane."

Kane sat there for a moment, understanding that he was being dismissed, but reluctant to leave with only limited information in hand. Finally, realizing the black-lensed gaze wasn't going to break, he pushed up from the chair. "Yes, sir."

Thrush switched off the wall display, and the section of wall slid back into place.

At the door, Kane hesitated, afraid to ask the question uppermost in his mind but finally even more afraid of not having it answered. "Can I ask you something, sir?"

"Of course, Agent Kane, though whether I answer it remains to be seen."

Kane nodded. "Where can I find Rouch?"

The black-lensed stare remained impassive. "I'm sure she'll be in touch, Agent Kane. At the moment, she's on special assignment."

Kane released the door and walked away. The headache slammed around inside his head viciously, but it wasn't the only thing making him sick now.

How the hell could Brigid get involved with someone like Lakesh?

*Find her! If you hesitate, she's dead!* the voice screamed inside his head.

# Chapter 25

"So all the old stories were true?"

Brigid listened to the wheezing excitement in the old man's voice. "Yes." It sounded unnaturally loud in the small room far below the Administrative Monolith.

"Division Master Frasier doesn't know the wealth of information he has in hand?"

"No. He's having me translate it as a matter of course. If he did, I don't think he'd let me out of his sight."

"Indeed," Lakesh agreed. "But we're presented with problems anew." Sorrow darkened his eyes.

"You never said why you called me down here," Brigid prompted.

"I sent for you, dear Brigid," Lakesh said, "because Director Thrush of the DEI has developed an uncommon interest in you."

Brigid felt as though ice water had been dumped in her veins. "Why?"

"I believe he's had his suspicions about you for a long time, but this is what ultimately tipped him off." Lakesh blew in the air pipe again and turned the wheelchair back to the comp station. A skeletal metal arm reached out and punched out commands on one of the keyboards there.

Brigid watched as a Sante Fe Ville med-tech report

flashed onto one of the display screens. She took out her glasses and scanned the report. "It's about me."

"Remember when you went into the med center two years after you and Kane were married? When you were concerned about not having children?"

Brigid remembered. Kane had been definite about it.

"Do you recall what the med techs told you?" Lakesh asked.

"They said there was no reason why I shouldn't have children," Brigid said.

"They were somewhat untrustworthy in that department, dear Brigid. I'm afraid your reproductive organs were damaged, scarred by the radiation you were exposed to last year."

The sadness erupted from Brigid like an artesian well feeding off a geyser. She'd never known such a strong emotion. Tears covered her face, streaking her cheeks.

"I'm so sorry, dear Brigid."

"It's not your fault, Lakesh." She wiped at her face with her hands. "How long have you known?"

"Today," the old man said. "I found it today."

For some reason, she felt extremely grateful that he hadn't tried to hide it from her.

*He has before. You're lucky you have him.*

"I sent for you as soon as I knew." He blew on the actuator to turn the wheelchair. "My goodness, child, and here I sit without arms to console you." Tears ran down the wrinkles in his face.

After a while, Brigid regained control of herself. "It must have happened when I was exposed to the radioactive isotopes in the Overproject Excalibur wing," she said softly.

Last year, she'd gone into the R&D labs on Beta Level with codes Lakesh had given her to ferret out information. The codes had come into Lakesh's hands at the cost of two agents, but the information had resulted in three antidotes to plagues that were introduced into Eastern Alliance lands. Once those antidotes were in Lakesh's hands, he'd garnered a lot of goodwill from the Eastern Alliance by providing them.

Unfortunately, Brigid had become exposed to radioactive isotopes that had been in one of the experiments. That had triggered her subsequent divorce from Kane. Their marriage had already been on the rocks due to the espionage work she carried out for Lakesh and all the lies she'd been forced to tell.

Kane had thought there was someone else in her life. It would have been worse to tell him that she'd initially gotten involved with him to get information about Director Thrush's agenda.

But when the radiation sickness had materialized, making her sick and causing her hair to fall out, she and Lakesh had found ways to hide it from her fellow employees. As an archivist for the Historical Division, she'd been alone much of the time, and Lakesh had helped her with her work, keeping her on task.

There'd been no hiding her sickness from a husband, though, and she'd forced the divorce, driving Kane from her life. The wig she'd worn hadn't drawn attention from anyone else, but Kane would have known everything.

He might even have turned her in himself.

When her hair had grown back, she'd opted for the shorter styling so she wouldn't have to keep wearing the wig.

"Our problems don't stop there," Lakesh said. "I fear that the director is on to you because of your ailment. The problem is, should you disappear now, it might draw attention to Division Master Frasier's project."

"And that would alert Thrush and DEI to those caches in Eastern Alliance lands," Brigid said.

"Yes. At a time when we and our allies are in poor positions to make something of our find." Lakesh looked at her. "My heart says for me to ask you to stay here, dear child, and simply drop from sight of the director and his evil forces. But my head says we must take the risk to insure that those documents are not found prematurely." He paused. "The decision rests in your hands."

Brigid only had to think for a moment. "I'll have to go back, Lakesh, if we're to have a chance at all. And I've fought the director for far too long to stop short of a goal that's so near to hand. I've given up so damned much for this, Lakesh." She thought of the children she'd never have, and she thought of Kane.

"I know, dear child, and I regret that such a decision should be forced onto you. However, if you're to go back, it should be soon. You're going to be late as it is. But before you go, I'll need the information you've uncovered. As a precaution of something happening to you, God forbid."

"Of course," Brigid said. She crossed to his comp and began inputting the information. She tried to be brave, but her hands shook continuously. Lakesh could only offer his sympathy, then watch her with haunted eyes when she took her leave.

She knew she'd seen the old man for the last time.

GRANT MADE HIS WAY through the caves with his escort. Most of them were small, narrow places. Some of them peered out over bottomless chasms, and twice he had to go under water to continue his journey.

They traveled by torchlight that wavered uncertainly. The cave system they traversed had been used several times in the past to get past the Mississippi Wall.

On the other side, they came up three miles beyond the wall, crawling out into a gully that overlooked the garrisons. No one appeared to have noticed that the Panther group had arrived.

He ate, grateful that he still had an appetite, taking it as a sign that the disease circling through his system hadn't started tearing anything down yet. In less than an hour, the trader consortium pack wag was scheduled to arrive. And Grant would catch the bus to Sante Fe ville.

His thoughts were concentrated only on revenge.

"CITIZEN, YOU'RE NOT CLEARED for Beta District."

Kane stared at the sec man who'd halted him when he got out of the elevator that took him up to the district. The indelible tattoo he wore that showed up under the man's ultraviolet light only cleared him to Cappa District. "Get the fuck out of my face." He slapped the DEI identichip onto the reader beside the man.

The sec man glanced at it, saw the clearance there, then stepped hurriedly back. "Yes, sir. Sorry about the inconvenience, sir."

Replacing the chip in his pocket, Kane continued on. The DEI badge was a blank check in the ville, unless Thrush put a lock on an area himself. His agents weren't supposed to be stopped for anything.

But he knew the director wouldn't have been pleased with the mission he was on now. Maybe if he hadn't been laced with so many tranquilizers, he would have been more fearful of skating so closely to insubordination. He walked down the Beta District street, knowing he stood out amid the green suits.

After leaving Thrush's offices yesterday, he'd gone home to his own dorm and slept for twenty-four hours straight, under the influence of the tranquilizers and his own extended fatigue. The director had never called with an assignment, and Kane's sources within DEI told him Thrush had been spending his time among the embassies.

The embassies had always held a special appeal for the director, Kane knew from talk that drifted down even from Alpha District. He'd had a hand in negotiating several peace agreements between the surviving nations himself. Kane had been told that by DEI agents who'd served as bodyguards during some of the summit conferences.

Thirty years ago, just as Thrush was coming into power in the DEI, the surviving nations of the world had started swapping ambassadors again. It was their hope and ambition to figure out trade routes and foundations for sharing tech and resources. Most people in the ville were of the opinion that isolationism was best.

Kane didn't have an opinion. He concentrated on the world that he lived in. Even across the Mississippi Wall was farther than he ever intended to go.

He found Brigid Baptiste's dorm easily. Mustering the courage to go in was a totally different matter.

When he finally did, it was anticlimactic: Brigid wasn't home. All he got for his trouble was a recording of the message she'd left saying she wasn't available. He knew from living with her that she never turned the messager on unless she was gone.

Some of the old suspicions and fears touched him, opening wounds he'd thought scarred over. Despite the drugs in his system, the hurt scored him more than the headache that pounded his temples.

Before he knew it, his hand was on the door and he was pressing the DEI identichip against the print reader. The door opened at once.

He hesitated before stepping into the dorm, recognizing the bits and pieces of Brigid scattered around the living space, remembering the smell of her perfume lingering in the air. Then he heard furtive movement inside the room.

He moved quickly, the door shutting automatically behind him. He left the Spectre holstered, not wanting to shred Brigid's dorm.

The blond-haired man erupted from the small bedroom, holding a small blaster in his hand. He popped off two shots that dug holes in the opposite wall, narrowly missing Kane.

Spinning deeper into the room and drawing the shooter out farther, Kane closed on the wall.

The shooter remained hidden by the doorway, taking advantage of the cover offered. He fired again, and the bullet plucked at Kane's coat.

Within reaching distance of the man, Kane knocked the blaster away with his left hand. The blaster popped one more time, sending a bullet digging into the ceiling. Drawing back his right arm, Kane drove his bionic hand through the wall, ripping through the thin material and slamming into the blond-haired man's chin.

The man flew backward, landing on the small bed.

Kane rushed through the doorway, expecting the man to come up fighting. The man rolled toward him, a knife in one hand. He drove it at Kane's face.

Flicking the bionic hand out, Kane grabbed the knife blade and snapped it off. He closed his other hand in the man's jacket. Before the man could defend himself, Kane backhanded him. Then he took the man's belt and used it to tie his hands behind his back.

He dragged the dazed man back into the living-room area, glancing at the comp display. Judging from the columns of symbols running across the display, someone already had a spoofer in place to foil the sec monitors in the dorm.

Common sense told him it was the man he'd captured, but the old suspicions in him suggested it belonged to Brigid.

He dropped the man in the floor and took a chair from the kitchen. Then he sat down to wait for the man to recover consciousness. The headache inside his skull pounded relentlessly. He shook out another tranq and wolfed it down.

"I GOT THE INFORMATION you wanted."

Grant looked up at the man and tried to focus on the words he was saying. "The dorm number?" The headache echoed within his head, sharper than it had when he'd been back at the St. Louis Outlands.

The man nodded.

They were down in the Tartarus Pits, under Santa Fe Ville proper, in one of the processing-plant rooms that broke down the sewage generated by the ville. The room was small and poorly lighted. Stains caked the walls, and the nauseous odor had deadened his sense of smell.

Grant had entered the ville by joining a sanitation crew taking a load of debris out of the Tartarus Pits. The guards were under contract by the trader consortium, and Grant's contact inside the ville had bribed them. Another man had provided the tattoo he needed to get through the security.

"What about the woman's?" Grant asked.

The man hesitated.

"Talk, goddammit!" Grant snarled. "It's not like we got a lot of fucking time here!" He was beginning to believe the increased headache was symptomatic of the plague he'd been exposed to. It had gotten much worse the closer he got to Sante Fe Ville.

"They don't want to give out her dorm number," the man said. He was broad and black, stooped from years of hard labor in the Tartarus Pits. "She's to be protected."

"Fuck that," Grant said. "Part of what I'm here to do is to protect that woman." He still remembered Kane under hypnosis, talking about the way Brigid was already dead. In the back of his mind, his doppelgänger slid around greasily, like a bad breakfast trying to come up. Grant didn't think it was his doppelgänger trying to regain control. Something else was wrong.

"I can't help you," the man said.

Pain stabbed through Grant's brain again, nearly ripping his control away. "Then get me somebody who can," he ordered. "And I mean now!"

THE BLOND-HAIRED MAN'S EYES flickered open and slowly focused on Kane. He smiled confidently. "You're treading on the skirts of treason, Kane," he croaked through blood-caked lips.

"You know me?" Kane asked. He sat in the chair, the Spectre naked in his fist. The man's words only hammered in the fact that he was well past the point of no return.

"Yes. Check my left breast pocket and you'll find an identichip. Run it through the reader built into the comp behind you."

"And what if it's coded with a command to summon your friends here?"

The blond-haired man's eyebrows rose. "Paranoia setting in, Kane? Starting to believe some of those conspiracies that these fucking ROAMers are spouting?"

Kane said nothing, but he knew who the man represented even if he didn't know the man's name.

"Or is it that you're simply too close to the problem to properly see for yourself what the truth is?" the man taunted.

"You tried to chill me," Kane said.

"I thought you were working with her. You're not supposed to be here. You were warned away." He licked blood flakes from his lips. "Run my identichip."

Reluctantly, Kane took the chip from the man's pocket and pressed it against the reader on the comp. The display filled with columns of symbols cleared for an instant, pixelating into an image of the blond-haired man. His name was Marko, and he was a special agent of the Department of Extraterrestrial Investigations.

"You see, Kane," Marko said, "we're brothers,

you and I." He sat up and turned, offering his bound hands to Kane. "Now untie me."

"What are you doing here?" Kane asked, ignoring the hands.

Marko waited for a moment, then sighed and gave up, dragging his hands behind his back again. "Your emotional involvement with this woman is why the director didn't want you to know anything about this."

"She's not involved with the ROAMers," Kane stated flatly.

"Oh, yes," Marko replied, "she is. I've been here trying to figure out in what capacity she's actually been serving them."

Despite the headache pounding in his head, Kane was putting it all together. "You're working with Rouch. Where is she?"

Marko paused, evidently taking time to weigh his answer. "We're tag-teaming the woman. Since Baptiste knows Rouch, I've been running close-cover on the woman. Rouch is nearby."

Mentioning the woman made Kane remember the night in the hospital, and the guilt was damning. He checked through the man's clothing, assuring himself there were no comm devices with open channels. He found pintels on Marko's jawline where a comm-tach would boot up, further identifying him.

Then the headache slammed into Kane with renewed fury as he struggled with what he was supposed to do, what loyalties he was supposed to honor. Brigid had lied to him and Thrush had lied to him. Who was more closely telling the truth? He held a hand to his temples, screaming at the pain that shot through his skull. When he looked back up, he saw

Marko lunging at him, pulling a razor-edged knife from his boot.

Without hesitation, Kane lifted the Spectre and shot the man in the chest. Marko's forward momentum carried him onto Kane, draping his corpse across Kane as the machine pistol's whispered coughing died away in the room.

Kane watched the man fall onto the floor. He slumped back in the chair and remained sitting there until Brigid returned home.

"ARE YOU ILL?"

Grant raised his head from his hands. He'd knelt down against one of the sandstone walls in the empty room that he'd been taken to. It had demanded a lot of skilled and desperate bargaining and serious threats to get into the inner sanctum of one of the ROAMers' hidden bases.

His grip on his doppelgänger's body was tenuous at best, and seemed to be fading with every second. He looked at the old man in the wheelchair, then at the only doorway into the room, knowing the man hadn't come by it. He smiled. "Still more hiding places, Lakesh? You never change, no matter what world we find you on."

Two guards in Tartarus Pits service uniforms stood on either side of the old man in the wheelchair. Blasters were naked in their hands, trained on Grant.

"You know me?" A look of surprise mixed with intense interest flashed on Lakesh's face.

"Yeah," Grant replied. His voice sounded strained even to his own ears.

"To the best of my knowledge, and it's the very best of its kind, we've never met."

"You know who I am?"

Lakesh nodded. "Grant, leader of the Panthers."

"Yeah, well, that's just here," Grant stated.

"By 'here,' you're referring to this world?" Lakesh asked.

"Yeah, I am." Before Grant could continue, another major stab of pain slammed into him, short-circuiting his senses. Everything went black.

# Chapter 26

*Cerberus redoubt*

"It was hard to find," Bry was explaining to Lakesh as his hands flew over the keyboard, altering the program codes that cycled over his monitor screens. "As you can see, the binary constructs I was able to tap into by accessing the Chintamani Stone's resonance created by its crystalline integrity is quite complicated."

To call the expansive programming Lakesh saw running before him *complicated* was ludicrous. He watched the columns of figures and coding speeding by him. "These are the codes you found inherent in the trapezohedron?"

Bry looked up at him and shook his head. "No. This is the code that I picked up coming in from the link to the other casement. I haven't even begun breaking into the coding embedded in the Chintamani Stone. I haven't gotten past its defenses yet."

"Then how were you able to discern this line of programming, Mr. Bry?" The amount of data was incredible.

"Because it's feeding back from the other casement," Bry said. "Not to it."

"Yes, I remember you saying that." Lakesh faulted himself for his inattention, absorbed by the program-

ming on the displays. "And you compared the link
between this casement and the last to find this?"

"Yes." Bry seemed tired but pleased with his ac-
complishment. "The programming is unbelievably intricate. The fascinating thing about this is that I think
it's possible to change the frequencies in the Chintamani Stone."

"Allowing egress into other such casements?"

Bry nodded.

The news captured Lakesh's attention, as well.
"There must be some reason Balam chose these three
worlds, though."

"The most intriguing part of this discovery,
though, is that we might be able to receive aud and
vid from the other casements. I don't know about
sending yet, but I really believe it's possible to receive those through the programming if we can receive this."

Lakesh's excitement flared to new heights. To be
able to peek in on other casements where the Archons
had applied their expertise might prove most enlight-
ening. But he shoved the idea away. He wouldn't find
out if any of the three people in the other casement
were killed. Those particular gateways might never
open. "Mr. Bry, the problem still remains whether
you are able to disallow this particular program and
help Kane, Grant and Brigid."

Bry's fingers kept striking the keyboard. "I'm
working on it now, Lakesh. The programming is complex, but I'm good at what I do."

"I know, friend Bry, that's why I brought you
here."

The steady drone from the jump chamber suddenly
dropped in pitch. Both men jerked their heads toward

it, startled. At the same time, the overhead lights flickered and the displays on the computer screens wavered.

"Another power fluctuation," Bry said tightly.

Lakesh poked an intercom button, opened a channel to the generator room and demanded, "Wegmann, what's going on down there?"

For a long, tense moment, there was no answer. Then the man's waspish voice filtered through the comm. "You're putting too much strain on the energy reserves. I've got one generator already out of alignment."

"What's the danger of overload?"

"Minimal right now. But if this keeps up, I'm going to have to take it off-line or we'll have a catastrophic system failure."

Lakesh dropped a hand on Bry's shoulder. "Whatever you can do, I've a feeling that it's best done quickly."

*Sante Fe Ville*
*Western States Coalition*

"ARE YOU ILL?" Lakesh repeated.

Grant tried to answer, but couldn't. He wasn't in control of the borrowed body, nor was the Grant he'd replaced. He knew he was lying on the stone floor of the little room, a pool of vomit spread out in front of him. Both of them were helpless.

Lakesh rolled his chair closer, peering down at Grant with bright-eyed interest.

Then, abruptly as it came, the pain left Grant's mind. But not the sickness. He roused himself slowly, finally managing a sitting position. "The WSC exposed us to a plague over in the St. Louis Outlands,'' he croaked.

"A plague?" Lakesh rolled the wheelchair back in startled dismay.

Grant showed him a crooked grin. "Yeah, must be a nasty thing, too, because the wall sec men are shooting at rabbits that get close to them. They were about ready to shit their pants yesterday morning after the plague was delivered.''

"And you deliberately exposed me to it without telling me of the plague's existence?" Lakesh sounded as if he couldn't believe it.

"I wanted to make sure you were properly motivated," Grant replied. "In my world, you sometimes work by your own agenda and don't give a damn about anybody else's problems. Not one of your more endearing qualities. In fact, I can't think of a single endearing quality that you do possess. This way, my problem is your problem.''

"Your world?" Lakesh asked. "Then it's true? The Archon Directorate has succeeded in splitting off the time line into a series of alternate worlds?''

"Damned right," Grant replied. His strength was returning, and the headache no longer existed at all.

"This could be a trick.''

"If it was," Grant said, "I'd have exposed you to the plague and not said anything about it. Or I'd have had this area flooded with sec men by now.''

"You do realize by exposing me to the plague, you could have doomed any chance we might have had against the Archons," Lakesh stated as harshly as his injured voice could allow.

"That plague's loose in Eastern Alliance lands," Grant replied. "How much of a chance do you think you stand against Thrush and the Archons without us?''

Lakesh remained angrily silent.

''You see my point, old man? This way you—'' Grant waved a finger at the men and took in all of the Tartarus Pits ''—and your buddies become carriers, too. If there's no antidote for this, then I'd just fucking as well chill us all. Thrush may live, and the Archons, but they won't have anyone to rule.'' He paused. ''Now I need to know where Brigid Baptiste is.''

''She's one of you?'' Lakesh sounded like he didn't believe it. ''But I saw her today and she said nothing.''

Grant thought about that, finding his mental clarity was getting stronger, as well. ''Did she have a headache?''

''Yes.''

''It's possible she's having trouble getting linked with her doppelgänger,'' Grant said. ''I noticed on my way into Sante Fe Ville that my own control over the fusion got harder. The Thrush of this world may have found a way to jam the process. He built a trap for Kane when he entered the gateway alone.''

''Kane? Agent Kane of the DEI?''

''Yeah.''

''For a time,'' Lakesh said quietly, ''Kane was Thrush's right-hand man.''

''Mebbe in this casement,'' Grant said, ''but we've been nothing but enemies with Thrush. Now I need to know where Brigid is.''

BRIGID BAPTISTE FROZE in the doorway to her dorm, looking past the dead man lying on the floor to her ex-husband sitting on a chair nearby. The headache had finally passed a few minutes ago, departing with the same mysteriousness as it had arrived.

Fear snaked along her back, freezing her into place for a moment. She looked at the big gun in Kane's hand.

"Get inside, Brigid," he said softly.

"So you can chill me, too?" She'd never heard him sound so tired, so exhausted. It touched the part of her that still cared about him, but it didn't take the fear away.

He glanced at her and shook his head. "I'm DEI, Brigid. If I wanted to, I could have chilled you when you opened that door." He pointed to the dead man. "He came here to chill you."

Looking more closely at the dead man, Brigid recognized him as the man who'd attacked her. "But you chilled him."

"Yeah."

"Why?"

Kane shook his head. "I don't know."

"And if Thrush finds out what you've done?"

"I don't know that, either. I thought mebbe we could talk, try to figure something out."

Brigid watched him, remembering all the love that they'd shared, love that had never truly gone away. It was funny in a way. When she'd first started to deceive him, she'd never dreamed of falling in love with him.

*Go to him. Trust him.*

Still afraid, but knowing that if she tried to leave he could shoot her down outside with impunity, Brigid stepped into the room. The voice in the back of her mind sounded stronger, more certain. She borrowed part of that confidence somehow and winnowed out the fear.

Kane stood, dropping his weapon beside the dead man.

Brigid had intended to stop just inside the door, but her feet wouldn't stop moving till she was face-to-face with Kane.

"My God," he croaked, and tears were in his eyes. He wrapped his arms around her, then kissed her passionately.

She held him tightly, pulling him to her as though trying to absorb him through her skin. She was so hungry for him, for his touch, that she couldn't stand it. "Kane," she whispered.

"I know," he said. He bent and picked her up in his arms, then strode across the dead man into the bedroom.

Brigid barely noticed the destroyed doorway. He laid her gently on the bed, then covered her body with his. She touched the bandage at the side of his head, wanting to ask about it, but willing to wait till later. If there was any time left, she wanted to spend it in his arms.

They worked with eager hands, tearing clothing out of the way, holding and cupping and tasting and caressing. Brigid was aware of the gauze bandage on his side, but she carefully avoided it as she continued to explore his body.

Kane pulled her legs apart and lay between them. She wrapped her legs around his hips as she pulled him into her. His hard length filled her, sliding into her silken sheath as if it was the most natural thing she'd ever experienced. She held him tightly, thrusting herself against him, meeting him stroke for stroke.

Then warm pleasure washed through her, and the voice in the back of her mind came forward again.

BRIGID WOKE in her doppelgänger's body. She was naked, which wasn't a surprise since she'd been an echo in the back of her other self's mind when the most recent events had taken place.

Rolling over in the twisted sheets, she found Kane watching her, his head propped up on one hand as he lay beside her. A troubled smile played with his lips.

Then he leaned forward and kissed her, an open-mouthed kiss that explored the inside of her mouth and set fire to her again. Brigid lost herself in the sensation for a moment, knowing she couldn't blame her other self for her actions now, and scared to death what involvement with Kane on this level would mean for her.

He dropped a hand to her breast, squeezing. Trailing his fingertips down, he touched the dampness of her sex, bringing back the sweet, aching memory of the explosion that had filled her.

But the touch was too much for Brigid, brought back all too clearly the risks she was taking by involving herself with him. She brought her hands up and pushed him roughly away.

"What the hell do you think you're doing?" she exploded angrily.

A wary, hurt look filled his face, competing with shock. "What's wrong?"

"It's over, Kane," Brigid explained, getting out of bed and wrapping a sheet around herself. "We're here now, and we're not—" she fumbled for words, amazed that she couldn't simply speak "—we're not doing that anymore."

"You mean making love?" Kane asked.

"That wasn't it," Brigid said. "That was just a means to achieve fusion with our doppelgängers and get into this world."

His brow tightened in perplexion. "What the fuck are you talking about, Brigid?"

Brigid pushed a stray lock of hair from her sweat-streaked face. Kane never called her Brigid; it was always Baptiste. Understanding dawned on her. "Kane, is it you?"

"Of course it's me." Kane got up from the bed, as well. His blue-gray eyes reflected the pain he was feeling.

"Which Kane are you?"

He acted like the question confused him. "I'm me. Who else would I be?"

"Did you pass out?" Brigid asked.

"No. It was good, Brigid, but I stayed awake." He grinned halfway, as if testing the water. "I was afraid to go to sleep, afraid I'd wake up without you."

Brigid thought furiously, remembering that Lakesh had told her about the tranquilizers Thrush had ordered Kane to take. Maybe those blocked Kane's fusion with his doppelgänger. Her own fusion was complete, and she found herself as much in charge of her doppelgänger in this casement as she had been in the last. "Does the word *Cerberus* mean anything to you?"

Confusion filled his features. "No. Should it?"

"Something's gone wrong, Kane."

"You mean besides the dead man lying in the floor in the other room? A man who works for the same guy I do?" He came closer to her, trying to put his arms around her again.

Brigid pushed him away. "Stay off me, Kane. I need to think." She walked out of the bedroom into the living room, staring down at the dead man.

"What's wrong with you?" Kane asked, following her.

Looking at him, Brigid knew he wasn't the Kane she needed, the one who believed. She said, "You don't know about the Archons, do you?"

"Brigid, what the hell are you talking about?"

"I'm talking about the aliens," she said, letting frustration tighten her voice. "The ones who caused the nukecaust and helped destroy the world, the ones who created a string of parallel earths to subjugate, as well."

Kane shook his head, all emotion draining from him. "That's crazy talk, Brigid. Stop. There are no aliens."

"There are, and you can deny them all you want to, but it won't make them go away. Thrush works for them, and DEI covers up any mistakes they might make."

"That's stupe talk," Kane snapped.

"That's the truth."

Anger darkened Kane's face. "I came here to warn you," he shouted, "that Thrush knew about your relationship with Lakesh."

"Lakesh knows about the Archons, Kane. He knows that they're hiding in the embassies. Over the last handful of decades, they've hybridized themselves, getting a strain of aliens that are almost indistinguishable from us."

"Crazy talk," Kane muttered.

"It's true! They're working together," Brigid went on. "By controlling the relationship between the surviving powers, they're going to set up trade routes and treaties that will give them control of what's left of this planet. They're calling it the Program of Unification. Lakesh broke into Thrush's files and discovered the whole plan."

"Brigid, stop!" Kane ordered. "Lakesh has seduced you to his paranoia."

"No," she replied. "No, he hasn't. I know the truth because I'm from another world. I'm not the Brigid Baptiste you know." She halted, knowing there was nothing further she could say from the vacant look in Kane's eyes.

"Goddammit, Brigid," he whispered hoarsely, "I thought I could help you. I'd have given my life to protect you. But not at the cost of jeopardizing the administration and all the work they've done. They've given us the life we have."

"It's all lies, Kane."

"Shut the fuck up!" Kane held his head in his hands for a moment, squeezing his eyes shut.

"You've got a headache, don't you? Have you been hearing voices in the back of your head?"

He opened his eyes and looked at her in wild disbelief.

"I know about those headaches," she said, hoping to break through his defenses, somehow make him see reason, "because I was having them, too. It's the other Kane, the one from another world, who wants to fuse with you and help me."

"You're way beyond fucking help. You've gone crazy, Brigid." Kane gathered his blaster, then his clothes from the other room.

Brigid left him alone while she dressed, knowing his anger mirrored the Kane she knew. She waited until he was moving toward the door. "What about Grant? Have you seen Grant?"

"Sure, I've seen Grant," Kane said. "A pic of him. He's a leader of the goddamned Panthers in the Eastern Alliance. And if you know him, then you're deeper into this conspiracy than I thought." He opened the door, but didn't go out immediately. "Why the fuck did I ever fall for you?"

"I don't know," Brigid told him, tears coming to her face for reasons unknown to her. "I guess we're just drawn to each other."

He stared at her. "Not anymore," he growled, and he walked through the door.

Brigid stood in the room with the dead man, wondering how the hell she was supposed to do anything without Kane in this casement, wondering if she could get back to the Cerberus redoubt. Then she heard a woman's voice behind her.

"You lost him, Baptiste."

Brigid turned and saw Beth-Li Rouch standing in her kitchen. A hidden door was open behind the woman, one that Brigid had never known existed. Lakesh had mentioned the existence of tunnels and rooms hidden throughout the ville, disguised by the architecture.

"In fact, you lose it all." Rouch tossed a package toward the center of the room.

KANE'S HEAD HURT and his senses spun. He still had Brigid's smell in his nostrils, the taste of her on his lips. He walked down the street from her dorm, noticing the night sky on the other side of the crys-steel barrier for the first time. He'd been gone for a long time. He wondered if Thrush had sent anyone out to look for him.

And he wondered what the hell he was going to do with the woman he loved so fiercely. He'd left her in the dorm with Marko's corpse. Thrush could easily pin the murder on her and use that to chill her or at the least stick her in the Tartarus Pits.

And what the fuck was she going to do with the corpse? Ask her friends the alien hunters to get rid of it for her?

He blew out an angry breath, knowing he couldn't leave her like that. He turned and retraced his steps, heading toward Brigid's dorm.

The explosion dawned like a nuclear sun, blowing out the front of Brigid's dorm and hurling chunks of flaming debris against the crys-steel barrier. The sound of the detonation rolled through Beta District, trapped by the crys-steel barrier that secured the district from neighboring areas.

"Brigid!" Kane yelled, running forward. But the intense heat of the flames drove him back, kept him from entering the dorm. He collapsed on his knees, going cold and numb inside as he witnessed the death of every hope he'd ever known. And in that moment of hopelessness, he felt the other rush past him to fill his mind.

# Chapter 27

Kane stared at the flames licking out of the dorm. "Baptiste!" he roared, knowing she wasn't coming out.

Onlookers began to gather, staring and gesturing at the burning dorm. Sec men could only be minutes away, Kane knew. He stood, feeling the ache inside him. With Baptiste dead here on this casement, the Baptiste he knew had to be back at Cerberus Redoubt. He couldn't afford to think any other way.

He walked away, fixing his thoughts on Thrush. His doppelgänger might not have had a clue what Thrush was really about, but he knew. And he intended to see the cyborg hybrid's schemes brought down.

A figure stepped out of the shadows, and he identified the man by the movements before he saw the face. "Grant."

"Yeah," Grant replied. He glanced back toward the fire. "Brigid?"

Kane nodded. "At least, the one in this casement."

Grant fell into step beside him. In the slashes of light overhead, Kane saw that he was wearing one of the Beta Level green suits.

"I thought you were some kind of bandit chief out in the Eastern Alliance," Kane said. He kept the dark thoughts of losing Brigid from his mind. He didn't

know how long he had before Thrush set the DEI on
his tracks.

"Not a bandit chief," Grant objected. "I was a
warrior king."

"How'd you get here?"

"Lakesh. Man's wired into every place that's any
place here in the ville."

"He couldn't save Brigid," Kane pointed out.

Without warning, the familiar shape of a Deathbird
rose into the air on the other side of the crys-steel
barrier. A searchlight crawled over the crowd gathered in front of Brigid's ruined dorm.

"No," Grant said in a quiet voice, "but he knows
where Thrush is, and how to get us there. Interested?"

Kane took a final look at the blazing pyre. Then he
slid his identichip against the reader and got through
the security and sec men. He punched up the code for
Epsilon District at Grant's suggestion. The destination
made sense because the security there would be most
lax. The fire blazed against the encroaching darkness
of the night. "Yeah." He felt his doppelgänger's loss
echoing inside him.

They took the elevator down, and Kane focused on
his anger, then walled it away. There was still a mission to be accomplished.

"So you were married to Baptiste in this casement," Grant said. "You gotta wonder about that."

"And divorced," Kane pointed out.

"Hell of a life the two of you lead," Grant said,
"no matter what world you're on."

"Yeah, well, the report I read on you stated that
you were a cannibal."

Grant grinned widely. "Had a leader of the Panthers name of Hooker. He started the cannibalization

myth, playing off old prejudices about all blacks being cannibals. We field-dressed the dead, buried the meat miles from where we chilled them. Struck terror in the hearts of sec men everywhere.''

Kane got out of the elevator when it arrived at Epsilon District. Grant took the lead. "Where's Thrush?'' Kane asked.

"At the Russian embassy on Alpha District," Grant answered. "They're having a gala event. We're bringing the party favors.''

"DO YOU UNDERSTAND the parameters of this exercise, Agent Kane?''

In the darkness filling the underground tunnel, Kane looked over at the Santa Fe Ville version of Lakesh. "You have your parameters for this mission," he snarled, "and I've got mine.''

Lakesh looked displeased, as though he'd bit into a bitter lemon. "Agent Kane, as Grant explained to me concerning your involvement with this particular casement, all you've got to do is alter Director Thrush's plans here to achieve your success. In fact, if you can expose his involvement with the Archons here, you'll serve to free this particular casement from his tampering, as well. As I've told you, Brigid Baptiste has given me maps of caches made by the Annunaki when they'd occupied the eastern coast.''

Lakesh had explained that bit of this particular casement's history. The Archons and the Tuatha De Danaan, another alien race that had been on the planet for millennia, had warred behind the scenes for the United States because it had the most potential of any of the nations.

The Danaan had established weapons and tech

caches in the eastern states, intending to strike at the Archons. Only the Cuban missile attack had come first, decimating their ranks. The location of those caches had been lost for the past two centuries.

Now, with the Panthers and the Eastern Alliance in a position to strike back, Lakesh felt certain that the Archon-based WSC would fall. The old man had already gotten the antidote for the plague the Panthers had been infected with, and determined that it could be ended with airborne delivery in the next week.

They were in a tunnel that Lakesh knew about, an old one that hadn't been arbitrarily filled in when the new Sante Fe Ville was constructed laboriously over the old. The sandstone bricks held spiderwebs and crawling things, and the smell of old death hung like a corpse's breath. While Thrush had been building hidden rooms and passageways in the new ville, Lakesh had been uncovering those secrets. But in the years since his contrived ''death,'' Lakesh was certain Thrush had kept layering in his secrets.

The embassy row in Alpha District was impenetrable by anything short of a full-blown attack. And that was where Kane, Grant, the Panthers who'd come in from the St. Louis Outlands and the men and women willing to aid in that assault from Lakesh's own Cerberus Underground came in.

''If we frag his ass here,'' Grant said, ''then mebbe we chill him all across the alternate earths.''

''No,'' Lakesh said. His voice was whisper soft, barely heard above the whine of the wheelchair's drive unit. ''The Chintamani Stone and Thrush have to be inextricably linked. Ask my doppelgänger on your casement. I'm sure he may have arrived at the same conclusion. If he hasn't—'' he smiled slightly in the reflection of the garish lights given off by the hand torches the party carried "—then I must not be as smart as I think I am."

Kane slipped another loaded magazine for the Spectre into his clothing. He was dressed in a formal black suit like Grant and all of the other men. The attire was provided by Lakesh, drawn from hidden stores the old man had been keeping and adding to over all the years of his silent war. He ignored Lakesh's comment.

"That was a small joke," Lakesh added.

"Very small," Grant replied.

"Yes, well."

The tunnel curved gradually to the right and descended. Less than twenty feet farther on, the tunnel dropped beneath a field of water. The lights danced off the water that filled the tunnel floor on around the curve.

Grant tested the water's depth with his toe. "Only inches," he said. He stepped in and kept going. Kane fell in behind him, followed by the whir of Lakesh's chair as the rubber tires pushed into it.

Kane focused on the coming mission, knowing it was going to go very quickly now. His identichip would get him through the main doors, but he was certain Thrush would have safeguards set up against him. He tried to keep his mind off Brigid's fate, but couldn't. If everything was going according to Hoyle, she'd be safe in the Cerberus redoubt. Back home.

The terminology surprised him, and he wondered if maybe his doppelgänger's presence in his mind wasn't still influencing him. This version of him was a gentler soul in a lot of respects, and he wondered how that had come about.

This version of him had had Brigid Baptiste and lost her. It was a sobering realization. Despite the difficulties of the relationship he had with the Brigid on this casement, at least there was still a relationship. As long as both of them lived.

For a moment, he wondered what those other lives he'd dreamed they'd shared had held for them. Then he put that out of his mind when he saw the elevator Lakesh had told them about.

It lay at the end of the narrow tunnel like a mouth yawning shadows.

"Agent Kane," Lakesh said, "you know the Chintamani Stone has to be linked to Thrush. For one to exist, so must the other. It remains to be seen if Thrush is the guardian of the Chintamani Stone, or if the stone is the guardian of Thrush."

"Mebbe we should try destroying the stone," Grant suggested.

"As with Thrush," Lakesh responded, "there are probably different versions of the Chintamani Stone on the various casements. Perhaps there is even one on this particular alternate earth, though I've never heard of it. If you destroy the stone on one earth, it's possible the other versions will keep functioning."

"Then why are these three casements so important?" Kane demanded angrily. What the old man suggested bordered on the insane edge of futility.

"The changes you seek to achieve," Lakesh said, "might indeed be effected, Agent Kane. But it could be years before you see them. Perhaps even after your life has past. But there was a reason."

"Fuck this," Kane said, stepping into the elevator. "Let's get on with it." The extra ammo felt heavy in the combat harness he wore under the Kevlar-lined jacket. He accepted the small bag Grant handed him. Inside the bag was a helmet that would defend him against the infrasound wands Lakesh had found out the embassy guards used. There was also a commtach that linked him to the frequency the interdiction team would be using.

"Settle for exposing the lies Thrush has promulgated, Agent Kane," Lakesh advised. "When you leave this casement, it might be good to have this casement's version of you around for the fallout we can expect here."

"I'll keep that in mind," Kane said. The elevator was large, one of the old freight rigs that had been used to transport materials to build the upper ville. When Grant and the rest of the team were on board, Kane hit the control panel.

"Godspeed, Agent Kane," Lakesh whispered in his dry rasp.

The elevator doors closed and it started up, groaning laboriously. Weak white electric light trickled through the cage.

"Man could be right about not being able to chill Thrush on all the casements," Grant said in a low voice.

"That's okay," Kane said. "I'll settle for chilling him once. Build on it from there."

EMBASSY ROW in Alpha District occupied the center of Sante Fe Ville near the top of the Administrative Monolith. As well as representatives of the remnants of two Russian nations, there were twenty-seven other embassies. Crys-steel bubbles formed canopies over each of the embassies, but each embassy had offices on the ground floor, as well.

According to Lakesh's intel, Thrush had replaced
a third of the ambassadors with hybrids that had been
genetically engineered from the Archon DNA. Gradually, he'd have people in all the embassies. Somewhere in the Administrative Monolith, Thrush had set
up a special hospital facility where the hybrids were
grown and cosmetically altered to look like the ambassadors they replaced. Lakesh had tried tracking the
facility by power usage but hadn't been able to isolate
the facility as yet.

Kane's target for the opening act was the Deathbird
hangar a hundred feet above the embassies. The elevator reached the top, on the same level as the mechanics shop where the Deathbirds were serviced. The
Deathbird roost had been one of the oldest and tallest
of the initial design components, giving the Deathbirds instant retaliatory capability over all the ville.

While working within Thrush's organization as the
ville had been built, Lakesh had hidden the existence
of the elevator. Extinguishing the light in the elevator,
Kane slipped on the infrared sunglasses, then took the
small, shaped explosives Lakesh had given him and
affixed them to the wall in a rough rectangular design.
He pressed the remote control to ignite the thermite,
burning through the metal in a second.

He kicked the section out and took the lead with
the Spectre in his hand. Mechanics on duty scattered
at once, but they were looking for fire extinguishers
instead of weapons. That changed rapidly when Kane
stepped through and started blasting down the members of one of Thrush's elite squads.

Grant and the others fanned out behind him, taking
over the hangar in seconds. Dead men littered the
floor.

Kane ran to the front of the hangar and peered down at the embassies. Looking over his shoulder, he found the man running comm on the operation. "Tell Lakesh to do it now."

Over the past months, Lakesh had gotten people into the service department working on the Russian embassy. Small bits of explosive had been layered into the building, concentrating on the nearest side of the crys-steel bubble and taking advantage of the structural weaknesses.

Grant had a team lock down the two access doors to the hangar to prevent any sec men from arriving on the scene too quickly.

Less than ten seconds after the message was sent to Lakesh, the crys-steel bubble over the Russian embassy shattered, and moonlight splintered all over its surface.

Kane raced back to the Deathbird Grant had commandeered, throwing himself into the copilot's seat. The rotors beat the air furiously, and they took off.

Handling the Deathbird with all the skill he possessed, Grant swooped across the sky and dropped toward the ruptured embassy bubble. Sporadic machine-gun fire raked white tracers across the sky, but only a few stray shots hammered against the Deathbird's armored hide.

"Hang on," Grant advised. "We're fixing to light up the night." He brought up the weapons systems, then started cutting loose with the 20 mm cannon and heavy machine guns. He cleared the hydroponics-garden area below, shattering more of the crys-steel barrier and killing everything that came within range of his weapons.

The main embassy building stood in a three-story box shape.

"Take out the wall," Kane called out.

Grant swung the Deathbird around as he swooped through the opening in the crys-steel bubble. When he had a lock on the main embassy building's front wall, he fired the rocket launchers. Roiling orange flames jetted up when the rockets impacted against the structure, blowing out the wall. Then he dropped the Deathbird on its skids beside the hydroponics garden.

Swinging out of the Deathbird, Kane ran toward the gaping hole in the building. Other members of the interdiction team followed him. He worked to remember the maps of the building he'd seen that Lakesh had shown him.

A man in the sky-blue uniform of an embassy guard stepped out in front of him, bleeding from a wound across the temple. Kane lifted the Spectre and blasted the man's face to bloody fragments. He ran past the falling corpse, his gaze sweeping the floor.

The embassy had been furnished in decadent opulence. Maybe some of it had been recovered and transported there from Russia. The walls were tall, covered by oaken slabs carved in bas-relief. Expensive vases and paintings decorated the large rooms.

Kane shot everyone in a sky-blue uniform, and killed anyone who had a weapon that he didn't recognize. He took the second stairway that he came to, following Lakesh's directions, half running and half falling down to the next level to where the personal quarters were located.

The hallway was filled with confused people milling around. Kane guessed they were personnel who'd been invited from other embassies, working on whatever machinations Thrush had engineered.

"Get down!" he roared.

All of them but three embassy guards went down. They fired at Kane, and the bullets from one of them hammered into the warrior's jacket with bruising force. Kane swept the Spectre over them, knocking them down and back, never stopping his forward momentum. He halted at the corner to reload, then slammed on the protective helmet Lakesh had given him. He added the comm-tach.

Ready again, he moved out at once, knowing Grant had his back as they broke into the rooms in quick succession. He fired into the locks, dismantling them in a rush of hot lead. They found a handful of men, but none of them were Archons.

Grant saved one of them in the last room. "I'm going to question this fuck. You keep looking for Thrush."

Kane didn't argue; they were working on borrowed time. He returned to the hallway, catching a splash of sky-blue to his left in his peripheral vision. He dived, twisting to land on his shoulder on the tiled floor, sliding along on his side, trying desperately to bring the Spectre up.

# Chapter 28

The embassy guard tried to alter his aim, but Kane beat him to it. The Spectre's line of whispered death tore through the reflective faceplate on the guard's helmet, ripping bloody chunks out of his face. By the time the dead man hit the floor, Kane was up and running again, taking the next stairway down.

"Got something," Grant announced over the comm-tach. "Puke in here gave up an ambassador named Cobalt. Ring any bells?"

"Hell yes," Kane replied. He swung around the next corner, the Spectre in both fists. He chopped a line of ragged holes through the wall and blasted down another embassy guard. Crossing in front of closed double doors, he opened one of them, peered inside and found a wet bar with an audience cowering in the floor. "Ambassador Cobalt?"

"No," a crying woman said. "No one is in here by that name. Please don't hurt us."

Kane started to turn, heading back into the hallway. Movement drew his attention to one of the women at the back of the room. He caught himself, lifting the Spectre in one hand as the woman dragged a small pistol from her purse. Without hesitation, Kane pulled the trigger.

The stream of 9 mm subsonic rounds caught the woman in the chest and knocked her back across the neat rows of glassware, shattering them into gleaming shards.

Kane took a CS gas grenade from his harness and tossed it into the room. The white smoke billowed out at once, filling the room with coughing and screaming people. He kept moving.

"Cobalt's one of the hybrids," Grant said. "He's supposed to be with Thrush on one of the lower floors."

The sound of gunfire filled the embassy. Fire alarms jangled, echoing all over the halls, and sprinkler systems sluiced water over the interior of the rooms. CS gas tainted the air.

Kane's breath tore raggedly through his throat. His eyes teared from the smoke already filling the building. Part of it was from the fires that had been started, and part of it was the riot gas that hadn't quite yet dissipated. His legs felt rubbery from the run through the hallways. He thumbed the magazine release on the Spectre, checking the load. The machine pistol's oversize clip still held thirteen rounds, and he had spare magazines in the combat harness he wore.

He pushed himself up, getting ready to go around the corner of the wall ahead of him.

An embassy guard came to a stop in the cross hallway. His white boots and gloves were stained with blood. He brought his assault rifle to his shoulder, his face covered by the hard shell of the riot helmet, its surface a sky-blue mirror.

Kane lifted the Spectre first, firing a 3-round burst, aiming for the reflective faceplate, hammering through with armor-piercing rounds.

The bullets cored through the faceplate and slapped

the helmet back. The dead man stumbled back and hit the floor.

Kane moved out, running hard, ignoring the burn of smoke and residual CS gas in the air. He struggled to remember the directions he'd been given, checking the markings tagged near the ceilings at the intersections.

He turned another corner and found he was right on track. The first-floor landing was ahead of him. Broad and white tiled, the landing held two giant Chinese dragon statues surrounding a flower-filled atrium in the center of the building.

Bodies were strewed across the floor, twisted in pools of blood and body parts. Most of them were embassy guards and a few of the rebels that had slipped across the Mississippi Wall for the raid tonight.

Kane glanced upward, spotting Thrush on the third level with two of the Archon hybrids, guiding them through the walkway. He thought about Brigid, about how she'd ended up. He raised the Spectre, set it on full auto and pointed it at Thrush and the two Archon hybrids. He squeezed the trigger, burning through the clip in a heartbeat.

The bullets chopped into Thrush and the Archons. The creatures fell, their overly thin bodies flailing helplessly as the rounds tore them apart. Thrush staggered, but he didn't fall. He held a hand up in front of his wounded face, light reflecting from the metal under the flesh and blood. "Kill Kane!" he ordered the guards below. "He's a traitor to the government!"

Immediately, a fusillade of bullets sizzled through the air where Kane had been before he pulled back to cover. One of them clipped the special protective helmet he wore, jerking his head forcefully enough to blur his vision and send a wave of nausea through him.

With shaking hands, he toggled the Spectre's magazine release, then rammed a fresh one home. He shot the bolt, stripping and chambering the first round. Then he took a stun grenade from his combat harness, pulling the pin and slipping the spoon. He whirled and threw it toward the knot of guards on the other side of the corpses.

The grenade detonated on the first-floor landing. The concussive wave crashed down the steps and lit up the marble-floored foyer with a bright orange flash. Kane felt the shock and the heat on the back of his head.

The rest of the interdiction team had taken up positions around the embassy reception hall, deploying like well-oiled parts of a machine, subguns leveled to cover every possible avenue of either escape or opposition.

Kane looked up the stairway, noting that four members of the embassy's security detail had been incapacitated by the stun grenade. His protective helmet's comm-tach buzzed, and Grant's voice filtered into his ear. "The west wing is secure, nobody here but a couple of hybrid grunts. The diplomatic staff must have been evacuated." The man sounded harried, out of breath.

"Resistance?" Kane asked, moving toward the first-floor landing.

"A little. Some of those bastards are armed with infrasound wands."

One of the stunned security guards on the stairs tried to bring up a weapon. Kane put a burst in the center of the man's chest, hammering him back down on the stairs. Then he shot the others to make sure, as well. He charged up the steps. "What about the ambassador?"

Grant didn't immediately answer.

Kane charged up the stairs. "What about the ambassador?" he repeated. They both knew Cobalt's security here in Sante Fe was coordinated through Thrush's infrastructure within the Department of Extraterrestrial Investigations. They had mapped his chosen evacuation routes from the embassy, which was actually a warren of tunnels. It stood to reason that Thrush would try to get Cobalt out through one of those routes.

"No sign of Thrush at all," Grant answered. "He may have been tipped off."

Kane grunted, not wanting to contemplate the possibility. That would have meant Thrush had some other source within Grant's people. Or he'd tracked Kane's own progress. "Stand by."

He ran up the stairs, keeping close to the curving, elaborate balustrade, taking three steps at a time, holding his Spectre autoblaster in a two-handed grip. The corridor was filled with astringent smoke. Through its shifting planes, he glimpsed four figures stirring feebly on the floor, their white faces streaked red from the blood oozing from hemorrhaging eardrums.

Kane stepped carefully around them, turning right beneath an arch into a long, carpeted hallway. Almost at once, a door opened at the far end of the hall, and a hybrid was framed there, with a fragile-looking infrasound wand in his hand. It flicked toward Kane, the three-foot silver length shivering and humming.

Kane threw himself against the wall, raising his side arm. Even with the special shielding inside his helmet, he wasn't sure he could take a direct hit, so he fired at once. The ultrasonic burst swept high, a barely detectable blur peeling long splinters from the wall over his head. The rounds from the Spectre caught the hybrid in the chest, hurling him backward amid a flailing of arms and a kicking of legs. The wand clattered to the floor.

Kane muttered beneath his breath, "So much for diplomatic immunity."

He carefully moved on down the hallway and paused by a window. He peered out past the broken glass. The grounds of the Archon embassy were filled with running, falling and shooting figures. Smoke boiled from a corner of the building, and flames licked out of a ground-floor window. An armored car trundled through the wreck of the wrought-iron gate, spouting 30 mm shells in a jackhammer rhythm.

He saw a Cerberus specialist surrounded by a pack of hybrids, their infrasound wands humming and popping viciously. The ultrasonic waves pulverized the man's joints and crushed the bones in his face. He opened his mouth to scream, and his teeth blew out of his mouth in a spray of splinters.

Kane put his blaster out of the window and depressed the trigger, firing a long, full-auto burst. Hybrids squealed as the high-velocity rounds struck them, knocking them down like puppets.

An explosion filled the hallway with rolling, thunderous echoes. A sheet of flame erupted, and the concussive roar broke the world behind him.

Looking at the wreckage of the embassy behind him, Kane knew they'd caused too much damage for

Thrush to cover up. People in Sante Fe Ville would know by morning that the Archons were among them, and the truth of that revelation would spread.

But that wasn't enough, Kane knew. Thrush had killed this world's Brigid Baptiste, and it was going to be a colder place because of that.

Then he saw Thrush muscling one of the Archons across the embassy grounds.

"I've got him, Grant," Kane called over the comm-tach. "He's over here." He ducked through the window, dropping to the ground below. Throwing himself forward, he ran in pursuit of Thrush, vaulting over the wrought-iron fence.

Thrush stopped at the black limousine parked in front of the embassy. Cobalt climbed in on the other side as the director slid behind the wheel.

On both sides of the street, Kane saw the citizens of Sante Fe Ville hiding in their shops and homes, witnessing the disintegration of the fabric of the lies they'd been told for years as the Russian embassy burned.

Thrush engaged the big car's engine, pulling away from the curb. The right front fender slammed into the car in front of it, crunching it in as though it had been hit by a tank.

Kane ran after the vehicle, lungs burning with the effort. He closed quickly, spraying the back of the limousine with autofire from the Spectre. None of the bullets penetrated the limousine. With a last burst of speed, Kane threw himself at the broad trunk.

He landed hard enough to knock the breath from his lungs, almost sliding off. Then he stiffened the fingers of his bionic hand and drove them between the metal and the glass of the back window, wedging in enough to purchase a grip.

Thrush turned around in the front seat and pointed a blaster at Kane. He fired, the muzzle-flashes flaring like blossoming neon roses in the shadowy darkness of the vehicle. But the same armor that prevented Kane's bullets from plunging through also protected him from Thrush's rounds.

One of the bullets struck Cobalt, throwing blood across the inside of the windshield. At least one of the others hit Thrush in the face, ripping away more of the flesh that covered his cybernetic infrastructure.

Kane didn't know if Ambassador Cobalt was alive or dead, but Thrush threw the blaster away and pressed a button on the dash. Without warning, a vibration ran through the limousine. In the next handful of seconds, the bumpy ride down the street leveled out, became smoother and faster.

Gazing over the side, Kane saw that the limousine had lifted from the ground, rising steadily. He tightened his grip on the car. Evidently the car had been modified with Archon technology. It flew rapidly upward, spiraling around the Administrative Monolith as it rose.

And everywhere it flew, everywhere it was seen, more and more of Thrush's lies were ripped away.

"Agent Kane," Thrush yelled, his voice coming back to Kane, "you've left me severely disappointed. How did you ever come to be seduced by Lakesh's doctrines after all I'd done for you?"

"Wrong Kane, asshole," Kane roared back, watching the hybrid cyborg's eyes widen in the blood-streaked rearview mirror. "I'm only one of the enemies you're facing across the lost earths." He wanted

Thrush to know because of the Brigid on this casement, wanted the creature to know especially so he'd realize that he and his plans weren't safe on any casement.

"You're from another casement?" Thrush asked.

"Yeah," Kane replied. "You're already dead there." He lied, knowing it remained to be seen if Thrush did exist in his world.

"Impossible! As long as the trapezohedron exists, so do I."

"We'll find out about that," Kane replied. He reached into his jacket and freed one of the grenades Lakesh had so generously given. He jammed it into the metal area he'd dug out with his bionic arm.

Thrush threw the flying car into a sudden whirl in the air, turning the car upside down.

Kane hung on by one arm, the cybernetic arm taking all of his weight with ease. He glanced down, wind whipping through his hair, seeing the streets of Sante Fe Ville over a hundred feet below and getting farther away.

"Kane!"

Recognizing Grant's voice over the comm-tach, Kane said, "Yeah." The grip with the bionic hand was easy to maintain, but the weight was straining his shoulder joint.

"I'm bringing the Deathbird up."

Getting his bearings, Kane tracked the Russian embassy by the flames jetting from the shattered bubble top. He saw the Deathbird whipping around, climbing quickly.

"I'm your only chance, Kane," Grant roared.

"Then bring it on," Kane growled, "because I can't hold on." He wasn't sure what Thrush was attempting to do. Maybe the hybrid cyborg was only interested in shrugging him off, or maybe the creature was indeed as mad as a hatter. Either way, it was coming to a close.

Kane watched Grant's Deathbird scaling into the air, only a few yards distant now. Despite the alien technology in the car, Thrush hadn't been able to outdistance the helicopter. Kane thought fearfully about the whirling blades of the Deathbird as it rose. He couldn't drop through them, and if he missed the helicopter, the fall would kill him.

Then he felt his doppelgänger speaking to him from the back of his mind, damping down the fear. His Brigid had perished, and his beliefs had all crumbled, losing his life held no terrors for him.

"Do you see, Kane?" Thrush taunted. "I can't be destroyed because the Chintamani Stone exists, and you can't destroy the stone because I exist. It's a conundrum, Kane. One that you'll never unravel."

"Fuck you, Thrush." Seeing Grant bring the Deathbird up into position, Kane pulled the pin on the grenade. "Grant!"

"I'm all over you," Grant promised. "Grab the ladder."

Kane looked up to see Grant had maneuvered the chopper overhead and tossed out a rope ladder. As Grant settled the Deathbird over him like a mother hen, he stretched, reaching out with his bionic arm and finally seizing the rope. As he managed a hold, the grenade on Thrush's vehicle went off.

The explosion of the grenade set off other explosions that ripped the air car into a ball of flaming debris that rained down over the Administrative Monolith.

"I'm on!" Grant yelled, watching the ground rising way too quickly.

The rotors screamed as Grant powered them up, slowing the Deathbird's fall to earth. Then it leveled off and Kane was able to crawl up to the copilot's seat.

A few minutes later, they landed in the street amid a circle of citizens. The Panthers had already taken to the streets, parading the bodies of the pure-bred Archons, as well as the hybrids. The bodies of the aliens hung from the streetlights, and already an army was gathering.

Beaten and bloodied, Kane crawled from the Deathbird. The crowd gathered around him and Grant, most of them frightened and confused. Questions and accusations were screamed at them.

But through it all, Kane heard one voice above all others calling his name. "Kane! Kane!"

He turned, tracking the voice with his pointman's senses, and saw Brigid Baptiste shove her way through the crowd. She was smoke stained and bloodied in a couple dozen places, but she ran to him. Breathless, she halted in front of him, her emerald eyes searching his.

"It's me, Baptiste," Kane said softly.

"You made it through," she said. "Thrush tried to block the fusion."

"Yeah. I thought I lost you, or at least a version of you, when I saw the dorm blow." Kane walked toward her, both of them revealed in the glare of the streetlights and the lanterns so many people carried.

Brigid shook her head. "Rouch tried to chill me, but I got out through the tunnel she used to get in. It took me a while to get to Lakesh and find out where you were.''

"What about Rouch?"

"I left her there," Brigid said. "She didn't make it out."

Before he knew it, Kane stepped forward and wrapped his arms around Brigid. Her arms closed around him, as well. But he didn't know if it was his own relief at seeing her alive or his doppelgänger's in the back of his mind.

"I was wrong about so many things," he said, but Kane knew the words were his doppelgänger's. His control over the doppelgänger's body was slipping. He felt light-headed, out of touch with this reality.

He bent down, kissing Brigid, tasting her lips against his, and he tried to hang on to the sensation, but it was ripped away between heartbeats and he knew he was going back.

# Epilogue

Wegmann looked at the feebly glowing power-consumption indicators on the console, then over at Lakesh. "Hardware failure," he declared. "We've got an out-of-phase thermal recycler."

Lakesh wasn't sure if that was really bad or merely an inconvenience, so he ventured, "What does that mean, exactly?"

Wegmann gestured to a huge wire enclosure. Within it rested three ovoid, vanadium-shelled generators. If the central complex two levels above was the brain of Cerberus, the subterranean room was its heart, pumping life and power to the entire redoubt. Opposite the cage sprawled a long operations and monitoring station. Liquid crystal displays glowed, needle gauges wavered and rheostats clicked.

"It means," the man said with a forced patience, "I've got to shut down one of the generators and reconfigure the power-load distribution. I'll have to take all nonessential systems off-line—including the mat-trans unit."

Lakesh stiffened. "The mat-trans has its own independent power source."

Wegmann scowled at him. "For normal operations, for transport to another receiving unit, that's fine. But with the way you realigned the system, it eats far more power than its own generator can provide."

Lakesh matched the man's scowl. "How long before we're up and running again?"

Wegmann shook his balding head. "I don't know. As little as three days, as long as a week. For starters, I've got to close off all the reactant injectors, vent the gases and reconfigure the entire homeostasis process."

Lakesh's lips compressed. "That seems like an awfully long time."

Wegmann shrugged. "You do what you want, but I'm going on record with this—if you operate the gateway like you've been doing, the best-case scenario is you'll lose anyone who is in transition. Worst-case is that we'll have a complete meltdown. We'll lose the entire redoubt."

Lakesh opened his mouth to voice an objection, closed it and heaved a sigh. "Very well. I'll expect regular status reports."

"When I've got something to report," replied Wegmann waspishly, "you'll be the first to know."

Lakesh turned and left the generator room without another word. As he closed the door behind him, Beth-Li Rouch stepped out from behind the cage enclosure. Quietly, she asked, "Think he bought it?"

A slightly scornful smile tugged the corners of Wegmann's lips. "Nothing is more convincing than the truth."

Beth-Li moved toward him, her step light and feline graceful. She reached for him, but Wegmann caught her hands, holding them away. She gazed searchingly into his face. "You knew the power failure was going to happen, didn't you?"

Wegmann's smile broadened. "Let's just say I overlooked a couple of measures to correct it."

Beth-Li cocked her head at a quizzical, teasing angle. "And the measures to fix the main problem? Will you overlook those, too?"

"That," Wegmann answered blandly, "depends on you."

KANE SAT OUT on the overlook outside the redoubt. Full night had bloomed, filling the sky overhead with a panorama of stars. It was quiet except for the sounds of the insects and the wind blowing through the trees and rocks below.

He was still tired, but he was too keyed up to sleep well. After the debrief they'd given Lakesh and the others, he'd gone to his room and gotten a couple hours of sleep. Then, when he'd awoken and couldn't get back to sleep, he'd given up, gone to the cafeteria and raided the refrigerator.

He sat cross-legged, bare chested and wearing only pants and his Sin Eater. He had three sandwiches thick with ham and cheese wrapped in a cloth napkin, a pint of pickles and a quart of milk. It was a simple meal for what he hoped would be simple thoughts. Only it didn't work out that way.

His thoughts were dominated by the other casement's version of him and Brigid. He wondered how their lives had progressed with the changes they'd made while over there. No one knew if Thrush was truly dead, but he hoped that that Brigid and Kane took a chance on the happiness that might be theirs.

Footsteps sounded behind him, soft and wary.

He knew who they belonged to without turning around. "Something I can do for you, Baptiste?"

"No, I just came out for a breath of fresh air."

"There's plenty of it." Kane sipped milk from the

quart jar. He wished he could say more, but didn't know for sure what he wanted to say or even whether he would have the words if he did know.

Brigid stood against the scraps of the chain-link fence, her arms crossed over her breasts. She wore pants and a blouse, but went barefoot. A blanket was folded in her arms.

"Did you hear that further jumps have been postponed?" she asked.

"Yeah. Can't say I was looking forward to another one. It'll give me time."

"To do what? Eat?"

He chuckled. "I was thinking more of getting around to fulfilling our agreement with Sky Dog."

Recently, he, Grant and Brigid had established contact with the redoubt's nearest neighbors, a group of Amerindians living on the flatlands beyond the foothills. A great deal of hostility and suspicion had to be overcome, since in the years after the nukecaust, the native tribes had reasserted their ancient claims over lands stolen from them by the predark government and returned to their ancestral way of life.

After Kane had gained a fragile trust, their shaman—a Cobaltville-bred Lakota by the name of Sky Dog—showed them the reason why he and his people had settled in the area. Nearly a hundred years before, Indian warriors had come into possession of a predark mobile army command post—refurbished and reengineered into an armored war wag.

Sky Dog was perceptive enough to realize that the exiles living in the superstition-haunted Darks were hiding from the forces of the villes. He proposed that if the war wag was made functional again, his people would be the first line of defense against an assault that might be mounted against the installation.

"It's past time to concern ourself with our world, not those belonging to others. Besides, we've got Thrush on the run," Kane added.

"Overconfidence will get you chilled."

He got angry at once. "And getting too timid will make sure you don't accomplish what you set out to do."

She shook her head. "Believe it or not, I didn't come out here to argue."

Kane released a pent-up breath. "That'll be a welcome change."

They were both quiet for a time, and Kane couldn't help stealing looks at her, thinking about how damned beautiful she was.

"How do you think things ended up with the Kane and Brigid of that casement?" she finally asked.

"I'd like to think they worked things out."

"Why?" Her emerald gaze pinned him.

"Because they deserved it," he replied. "They loved each other."

"But they fell apart."

"They were pulled in different directions, Baptiste. Passions do that to people."

"So the secret is for both people to have the same passions?"

"No. It'd be like learning to fight from the same person over and over."

"You think a relationship between two people has to be like a fight?"

Kane pulled a face. "No. That's a Mag comparison. You train against different fighters so you learn different styles. Think about reading the same book over and over again. You don't learn anything new once you've absorbed all the knowledge it has to offer.''

''But you may have to read it over and over to get it all.''

''The same way you have to fight an opponent over and over to fully learn those skills. But a relationship, Baptiste, isn't a lesson. It's a series of lessons. At least, that's the way I believe it should be. You're going to have your differences—that's how you grow.''

''And what made you such an authority on relationships?''

He shook his head, feeling slightly foolish. ''I'm not and you know it. It's just my opinion.'' He felt exposed all of a sudden.

''It's such a risk,'' she commented quietly.

''Yes.''

''What do you do if you're wrong?'' Her emerald eyes bored into his, soft and liquid in the moonlight.

''I don't know,'' he told her. ''I've never taken that risk. The relationships I've had, Baptiste, have only been superficial.''

''Why?''

He shook his head. ''Mebbe that was all they were meant to be.'' He knew the questions were all coming his way, but he let it lie. Their experiences in the other casement had touched them more deeply than either one of them wanted to admit.

''She betrayed him.''

''Yes. But now he knows why.''

''And that's going to make a difference?''

''Mebbe. I hope so.'' Kane looked up at her, and in the moonlight he remembered the visions that had skated through his head when he'd seen Brigid in other times, other lives. He spoke again, his voice softer. ''You're asking me questions I don't have answers for. What I have are most of three sandwiches and nearly a quart of milk, and the moonlight. If you've a mind, you're welcome to join me, Baptiste.''

She hesitated for a moment, then she sat beside him and accepted one of the sandwiches. ''I'm cold,'' she told him.

He helped her spread the blanket around their shoulders, wrapping it over their backs to block off some of the cool breeze. They ate in silence, sharing the meal he'd made, and Kane luxuriated in the quiet of the night, feeling her heat soak into his side.

But Kane knew it was only the lull before the storm. There was still one more casement to explore, and no one knew what it would hold—except for the deadly constant that was Colonel C. W. Thrush.

ABRAMS LOOKED at the distant jagged peaks looming against the backdrop of stars. The Bitterroot Range reminded him of fangs, and the glittering constellations above were like the multitudinous eyes of a continent-sized spider, waiting hungrily for prey to come within reach.

Abrams repressed a shiver as a chill wind gusted across the flatlands and caused the flames of the campfire to flutter and flicker. Black shadows writhed across the ground. On the far side of the camp, colossal aspen trees rose amid tangled, thorny thickets. He didn't like the woods, either, his imagination populating them with all variety of menaces, from mutie wolves to mutie people.

Nearly thirty years had passed since Abrams had

worn the combat armor of a Cobaltville Magistrate. During those years, he'd become the administrator of the Magistrate Division. He'd liked his position and he'd been good at it. Now all of that, as well as his life, was on the line.

He was tall with a neatly clipped gray beard that was presently stained white from the road dust he'd been exposed to all day. Judging from the dryness hitting the back of his throat with every breath and the heaviness in his lungs, he'd also been inhaling that dust. Sitting on the outside of the camp where the Mag force had bedded down for the night after a day's hard travel, he watched over the other eleven men who sat around the two Sandcats they'd brought with them from Cobaltville.

Abrams hurt all over, especially the leg that Kane had lamed. He'd forgotten how much the Mag armor could chafe when a man had to wear it all day. And he stank. He'd forgot about that part, too. He'd have given anything for a bath and a bed, but he didn't know when he'd see either one of those again.

He was still resentful of Baron Cobalt ordering him to take a Mag team over the road himself instead of simply assigning a team to it. But the baron had told him more than he should have, had revealed more of the baron's weaknesses than a man trained to follow command should ever know.

Baron Cobalt had told him that Salvo had been telling the truth about Lakesh working with Kane, and the baron had told him he hadn't been in touch with the Archons. Both of those declarations had shaken Abrams's belief systems.

He drank his lukewarm coffee sub and accepted his lot with a warrior's stoicism but the resentment of an experienced man who'd suffered a change in the status quo. Looking up at the starlit sky hanging over the Bitterroot range ahead of him, he realized that if all went according to plan, the squad would arrive at the foothills by midday tomorrow.

Somewhere in that mass of mountains was a buried redoubt. Abrams knew that for certain. Once, it had been called Redoubt Bravo, but Lakesh had pronounced it unsalvageable. At that time, Baron Cobalt had trusted the old chief archivist of the Historical Division. That was no longer true. In fact, if the baron's information was correct, Lakesh was an even bigger traitor than Kane.

Baron Cobalt had declared that the redoubt was actually the hidden base that Kane and Lakesh were operating out of with other members of their team. Abrams sipped his coffee sub again, watching the other members of his own team. Sometime over the next two days, he'd find out if the redoubt actually was abandoned and unsalvageable or if Kane was holed up in it.

If it was abandoned, Abrams was convinced Baron Cobalt was going to be angry enough to have his head from his shoulders for proving him wrong. And if Kane really was there, even with a full force of twelve Mags, Abrams knew they were going to be in a fight for their lives. There would be no stopping twelve Mags, but Kane and Grant would undoubtedly kill some of them.

Either way, the day the Magistrates arrived was going to be a day that changed his life. And Abrams was determined it would change the lives of anyone who might be living on that mountain ridge.

# An enemy within...

Stolen U.S. chemical weapons are believed responsible for attacks on Azerbaijan and on a merchant ship in the Caspian Sea. While all indications point to Iraq, Bolan and the Stony Man team are sent to track a much more insidious enemy....

Available in July 1999 at your favorite retail outlet.

---

Or order your copy now by sending your name, address, zip or postal code, along with a check or money order (please do not send cash) for $5.99 for each book ordered ($6.99 in Canada), plus 75¢ postage and handling ($1.00 in Canada), payable to Gold Eagle Books, to:

| In the U.S. | In Canada |
|---|---|
| Gold Eagle Books | Gold Eagle Books |
| 3010 Walden Avenue | P.O. Box 636 |
| P.O. Box 9077 | Fort Erie, Ontario |
| Buffalo, NY 14269-9077 | L2A 5X3 |

Please specify book title with your order.
Canadian residents add applicable federal and provincial taxes.

GSM41

# Take
# 2 explosive books
# plus a
# mystery bonus
# FREE

Mail to:  Gold Eagle Reader Service
          3010 Walden Ave.
          P.O. Box 1394
          Buffalo, NY 14240-1394

YEAH! Rush me 2 FREE Gold Eagle novels and my FREE mystery bonus.
Then send me 4 brand-new novels every other month as they come off
the presses. Bill me at the low price of just $16.80* for each shipment.
There is NO extra charge for postage and handling! There is no minimum
number of books I must buy. I can always cancel at any time simply by returning a shipment at your cost or by returning any shipping statement marked
"cancel." Even if I never buy another book from Gold Eagle, the 2 free books
and mystery bonus are mine to keep forever.                   164 AEN CH7R

_____
Name                          (PLEASE PRINT)

_____
Address                                                    Apt. No.

_____
City                          State                        Zip

_____
Signature (if under 18, parent or guardian must sign)

* Terms and prices subject to change without notice. Sales tax applicable in
  N.Y. This offer is limited to one order per household and not valid to
  present subscribers. Offer not available in Canada.

                                                           GE2-98

# From the creator of

## comes a new journey in a world with little hope...

# OUTLANDERS

**OUTLANDERS**

| | | | |
|---|---|---|---|
| #63814 | EXILE TO HELL | $5.50 U.S. | ☐ |
| | | $6.50 CAN. | ☐ |
| #63815 | DESTINY RUN | $5.50 U.S. | ☐ |
| | | $6.50 CAN. | ☐ |
| #63816 | SAVAGE SUN | $5.50 U.S. | ☐ |
| | | $6.50 CAN. | ☐ |

**(limited quantities available on certain titles)**

| | |
|---|---|
| **TOTAL AMOUNT** | $ |
| **POSTAGE & HANDLING** | $ |
| ($1.00 for one book, 50¢ for each additional) | |
| **APPLICABLE TAXES*** | $ _____ |
| **TOTAL PAYABLE** | $ _____ |

(check or money order—please do not send cash)

To order, complete this form and send it, along with a check or money order for the total above, payable to Gold Eagle Books, to: **In the U.S.:** 3010 Walden Avenue, P.O. Box 9077, Buffalo, NY 14269-9077; **In Canada:** P.O. Box 636, Fort Erie, Ontario, L2A 5X3.

Name: _____

Address: _____ City: _____

State/Prov.: _____ Zip/Postal Code: _____

*New York residents remit applicable sales taxes.
 Canadian residents remit applicable GST and provincial taxes.

GOLD EAGLE

GOUTBACK1